The Gift

The Gift

A NOVEL

DAVID FLUSFEDER

Fourth Estate

An Imprint of HarperCollins*Publishers*

Published in Great Britain by Fourth Estate.

HarperCollins books may be purchased for educational, business, or
sales promotional use. For information, please write: Special Markets
Department, HarperCollins Publishers Inc., 10 East 53rd Street,
New York, NY 10022.

FIRST U.S. EDITION 2003

Printed on acid-free paper
Typeset by Palimpsest Book Production Limited, Polmont Stirlingshire

Library of Congress Cataloging-in-Publication Data

Flusfeder, D.L., 1960–
The gift/David Flusfeder.
p.cm
ISBN 0-00-715773-8
I. Title
PR6056.L77G54 2003
823'.914—dc21
2003041752

03 04 05 06 OS/RRD 10 9 8 7 6 5 4 3 2 1

The Gift

One

After the weekend was over, when we were driving home from Barry and Sean's house and the twins were at last beginning to whisper themselves to sleep in the back seat, I said to my wife that we must buy our hosts something. We had taken Barry and Sean's hospitality, as we had so many times before; we had to give something in return, maybe a good bottle of champagne, vintage, the label that Barry approved of.

They don't want anything, Alice said. They like having people to stay. Anyway, what do you get the people who have everything? Anything they want they can get themselves.

Something well chosen. The price isn't important.

I don't know. But if you really want to get something we can give them something for the house.

Yes, that's a good idea, I said.

I found what I thought I was looking for in a film memorabilia shop. An Italian poster for one of Barry's movies. It was a very big poster, but Barry and Sean lived in a very big house. The poster cost more than I had dreamt of paying, which seemed to be part of the joy of the giving. The boy in the shop, whose plump hairless face was punctuated with little metal studs, slipped it inside a protective cardboard tube for me to carry.

I showed the poster to Alice and I felt very proud.

Look, it's perfect isn't it? Just look at those colors.

I don't know. I'm not sure. How much was it? These things cost a lot, don't they?

Don't worry about it. It was a bargain. But it's perfect isn't it?

No it's lovely, it is, but I thought we were going to get them something for the house.

This is for the house.

Yes but have you seen any posters in their house? I've got a feeling it might be vulgar to advertise your own movies? I was thinking candlesticks.

We can give them candlesticks as well.

No that's too much. It's embarrassing. We have to give them one or the other.

Well, which do you want? Do you want to give them candlesticks?

We'll give them the poster.

Only if you want to.

I knew I was looking like a child when I said that, a boy unsure of love who was threatening to cry if an ice cream wasn't bought or his boots not tied for him.

Yes I want to. It's a very good choice.

We had been invited to have dinner with Barry and Sean at an Italian restaurant in Chelsea. I took the poster along. I left it in its cardboard tube with the cloakroom girl.

Alice walked ahead of me into the restaurant. (She is more adept in this kind of world—I might even have pushed her to go ahead.)

The maitre d' stood tolerantly in front of us as we looked and listened for Barry's unmistakable head.

There. I heard it over there.

4

Like bells from a miniature traveling church, the trinkets in Barry's hair tolled through the restaurant. Shiny metal fetishes, seaglass pendants, polished leather scroll-cases, hooked and tied and dangling from wild grey and black curls. Sean waved as we approached. His head was shaved, restaurant lights glared off his scalp, the blubbery W of male pattern baldness.

When I first met Barry, long ago, when Alice still worked for him, I'd been struck, principally, by the unnecessary magnitude of his wedding present to us and by the things he wore in his hair. I'd fearfully assumed that the producer was deep into primitive religion, voodoo, gris-gris, dark practices. I later realized—or, as it usually happened, Alice explained to me—Barry wore heavy things in his hair to show that he could, and to remind the world that Sean, his younger lover, could not. He added to them periodically, like a charm bracelet.

Also at the table was Dylan. I had hoped she would not be. Dylan had close-cropped hair and a handsome, unnecessarily young face, like a rock star's. She outshone everything and could be mean to people. Once she had been a young writer of passionate plays as slim and delicate and poetical as herself. Then she had alchemized one of her plays into a film and now she was middle aged and was a movie director in Hollywood and her body and her vanity and her appetites had expanded into the space the world gave her. Critics praised her. Foreign governments awarded her medals. Women admired her. Men adored her, especially gay men. She had a variety of children, including one with her current husband, who had once been her ambitious, watchful assistant.

I reminded myself not to try talking to him tonight. I often did try, because he always seemed so anxious and

5

watchful, but he didn't like to be pitied, especially in public by someone like me.

And you remember Phillip.

The husband looked watchfully away. Sean repeated the statement a couple of times before Dylan noticed that she was meant to respond.

Yes, of course.

Dylan smiled lamely. I winced. Of course she didn't remember me, she never did, despite having met me at least a dozen times. She realized she was meant to say something more. She concentrated very hard. Lines emerged in surprising parts of her face.

You're a doctor aren't you?

No, I said and my smile hurt my teeth. You must be confusing me with someone else.

No it's you, something to do with noses.

We last met after a preview. I talked to you about Sinology.

You see? I knew that.

Dylan went back to talking about herself for the benefit and applause of her claque of hustlers, actors, flunkies, and starlets, who were hungry for everything she had to say, do, and imagine. I avoided looking at Alice. She'd be either angry or humiliated or both. Sean was trying to offer support. I felt grateful for this, but unconsoled.

A Sinologist has nothing to do with noses.

Dylan kept on talking. She was telling a very beautiful woman at the table about a dress she'd recently bought at a shop in or called Scandinavia.

I said, A SINOLOGIST HAS NOTHING TO DO WITH NOSES!

Conversations stopped. Everyone, apart from Alice, was looking at me.

Sorry. I didn't mean to startle anybody. Just wanted to tell you, so you'd know, a Sinologist is someone who studies China.

I detected a lot of wariness. Dylan's crowd all waited too long a time to respond, and when they did they did it all at once.

What, like pottery and plates you mean?

That's a very fancy word.

Dinner services?

I couldn't tell whether they were laughing at me or not. I had to assume they were not.

China. Its history and culture. Chinese civilization is what a Sinologist studies. Not dinner services.

Why?

I'm not an expert in it. It's not my job or even my main interest, I was just talking to her about it once—What do you mean, why?

Why China? Why not study something closer to home?

Do you read Chinese?

It was a great civilization. Perhaps the greatest. No I don't read Chinese.

We have a lot to learn from it?

I suppose so.

What did he say?

He says he supposes so.

How can you study it if you're not at home in the language?

I didn't usually have to explain myself like this. I was being made to feel stupid, but what was worse, the subject itself, China, and broader than that, just being interested in things, was being cheapened by my attempts to justify it to a table of people who had no sympathy for me or it.

I've always preferred the Japanese, Dylan said as if this

was what the table had been waiting for, her final word, and now the attention could move back to something more interesting, herself. Already, people were beginning to remind her of recent triumphs and other directors' disasters. I knew I should let it stop there. I'd have known it even without Alice looking at me in an increasingly familiar way.

Look. It's like the Greeks and the Romans, all the best Roman stuff, the philosophy I mean, and art and gods, that all came from the Greeks. The same with the Chinese and the Japanese. The Japanese took everything from the Chinese.

That means that the Japs were more successful.

In a way. I know what you mean. I wouldn't argue with you about that.

I've always preferred the Romans to the Greeks, haven't you? Dylan said to Barry.

I know what you mean, Barry said. Sexier somehow.

Dylan had a most charming smile. It made people fall in love with her and believe in her and lay themselves down for her genius. She used it now, to prevent me from saying anything more.

The case against Sinology and its representative had been proved. Quiet conversations began in different parts of the table. I could assume that the next time I met Dylan, I still wouldn't be remembered; all that had happened was that I'd blurred the film director's image of me, which was another kind of defeat.

I'm a writer, I said.

No one met my eyes. Conversations became louder. My glass was empty.

I'm a manual laborer, I said.

I announced this a number of times with increasing force

but no one responded or gave any sign of hearing me. Alice had gone, to the Ladies, I supposed.

At the end of the meal, after the bill had been divided and the credit cards returned (Dylan's a classier shade of platinum than Barry's), Dylan was still waiting for her coat and Barry was watching Sean perform stretching exercises on the pavement, where we joined them.

Are you coming on with us? Sean asked. We're going to a party. It might be good.

We can't, I said.

Babysitter, Alice said.

You should come, Barry said keeping his tone carefully neutral so it was impossible to tell whether he wanted us there or not.

Here this is for you, I said in an effort at offhandedness. I saw it, we thought you might like it.

I unfurled the poster, held it up to be seen by the light of the restaurant window.

Oh, Barry said probably not meaning to be unkind, the Italian, those, I've got hundreds in the office.

Sean saw my disappointment but not, I hoped, my sudden surprising fury.

It's very nice of you. Thank you, Sean said.

For the house somewhere, Alice said in a poignant if vague attempt at loyalty.

It's very thoughtful. It's lovely.

Sean gave us goodnight kisses. Barry waved. Dylan emerged with her claque around her.

In the car going home I said it, before Alice had the chance to,

We should have got them the candlesticks.

That night I walked down long narrowing dream corridors, holding a very small woman in the protective cup of my hands, needing to release her to her home and taking my duty well. I squeezed through a small doorway into a square gray room, which together we inspected for mouseholes. The wainscot had no gaps, except for the tiny door she squeaked out the discovery of on our second turn around the room. I nudged it open with my toe and set her carefully down. She stood in the doorway, smiled, beckoned me in. I crouched, I curled, I made myself little, the doorway was still much too small for me. Reluctantly she turned, started walking, pausing once to look back ruefully, and disappeared down a tiny darkening corridor.

It was always hard to adjust to the day after one of my vivid dreams, and I had been having these dreams with more frequency. It took longer for the room to find its usual shape, for the edges to be filled in.

Alice rolled to face me. She stroked my face.

We shouldn't go out with them, it always puts you on edge.

You think?

Look around you. Be proud.

I looked around at the uncluttered walls of our bedroom. This was the fifth house we'd had in our nearly twelve years of marriage, because Alice liked to keep things new. And it was by far the biggest. We hadn't worked out yet how we were going to pay for the house (each month we dipped into our building society savings to top up the mortgage). Nor did we know how to fill it. The girls still insisted on sharing a bedroom. Most of the rooms were unused. Alice had invented names for them: the library, the morning room, the blue room—which had so far remained red. Our bedroom was called the Chinese room. But I had resisted buying anything Chinese to put in it. It has to be the right things, I insisted. Not chinoiserie junk.

You keep thinking it's all going to be taken away.

I pushed away my wife's legs, which were crushing mine, and waited for the first sounds of need from the twins' room above. The sun was streaming in through silk curtains, casting shadow faces on to the rise of bedclothes over the innocent potency of my early morning erection, Alice turning beside me, too early to try? Of course not. I kissed her shoulder. She pushed drowsily towards me, Flying Butterflies.

She was turning and stretching, her arms and eyes opening. Her breasts were about to escape from the cotton cage of her nightdress.

Kiss, she said.

Her mouth was open, she tasted musky, night dreams. Her tongue dipped past my lips, a hand stroked my buttocks.

I kissed her mouth, her eyes, wriggled down to find her breasts with my mouth. I kissed and lightly bit her left nipple, then went to find her right but misjudged, came short, nuzzling only the near side of her right breast; she helped me out, nudging the breast towards my mouth with the side of her right arm. I stroked her arms, her shoulders, her breasts, caressing her body throughout, as I had been taught. A shallow stroke of my jade peak into her lute string—*One*, I whispered—and then a deeper one, black pearl. *Two*, we both said.

Three shallow, one deep. Five shallow, one deep. Nine shallow, one deep, that was the best, recommended by all the Tao masters. Nine to the Water Chestnut Tree, one to the Deep Chamber. The same pattern of ten thrusts repeated a hundred times, that was all, if you broke it down it sounded easier. One thousand loving thrusts. We—I— had never got there.

At four hundred and ninety-seven, sweating much more than the Taoist masters of loving would condone, I ejaculated.

I think I made it, I lied when my heartbeat was calming down and my breathing returning to normal.

That was four hundred and ninety-seven, Alice said.

Are you sure?

I was almost there.

Our yoga instructor Ken once said, *A man of twenty can have one emission every four days. A man of thirty can have one emission every eight days. A man of forty can have one emission every ten days. A man of fifty can have one emission every twenty days. A man of sixty should no longer emit. If he is exceptionally strong and healthy he can still have one emission monthly.*

In case we forgot this central tenet of the Taoist art of loving, Ken, a short squat man with matted whorls of body hair and large sweat stains under the arms of his T-shirt, photocopied this wisdom and gave it out on a yellow sheet to every couple in his class. Each week we would receive one of Ken's yellow sheets, at the end of the class when the couples were recovering from the exertions, small italic photocopied scrawl, always headed with a few untranslated Chinese characters, which, I sometimes suspected, were invented by Ken.

Alice kept the sheets in a green ring binder in the kitchen, on the same shelf as the recipe books. Before our first enthusiasm for Ken's teaching began to dwindle, it was more often kept in the bedroom, on Alice's bedside table, underneath her contact lens case.

To achieve one thousand loving thrusts, Ken had told the class, was within any man's capacity; it was just a matter of practice, half an hour of Taoist loving.

When a man loves once without losing his ching, he will strengthen his body. If he loves twice without losing it, his hearing and his vision will be more acute. If thrice, all diseases may disappear. If four times, he will have peace of his soul. If five times, his heart and blood circulation will be revitalized. If six times, his loins will become strong. If seven times, his buttocks and thighs may become more powerful. If eight times, his skin may become smooth. If nine times, he will achieve longevity. If ten times, he will be like an immortal.

One thousand loving thrusts. In the early days of Ken's tutelage (and long before the class was banned from the community centre), in the night following an inspiring session side by side with other Clapham couples in holiday T-shirts and baggy sweat pants, we had made it nearly to nine hundred and fifty. Only twice since had we broken the nine hundred barrier.

When both parties are as spiritual as immortals they can unite deeply without motion, so ching will not be stirred. At the same time the couple should imagine that there is a red ball as large as a hen's egg at their navels. They can thrust very slightly. But if they get excited they should retreat. In twenty-four hours the couple can practice this form of union

13

dozens of times. By practicing this they can also live a long time.

We are not as spiritual as immortals, Alice said. You're just being lazy.

I was five years old when I decided to become immortal. My future life stretched godlike across time infinite. I was six when I broke the news to my parents. One late afternoon after school, bicycling in the park, the thought occurred to me that if I became a doctor I could invent the miracle drug that would enable me, and—I generously supposed—others, to live forever. I cycled rapidly home to tell my parents the good news. My mother was out, at the shops. My father was in the lounge, sitting in the TV chair, composing a letter to a newspaper. My father often wrote letters to newspapers.

I'm going to become a doctor!

My father pushed his reading glasses further down his nose and looked sceptically at me.

Why?

Which is when I experienced the first disagreeable stirring of shame—which led directly to the secret pride of my first successful lie. I knew my father well enough by now to recognize that if I revealed the real reason I would have a loud speech made at me and be condemned.

Because, I said.

I waited for inspiration to arrive.

Because I want to help the masses, I said.

That's a good boy, my father said.

By the time I was eight I was going to be a world-famous footballer. Everyone told me so. Teachers at school, admiring schoolfriends, teammates in the London under-tens, my mother and even my father.

My father approved of football. It was the people's game, working class, played in barrios and ghettos worldwide. With the right ideological apparatus it could be a force for international communism. I set myself diligently to the task of becoming a world-famous footballer and, therefore, revolutionary. I practiced heading against the block of flats where we lived until the widow whose bedroom was behind the wall I was using came out with her poodle yapping. I developed my weaker left leg by practicing corners with it; I built up my stamina on long training runs invigilated mercilessly by my Marxist father tottering behind me on a woman's bicycle through the streets of south-east London. My rise was prodigious. At ten I was the second-best player in the London under-twelves. Like Stan Bowles I was a stylish, shaggy-haired number ten capable of a blistering shot with either foot, of finding the miraculous pass, and with a gift for dribbling that I used seldom and apologetically, because my father had trained me into believing that the player must subordinate himself to the team and not indulge in displays of bourgeois individualism.

My progress brought respect to the household, photographs in the local newspaper, and, in some way I never quite got to the bottom of, funds for the local branch of the British Communist Party (Marxist-Stalinist splinter). Everything was good, effortless, charmed. *Lucky*. At the same time I couldn't entirely ignore the feeling of anticipation thwarted. A small disappointment lurked in the shadows of all my future monuments and glory, because, after all, I was not going to be immortal or truly miraculous; I was only going to be a footballer.

At fourteen I was playing for England Schoolboys. By this time I was sure of two things: my good luck and my destiny. I had—but never would dare say this out loud—a guardian angel. I didn't have a name for the angel or even an image of her in my head, I vaguely supposed her to be female and beautiful, but I knew for certain that I was being watched over, protected, helped, anointed.

The ball I passed blind would always find a teammate running on to it. If I hadn't prepared for an exam then, miraculously, the teacher would fall sick, the examining board send the wrong papers, the school be evacuated on a bomb hoax morning. The bus I failed to catch was always the one that broke down.

You're a very lucky boy, my father often said reproachfully.

When I was fifteen I was at a junior tournament in China with the England under-sixteen side. The Friendship Games. I had recently accepted that I was not a natural number ten in the Stanley Bowles, Tony Currie mould. (And I was still Philip then; I hadn't yet added the second, distinguished 'l' to my name.) Testosterone had given me weight and bulk. I was a midfielder now, the incisive pass, the bustling run, tracking back to break down opposition attacks, then bursting forward into the penalty area, sliding in to toe-poke a goalscoring touch on the speculative ball crossed from the wing.

The captain of the team, Lee, was playing his final game before his birthday. The coach, Smithy, an assistant manager with a first-division side, had told me that I was going to be the next captain and a fast-tracked shoo-in for a future England player. Life and the future were good.

A cool spring day in the national stadium in Beijing. England versus Spain. I jogged out in my usual fourth position. Schoolchildren waved tattered red flags and bunches of white flowers. Members of other teams in national-color tracksuits sat around the pitch on the cinder athletics track. An exchange of rosettes. A few nasty glares exchanged by opposing players. Doughboy, the team enforcer, spat and then excavated each nostril in turn. I did my usual stretching exercises. And the game started. Lee kicked off to Richard. Richard tried to side-step the oncoming Spanish schoolboy but failed and was tackled. Doughboy brutalized the player with the ball, which rolled lamely towards me. I just had time to control it with my left foot before the revenge tackle came in on the back of my leg and I crumpled hard to the ground in pain worse than any boy could bear. My left knee had been shattered.

Bad luck, all my teammates said, gathering around my bed in the Beijing hospital. They wore their blue England blazers and regulation gray trousers and their hair was wet and combed and crispy-gelled, and they all looked very pale and miserable. But in the way that they looked at each other when they weren't looking at the cataclysm of me there was also a clear relief that this awful event had happened to someone else and that their own legs and careers and futures were still safe. They had won the game and were getting ready for the next and their world was no longer mine.

I spent a week in a Chinese hospital, waiting to be flown back home. The doctors and nurses were pleasant, but distant, issuing instructions with mime, their eyes behind glasses never quite looking at me. The one book in English was a collection of Chinese ghost stories, printed on thin government paper. I lay in my bed, my leg held up in traction, breathing in between pain and throughout it, eating food that was white or slightly yellow, and I read about brides who really were foxes, and dreamers who dreamed a whole life after passing through cracks in pillows. It was the first time I'd ever found in a book or maybe anywhere a sensibility that felt like my own.

And then I returned home.

Bad luck, my family said when I was wheeled off the plane, left leg encased in Chinese plaster. My father drove us back home in silence in his taxi.

After the operations, and after my leg was released from its final casing of plaster, deathly pale, scaly and shiny, rickety thin, I limped along for one more season of football using a body I was no longer sure of. I was slower than I used to be. Ungainly taller too. I learned how to appear indifferent, even to smile, when less gifted boys slipped the ball between my legs and dashed past while I was still cumbersomely turning. For the second half of that final season I was never more than a substitute. My father, watching from the sidelines as he had always done before, was heartbroken. Perhaps, although this was never said and the thought may have been the product of my over-generous imagination, he blamed himself, he lamented, for pushing his son too hard, for putting such strain on growing bones and ligaments, on a boy's fragile physique. He might even have used against himself the hateful word *oppressor*. It was around this time that my father let his hair grow and enjoyed a brief mid-life apostasy as a Trotskyite.

I though was undiminished, perhaps even strengthened. Particularly in my bedroom, behind a closed door, away from the burning scrutiny of my father's revolutionary vision. Now that I knew my achievements weren't going to take place on the football pitch my anticipation was allowed to grow again. No one puts up monuments to footballers. I was destined for something grander.

At university I coached the football teams and studied English Literature and Hotel Management and, surreptitiously, Chinese Culture. Other members of the England under-sixteen team went on to professional careers—Doughboy became the most famous, and was the only one to play for the full England team. I followed the glorious part of Doughboy's career in days-old newspapers on the Caribbean island where I became assistant manager of a sports hotel complex, and where I met Alice, on a holiday with her friend Molly, both of them temporarily wanting little more from life than a tranquil breeze, white-sanded coves, rum punches, and friendly sports instructors.

I met Alice the first time by the hotel jetty. I was wandering down, in my shorts and cap, to help out Nikki the Austrian boating instructor who, I had realized the day after recklessly giving him the job, had never before sat in a boat. Molly was drying her hair on a hotel towel. Like the rest of the group of guests she was watching frantic Nikki, his long highlighted hair wet with exertion, his ski-sunglasses atilt, trying to tug Alice out of the kayak she was wedged inside. Alice was crying and laughing and she was the most beautiful woman I had ever seen.

It was an effort to get her in, said Molly.

I think my clothes must have expanded in the wet, said Alice in between tears and giggles.

Fucking Hottentot, said Nikki. Her ass is too big.

What are you going to do? asked Molly.

We'll have to cut into the boat. Get a saw, Nikki.

I cut her free and lifted Alice on to land and Alice wiped

the tears away from her face and kissed her rescuing hero with one foot lifted behind.

We had dinner together that night, and drank Planter's Punches on the veranda and smoked marijuana in Nikki's room. We were together every night after that, until the final one, before she was due to return to England. On the restaurant veranda, looking down to the jetty where we had first met, I told her something about my destiny.

I believe it, she said. I knew there was something special about you.

After she returned to London, I pined. I followed her back in the end, visited her in the mews building in Soho where she worked for a movie producer, an exiled New Yorker called Barry. The courtship renewed. Alice found me a job as a proofreader at Molly's legal firm. It was Barry who gave us our most lavish wedding gift, a full dinner set of Italian crockery, after we married in the untropical sunshine of Battersea Park.

I poured milk into identical bowls while the girls stared at their father through identical eyes.

I could do the basic tasks without thinking about them. It was all done in an hour and a half, from being woken up by the first twin (usually Daphne) to being back at home having delivered them to school. I had looked forward to becoming a god in my children's imaginations, to being something magnificent, big and glorious and impossible. It didn't work out that way. My children treated me lightly. They were pleasant enough about it most of the time but they tended to treat me as a small child with outlandish responsibilities who needed to be protected from the world and himself. They took it in turns to hold my hand on the short walk to school, as if they were worried I might fall over or stray if allowed to walk unattached.

Usually I could block out most of the patter and chatter. Usually the girls didn't require anything from me beyond a *Yes?* or *Stop doing that!* or *Serves you right* or *No, you may not go to boarding school.* And approaching the school gates, I always felt reassured: Everyone here was the same. No one was as rich or poor or happy or miserable as he had hoped to be or feared he would be. I didn't feel judged in the school playground. Everyone here had fallen or risen to the same level of disappointment.

May we have a pony please?

They didn't talk to me as much as they'd used to. Alice said the same. The twins had withdrawn from us, except to demand things. It is hard to accept that your daughters find you less attractive than other men—and these men, your all-conquering rivals, are nine or ten years old.

A what?

A pony *please*.

May we—

Have one please.

A pony—

Please.

At least they'd come down from begging for a horse, which had been the dominant subject of the previous week. They'd come to me with photographs of stables and stoical hairy-faced horses, which they'd decorated with little red hearts along the sides of the pages.

Of course not.

Please.

I had some sympathy for their needs. I rather thought that girls should have ponies. Alice felt the same but we had both decided against it, for different reasons. She didn't think we could afford to buy ponies, which was true. And I was on a new policy, of not buying with gifts the affection of anyone I hoped would love me. Which was a speculative policy and possibly a self-defeating one.

No. I'm sorry.

Nobly, I managed to resist the easy temptation of blaming their mother. The twins ran off, joining the back of the line disappearing into the school. I watched them go, swallowed my goodbye and final kisses, started my own way back through the obstacle course of parents' eyes and unavoidable pleasantries.

Hello.

Hello.

How are you?

Oh. Hello.

You've grown a beard, Richard observed. It's deeply ugly.

Everyone says that.

The twins complained my beard was too rough against their skin. Alice said it made my mouth look like a sideways vagina.

Richard, whose loss of the ball in the Friendship Games had led to my injury, had turned pro at eighteen, worked his way down the divisions and then enjoyed a golden time in Tampa Bay as a player/assistant coach. He retired with a pub for his parents, a couple of hairdressing salons for his soon-to-be ex-wife, and a launderette business for himself. And now, as a result of some occult sociological movement, we lived in neighboring streets and had similarly aged children at the same school. Richard's children had only recently arrived from the private school they had used to go to. A problem with bullying, Richard said. Alice explained to me that this meant that Richard could no longer afford to pay the school fees.

It was reassuring in a sort of way. We used to get drunk together and train together. Now we turned for home together after watching our blue-sweatered children disappearing through the same doorway. A group of hard-looking women with blondeish hair pulled hard back were sucking at cigarettes in a rain shelter. Patient bald fathers carried their children's school bags. A small mousy man who always wore a fleece-lined waistcoat and had a spaniel on a lead walked past with his usual inexplicable confidence.

I don't get him, I said. He's so cocky.

He's part of a sex ring.

A what?

Sex ring.

You're making that up.

I'm not. There's at least two here.

What, you mean like pedophiles? That's horrible.

Swingers, group sex. Organized on class lines. There might be more but those are the two main ones. That guy is one of the organizers of the working-class one.

No. I'm sorry. I can't believe it.

It's true. They meet on Wednesdays and Fridays. Fuck each other senseless and drink fizzy wine.

You never really know what goes on in private in other people's lives, or even sometimes your own. So this is what he did? Did Alice go there too? Girls' nights out?

Have you gone? You gone to one of these?

Of course not. But it does go on.

Along class lines.

That's right. But there's some movement between the two groups. They're all at it.

No.

It's true. I'll see you later. I forgot to give them their lunch money.

I walked slowly back through the playground, greeting anyone whose eyes I failed to avoid.

Hello.

How are you?

Good morning.

Hello.

Were these all invitations? A form of recruitment? The cocky little man walked ahead beside a handsome, much taller woman. Had they been at it the night before? I've never been to an orgy. I imagined lined flesh, swinging breasts, bouncing cocks, sweat on skin, abandonment, mixed in with the idlest most banal gossip. Had the cocky man last night been fucking the handsome woman while the woman vicar signing a petition sodomized him from behind with a dildo harnessed around her own low buttocks? Do they video these things? The architect, the one with the heavy rimmed glasses who had videoed the summer concert, did he wander among the pink puckering aging flesh, naked except for a spare battery pack belted around his paunchy middle?

Hello.

Hello.

I was being invited to sign a petition held on a clipboard by the architect's wife, who was also the head of the PTA. She had never talked to me before. I had always sensed her disapproval without knowing quite why but accepting her verdict, without doubt or complaint. I had heard her complained of. She was a snob, people said. That did not bother me so much. I just found it unbelievable that I was part of a peer group that included women who looked like friends of my mother.

Would you sign this petition? It's to get a lollipop lady.

Was that a wink or a nervous tic or was I just imagining it? The architect's wife was very thin and wore long skirts and sensible blouses.

It's a very dangerous junction. Matilda nearly got knocked down the other day by a cement mixer.

Oh I see. Yes.

Matilda was the name of her daughter, who had a pretty, candid face and often wore a toy belt with carpenter's tools. The architect's wife was holding the clipboard out at me, at arm's length as if to avoid any personal contact. But at night, perhaps, in the sex ring parties, she was the opposite. Abased, abandoned, taking on all comers, rising high on passion and flesh. Exhibiting her own need in the sight of everyone else's. My thoughts were embarrassing me. The architect's wife's arms were thin and freckled. I imagined them held by the cocky man, tightly clasped, while one of the hard-faced women went down on her greedily sucking, one of those occasions when the sex rings all joined up together, like the Olympics.

Here.

What?

Sign your name here. If you agree.

Oh. Yes. Sorry.

I signed my name. Wrote my address down clearly. Was this the way in? I didn't know if I wanted to go. I did know I would like to be invited. I imagined the architect and his wife in bed at night with clipboards. Going through the names and addresses, the architect toying with his wife's nipple rings while they read out the names on her petition lists and discussed whom they wished to fuck.

Thank you.

I was being dismissed. I shook my head vigorously, to try to clear it.

That night I dreamt I was making love to someone who was not my wife. The dream woman was someone I had never met before nor even imagined before, but in the world of the dream she was the woman I had been waiting for all my life, the woman I had been expecting. She wasn't especially beautiful, but something in her matched something in me that I had never recognized so clearly before as being intrinsically myself. Just before I woke

I realized that the woman was tiny, and that I didn't loom over her as much as I usually did. When she left to go through a door I couldn't enter, the door wasn't as absurdly small for me as it usually was.

When I woke up, I looked at my wife sleeping and I felt ashamed. Alice was beautiful. She looked like a Eurasian princess plumped by neglect. Her father had been a colonel in the army, her mother a perfect military hostess, her childhood a succession of identical army bases in different parts of the world. Sometimes I invented a preferable lineage for Alice, a sad Irish princess sired by a mysterious Russian adventurer, who had lost her way to a foreign court, where, unacknowledged, she had been condemned in exile to eat the crumbs of sweetmeats fallen from the royal table. She had long brown hair and high cheekbones and I felt ashamed and I felt guilt and also a longing for the woman I had been making love to in my dream.

I dreamt about her again the next night, and this time I was smaller again and the dream was explicitly erotic and I managed to pull myself out of sleep. After I awoke I patted nervously around for seminal dampness and was so grateful not to find any and so anxious about ejaculating if I allowed myself to fall asleep again in this state, that I started caressing Alice in the way that she liked best, rubbing the small of her back deep to her tailbone. It was one of our signals that intercourse was being suggested that allowed either of us to pull discreetly, relatively unhurtfully away. Alice half-sleeping stretched her body against mine. I made love to her and tried to recapture the image of the tiny woman in my dream and neither of us counted out loud but we got up to seven hundred and two.

Alice didn't like the phrase dinner party, it was too pompous she said, sent out the wrong messages, pretentious. She preferred to invite her friends to a supper party, for which Barry and Sean were, as usual, late. Sean was coming in from Los Angeles, Barry had met his plane, called up on the mobile from the airport. They were on their way.

Barry's fuming, said Alice. It's usually him in LA and Sean doing the housewife stuff and chauffeuring.

I thought he ran a shoe shop or something, said Molly.

When they met he did. Now he's working as a set designer. He's doing very well.

I love this wallpaper. Where did you get it?

The secret message of the invitation was Admire Our New House. Guests had dutifully scattered around, stroking soft furnishings, making praise, except for my father, who had found the most uncomfortable chair in what Alice called the drawing room and what I persisted in calling the lounge and had remained there waiting for things to be brought to him.

The twins had been allowed to stay up to receive the first coats and hand out olives on the rough brightly colored dishes they'd made in their pottery class. I finally persuaded them upstairs to their new bedroom, where they still insisted on sleeping in the bunk beds from the old house. The house terrified me and I think them too. None of us was yet convinced by Alice's theory that you make a decision and then everything else just falls into place. I bribed them to remain there with the promise that they could wear whatever clothes they wanted in the weekend ahead and go window-shopping for lacrosse outfits. I closed my eyes as I went down the stairs.

In the lounge my father was sitting beside Alice's mother. Both our surviving parents had lent us money for the house. The tacit understanding was that this would never be referred to, but it did confer on them certain rights, such as being invited to dinner—or supper—at least once every month, although seldom together.

My father glared angrily at his privileged son. I offered him olives.

I don't like olives, never did, confided Alice's mother who was gracious and lonely.

I like them green, said my father. I like them with that little red thing in the middle. Phil! Do you have any with the little red thing in the middle?

Pimento, said Alice's mother.

Bless you, said my father.

Sorry, I said. I refilled my mother-in-law's glass with champagne. She held her free hand over her hearing aid to hide it and flashed me her woman-of-mystery smile. She sat half an arm's length from her champagne flute and leaned forward elegantly to sip.

What are you doing these days? asked my father. Still those stupid booklets?

My father didn't drink champagne. I handed him a bottle of North Korean wine and the corkscrew.

I'm writing a movie, I said and I had no idea why. It

certainly wasn't true, although the thought had occurred to me. Probably I had just said this because I was tired of the kinds of conversations I always had with my father.

That stupid corkscrew. When are you getting a proper one?

There's a trick to it.

The trick is getting a corkscrew that works.

Let me help, said Richard. I think Alice wants everybody to come in and sit.

Everybody else was already sitting at the dining room table, and inspecting the plates that held black squid-ink spaghettini with anchovies and parsley. My father grumbled to Alice's mother about the exploitation of workers in the pasta industry.

We've been talking about you, Molly said.

Superstition, Alice said.

I'm not superstitious.

What position did you always come out in the team?

Fourth.

Why?

I just did, that's all.

What about you?

Me? Richard said pointing to his chest. I had a ball in my hands, had to have a ball in my hands, 'd bounce it twice against the changing room ceiling.

Why?

There's no why. Just did, that's all.

And Lee. Do you remember Lee?

Yeah. He came on to the pitch bare-chested.

Put on his shirt last thing.

And Doughboy.

Always had to have a poo last thing before the game.

Said he liked feeling clear.

We called your man here professor, Richard said to Alice.

Well that's no sign of favor, said Molly. Doesn't any player whose knuckles don't drag on the ground get called professor?

It's not like that.

Isn't it?

What about that friend of yours? Alice said.

What friend?

The one who lost his job because of that pooing thing.

When we met we crapped and shat.

Phillip!

It's like a poem isn't it? When we met we crapped and shat.

What's he saying? asked my mother-in-law.

Once upon a time we crapped and we shat. Nowadays we don't do anything ruder than poo. And the same with all our friends. It's child-led. Because our kids use a word so do we. Shouldn't it be the other way around?

Don't change the subject. What was his name?

Smithy, said Richard who was rightly convinced that Alice despised him and was always looking for ways to ingratiate himself with her.

He wasn't our friend.

He was our coach.

Yes. And what was it that Smithy did?

He perched on a chest of drawers.

And?

He crapped into a paper cup. He *pooed* into a paper cup from a great distance.

Thank you Phillip.

Didn't miss with one, said Richard enthusiastically, lifting his arms in victory, showing the wear on his all-in-one dinner suit. It was like an air rifle. He had a very pulsey diet I think, just hammered these little turds into the cup.

Thank *you*, Richard.

Makes you wonder how he got that good, I said.

I always wondered about that, Richard said. Was he like that to begin with or did he train?

He must have had a natural thing for it, but all the same.

How did he find out? Think how messy it could have been at the beginning of his career.

And they called *him* professor? said my father. Think what geniuses the rest of them were.

That's rather my point, said Alice drily.

I don't understand, said Alice's mother. Why was this man doing this?

We'd lost a game. He was trying to cheer us up.

He was very good for morale, Smithy.

Phillip of course is in denial about his football career, Alice said to Molly. He never really got over losing it.

I don't think that's true, I said.

You see? Exactly. You know how they always used to have pubs? After they retired? Well his would have been called The Wounded Footballer.

That's not a bad idea, said Richard hopefully. Could have it decorated with X-rays and scans of famous injuries. Cruciate ligaments. Hamstrings.

Broken legs.

And shattered knees.

Keyhole surgery.

You had keyhole surgery didn't you Richard?

I did.

Where did you have it?

At the Chelsea and Westminster Hospital.

No, I mean which part of your body.

On my keyhole of course. Boom boom!

After you with the bottle, said Molly.

Everything I do I do with love, Alice's mother announced. It was a recent habit of hers to respond to accusations and criticisms that no one else had heard or thought. Her husband had died two years ago. Alice said she thought her mother might be getting Alzheimer's disease too.

I refilled everybody's glass, then picked up the next bottle to open. This wasn't so bad. Wife, father, mother-in-law, friends, this world. Small-potatoes paterfamilias smiling benevolently on the bowls of vegetables and char-grilled strips of fish.

Isn't this Swiss chard lovely? Is it organic?

We get it delivered.

It's delicious! I hope it's not fried. You know I don't do fried.

Steamed. Just a little pepper and lemon juice, that's all.

You do everything so well, said Molly unenviously.

It had been one of my pre-supper party functions to make the list of what the guests did and didn't do. Richard smoked and drank and ate anything and everything. Barry didn't smoke or drink or eat meat or fried food. Molly did eat white meat but she didn't eat fried food or dairy products and when I had made the list she didn't drink alcohol either, but since then she had fallen off the wagon and now she did again. Alice's mother didn't smoke but she drank and would eat anything, in very small portions. My father disapproved of most things but would drink cheap red wine from communist countries and peasant collectives and smoke cigars as long as they were Cuban. Sean was allergic to shellfish but ate everything else; he drank but didn't smoke. There was a sub-list, that seldom needed referring to, of what drugs everyone took or didn't take. Barry had given up the most drugs. Richard had given up the fewest.

And now we were talking about Alice's work. Or, rather, Alice and Molly were.

Phillip?

Sorry. Any more wine anyone?

You've got that glazed look in your eyes, said Alice. He gets that every time we talk about my work.

I don't.

He hardly knows what I do.

That's not true.

I tried to squeeze on to my face a smile that would express good humor, pride in my wife's accomplishments, and the gentlest plea for this conversation to be interrupted.

You rebrand things, I said. And people.

What are the names of my colleagues? What's the job I'm most proud of?

Well, your boss is called Lionel. And there was that magazine wasn't it?

How about a little more recently than that?

Well, how about that comedian? The one who kept hitting his wife?

Quite. Is that the doorbell?

Alice liked issuing implied instructions in public. It was part of what she required from marriage. And the big house that her friends could admire.

Barry and Sean stood shivering in the doorway. Rain filled the night behind them.

Sorry we're so late, Sean said. The traffic.

You're always late.

Barry on his own always arrived, punctually, twenty minutes after he was meant to. Sean was worse. Sean was kind and warm-hearted and good at most things except for leaving one place and going on to the next. But I had only meant to think the words not say them.

Sorry.

No you're right, said Barry.

We're always late, we shouldn't be, said Sean.

Don't worry about it, come in.

Barry and Sean's arrival provoked a flurry of hellos, half-rises from chairs, air kisses and anxious smiles.

Oh. I nearly forgot, said Barry. We got something for you.

I had heard these words before from Barry, *We got something for you* . . . lines of cocaine ensuing, invitations to movie premieres, gifts of glamor and novelty that Alice liked and which I could not raise on my own. My heart sank. Ever since the failure of the poster I had been expecting this, a reprisal.

Barry held out his hand. Sean passed him a plastic supermarket bag. For a moment I was relieved. It was only a bottle of wine that was emerging to the accompaniment of tinkles and chimes from the thimbles, amulets, hooks and polished seaglass tied into the movie producer's hair.

Thank you, I said somewhat complacently. It was an old, distinguished bottle, deep red, gold coronet on the label, scratches on the foil, dust on the neck, obviously vintage and good, but not too humiliatingly thought-ful a gift.

It's a bottle of wine, Sean said.

And something to open it with, Barry said.

Oh.

Barry reached past into the plastic bag and pulled out

an object which was large and intricate and made of green translucent glass.

We saw it in—where did we see it?

Venice.

We saw it in Venice. Thought of you. Here. Let me show you. You fit it over the top like that. You don't even need to break the foil, just lower the lever and lift it again and—

And Robert c'est notre uncle.

I did as I was told. I took the green glass apparatus and applied it to the bottle of burgundy that Barry had brought. The neck of the bottle went inside a narrow aperture. I lightly lowered and then lifted the lever and, with a satisfying slurpy pop, the cork was removed.

It's a corkscrew.

Yeah of course it's a fucking corkscrew. But it works, that's the point. We got tired of watching you struggle always.

I was saying the same thing! Richard said.

No you weren't, my father said. *I* was.

It's very pretty, I said.

It's gorgeous, Alice said. Thank you.

It's Italian, look. Limited edition.

I looked. On the base the designer had etched his or her name in a series of unreadable flourishes.

It's number four of fifty. Number three's at the Cipriani. Spielberg's got number two.

And number one?

Well, we don't know for sure. But we *heard* . . .

Heard what?

Vatican City, said Sean.

The Pope, said Barry.

Wow, said Richard.

Who? said my mother-in-law.

Thank you, said Alice.

Excuse me.

I went into the kitchen to smother my sense of defeat. On the refrigerator door, among the fridge magnets and school timetables and photographs of other people's children and invitations and postcards and letters of praise from Alice's clients, I looked for evidence of my own life and failed to find any. I cleared a space around the sink to stack up the first dirty dishes of the evening. This had happened before. I expected it to happen again. If ever I tried to make a gift to our benefactors I always received something back that made my offering paltry.

The twins came down during supper, even though they had been bribed not to.

We're, said Daphne, Not tired, said Chloë.

They stood inside the doorway of the dining room blearily rubbing their eyes, wearing tie-dye T-shirts that dangled to below their knees.

Back to bed darlings, Alice said.

The darlings shook their heads. White-blonde curls tumbled.

They're so beautiful, said Molly whose three children were boys and whose house was a terror zone of curses, chants, nasty videos, mud, brutality, and guns. Sean poured her more wine.

Not at this time of night they're not. Say goodnight to everybody.

Sean's here!

And Barry, said loyal Chloë not wanting to upset their second favorite adult.

I told you.

Sean opened his arms and the twins ran inside. They

rested their heads against his well-muscled shoulders, looked adoringly up at his face.

You really should go back to bed, Sean said.

Daphne looked at Chloë.

We want to go to boarding school, Chloë said.

You're not going to boarding school, I said lightly as if this were a game we liked to play and not a bitter war between a would-be loving parent and a pair of daughters who dreamed a better life for themselves from the girls' books of previous generations.

Chloë looked at Daphne.

May we have a pony please, Daphne said.

No. Go to bed.

Or a dog.

We'd like a dog.

You're not getting a dog. Go to bed.

The twins lavishly sighed.

We'll go up to bed, said Chloë.

If Sean comes up with us, said Daphne.

Only for a minute. If your parents say it's OK.

It's OK, said Alice.

's OK.

Sean got up. The girls clung to his shoulders, hooking their legs around his waist, monkeys on a tree. He carried them out.

Sean's very good with children isn't he?

In the same way that Barry was with people. He made them feel only accidentally unimportant. And that he was just an ordinary Joe, from Brooklyn or New Jersey or wherever it was he came from. He was asking Richard what he did, and including everyone else in the conversation if they wanted to be, without coercion, and then he gave them something that sounded intimate about himself. He probably saw this as publicity, or audience research, or it was habit, or he was a genuinely nice man whom I judged too harshly.

I used to have a cat, said Barry. He was called Lucifer Sam. After the Pink Floyd song.

Uh oh, said Alice. He's going to talk about Syd Barrett again.

Alice was allowed to make fun of Barry, as was Dylan. If Sean was permitted to, he only did it in private, behind locked doors.

I wasn't actually. I intended to be talking about this cat I used to have.

Who's Syd Barrett? Richard asked, abruptly shifting his loyalty and desire to please from Alice to Barry.

When I first came to London, was this guy, the prettiest star in town and the cleverest, who was on his way to becoming the maddest.

You see? said Alice. I knew it.

There was something about Barry talking about Syd Barrett that made him different. It wasn't just the reverence in his voice, the lines that disappeared from his face; there was a simplicity about him: He became a young man who hadn't achieved anything yet who adored a pop star.

He was the bee's knees, the face, the guy who took more drugs than anybody else. He was gorgeous. I was twenty-two, just got off the boat, I lived in Chelsea.

Did you sleep with him? Molly asked, beginning to be interested.

No I did not sleep with him. There was too long a line to do that, and by the time I came along he was already beyond that kind of thing. He had this Eskimo girlfriend. He fell apart, disintegrated. Kaput.

When did he die? said Richard.

He didn't die. Or at any rate only in a manner of speaking.

What manner of speaking?

It left him. He was a star and then he wasn't. He was a genius and then it was gone. A living dead star, he's the only one. Nada. Can you imagine? Summer of love. All the drugs you want, the sex you want, when it gets too much you sit down with your guitar or piano or whatever and write a song, and everything's rosy it's a beautiful day. And then it goes. He can't write songs, can't sing in tune, doesn't remember how to play lead guitar any more, can't even play rhythm guitar because he can't keep rhythm. Although maybe he never could, I don't remember about that.

What happened to him? said Molly.

He lived by himself and got madder and fatter in Chelsea Cloisters. His band without him, bunch of schmucks, became enormous. His hair fell out. Shaved his eyebrows. Ate a lot of pork chops and drank Guinness at the pub and watched TV on the biggest set he could buy. He was twenty-one when he had his first hit record. Twenty-three when he was kicked out of the band. Twenty-five he was back in Cambridge again living with his mother. The starlight left him. Isn't that kind of glorious?

I don't know. Is it?

He was a beautiful boy, everyone wanted a piece of him. Then he went bald and fat. Pork chops and Guinness. He had violet eyes. I guess he still does. But that wasn't what I was talking about. I was referring to Lucifer Sam.

Your cat.

Yes my cat. He was very strokable. People need things to stroke I think. He used to climb my neighbor's tree and get stuck and cry and my neighbor used to fire this BB gun at him to make him come down.

What's a BB gun?

It's like an air rifle, what you call an air rifle.

My neighbor, said Alice's mother, who is an old lady, older than me if you can believe! is very lonely.

Barry stared at Alice's mother. He still hadn't finished his anecdote about Lucifer Sam and he was deliberating with himself whether to go on with it or let Alice's mother say whatever it was she was going to say. He opted for silence, which was honorable. He rubbed his face. Barry's face was very attractive. His nose was maybe slightly too small for the rest of his features but that was the only complaint to make. He looked like a fairground gypsy, a dangerous man who made girls scream by turning them too fast on spinning machines. I liked Barry's face. Sometimes I liked it better than I liked my own.

My neighbor let in a man. She doesn't have many visitors. I go once a week to check on her. She isn't very strong and doesn't see so well. She can't really look after herself that's the truth of it, but she doesn't want to be in a home and hasn't got anyone to look after her. She has a daughter who isn't like Alice.

This was an obscure compliment but no one sought explanation. Most of the company stared straight down at their plates. Richard inadvertently met Alice's mother's eyes, which gave her the energy to keep on talking.

The doorbell rang, you see.

Yes, said Richard. I see.

And my neighbor, who's quite a vain woman and quite a garrulous one too if the truth be told, wasn't expecting anyone, but she did what she always does whenever anyone calls. Even if it's me and she knows it's me, I have a customary knock, so as not to alarm her. Two loud ones and then a little one and then another loud one and then a little one, so she knows that it's me you understand.

Yes, said Alice, we understand. Get on with it.

I'm sorry. I don't want to bore anyone.

You're not boring anyone. It's a very interesting story. Go on.

If you're sure?

Mother!

What was I saying?

Your neighbour.

You have a special knock.

She does something she always does when—

That's right. Thank you. (She rewarded Barry with a flashing smile.) She always combs her hair and pins it up at the side. She's quite vain, and very proud of her hair, which is nice it's true. A very nice color white. She's always pleased when someone comes to call. So she combed her hair and pinned it up, and it was this man, you see, from the Gas Board. Well he wasn't from the Gas Board but he said he was, and she's a silly woman not to check credentials, and she opened the door and he hit her over the head with a baseball bat. I've always wondered, you know, about baseball bats. Who plays baseball in this country? It's an American sport isn't it?

That's a good point.

It's a very good point. You always hear about people hitting people over the head with baseball bats but who sells them? They must know what they're going to be used for.

They should be banned.

They should.

Excuse me. What happened? To the woman. Your neighbor.

Oh. She's in hospital. Touch and go. She's more or less a vegetable now. Doesn't recognize anything. Mirrors frighten her. They don't know why.

Sean came back in, alone, giving the thumbs-up sign.

How did you get them down?

I said that at *our* party they could stay up all night long if they wanted. Just so long as they went to bed now.

We're thinking of having a party, Barry said.

In the summer, Sean said.

Everyone here's invited.

For your birthdays? said Alice who remembered everyone's birthdate and sometimes plotted astrological charts for her most loved friends.

Their birthdays are two days apart, Alice said.

Yeah, Sean's two days older than me.

How old actually are you?

No one knew how old Barry was except for his mother and maybe Sean.

As old as I want to be, Barry said. Pass me the corkscrew. Your guests are going dry.

The moment I had dreaded came. My father started to talk to Barry.

Hey. Mister Bigshot. My son has written a movie.

Barry stared closely at my father who stared beakily back. As he aged he raged and as he aged and raged his body shrank and his skin hung speculatively and forlornly around his bones, as if it had lost its cellular memory.

I was used to being blamed by my father for the survival of late capitalism. My lack of class consciousness had somehow corroded the machinery of history. But this was more embarrassing. The dry humiliation of being boasted about by an idiot parent who didn't realize who he was talking to. Nor was this information true. I hadn't written a movie. For some reason this had lodged in his head as a fact when usually nothing I said ever did.

Tell me something, demanded my father.

Yes? said Barry very politely.

Tell me this. Since Eisenstein what's the pictures ever done for the working class?

You'll have to excuse my father. He never got over Russia losing the Cold War.

Well, all I can say, Barry said his hair chinking as he shook his head for emphasis, is I'm sure your son has written a very beautiful movie.

Can you eat beauty? I don't think so.

Sean leaned forward. This is terrific news! he said. When can we read it?

Alice too was pleased. I *knew* you were up to something, she said.

She was seeing this as evidence supporting her theory. Make a decision, make a change, and everything else will adapt and grow to accommodate your will.

What's it about? someone asked, I couldn't tell who, because I was looking at the table through half-closed eyes, making diabolical shapes out of the veins of the soft cheeses.

Good question, I said.

I'll tell you one thing, said Barry—which meant that he was probably about to tell me at least two things or maybe none—Bud's coming to town soon for Dylan's latest, and we're looking for future projects for him. If there's a part for Bud we might all be very happy.

Oh, *Bud*! said Molly. What's he like?

Very gentle, very talented.

I had met the film star only once, been pleasantly surprised by a polite young man with clever frightened eyes and a bad complexion. The film star had been with a plump, older woman who mothered him.

Is there a part for Bud? said Alice.

What's the script about? asked Sean, and I couldn't tell whether he was being genuinely curious or secretly malicious. Sean was very warm and caring and looked after Barry and whispered the names of the celebrities he was talking to when they were out together in public, but it was all so perfect. Sometimes I wondered what, if anything, was beneath. Did Sean spill all his swallowed bile when the lovers were alone? Or maybe there was just nothing there, and what passed for universal amiability was in fact pure empty-headedness. Even Alice said she didn't know.

It's not quite finished yet. Actually I don't really like to talk about it until it's done.

Dylan's like that, said Barry. Keeps everything to herself and then just goes away and does it. I understand. But tell me something. Does it have a spiritual element? Bud's very keen on the spiritual side these days. As we all are. Does it have a spiritual element? I bet it does.

Yes. It does. It does have a spiritual element.

I thought it would. And what else? Sex?

Oh, that reminds me, I said and hoped the desperation didn't show, I heard a curious thing the other day. About sex.

Are you changing the subject?

Sort of, yes, but anyway, I heard this story about the parents at our school—the twins' school—

Which they hate.

They do not hate it. Someone's put this Enid Blyton schooldays thing into their heads, it'll pass. It's a good enough school. But someone was saying that there are these sex rings there.

What? Like pedophiles?

That's what I said. No. Group sex, swingers. They have these parties. They're all at it apparently. And the interesting thing is, *you'll* like this (I pointed to my father because I would do many things, perform most contortions, rather than say the word Dad), it's organized on class lines. Apparently.

The guests looked at each other. Alice looked at me.

And who told you this?

I don't remember. Someone in the playground. A parent I suppose.

It was me. *I* told you that, said Richard.

He was pulling your leg. Weren't you Richard?

Of course I was. I didn't think you believed me.

Well, I didn't know. I wasn't sure. I said it was something I heard.

I bet you've been trying to get an invite ever since. Did you try to get an invite?

Of course not.

People took it in turns to laugh at my gullibility and then they did it all together. It was probably what would make our supper party memorable.

Look, I don't know, how are we so sure it isn't going on? How do you know what goes on behind other people's doors? Bedrooms, sex lives. I mean, our own is enough of a mystery.

Warning bells ringing in my head, warning lights flashing in Alice's eyes, made me stop. Barry used the new corkscrew to open another bottle of wine and I vowed to get him a better present in return.

Barry and Sean were the first guests to leave. Richard and Molly were the last. The wine and the Armagnac had been finished and the marijuana smoked, and the chocolate and cheeses eaten, and they were still at the table. Neither wanted to go home because that might mean they'd have to leave with each other and neither seemed to want to do that. I asked for ideas for gifts for Barry and Sean.

Richard answered first.

Red shirts. They're very in. His and his red shirts. They'll love you for it.

You think so?

Sex toys then. They're mad for that kind of thing aren't they, poofs?

I don't know.

Or a penis extension? What size are their penises?

Penes, I think it is, actually. Plural.

Fuck off. Pea-knees. For fuck's sake. How big are their knobs?

I wouldn't know. Why would I be looking at their, knobs?

Maybe you go swimming with them.

I don't go swimming with them. Would you be quiet please.

Molly said,

Portrait. Get them a portrait commissioned. I have a cousin. She's very good. She did those legs you like so much.

Have you seen her cousin's legs? Alice asked Richard.

No. I don't suppose I have.

Do you want to see them? Molly said.

Why not? Richard said resignedly.

The last two guests departed, holding on to each other. Alice and I were left contemplating the ruins. Cigarette butts in the brie. Pools of candlewax and streams of wine on the refectory table. Towers of plates with cutlery sticking out at the sides.

We'll do it tomorrow.

You mean *I'll* do it tomorrow. Come on. It's twenty minutes' work. Let's just get it done. Is that rain? Isn't it nice? Be good for the garden.

We got it done and it was all reassuring, husband and wife together, a team of two, loading trays with plates and glasses and cleaning the table and transporting all the debris to the kitchen where we loaded the dishwasher and washed the pots and pans and crystal and wiped down surfaces and threw out empties into the recycle bin and bags of supper party waste into the wheelie-bin. And when the kitchen had been returned to order we opened the doors to the garden where the rain was still pouring down and something took hold of us and we danced. Husband and wife swirled on the rain-damp floor.

We stopped to look at the storm. We stood in the doorway and watched the night weather, the sheets of lightning above neighbors' trees, the rain coming down hard over our camellias and ferns, splashing against the creosote roof of the shed, shining a brilliant white out of the column of stones that made the artificial mountain at the top of the garden. Water overspilled the twins' paddling pool.

Thunder hit again, cracking directly overhead; it moved us both to clutch one another. She raised her free hand to touch her chin, and so did I; one of us yawns and the other catches it. This is how it is, becoming each other's reflexes, the rain coming down, the boom of thunder, the weight of bodies.

It was a very nice evening, Alice said.

The food was very good.

You think they liked it? Barry left most of his.

He's always on a diet.

That corkscrew's very sweet.

We'll get them something better in return.

What?

I said, we have to get them something in return.

I don't think that's what you did say.

No. I just think we have, I have—*we* have, to show that we can give them something as nice as they get for us. Nicer.

That's not the point of giving things.

Of course it's not. But it's about being thoughtful. Even if we're not as rich as them I want to show we can be as thoughtful as them. *More* thoughtful. I'll lock up the house. See you in a minute.

Alice gave one of her searching looks. She made a noise in her throat and went up to the bedroom. I swigged the dregs from the final bottle and locked up the house.

In return for the corkscrew, I gave Barry and Sean a kaleidoscope bought at a decorative arts fair in a tent in Battersea Park. A bearded Canadian in dungarees glowered behind a table of toys he'd made out of nineteenth-century industrial machinery. The cylinder had been handcrafted out of a cotton-mill bobbin, with brass end rings and a glass prism the size of an egg. The kaleidoscope was large, charming and expensive, and I wanted it so much for myself that I thought it must be the perfect gift for Barry and Sean.

I gave it to them at a dinner. They played with it most of the evening in the restaurant, even lent it to the chef, who, the maitre d' said, wanted it to inspect certain sauces and soups in the kitchen. The kaleidoscope was, Barry said in his thank-you note, a most delightful gift.

In return for the kaleidoscope, Barry and Sean took our family skiing. It was never actually said that the skiing trip was in return for the kaleidoscope, just that a chalet had become available, and that Alice and the girls and I could fly on tickets that Barry and Sean had earned with frequent flyer air miles. The children's faces showing innocent avarice were impossible to refuse when I made the mistake of handing them the travel brochure photographs of jagged peaks, pots of fondue (the girls, like their father, love cheese above all foods), of mountain girls in woolly bobble hats and red check coats tobogganing down pure white snow.

It is good, said Barry as he drove us from the airport to the chalet, to be reminded of the sublime.

He meant the mountains, which we could see through the living room window of our chalet, pyloned with ski lifts, white and indifferent and raw.

The first day was spent hiring ski gear, which I paid for, or rather Alice did. The second day was spent on the nursery slope where Alice executed slow graceful half-balletic moves that sent up little flurries of snow powder around the edges of her skis. I thrashed wildly about, scattering tiny children on tiny skis, trusting to my balance to keep me up, which it normally did, and everything was fine except when I had to stop, because when I angled my skis towards each other to brake, my stronger right leg would use my weaker damaged left as a pivot to skim wild circles around. After a day of this, and the twins having landed in the society of a snowboarding French family, led by a severe but bribable Swiss governess, I felt ready to make an exhibition of myself on the mountain.

Sean was designated to be Alice's guide. Barry looked after me. I didn't mind falling, there was even a bruising kind of pleasure to it, and I did it quite often, in between exhilarating white flashes of speed. I did mind the variety of transports that carried us up different parts of the mountain. The worst was the T-bar, an inverted iron cross suspended from a weary clanking chain, that lifted us along, our skis jittering and twisting against mountain ice, while Barry and I regarded one another with wary terror, as if daring the other to spill our unbalanced weight out of control.

Either on my skis, or rolling over on my sides, or on my belly and face shoveling through the snow, I kept up with Barry, who skied as if he were making a telephone call (which sometimes he was), very efficiently, with the occasional intimate flourish. I waved him away at the final slope, which went at an angle of about forty-five degrees down bare ice. Barry, contemplatively, added himself to the zigzag of skiers coming off the mountain. I passed him quickly, skidding, sliding, tumbling, head over heels, one ski twisted on the ice, my knee lacerating, the other ski uncoupling from my right boot and staying where it fell, about six inches or so from my grasping hand. When I pushed with my good leg against the ice the ski was now about thirty inches away and I was slipping still further down until Barry, my triumphant angel of the slopes, rescued me.

My leg was undamaged but I was happy to stay at the nursery slope after that, watching the twins' flirtation with a dashing pair of black-haired brothers in matching blue gilets and lambswool inflame into a love affair. Chloë had her heart broken first, when the older brother left her for an American heiress with her teeth in a brace. Daphne never gave up hers, even when his duplicities became too much for any onlooker to bear.

Barry and Sean and Alice kept me company the first day, on a blanket in the roughest corner of the nursery slope, where we wrote postcards home and picnicked on ham sandwiches and hot chocolate and exquisite miniatures of brandy bought from the cafe over the way, avoiding the yellow bus carrying skiers up to the cable car.

They had more postcards to write than we did. Sean looked up the addresses on his Palm Pilot, and Barry closed his eyes and put his hands behind his head and dictated quick witty messages that never quite duplicated each other.

Don't want anyone thinking they're getting the same as everybody else, he said.

That's a real skill, I said.

Just a knack, said Barry modestly. But listen, if you've run out of friends to write to—

I'm sure we can think of some more.

—then you might be interested in this technique that I know.

What kind of technique?

I learnt it from my AA sponsor. What you do is you write postcards that you never send.

Why would you want to do that?

Because you're writing your secret thoughts to people. You know, tell your father how he fucked you up, all the stuff that you would never disclose because people'd hate you for it. And then you destroy them. The postcards I mean. It's kind of cleansing. You want to try it? I got one or two spare.

I liked the idea of seeing my secret thoughts on post-cards. I did not know what they were and I was curious to read them. Barry offered me a couple of postcards from Sean's unwritten stack and I looked at Alice and she looked at me.

No, I said. Better not.

I grandly released them from any hostly or wifely obligation of sitting it out with me for the last two days. We gathered in the evenings when, after Barry and Sean had finished praising Alice's extraordinary flair for skiing, Sean would retire with the twins to be their confidant, and Barry and Alice would beat me at Scrabble if I wasn't pretending to be writing my film script.

On our last night they asked me about it. The twins were in their bedroom sobbing about love and Barry and Sean and Alice waited with anticipatory pleasure to hear about my script.

You have these stories, Chinese stories, a dreamer dreams a whole life. There's one, a monk has a pillow, it's made of cypress wood, and it's got a—

What's the point of having a pillow made of wood? That's dumb.

Barry began to laugh, his worst laugh, a nasty braying, which embarrassed me because it was the laugh he used in ignorance and contempt and was unworthy of him.

I don't know. In some stories it's jade. Maybe it's good for your back, I don't know. But the point is, he has this pillow, cypress—it could be jade, it doesn't matter—and it's got a crack in it, that's the important thing. So the story is this. A merchant comes to visit the local temple, to pray for good fortune, and the monk there asks him if he's married. He's not, so he's allowed to sleep beside the cypress pillow. The monk tells him to go inside the crack in the pillow and the merchant doesn't know what he's talking about but somehow, suddenly, he can.

I made myself go on. For a moment I had been disabled by envy for characters who live in stories, for men who can slip inside cypress cracks. Barry and Sean were, as far as I knew, unmarried; perhaps they, unlike us, were permitted inside cracks and pillows.

And it's like a fairyland in there, he goes through the outer vermilion gates and then through the inner yellow ones, into a palace built of jade, high terraces studded with precious jewels. He lives there, he has a place there. The Grand Marshal arranges a marriage for him. A good marriage. He raises six children. He's made Assistant Director

55

of the Imperial Library, then he's promoted further, to be the Attendant Within The Yellow Gates. He never thinks of going back, to the outside. He is happy. Life is good.

I sighed. Alice sighed too.

But then. But then he gets into trouble.

What sort of trouble? Sean asked.

Oh. You know. An influential enemy. Gossip in the court. That sort of thing. He loses his job. His wife dies. His children turn against him. Everything goes wrong. And then he hears the monk's voice, telling him to come out, and he does, he comes back out through the crack in the pillow again. He's lived many years inside it but when he comes out, only a moment has passed.

Barry poured us all another glass of Glühwein.

Is that it?

Yes.

That's not your film idea is it? said Alice.

No, I said quickly. Of course not.

Barry wouldn't accept any money for the skiing holiday. So, the next time we stayed at Barry and Sean's house, I brought along a rose bush.

Roses. For the garden, I perhaps unnecessarily explained.

And received in return two Cup Final tickets at the side of the royal box. The tickets had been intended for Bud the movie star, but he hated sport and appearing in public both, so Richard and I sat between an Arabian monarch and a party of Bulgarians, and one row behind Doughboy, now bald and plump and prosperous, but still regrettably playful. I escaped from him in the players' lounge after the game, where he had Richard agog and delighted with talk of the fast money that could be made from Asian betting syndicates and Balkan television rights.

And now the onus was back on me.

In the shed in the garden was my office, and inside it, on an erratically weathered Saturday, I sat sipping unsweetened coffee on an orthopedic chair whose wide wheeled base filled the floor space. The chair was angled away from the PVC window that let in light that was either searing bright or dirty gray. The desk was made of pine and covered by papers and coffee mug stains.

It was late morning and I was sighing a lot and the garden was noisy and these were the things I had to attend to: Tax bill; MOT; resident's parking permit application; breadmaking machine manual; movie script with a spiritual element in it.

I forced the official mail unopened into an already bulging large brown envelope on the darkest corner of the desk. I angled the anglepoise to shine on three drafts for the instruction manual—the Korean original, the first English translation, and my first improved version. I leaned back on my chair. I looked out of the window, narrowed my eyes against the glare. A pigeon on top of a fence-post was abysmally cooing. I sighed. I picked up the pair of porcelain Chinese dogs that Barry had—it had seemed at the time innocently—given as an anniversary present, and dropped them on the rug that covered most of the tar floor and watched them bounce.

After replacing the dogs in their dust paw prints on the windowsill, I sat down again, this time on the floor, in the north-east corner of the shed, with my head against the photograph of a jade mountain I'd torn out of a book on Chinese art and blu-tacked to the wall. I closed my eyes; I exhaled.

A breathing exercise to lift me up again. Fifty breaths from alternate nostrils and swiftly back at the desk and the manual. The trouble-shooting guide was missing from the literal translation. I had put off doing this, at first as a reward, something enjoyable to invent after the drudgery of alphabetizing the recipes, and double-checking the measures, each teaspoon and tablespoon and cup-sizing, and Anglicizing the Americanisms, and chopping away the wild neologisms and ugly coinages (*now make the proof to the dough!* or *yeastify with teaspoons two*), but then I had put it off because I just didn't have the creative heart. I had resolved to get the work done if the promised free machine ever arrived from the company. But that had been sitting for a week under the table, still in its box, next to ungiven gift-wrapped packages, another subtabular object for my shins to crack against.

I had done this kind of exercise dozens of times. It shouldn't take longer than ten minutes. There were eight trouble-shooting problems and solutions in the Korean original and they no doubt followed a typical formula. I opened a file on the computer. I made a start.

1. Problem: *i*-BreadMaker™ does not operate when start button is depressed.
   Solution: *i*-BreadMaker™ is not switched on.
2. Problem: bread does not rise.
   Solution: insufficient yeast has been added.

3. Problem: bread rises too much.
   Solution: too much yeast has been added.

I had reached an impasse. I shut my eyes, the better to imagine what else could go wrong with making bread.

4. Problem: bread tastes disgusting.
   Solution: don't eat it.

I exited the file without saving it, won three games of FreeCell and lost twenty of minesweeper at the expert level, then opened a new file.

1. Problem: need to buy perfect gift for Barry and Sean.
   Solution: buy it.

After the humiliation of the corkscrew I had gone out and bought candlesticks, Alice's original suggestion. I had been pleased with them at first, 1930s, solid silver, not plate, tastefully ornate, hinting at kitsch and grandeur both. And then I had rejected them. Too obvious, too much an imposition of my own taste. I had to learn how to learn from Barry and Sean themselves. Why had the corkscrew been such a good gift? Because it was a beautiful object in itself but more importantly it corresponded to a lack in my own life that they had been sensitive enough to notice and rectify.

Question: What is the perfect gift?
Answer: The perfect gift is an expression of the recipient's

character as appreciated, and rewarded, by the giver's sensitivity, friendship, and love.

I exited this file without saving it, switched off the computer straight away to avoid playing computer games, then switched it on again for a game of hearts.

The candlesticks had gone beneath the table. I had intended to return them to the shop but hadn't got round to doing that yet. I had looked through magazines; I'd taken window-shopping crawls down Northcote Road, Clapham High Street, Fulham Road, King's Road and New King's Road, Bond Street and New Bond Street, Knightsbridge, Camden Lock, Portobello Road, Camden Passage. I had poked through the bedrooms, living rooms, kitchens, and bathroom cabinets of friends, looking for desirable objects, necessary things. I had searched, I had failed, I had despaired. And I had avoided consulting Alice, because it mattered so much. It was something I had to do on my own.

I was getting too behind in the game. If I didn't do something good now, I was close to defeated. I cursed myself, I cursed Alice, I cursed the world, for allowing the ski holiday to happen. (If only . . . I briefly dreamed of my knee having actually been hurt on my ski accident, if only Alice hadn't turned out to be so good at skiing, if only Daphne and Chloë hadn't been receiving daily twin heart-stamped envelopes from what Alice told me was the smartest arrondissement of Paris.) I stopped short of cursing the twins, careful not to bring any calamities down on their unsuspecting heads.

A soft knock came on the door. The time was approaching lunch. Alice often sent the children, as emissaries.

Daddy?

The more sensitive twin, Daphne, came timidly into the shed.

I lifted her up as I used to do at the old house and sat her on my desk, but the desk was higher here and she might have grown heavier since the move, and the maneuver was a struggle for both of us, which ended with me panting and her sitting on the desk with her jumper pulled half over her head.

Can we have a rabbit please? Muffled-voiced Daphne.

No of course you can't.

Please, she said as her face appeared striped with red from where the ribs of the jumper had burned against her skin.

No. I'm sorry.

Please get us a rabbit?

No.

We don't want a regular sort of rabbit, a scruffy rabbit. We want a chinchilla.

No.

Why not?

Why not? Because I don't want animals around me that eat their own poo, they'll escape from the garden, make a mess in the shed.

You don't keep them in the garden, you keep them in the house, it's nicer for them that way.

That's even worse.

Something about what I then showed her pleased her, gave her hope. She carefully rolled up her sleeves exactly as Alice did. She pushed on with what she thought was her advantage.

They hardly take any looking after, they learn to use a litter tray, just like a cat. It's true.

That's brilliant.

Even if it was fraudulent and perhaps despicable I loved

this tender moment, the look in her face corresponding to the look in mine.

You mean we can have one?

Of course not, but thank you. I will get you something but not a rabbit. I promise.

I kissed her on the brow, carried her disgruntled out of the shed, along the garden, deposited her at her place at the kitchen table.

I put on my jacket. I tiptoed into the hallway carrying my boots, hoping to get out of the front door without being seen or heard—and was intercepted by Alice.

What are you up to? Lunch is ready.

I'm not hungry.

How's the script going?

It's, going. Coming along. Can't rush these things.

Have you finished the manual?

Nearly.

Have you done the parking permit? The tax return?

This afternoon. I'm going to do that this afternoon.

You said that yesterday morning. And you said that last week. Have you booked the car in for the MOT? Where are you going? You know how much it means to them to have lunch with you.

I'm going out.

Where out?

Just, you know, out.

I airily waved a hand. She blocked my way. I tried to look mysteriously casual. As if I might be trying to hide an affair I was having, as if I was on my way to a rendezvous with a secret, tiny love.

You're looking for a gift aren't you? For Barry and Sean? I know you are. You've got yourself in a spin over it. Calm down. *It doesn't matter.*

I'll see you later.

I hoped she didn't see how hurtful her words were to me. Of course it mattered. It mattered terribly.

I'll see you later, I repeated confidently, smiling fatuously at Alice's departing back, which was broader than remembered.

I walked to the pet shop on the high street, where I found on a pinboard a card advertising chinchilla rabbits from an address in Fulham. In my delight I took a cab to get there.

The chinchillas for sale were part of a family that had free run of a pair of rooms that stank of staleness and rotting herbs, a smell, which I only realized on the way out, originated in the very stern woman who lived there rather than the livestock that surrounded her. I sat on a shattered Draylon sofa and answered many questions about my capacity for chinchilla loving before she could bring herself to accept my money. I sneezed more or less throughout because, it transpired, I was allergic to long-haired rabbits.

I carried them back in a traveling cage to reveal my excellence to Alice.

Look. Rabbits.

For the girls? I thought—

No not for the girls. For the boys. They're chinchillas. They're called chinchillas. Well these are called Mitzi and Fritzi but you know what I mean.

Neither of us said anything for a while because I was too busy sneezing and Alice was watching in some degree of horror. When the nasal eruptions had subsided and most of the mucus mopped up, I was able to speak again.

Barry and Sean, their birthday presents, one each. They live in the house, the rabbits I mean, chinchillas, they're very clean, they use a litter tray, isn't their fur beautiful? It's

63

so, gray. And blue. And that pearl color. Aren't they cute?

They're a bit annoying looking. Why are their noses doing that? Are they clean?

The woman who sold them, said rabbits are cleaner than most children.

Most animals are—What do you mean *sold*? How much did you pay for those things?

They always say, Barry and Sean do, how they'd love to have a baby, I thought it would be much the same thing, in a way, something small and warm to look after. Two things. Don't you think? And he's always talking about that cat he used to have. Lucifer something. The one who used to get shot at in trees. People need something to look after, to hold and feed and stroke. It's a human need.

Did you know they eat their own shit?

Who, Barry and Sean? That's disgusting.

Don't be facetious. You know what I'm talking about.

Are you saying you don't think it's a good present?

Yes. It's. A. Very. Good. Present. I'm very proud of you. You're a very clever man.

I have to put them somewhere warm. They're quite young you know. How about the wardrobe?

Alice stared in the stoical way she was increasingly adopting, of someone who had been condemned to witness infinite folly for an infinite amount of time, and therefore no new manifestation of zaniness could surprise her, even in her husband.

They're not a couple are they? By morning the wardrobe will be full.

They're girls. Females I mean. They're sisters. Mitzi and Fritzi. But they can change the names if they like. I don't think the rabbits will mind. We can bring them to the birthday party. Haven't they got a very intelligent look about them?

She swallowed her intended reply. I assumed that it was discarded as being too wounding, even for me.

The sound of the chinchillas scratching against the cupboard doors through the night kept me awake. My excitement at having found the perfect gift would have kept me awake anyway.

I was in the kitchen with Sean. Sean was washing the CDs in a solution of his own mixing while I dried, a pleasant domestic task. Alice was in the attic bedroom putting the final inexplicable touches to her party dress, while the girls guarded Mitzi and Fritzi and pushed thin shavings of carrot into their cage. The twins loved Barry and Sean but they had come to love the chinchillas more. I asked Sean about the film he was set designing but Sean wanted to talk about my film instead.

Barry's very excited about it. Says he always knew you were peculiar enough to be a scriptwriter. I think he means that as a good thing not a bad thing. He's very glad there's a spiritual element. You're finishing it soon aren't you?

I hope so. Where *is* Barry?

Here soon. Meeting in Soho. He's catching the train back. Help me with the ashtrays?

We put out ashtrays from grand hotels in Norfolk party rooms. The house was filling up. In the screening room by the kitchen stairs Barry's fleecy flunkies were bickering over which videos should be playing at the party. The tarot reader was setting up a table in the first floor library. In the drawing room, by the piano, Sean showed me a black cardboard photograph album Barry's mother had sent over from New Jersey.

It's her way of showing she accepts me, Sean said. Finally.

I politely turned the pages. I was looking for Barry but kept finding the wrong child, in different clothes in different seasons but always the same appearance, bottle-glassed and snaggle-toothed, a teenager's skin richly pimpled, teeth thoroughly braced, nose long and crooked.

Is that Barry's brother? I didn't know he had a brother.

That's *Barry*. He got his face fixed after *The Killing Kind*.

Oh. It is isn't it? I see him now.

Only his hair was the same madness of shape and texture, if not quite the same color.

He said once that he didn't think anyone had ever listened to him when he was a child. Even when he pointed out the mistakes they kept making. When he was a teenager he tried shouting. That didn't work either. That's why he talks so softly now. To make sure people are listening. His parents kept putting these awful apparatuses on him. You know he wore orthopedic shoes until he was seven?

No. No, I didn't know that.

In the front hall we strung fairy lights over the fireplace and along the tops of portraits of somebody's Georgian ancestors.

Where's Alice and the girls?

Upstairs. Getting ready.

Still by the cage probably, curling around it, incanting schoolgirl prayers, protecting it with fetishes made of their own hair. They still believed against hope that it was all a game of mine, a giant fatherly tease. Even Alice wanted me to give the rabbits to the girls. She wouldn't admit it but a part of her responded in the same maternal way to rabbity features and soft gray fur and seeming helplessness. It was a mercy to Mitzi and Fritzi that they would be staying here. Already the cat litter floor of their traveling cage had become piled high with unwanted offerings of carrot and lettuce.

The first guests arrived. Discarding coats, displaying party clothes and anticipatory smiles. Air-kissing Sean, each other, themselves. And Barry had yet to show.

I carried the washing-up rack of CDs to the stereo cabinet in the hall, my suit jacket left behind on a kitchen stool. Without the jacket I was dressed much the same as the catering staff which depressed me.

At Barry and Sean's parties the usual suspense was whether the hedonist celebrities were going to outnumber the on-the-wagon celebrities. Tonight (with the balance seeming tilted towards the hedonists) the question was whether Barry was going to show. There was no sign of him. The house was filling up with guests and birthday presents and the primary host still wasn't there.

What do you do?

I'm. I'm a writer.

The question had taken me by surprise. (I was at the open wardrobe in the hall and trying to decide between jazz, rhythm & blues, and Syd Barrett. The cover of the Syd Barrett CD had a picture of the singer, wild dark hair, perfectly handsome English face, which in another lifetime could have belonged to a World War One hero, a diffident flying ace.) In Barry and Sean's circles it happened quite a lot. Someone would ask me what I did and I would be taken by surprise and sometimes I would answer honestly and wish immediately that I had lied.

The woman looked nice, quite endearingly shy, a little

awkward in her dress that was so obviously new, still shop-creased.

Do you work with Barry?

I'm not that kind of a writer.

What kind of writer are you? Have I heard of you?

I'm a technical writer, I said.

And wished I'd lied, invented something glamorous or stupid. The woman wrinkled her nose as if what I'd said had confirmed something disappointing she'd already smelled, and when I turned back to her after putting on the jazz CD she was gone.

I was next to her again some time later. (The jazz had been removed and replaced within minutes by a bartender, who had set up in front of the stereo; I took this as a sign that I should relinquish my DJ duties.) Sean was at the center of a group of slightly malicious film agents dressed as fauns with gold body paint and bronze leaf costumes who were asking where Barry was. He was waving his hand in the direction of the sky and said he thought Barry might be coming by plane. Someone mentioned helicopters, which bored the woman from before, who turned randomly to me. The creases in her dress had been smoothed away and she looked more beautiful than before, which was perhaps because her beauty was more special than I'd thought or because of the sea breeze cocktails I'd been drinking.

He's not coming is he?

Doesn't look like it.

I had presumed she remembered me from our first conversation but her next question showed she hadn't.

What do you do?

It was seldom in this circle that anyone was given a second chance.

Me? I'm a Chinese garden designer.

69

You don't look Chinese.

No. I mean, I design Chinese gardens.

In China?

No. Here.

Oh.

I apply classical Taoist principles to gardening.

That's interesting.

Do you have a garden?

It's very small.

Smaller the better.

It's south facing and it doesn't get any light and anything I try to plant in there just dies.

Using certain occult practices that few people in the West have survived the knowledge of, I can make the darkest garden bloom.

Really? Are you telling the truth?

I summoned up all my attributes of sincerity and poise to murmur,

You might have seen me on TV.

She stared dubiously at first, and then with enthusiasm.

Oh yes. I think I have. You're on that program, on Wednesdays.

That's right.

I'm sorry. I didn't recognize you with that, you know, beard.

You don't like it? Most people don't.

No I don't *not* like it, it's just I didn't recognize you at first. But of course, it's you. I recognize you now. You're very good.

I looked modestly at my hands. I was proud of them for once, they mixed with the elements, and made things grow.

Do you have, you know, private clients?

Sometimes. If the job interests me. But I have to warn you. I'm expensive. Very.

God. I'd pay whatever it takes. You might be a godsend. What sort of things would you plant in my garden?

Whatever would give you most pleasure. Flowers. And shrubs. Maybe a tree. Certainly a mountain of some kind— at least symbolically, a few stones will do. The garden must represent the world, all its attributes. Running water. Perhaps a fountain. But I couldn't possibly say without seeing the garden first. Getting my hands and face in there.

Of course. But—

I'll get you my card. It's in my jacket.

I could have enjoyed this conversation for hours, and it seemed to be developing an erotic subtext that was enjoyable too. But Dylan was approaching, and there was a small possibility that she might remember that I was not a Chinese garden designer.

The film director smiled in a very friendly way, which, despite the animosity I felt for her, was flattering. She put a hand on my sleeve and spoke in a confidential tone.

Do you think there's a sea breeze available? Two of them. And maybe whiskey? We'd prefer Irish.

I don't know.

Do you think you could find out for me?

I suppose so.

I headed towards the bar. I didn't get there because Alice called me over. She was talking to a small plump man, which was the physical type that she liked best.

Have you seen the girls?

No. Have you seen Barry?

We don't think he's going to come, said Alice. We think

he's having an affair. Are you on your way to the bar? Could you get me something?

My hands will be full. I seem to be fetching a round of drinks for Dylan.

She probably thinks you're a waiter. You look like a waiter.

I thought you were a waiter, said the small plump man.

Oh. Fuck her.

I pushed back into the crowd. I saw the film director and mouthed the words, Fuck you. Dylan shook her head, raised her hands, apologized for not being able to hear. I bloodily executed a thousand Welshwomen in my head and went to look for my jacket which I found crumpled on the kitchen floor. I brushed away cigarette ash and obscure food stains and put it back on and immediately felt far too hot. I wandered through rooms looking for someone I recognized. I stood for a while on the edge of a group that contained Dylan's husband but he didn't look at me despite my amiable gurning. I hunted for the consolation of my daughters. They were wearing pink satin dresses and diaphanous angel wings and flirting with elderly homosexuals in the library. They ignored me too, ostentatiously unforgiving.

The next time I saw Dylan, she was at a center of a group of tall women and short men, one of whom might have been the man my wife had been talking to before. They were all talking about Barry. It had been generally agreed that he was not coming to his own birthday party.

I was sweating. The night was warm and the house was hot, and my suit, which was my best, was made of thick wool. I put a hand on the film director's arm and steered her a couple of steps away from the group.

Hello, I said.

Hello. How are you?

I'm not a waiter.

No. I know you're not.

Dylan concentrated very hard. She remembered something. She was pleased with herself.

You're the one who isn't the nose doctor. I remember you.

You thought I was a waiter before.

Did I? Did I?

I silently shook off my jacket. Dylan had the decency to look ashamed.

Oh. I'm sorry. It's just that your—

I know.

Dylan waited for me to say something more. As a consequence of her shame I had earned the grace of her conversation.

What have you got them? I asked.

Who?

For birthday presents. What have you got them?

Oh I don't know, I expect he'll have thought of something that's probably quite good. Do you have any cocaine?

No. I don't. But it's hard isn't it? To choose gifts for people.

Have you seen Bud? Bud's supposed to be here, Dylan said with the annoyed complacency of someone who had just realized that she was the most famous person in the room.

I don't know Bud.

If ever I talked to someone famous I always talked too much, as if I had to get as many words spoken in the short time allotted, before an invisible red velvet rope was hung in front of me again, or else it was a form of aggression: I needed to display myself, to show no person was any better than me, and if it looked that way it was all an accident of fate or luck.

To choose gifts for people. It makes me feel bad sometimes, you know, we're often here and they're very hospitable and I want to get them something that they'd like. I mean, I was going to get them some candlesticks and they're nice but not really special if you know what I mean.

If the rabbits didn't take, I didn't know what I was going to do. Already I was beginning to dread what I would receive back in return. (*We got something for you . . .*) But whatever it would be, the obligation was going to be on them now. I was about to issue a serious challenge to Barry and Sean's superiority.

If it was up to me, Dylan said, if I had the time to arrange it, you know what I'd do? I'd commission a painter to do their portrait. They're a very beautiful couple don't you think? I mean, Sean's very good looking isn't he? And I know Barry makes an idiot of himself with his hair, but he's very handsome isn't he? A portrait would be good, if you could get them in the same room at the same time. Though I suppose they can do it from photographs.

Yes. I've been thinking along those lines myself, I lied.

Dylan started to look around. We'd had enough time, her debt had been decently discharged, she could find a reason to go now. Or else she could just leave.

Goodbye, she said.

Do you still write plays?

I had liked Dylan's plays. They were passionate and strange, with depths of tenderness and violence.

What's that? I'm sort of writing a novel. I've been writing it for years. Plays are finished, don't you think?

I've thought of writing a novel.

Dylan stepped away and looked wildly around for escape. I realized, with some embarrassment, that people like Dylan were always being told this sort of thing by people like me, and I hated myself for being so predictably irritating. Hello! I'm a waste of space who wants to talk about the book inside me! Dylan had given me a graceful moment of her time and it had been even more boring than she'd expected.

It would be an honest book.

Really.

Yes honest. I've always thought, well often thought, I do have other things, ha ha, but if you're a novelist it must be very hard. You know, if you want to write about the world you live in there must be so many people you can't be rude about. Famous rich people know other famous rich people don't they? You can't afford to alienate them, can you? Career to look after. You've got lots of children haven't you? What about the school fees? You can't afford to take the piss. And then if you play your cards right you get prizes and titles and suchlike. You'll probably be a Dame soon. You don't want to prejudice that, do you? I mean, unsuccessful novelists probably write honestly and satirically all the time, but who wants to read them? I don't. And anyway, readers want glamor don't they? Successful men, beautiful women. Maybe they don't want to know what really goes on. I don't know if I do. When it comes down to it. At the end of the day.

I realized that I was making very little sense. I ordered myself to stop talking. I forced my mouth shut.

Do you know what Kafka said? Dylan asked.

I don't know. Maybe.

It was in a letter to a friend of his, I learned the whole

paragraph by heart once to impress a boy. I might still be able to remember it. If the book we're reading is how it goes. If the book we're reading, he says, doesn't shake us awake like a blow to the skull, why bother reading it in the first place? So that it can make us happy, as you put it? Good God, we'd be just as happy if we had no books at all, books that make us happy we could, in a pinch, also write ourselves.

That's very good.

It goes on. What we need are books that hit us like a most painful misfortune, like the death of someone we loved more than we love ourselves, that make us feel as though we had been banished to the woods, far from any human presence, like a suicide. A book must be the axe for the frozen sea within us. That's what Kafka said. The axe for the frozen sea within us. He's right, isn't he?

Did you impress the boy?

What boy?

The one you learnt the poem for.

It's not a poem. It's from a letter to a friend of his. I don't remember. Probably. I think that's Jerry over there. I'm supposed to be nice to him. I'll see you later.

I thought more fondly of Dylan after that. I realized that despite everything, Dylan considered herself a failure too.

She's a genius isn't she?

The most beautiful woman that I had ever stood close to was gazing at Dylan with awe and desperate sexual longing. My appetite for the party was gone after that. I climbed up towards the attic. I pushed through couples flirting on the stairs, past mustachioed dancers on the landing. I lingered in the doorway of Barry and Sean's bedroom, where a very tall male writer dressed as Elizabeth I, with courtiers surrounding, was very regally having his fortune told by the tarot reader. Mostly men filled the bedroom, sitting on the bed, sitting on the floor, leaning against window and wardrobe and wall.

We're about to start playing a game.

You can play too.

Have you got a partner? Where's your partner?

Are we playing or not? said a slightly malicious film agent.

The rules of the game were explained to me by a burly man in tweeds: Remember a day, a moment, when things were good in a love affair. Offer it to the audience. There was one condition: The moment must be strictly between the two lovers and may not involve a third.

Triangulated desire is what we're trying to eradicate here, he said in conclusion.

Oh sit down you great poof, said the film agent.

What about animals? Are animals allowed? asked a muscled young man in gym singlet and ripped jeans whom I recognized from a poster in the twins' bedroom one house and several generations of girlish lust ago.

You can shut up too.

I found a space to sit beside the burly man, crouched, beneath the window. The first declarer got up. He remembered a day on an African beach building sandcastles. Then the sex that was had, in mud and sun.

Bloody nostalgie de la boue, scowled the very tall writer.

Baking bread, is what another man remembered.

Bloody Pollyannas.

Dangerous sex in a New York club.

Bloody arseholes.

That one anyway was disallowed, despite the arguments of its declarer, a TV chef, because of its public nature, its requirement of others.

A woman remembered an argument in the kitchen, throwing cherry tomatoes at her husband, watching them splat sticky viscous against kitchen walls.

And then we had the greatest shag.

All roads lead to sex, murmured the tweedy man beside me. Would you like me to give you a blowjob?

No, I don't think so. No thank you.

The turn came around to me. I stood. I had been thinking very hard.

Running in on goal, my father on the touchline, cold air in my lungs, opposing players falling away, their goalkeeper rushes back to his line then comes fast-forward towards me, legs and arms out wide, trying to narrow the angle, I slip the ball between his legs, skip over his flailing arm, the big empty swat of his hand, nothing in front of me except for an empty goal net, a black and white football rolling towards it. That had felt very good, I had been happy then, but it didn't apply, there had been at least three: father, football, me.

Sitting on a wooden bench in the minibus on the way to the Southern Counties Final, Smithy driving while massaging Lee's injured upper thigh, Richard losing money hand over fist in the brag school opposite me, Doughboy winning the argument with the center-backs over whose turn it was to be DJ, the two goalkeepers playing slapsies; and I, The Professor, read a book of Chinese legends. That wasn't the point: that was just me being happy on my own.

Being fitted for my blue England blazer, a gray-haired tailor in a waistcoat, tape measure around his neck, breath smells of milk, cough sweets, and cigarettes, he yanks my arms full-length down, jerks my head to correct the angle of my shoulders while my mother, soon to be dead, sits on a gray plastic chair with the outer layers of my school uniform on her proud, doomed lap.

The twins. The day they were born, my heart swelled with a terrible tenderness. Alice's exhausted triumphant face, the rip on her belly which the surgeon had pushed both frantic hands inside. The night Daphne fell out of bed and Chloë didn't. The girls singing happy birthday to me with trick candles on the cake they'd made and on their heads queenly crowns beneath which identically textured blonde-white hair swung in identical braids. The implacability of their silence and disregard, when they were punishing me for the crime of not providing something they wanted, which merged into Alice's.

I excluded thoughts of the twins because that was against the rules of the game. Romance was being celebrated here, especially precious because of its necessary end. Expectant faces waited for me to speak of a moment between two that had no need of a third or a fourth. My audience. My already restless crowd.

Alice in the back of a cab blows me a kiss. I'm on the pavement waving as her hand comes towards me, as if the taxi had no rear window, as if there was no distance between us, getting larger. That was anticipation, mine. It wasn't a moment equally shared by two.

This was me at last in the spotlight and men were looking away from me with embarrassed mocking faces and I was about to fail. Our honeymoon? The first time we signed a contract on a house? I would have liked to say a thousand but we never got there.

Nine hundred and fifty, I said.

Nine hundred and forty-two. Actually, said Alice who was standing just inside the door.

Bloody anal retentives.

Excuse me.

Like the player who has missed a penalty, I slunk away.
I made my way into the attic. Daphne and Chloë had fallen
asleep holding on to the rabbit cage, their little fingers
gripping tight, strained white at the knuckles.

In the morning, a few guests managed to repair themselves
enough to stagger into the kitchen for breakfast. Alice was
eating toast and marmite. The slightly malicious film agent
was huddled inside the fur coat he was using as a dressing
gown and sipping at a large bowl of rice krispies. The
very tall writer occupied the head of the table, where
he declaimed obscure statements and guffawed. Sean was
baking croissants. Dylan had already left; she'd taken a
cab to meet a helicopter to catch a plane to Wales, where
she would be going horse riding. And Barry hadn't come.
I heard it whispered, by the agent to the writer, that it
wasn't a coincidence that Bud hadn't come either.

He called didn't he, said the slightly malicious agent
more loudly when Sean approached with croissants. You
know what trains are like.

And planes, Alice added.

Yes, and planes. You know what trains and planes are
like. He meant to be here.

Something might have happened to him.

Like what? said Alice.

Barry's indestructible, said the film agent.

Barry's frightened of dying, the very tall writer said
matter-of-factly and then guffawed. He's getting old and
he can't face it and he's trying to get you worked up, where
do you think he is? I'll tell you where he is, he's in a hotel
room smoking crack with rent boys and he's staring into
a mirror and tying something new into his hair, an anvil,

that's it he's got a fucking anvil hanging off him by the follicles and he's trying to make you jealous because he's old and you're not and he's terrified of losing you. Ha ha ha. He's closer to death than you are. Ha ha ha ha ha.

Alice and I looked at each other and the film agent looked at us, insecure in the knowledge that we knew something he didn't. We knew that what the writer said was not true. We knew what people in the film industry did not—that Sean had a heart murmur as a result of taking too many body building steroids and was probably closer to death than Barry, whose only medical secret was an embarrassing skin disease.

Where are the girls? Sean asked. Don't they want breakfast?

Alice said, They're upstairs. They're guarding.

Guarding what?

Oh, I said. You'll see. It's a surprise. Back in a minute.

I ran up the stairs, glimpses of bodies along the way, party aftermath carnage, up to the attic, where my daughters in anoraks against the cold sat grimly beside two gray rabbits in a traveling cage. Four pairs of eyes (two blue, two brown) warily regarded me. I stepped forward. I reached for the cage and so did my daughters.

I fought my children for the traveling cage. I battled to pull it away from the clutch of four small hands. I made myself hard, I smothered the sound of twin hearts crying. They pleaded with me, they begged; I was strong, I was resolute.

No, I said, these are not for you.

I seized the cage. I took it downstairs. The chinchillas shivered on their journey.

This is for you, I said to Sean. Gifts. For you and Barry. Happy birthdays.

They are *adorable*, said the slightly malicious film agent.

Are we going to eat them? said the very tall writer.

Thank you, Sean said, I think they're beautiful.

They're for the house, I said. They're house rabbits.

The rabbits twitchily inspected Sean. I blew my nose. Sean looked at the rabbits and smiled.

Shamelessly, Alice, seeing the success of the gift, joined in with the giving.

They're toilet trained. They can use a litter tray just like cats.

I think they're beautiful. What are they called?

They're called Mitzi and Fritzi, but you can change that if you like.

I wouldn't dream of it, Sean said.

Now was I smug. I broke my own rule and bought a canary for the girls, which helped them to forgive my treachery. The world benefited from my expansion. I finished my manual labor, I dealt with all my correspondence, even the most irksome. I was a sexual creature, satisfying my wife almost daily (741, 750, 679). Much of the day I smiled. Often I whistled. I made the first sketchy outline of a movie script.

The thank-you letter was signed by both Barry and Sean and, in a cutesy way that would normally have made me nauseous, footprinted by Mitzi and Fritzi in bright poster-paint blue. The boys' gratitude was clear, their humiliation evident. I was, for once, ahead of the game.

I received a phonecall from Barry the day after the thank-you letter. I was in the living room telling Alice an old Chinese story, in the hope that she might think it might be a good idea for a movie.

There's these two friends who get lost looking for herbs in the mountains. They've been walking around for days, nothing to eat, nothing to drink, and then they see a peach tree at the top of a mountain peak. So up they climb, it's a tough dangerous climb, but they manage it. They get to the tree. They eat peaches and they're refreshed now, so they go back down, and they come to a stream, where there are these two beautiful girls they've never seen before but who somehow seem to know them. The girls call the men by their names. What took you so long? they say. We've been waiting. The girls take the men home, a building with a bamboo roof, beds draped with scarlet satin curtains, gold and silver bells. Ten maids standing at each bed. They stay for ten days. Then they want to go home.

Why would they want to go home? It sounds like male fantasy come true.

Maybe they've got work to do, or families, or something. I don't know. They might just be homesick. That's not the point. Anyway. The girls persuade them not to go and probably, you're probably right, it's probably not that hard to persuade them. So they stay on, for another seven months, and then they do leave, because they're still bound by worldly concerns. Maybe they're not ready for paradise yet. The girls throw a farewell party for them, you know, music, dancing, a banquet, and then the two friends set off for home, but when they get there, this is the thing, the town is unrecognizable, all their family and friends are dead. Finally they find their—hold on, I don't know if I'm going to get this right—great-great-great-great-*great*-grandchildren, who tell them a story about these two ancestors who had gone up to the mountains seven generations before and couldn't find their way back . . . Well? What do you think?

Fortunately the telephone rang, which meant I would never need to know what Alice thought. Unfortunately, it was Barry.

Phil! We *love* the rabbits, it was so clever of you to know.

Now was I uneasy. I detected hidden threat, a promise of

reprisal. I made sure that the subject of a return gift would be difficult to reach.

It was a great party. We were sorry not to see you there.

Barry took a while to decide on his reply. He breathed hard on the other end of the phone.

Yeah, he finally said. Me too. Look. I'm going to talk about this subject once and then if you're my good friend we won't talk about it again. Are you my good friend, Phil?

Yes. I hope so.

I know so. So listen. It was pathetic of me, but I just couldn't bear it. You know how old I am? Fifty-five years old. Fifty-five. Five-five. I'm closer to seventy than forty. This is not a matter for celebration, you know what I'm saying?

I think so.

But hey. Of course. Talking about birthdays. It's the birthday isn't it? The *births*-day. When's the party? Tell the girls we'll be there.

It's next week. Saturday. But you don't have to.

I know we don't have to. We *want* to.

The twins'll love it if you're there, you know that, but you know what it's going to be like, high-pitched screaming, lots of it.

We'll be there. Jesus, it seems like it was their births-day only yesterday. Man, time flies. Does time not fucking fly? What does time do?

It flies.

Damn right it does. You never said a truer word. Except when I'm pissing. Do you know how much time I endure pissing every day? Standing at a urinal waiting for my dick to stop dripping? Sometimes I swear I could kill myself out of the boredom.

Oh.

Look. I shouldn't have missed the party. It was mean of me and bad of me but it happened and whatever. Sean's cool.

Is he? Good.

Yeah, I had to do some things but it's cool. But listen, while we're on the subject of *things*, I got, we got—

Sorry Barry. That's the oven alarm. I have to go. I'm cooking dinner. Bye now.

Fuck the oven. I just want to say—

Sorry Barry. Speak to you soon. Thank you for calling. Best to Sean. Glad you like the rabbits.

I avoided Alice's eyes. On my way out of the living room I offered Django the canary a pellet of seed and made no sound when he pecked at my fingers instead.

We had got to one hundred and seventy-two when Chloë came crying into the bedroom.

Look, she said sobbing, LOOK!

She tenderly held out a finger for us to inspect.

Wha' happen? I said withdrawing from Alice's jade chamber, covering my throbbing jade peak with the duvet cover.

Did you have an accident darling? asked Alice pulling down her nightdress.

Chloë, through her tears, shook her head.

It hurts, she said.

We looked at the finger for signs of injury. There was none. I looked to Chloë's face for clues and then to Alice's for theories.

When the sound of Daphne screaming pierced everything.

I pulled myself out of bed, walked away tent-pole hunched, found my way into a dressing gown and ran into the twins' room, where Daphne sat sobbing on the floor, holding up a bleeding finger. I kissed away the blood. Chloë, who had followed me in, lifted her own, undamaged, finger for me to kiss also.

And so begins the flurry of early morning activity, the brushing of teeth and sniffing of yesterday's knickers and burning of porridge and jamming of emergency toast until everyone is in the kitchen seated and dressed and eating breakfast. The twins were self-regulating and self-maintaining in most things. With a slice of toast in my mouth and a mug of tea in my left hand, I could concentrate on trying to understand the *i*-BreadMaker™.

It doesn't work, I said.

The remote control unit was the most heavily buttoned and variously colored I had ever come across. The *i*-BreadMaker™ itself was sleek, handsome, chrome, uncluttered. Before it would consent to perform I had to set or confirm or at least disable the machine's calendar and clock.

Look in the manual, Alice said.

I *wrote* the manual. What help's that going to be?

A twin went past and my hand automatically went out to stroke her hair. I loved the feel of the twins' hair. The fizz of blonde electricity against my tired skin.

Let me have a look, said Alice.

Hold on, I haven't tried this yet.

Alice reached for the machine and I pulled it back towards me and the lead knotted around her wrist and the *i*-BreadMaker™ came crashing off the counter and landed on Alice's foot. For a moment there was stillness, a long moment of silence filled with expectation, the perfect present, heavy with the past, the future inside it aching to be born, like the breath-hold of a crowd waiting for a penalty to be taken. Then Alice shrieked and crumpled to the floor holding her foot. We went to tend her, one twin stroked her face, the other took hold of a hand. I reached for my wife's foot, which kept wriggling away from me.

It's broken, said Alice.

Are you sure?

The twins cooed at their mother, soothing the sweat away from her forehead. Her skin had turned very white. I picked up the machine, which appeared resolutely intact, and replaced it on the work surface.

My toe. It's broken.

I dropped the twins off at school and then took Alice to the hospital. We waited on pink plastic chairs between a woman who groaned and a man with pleasant breasts who had a bandage on his nose. Half a day later Alice's broken toe had been wrapped inside a bandage strapped around the neighboring toe. The slightest pressure on her damaged foot sent her wincing with pain.

It's just bad luck, she said.

As I eased her into the Volvo my jacket caught on the corner of the passenger door and ripped.

That too, she said.

I took these events personally. I vowed to keep a vigil on the twins. Their conception and birth had been miraculously lucky. After being told that we could not combine to produce children, that the motility of my sperm and the shape of Alice's womb would not permit it, perhaps we might want to consider IVF treatment, or the fostering of a thirteen-year-old with a borderline personality disorder . . . ? Alice had conceived and, eight months later—premature, the twins had been delivered by cesarean section—two tiny jaundiced girls had arrived, with yellow chests and faces and blue fingers and toes, who only became themselves after the intervention of tubes and heat and breathing apparatus. Daphne had been the sicklier one. In their infancy I had watched over them both with a scrutiny strong enough to battle misfortune.

I left Alice lying on a sun lounger in the garden, with a glass of elderflower cordial, a ring binder of rebranding notes and the sometimes-working telephone. I made the short walk to school, into the playground through blue clouds of children.

How're things?

What?

How're things?

I had heard Richard's question perfectly well the first time. It was a new habit I was experimenting with. Perhaps wilful deafness could be a consolation of middle age.

Stop that!

The twins carried on with what they were doing.

Things. How are they?

Fine. Good. Everything's very good. Alice broke her foot today. I mean, apart from that things are good.

That Molly's quite a firecracker isn't she?

Is she? I don't know. I suppose she is.

Do you want to come in on something?

Come in on what?

It's a sure thing. Doughboy. He said you could come in on it.

Really? Why?

Said he feels sorry for you. Actually he said I could only come in on it if you did. You want to?

No. No I don't.

It's a sure thing. It'd get me out of a hole. You could bet the house.

I don't think that would be a very good idea.

You know what I'm going to do? I'm going to stand right here and convince you and you're not going home until I've done that. I WANT YOU TO GIVE ME YOUR MONEY! You ready?

Richard's appearance and, therefore, Richard himself, was sinking. In his happier moments, he wore his wealth on his sleeve, blinding the world with peacock displays of latex and leather and gold. But today, blocking me from leaving the playground, his skin was sweaty and raw, his football shorts and denim jacket looked, and smelled, as if they had been used to douse a chip-pan fire and then left out in the rain overnight to be washed.

Excuse me. I forgot something.

I could not bear to add to his disappointments. It felt craven and stupid but I turned and led the twins back towards the school buildings. In the corridor I met the garrulous Miss Abbot, who was pleased to see me. She said so.

I had been hoping to have a word, she said rather coyly as if I had wheedled this out of her. She took me into a classroom.

Is there a problem?

Problem? With the twins? No. Not at all. Delightful girls. Marvellously undisruptive. I only wish they'd sometimes, show more *appetite* for joining in. They're very exclusive you know.

Twins are often like that I think.

Yes I know, that's what I hear, but—

We used to take them to Twins' Club, and that was dreadful.

I looked over to the girls in case I was in danger of hurting their feelings, but they didn't seem to be listening. They were sat neatly at a desk passing back and forth a square of paper on which they were taking it in turns to add to a drawing of what looked like a lacrosse player.

Yes, dreadful. It was like being in a loony bin—that's probably not the right phrase is it? What do you say these days? It was like being in a *special* place. Special needs. All these pairs interacting only with each other.

Yes yes quite, said Miss Abbot eager to have a turn to speak, which I denied her. I knew her chance would come and she would exploit it to the full so I felt no guilt at delaying it.

It's quite recent, you know, the twins, the way they've been acting.

Recent—

Yes. A couple of months. A few months. That's all. They've become obsessed with public school, boarding school. They seem to be having some sort of Enid Blyton fantasy about school. It's out of the question of course.

I stumbled. I fell. Miss Abbot took over.

It's so very fascinating isn't it? They say that adolescence begins that much earlier these days. And the twins are approaching the very *cusp*. I wondered? Wondered if, a pet might be quite a good idea? I rather think they need to learn to move *outwards* (Miss Abbot—horsey faced, sparkling blue eyes—threw her arms forward) rather than *inwards* (Miss A pulled her arms back, made as if to hug herself) all the time.

A pet.

The twins looked guilelessly innocent, betraying no sign of being in collusion with their teacher.

Yes. Exactly so. A pet. To learn to love something that is not them.

We have a canary. He's called Django.

Can one love a canary? Truly? I don't know if one can. I was thinking, really, of something furrier.

After enduring a half hour of Miss Abbot's lesson on the meaning of love I timidly re-emerged. In the crooked concrete playground, Richard was nowhere to be seen, not on the wooden bridge where younger brothers and sisters were briskly injuring themselves, not hiding behind wind-bent clumps of trees planted in honor of suffering children in poorer parts of the globe. I turned to shepherd the twins out into the playground, and turned again to find myself blocking the way of the architect's wife who was trying to get through.

She looked surprised to see me, perhaps even flustered.

Oh, she said. Are you going in?

In?

To the meeting.

I could feel myself blushing, and hoped it could be put down to the wind that was hurtling around the playground, bouncing the school door between my hand and the post.

No yes, I managed to say and then, more suavely, Yes.

I held the door open for her and a sleeve of her nylon windbreaker brushed against my hand.

I should take the girls home first.

Oh they can stay outside. Someone will be keeping an eye on them in the playground.

Her very daring remark made me blush again. The children in the playground, at any moment able to climb on shoulders and peer in through high mullioned windows to witness the depravity on display. And a bored supervising teacher ambling over to see what the children were getting so excited about. This was all part of it, I supposed, the thrill of exhibitionism, the excitement taken in a pleasure that could any moment be discovered, interrupted, compromised, condemned. I wondered if any of the teachers were in on the sex rings, quite likely the middle-class one, and maybe the working-class one too, SATS papers and homework books lasciviously abandoned in favor of a bit of rough. The boring tone of all those notes in the girls' school bags signed by the *liaison officer* between staff and parents suddenly became erotically clear.

93

She led me down the corridor. The architect's wife was carrying a supermarket carrier bag filled with what in more innocent times I would have assumed to be PTA newsletters and traffic petitions. She held her bag tightly to her chest as she walked, her head jutting forward protectively, or excitedly.

I was the only man at the meeting, apart from the speaker from the council traffic department but he didn't seem to be aware of the sexual uproar in the room. School mothers and I sat on a semicircle of small wooden chairs. The council man facing us had obviously made this presentation many times before. He was able to switch the rest of himself off while he gave his speech about pedestrian crossings (pelican and zebra, raised and flat), traffic lights, belisha beacons, bicycle lanes, bicycle locks, the human train of children as a means of walking safely to school that was particularly popular in Croydon and Norway. Some of the women leaned forward, lips slightly parted, hands opening and closing on thighs, the rustle of denim and skirts. Others sat back, arms crossed, eyes flicking casually around the room resting on me, appraising me no doubt, the curiosity, or disappointment, of fresh blood, new flesh. I slumped deeper on my chair. My eyelids lowered, protection against the councilman's drone, the women's scrutiny.

When I woke up the man from the council was gone. The women still had their clothes on. No boxes of sex toys had emerged from the bag of the architect's wife.

Well that was very helpful, said one woman. *Not.*

It's exactly what he said last year, said the architect's wife.

The women got up from their chairs, stood in groups, organized perhaps on the principle of shared sexual preference or perversity.

94

Is that it? I asked.

Perhaps you'd like to volunteer? said a woman I had never seen before. I wondered if she was the liaison officer. She had cropped gray hair and a smooth, unlined boyish face, and wore what appeared to be a leotard under her army greatcoat. Her green eyes gazed at me quite coolly and thrillingly.

No, I said. Thank you. I don't think I'm quite ready for that yet.

Sean was in the bedroom with a basket of muffins for Alice.

You poor love, he said. In the wars.

He sat on the edge of her bed and lightly kissed the bandage on her toe and held her hand and took her on a muffin tour.

There's blackberry and blueberry, and chocolate chip here, and double chocolate there, and I think this one is cherry, and those ones are plain.

Thank you Sean, she said looking at me. You're very thoughtful.

It hadn't occurred to me to buy a basket of muffins for Alice. But then I suppose it wouldn't have.

Phillip? Will you get something for Sean. A drink.

What would you like to drink, Sean?

Cup of tea would be nice.

Not the way I make it.

Sorry?

Excuse me. A joke. Alice?

Tea. Use the pot. And bring plates for the muffins.

I left the bedroom telling myself to curb this tendency to make vaguely malevolent remarks to my friends and loved ones. Alice, I noticed, was beginning to treat me like a retarded servant she was keeping on out of some loyalty, an oath made long ago to a concerned failing parent.

When I returned, with plates for the muffins and cups and the pot of tea dripping onto a tray, Sean and Alice were talking very earnestly and softly. From the way they broke off as soon as I came into the room I realized that what they were talking about had either everything to do with me or absolutely nothing at all.

Sean's just been telling me about the rabbits, Alice said.

That's right, said Sean. They're thriving.

That's good to hear.

We love them. Barry especially.

Great.

They've really got their own characters you know. Mitzi's the daredevil. Fritzi's kind of calmer.

I tried to imagine a daredevil rabbit. I couldn't even imagine a calm rabbit, so I gave up the exercise.

How's the toe? Sean said. Does it hurt very bad?

Only when I'm cold or the weather's wet or when I get tired. Have another muffin.

Try to stop me.

How's Barry? I asked.

Rushed off his feet. He's in his element. He loves it, the start of a new movie. I don't think he loves anything more.

Sean?

Umm? he managed to say through clods of muffin, perhaps cherry.

What did you and Barry get each other for your birthdays?

Sean chewed very slowly. He looked at me as if wary for a trick.

Barry got me a suit. Made to measure from Savile Row. I've never had a made-to-measure suit before.

Wow. That's good. And?

And what?

What did you get him?

It was tough. It's tough to think of presents for Barry.

Is it? Is it really?

Alice kicked me with her good foot. Sean didn't notice or just pretended not to.

Yea, I can't get him things to tie into his hair because he likes to collect those by chance and short of bringing Syd Barrett to see him, what can you do.

Short of what?

Finding Syd Barrett for him.

Really? That's an idea.

Phillip!

It was a joke, Sean said. You know, he likes Syd Barrett and, it was a joke.

I didn't like the way Alice was looking at me. I endeavored to ask only appropriate questions and make appropriate answers from now on.

Yes. Of course. I understand. So what did you do?

I made him something, a collage. Photographs and so forth. Our time together. I even found some old ticket stubs. Stuck them on, keepsakes. I thought he might hate it, even after all this time I still can't tell when he's going to be sentimental and when he's going to be . . .

Cold?

No. Not cold. Just not, really, you know, interested.

And? Was he interested?

Yea. He was. Hung it in our bedroom. I said it should go in the loo but he insisted. You're going to have to see it next time you come. You haven't been for ages. When are you planning on coming?

Soon, I lied. Very soon.

For their birthdays, the twins received:

Seven items of jewelry.

Four software programs.

Three lipsticks, four mascaras, one eyeliner.

Two brassieres.

An optic-fibre light that revolved and shone different colors.

A lewd leather thong.

A jigsaw puzzle.

Two novels (one—boarding school—from Alice's mother; the other—Marxist doctrinal—from my father).

A book to develop telepathic, telekinetic, and pre-cognitive skills.

Five CDs.

Three DVDs.

One video.

Two goldfish.

For their birthdays, the twins also received:

A day of domestic sweetness from their mother and me.

It began with us in (improvised from napkins and staple-gun) his-and-her chefs' hats bringing them their favorite celebrity-sponsored breakfast products in bed, along with the morning post of birthday cards and presents.

Alice sat on the edge of Chloë's bunk. I balanced on the ladder to Daphne's. Indulgently, we watched them unwrap their presents and open their cards. We stayed with them until it became over-apparent that it was the parents who were being indulged in this ceremony rather than the children.

The day included ice-skating in the morning, and a highly successful and unembarrassing birthday party in the afternoon, where multicolored non-alcoholic cocktails were served in pink and blue glasses with plastic elephant stirrers and dainty paper umbrellas. We gave them the goldfish and agreeably they were, or pretended to be, pleased. We also granted them a post-facto written permission to go to bed whenever they felt like it; and life felt good for both Alice and me as it always did when we conspired together to make our day into something better than it might have been.

For their birthdays, the twins also received:

Riding hats and jodhpurs and black velvet jackets and a pair of ponies from Barry and Sean.

We got up to two hundred and thirty-two and Alice and I both lay furiously in bed. The photographs of the ponies, taken on their new location in Barry and Sean's stable yard, had remained in my furious line of vision even after the twins had finally consented to go to sleep. Barry and Sean had given us something as well, a large red-enameled flowerpot that they had chosen for our front hallway.

It was helpful, I discovered, and calming, to ascribe a numerical value to every gift exchanged.

Begin with 100. An arbitrary index measuring the weight of Barry and Sean's combined benevolence and generosity to Alice and me over the years. My first effort at repayment, the poster, could most optimistically be called a 3. Their bottle-opener had to be at least a 9. So, my first efforts at repayment had caused the debt to rise to 106.

The table I drew up that resulted from my calculations looked like this:

Poster	3	**97**	Bottle opener	9	**106**
Kaleidoscope	5	**101**	Skiing holiday	15	**116**
Rose bush	7	**109**	Football tickets	5	**114**
Rabbits	15	**99**	Muffins	2	**101**
			Flowerpot	3	**104**
			Ponies	25	**129**

We were well behind. Too far behind. The all too brief glory of the rabbits was already squandered. And it was hateful of Barry and Sean to bring the twins into the competition. I couldn't let them get away with that. In revenge for Barry and Sean's gift of the ponies, I bought the twins a dolls' house with money taken from the building society. It was made of light wood, a grand Georgian house with two chimneys and a tiny steeple topped with a golden crown. A pair of staircases at the front angled away from each other and then joined at a first floor gallery door. The dolls' house came with a six-legged mahogany table, which I carried up from the Volvo, sweating, straining, hurting. I found a space for it in the twins' bedroom, between their make-up box and illuminated globe. I mounted the house on top.

The girls looked up with some degree of wariness that reminded me of their mother.

A gift, I said, late birthday present, for you.

That's very kind of you, they said stiffly.

Look, you see here, it opens in flaps. That comes away like that and, and, that like that.

I opened up the walls, which were hinged at the sides. The twins looked at each other and stifled simultaneous looks of disappointment and pity.

Look there's the sitting room and there the music room, and upstairs, that seems to be the sewing room and there's the bedroom. And those curtains, you want to feel them? They're made of real chintz. That's what the woman in the shop said.

Thank you, said Chloë.

It's very pretty, said Daphne.

You're going to have to be very careful with this. It's the detailing, the craftsmanship that's so impressive.

My words trailed away as I realized I was trying too hard to sell the house, like a gargantuan estate agent with his miniature prize.

Yes, the twins said.

You're not too old for this kind of thing, if that's what you're thinking.

No, said Daphne.

Of course not, said Chloë.

It's a real collector's item.

I made myself silent again. Sympathetically, the girls fingered the furnishings, pulled apart and drew shut again the chintz curtains.

We'll have to get you some dolls to put in there, I said.

The girls nodded politely and dismissively. I left their bedroom.

I felt confident that, despite the twins' cool reception of the gift, they would warm to it. I went back to my numerical table. I subtracted ten points from the ponies and then scrupulously reinstated them. I did not want to be guilty of false accounting. Nonetheless I felt immediately more energetic than usual. Things could go my way after all.

The only thing I could think of that would bring the index of obligation back towards zero was the gift of Syd Barrett. In the meantime I had to be thoughtful, considerate, generous, and prolific. I called a mail-order food company and sent Barry and Sean an organic picnic hamper of fruit and vegetables and cured hams as a holding operation until I could think of something better.

Django flourished under our care for several weeks before he suffocated in heavy darkness beneath the blanket that Alice hung over his cage to signify night. I took a shot of brandy and told the twins that Django had felt no pain. The funeral service was performed in the back garden. We buried him by the artificial mountain.

Something's missing, I said to Alice.

What? Django?

No.

There was an absence in my air. My guardian angel was gone. I felt unprotected, exposed. So this, I finally realized, is how people live. I took the sorrowing twins to school. Alice went off to rebrand things. When I got back to the house I went into my shed and waited for more things to go wrong.

The telephone rang and I made the mistake of answering it. It was Barry.

Hey. Phil. Thanks for the food.

Don't mention it. I hope you liked it. The ham looked really good I thought.

Yeah. Looked good. Couldn't eat it though. Vegetarians don't do ham too much.

Oh. I'm—

And the meat juices got kind of drippy over the

asparagus and the—what's that thing called? An ugly fruit? Appropriately named, I would say, but don't worry about it, we'll pass it on. There's an old age home nearby. They'll love it. I mean, it might be kind of risky and all, with various botulisms and whatnot, things that lurk in meat, but I'm sure it'll be OK.

I'm very sorry. I forgot. I—

But listen. I, we, got something—

Sorry Barry. Someone at the door. Got to go.

Fuck the door. I'm—

Sorry Barry. I'm expecting a parcel.

I wiped the sweat away from my forehead. I replaced the receiver and the telephone immediately rang again. I watched it ring. It stopped, and started again. I turned off the volume on the bell. Feeling as if I was being watched, I left my shed, walked through to the front door, opened it and closed it again.

No parcel, I said out loud for the benefit of any listening devices planted in my house. I'm expecting a parcel.

I ignored the ringing telephone and went back to the shed.

Fuck, I said.

I knew that Barry had something up his sleeve. There had been an offer about to be made, a gift to be bestowed. The organic hamper had been a disaster and I still owed them, for Sean's muffins, the flowerpot in the hallway, for everything. He was belittling me. I went into the house to look for alcohol. The telephone was still ringing.

The telephone was a new one. I had been given it by the company I had done a manual for. I picked up the receiver, weighed it in my hand, was impressed at how light machinery was these days, and threw it across the room. It bounced off the sofa, slid along the coffee table, banged to the floor. When I picked it up, I heard something disattached rattling inside it.

Fuck, I said.

This was my life. I had expected it to be different.

When Alice came back from work she found me standing by the living room window, looking out at the street through a face-shaped gap in the curtains. She gave me a look of low-intensity disappointment and went to make the children their tea.

Someone's disconnected the phone, Alice said. Was it you?

Yes. No. It might have been. I was trying to connect up the machine the company sent.

Could you plug it back in please.

I plugged it back in. Stared at it. I had been expecting it to ring instantly. It did not. The phone was silent, menacing. Which was worse in a way. I tried to think clearly. I was in a big dark hole.

At Richard's launderette party on Battersea Rise to commemorate the end of his career in cleaning our depressed host took hold of me by the arm and wouldn't let go.

This used to be the jewel in my crown, said king Richard (dethroned, deterred, bankrupt). Classy. I could charge double a service wash what I could get in Peckham.

I've got to do something, I said.

Good for you, said Richard. I'm going to get a blowjob.

I'd like your help.

Molly, I tell you, it's the quiet ones who are always the wildest.

The electric clothes spinner, which had not found a buyer with the rest of Richard's stock of machinery, was the centerpiece of the party. It was filled with vodka and a fruity caffeine drink.

The baggy white and yellow striped clown's suit Richard was wearing was spotted with splashes of vodka and fruity caffeine drink. He grinned at me, then the grin dropped away and he clutched my arm. I hoped he wasn't as desperately sober as he appeared.

It's hard, isn't it? No one tells you it's going to be this hard. You know how much money I've got?

Um—

I've got no fucking money. Less than no fucking money.
There's about ten directions I've gone bust in. I owe to the
bank, the credit cards, the building society, the loanshark,
my lawyer, my ex-wife's lawyer, the courts, the brewery.
That's about ten isn't it? Maybe six.

The brewery?

My parents' pub. They're about to lose it.

Oh.

No one tells you do they. They always say it's going to
be so fucking easy. Just bish here, bosh there, a dib and
a dob, we're all in it together, but they don't tell you
about a bunch of cunts who are just lurking to screw all
the happiness out of you. Do they?

He goggled at me. He held me by both arms.

At least you're going to get a blowjob.

That's true. Yes. There is that.

He relented. Then gripped harder again.

And you know whose fault this is? DO YOU KNOW?

No. I do not.

YOURS. It's your fucking fault. I had a chance. *We* had
a chance, to get some action, to make some easy money and
you wouldn't do it. I'd've had all this still, and more.

What easy money?

Doughboy. His Balkans. Do you know how many Balkan
FAs he's got a share in? Do you know how much money
we could've made by now? And still could. But instead—
this!

He waved his arm dramatically around his ruined
launderette, knocking over four glasses that were perched
on the side of the electric clothes spinner. Three smashed,
one survived the fall and rolled between a sun-tanned pair
of legs that belonged to Richard's ex-wife Lisa.

But you said you wanted my help. I'll show you what

friendship means. What? Just say it. You want my help, let's do it. You want me to kill someone for you? Is that it? Just give me his photograph in a brown manila envelope and the cunt I tell you the cunt is good as dead. Is he here? Is he here tonight?

Richard experimented with a range of squints as he looked around the room and tried to focus on the faces of his friends and ex-customers and current creditors.

It's not your wife is it? I don't think I could kill Alice. It wouldn't feel right.

It's not my wife.

Good. That's a relief. You know, Alice, she's a diamond. You've got to woo them, women, keep on wooing them, over and over. It's the only way to keep them from realizing what a fuck-up you are . . . Who is it then? Who do you want me to kill?

No, I mean. It's not anyone. I don't want you to kill anyone for me.

I would. I'd do it.

Yes. I know you would. Thank you.

Because I would. You know that.

Yes. I know that.

Then what is it? What the fuck is it?! WHY ARE YOU FUCKING WASTING MY TIME!

Guests had turned their attentions our way. The man Richard detested above all, Rajiv Patel, the dry-cleaning king of south-west London, was smiling amiably over. As was Richard's ex-wife, and Molly, and Alice, and Doughboy and Lee comparing Ferrari key rings, and there was a surprised gratitude in the way we were being looked at (except by Alice, in whose eyes I could read incipient blame for any disruption, any social peculiarity) as if something interesting might at last be about to happen here tonight.

So I hugged Richard very tight, partly to shut him up and partly because, as I could feel by the way his body just let go when I held him, this was what he wanted; it gave him, if not strength, at least some comfort.

I carry-walked him over to where the mothball-dispensing machine used to be, sat him down on the chair the crooked manager's crooked friend used to sit on, and let go when I could be sure that he was not going to fall. His eyes were closed and damp.

After I separated Molly from the dry-cleaning king of London (SW) and steered her towards Richard's chair, I had to accept that I could not ask Richard for help to find Syd Barrett for Barry.

Doughboy stopped me on the way out. He repeated the offer of a sure thing that Richard had told me about. Any investment returned ten-fold.

You know the expression there's no such thing as a free lunch?

I think I've heard it.

Well there is. And this is it. Free lunch, free dinner, free full fucking English breakfast. For the rest of your fucking life. Ten grand gets you a hundred.

He jangled the change in his pocket and I jangled mine in a smaller sort of way.

Your mate wants in but I'm not letting him. I'm letting you.

That's very nice of you.

Not nice. Not nice at all. I have bad dreams sometimes and you know whose face I see in them?

No. No I don't.

Yours. You remember when you got tackled that time? Your knee?

Yes. I remember.

It's the face you had then. When that happened. Sort of looks like this.

Doughboy's plump prosperous face turned into a mask of terror. His future was gone. His present had been obliterated in a screech of pain. There was no hope for him, for any of us, all we had to look forward to was making some kind of lives for ourselves in the long lingering aftermath of calamity. Then he relaxed, facial muscles softened, and he slapped me hard on the back.

And you know the interesting thing? Lee has it as well. Now I know perfectly well I don't owe you a thing but my anger management counselor reckoned if I did something for you then I might stop having these dreams. So what do you reckon? Quids in. Everyone's a winner. I'll even let your mate in.

On the way home, I told Alice about Doughboy's offer.

You're not actually considering taking him up on it?

No, of course not.

Kindly, she did not then deliver the scathing words that she was so obviously thinking.

Have you finished your film script yet?

No. Not quite. Not yet.

You're in a bit of a rut aren't you?

A rut? I don't know. Maybe. I don't think so.

Barry's quite worried about you. He said he thought you needed a change.

Oh. Did he?

Bud's coming back into town soon. Barry thought you might enjoy showing him around, the sights and things.

What—being his driver, you mean?

No, not driver. Friend on the ground is the phrase he used.

He had more money than me, therefore he thought without question that I had to do what he said no matter how humbling. I was annoyed at myself that the subsequent revelation had taken so long in coming: It took serious money to compete with Barry and Sean.

The following day, after switching off the ringers on all the house telephones, I sneaked out of the house and withdrew our savings from the building society and dropped the cash off with Richard to give to Doughboy. I further justified the action by telling myself that I was doing it for Richard as well as for myself, which was perhaps even true. And then gave myself a virtuous alibi by going to the supermarket.

In the supermarket I amused myself by selecting items I didn't usually buy, but had previously admired or been appalled by in other people's trolleys. I selected pieces of stem ginger soaked in Italian brandy in a plump little bottle. Recycled toilet paper with novelty cats printed on each sheet. A mountain of cartons all attached together that promised (*New Taste Sensation!* it said on the packet, *Flavors Of The World!*) to assemble into an authentic Peking duck banquet. Teeth-rottingly sweet things in holiday wrapping. Instant snacks endorsed by cartoon celebrities.

I was also looking for the joke anniversary gift for Alice that would go along with the proper one that I hadn't thought of yet. I couldn't choose between a chocolate paperweight in the shape of the Leaning Tower of Pisa and a miniature bicycle pump in the shape of a bicycle so I put them both in the trolley. For a moment I was trapped. On one side a mother with a super-wide trolley whose front wheels had jammed was trying to force her shopping and her five children along the aisle. On the other, a well-dressed young man was sitting cross-legged dreamily opening the tops of and sniffing bottles of cleaning fluid. I squeezed on past the dreamy young man and in celebration tossed some doughnuts into the trolley and a large tin of dog food and then a second.

I was about to pay with the building society Visa card, but then realized I couldn't and would have to use the current account Switch instead and forgo the self-initiation of the bookmaker's next door where I had intended to explore whether the pleasure of gambling, on horses or anything, was available to me. With no way of hiding from Alice's monthly scrutiny the money I expected to lose, I killed time instead looking through music magazines to see if I could find anything about Syd Barrett. The small ads of the fifth magazine I looked at announced a monthly meeting of Barrett devotees. I ripped the page out without any rigmarole of trying to disguise what I was doing, but no one seemed to care anyway.

On the way home I bought flowers for Alice, from the florist's she liked, because I had resolved to take Richard's advice and woo her, over and over again if necessary. I booked us a table at the latest restaurant her boss Lionel was a backer of. I bought chocolates for her also, and a vegan deluxe picnic basket to send to Barry and Sean.

The flowers went into a vase next to the larger bouquet sent to her by a grateful client. The chocolates went to the twins because Alice had gone on a diet. I canceled the reservation because Alice was going to be rebranding late into the evening. I calmed my resentment, telling myself that none of this was rejection because Alice didn't know yet that I was wooing her, over and over again.

Once a month, Alice conducted weekend courses for clients. She had been to Scottish castles, Spanish paradors, Ibizan beach resorts, Walthamstow dog track. Today, because of her damaged foot, Alice was mind-melting in our garden, sitting in a cross-legged circle on the overgrown grass with a rapt group of woman clients. *This is not a seminar*, I had heard her saying on my way into the shed, *and all that the word implies. Ejaculating information. Spitting.* Crouching at my desk, earplugs on listening to music Syd Barrett had made before his decline (loud buzzing sci-fi guitar and a pleasant, very English voice either drawling out the words or half-shouting them as if to get the attention of someone impossibly far away), hoping I was out of view, I sometimes saw the tops of keen female heads.

The need to go to the toilet finally pulled me out of the shed. I stumbled, smiling, bladder bursting, trying not to feel like the beast of the garden. I wasn't allowed past. Alice smiled at me most sweetly.

You wouldn't mind? she said.

I'm just on my way—

Help us out for a moment. Here's a case. Phillip Wilson, aged thirty-nine. Rebrand him.

I really have to go—

Stay still for a moment. Let's see what fun we can have.

Girls with bare midriffs looked at me condescendingly. I tried not to stare too obviously at flat unmaternal bellies.

A suntan might help.

Very good, said Alice.

The beard obviously, said one.

Has to go, said another.

Yes, said Alice.

What's his market identity?

What's your market identity Phillip?

I don't know, I said hopping heavily from foot to foot. I really have to go.

He's what's called a technical writer.

That's no good.

Obviously. So let's try something else. How could we start?

The ABC?

Which stands for? Gisèle?

Animal, book, color. He's quite white isn't he?

Something about him says Great Expectations to me.

For a moment Alice was thrown off-stride but then, professionally, she recaptured the rhythm.

That's great, Jenny. Excellent intuition. How about animal? Anyone?

He does look a bit like one of those, what do you call them? Sort of bear things with funny feet, no, sorry, I'm thinking of somebody else.

The rest of them shook their heads. I had failed to remind them of an animal.

Does he do anything else?

Phillip? Do you do anything else?

I'm sorry. I really have to go.

Why don't we call you a scriptwriter?

Well no, maybe yes, I'm trying to write one, I haven't really finished it yet.

Scriptwriter it is then.

Despite my discomfort it was an impressive sight watching Alice at work. The women in the garden all hungered for her approval. They became more confident, even better looking, when they received it.

Parties?

For what purpose?

Meeting people.

Being seen.

And?

Getting written about.

Better. Where?

Trade papers?

Far too tentative.

A frighteningly thin one stroked her mustache.

Diary items?

Good. Yes. How would you word them?

What's his name again?

Phillip Wilson.

Oh. OK. Phillip Wilson, thirty-six—

I'm thirty-nine.

Ssh, said Alice.

Phillip Wilson, thirty-six, the hottest scriptwriter in town or something like that, was among those seen at . . .

Shouldn't we say he's working with somebody big?

And could we say he's having an affair with someone?

We could. Does anyone have any suggestions as to whom?

They went around the circle, ovulating suggestions, pop singers, film actresses, porn stars.

Excuse me.

I broke, running full tilt at the house, managed to hold on until I got to the downstairs toilet, my urine thundering into the bowl.

I hid out in the house for the rest of the day until it was time to pick up the twins from school.

It would be fun, rebranding, Alice said later as we were sat in front of the television.

I was watching the telephone. She was compiling a list of people to invite to our anniversary party.

It'll be good for you. Blow the cobwebs away. Let's do it, it won't cost much at all, PR for a couple of weeks, maybe just a week, haircut, shave, sun ray lamp. You wouldn't mind doing that would you?

I suppose not.

We can take some money out of the building society account.

No. We can't do that.

Why not? I think it's a justifiable expense, don't you?

I tried smiling at her.

What are you doing that for?

Doing what?

Making that face. It's strange.

Can't we just wait for a bit? Wait until I've finished the script? I don't want to pre-empt anything.

No, she said. You probably don't.

Don't want to run before I can walk. Take things for granted. Count my chickens. I mean—

Just say yes to something for once. Trust me, it'll be good for you. Take some money out of the building society, a couple of thousand. And look. Can you do these invitations, send them off? Everything's there. I've made the list. You just have to write out the envelopes. And send them off. You can manage that, can't you?

I expect so.

And you'll go to the building society tomorrow.

I can't go to the building society.

Well then I will then.

You can't.

Why not?

Because. It's. Got, no—Your foot, I mean. It's supposed to rain tomorrow. You know how bad your toe gets when it rains.

That's very sweet of you but I'm not an invalid. I have to get about.

We need the money for something else then.

For what?

Umm. The school fees. I think, yes, I think. The twins. Boarding school.

I thought you were all so dead set against it?

Well yes, but maybe I was being selfish, I don't know, I'm not saying I'm *for* it, just that I'm reluctant to spend all that money on me, just in case we do decide. That we've got to think quite hard about it. Think quite hard about that one.

It seemed I'd got away with it. Alice didn't mention visiting the building society again, and in return all I had to do was carry a pile of invitations to the shed and then return to look interested for the rest of the evening as boarding school brochures were put in front of me.

I wrote my film script. Sitting in the garden shed, the house overfull, spilling out sounds around me, girls at play, pop music, a ball bouncing against the shed wall, violent laughter, a small voice pleading for mercy. This torrent of activity I envied for its unthinking disturbance of the world.

I couldn't think of a better title than Wang The Unlucky Scholar so that was the one I used. It was an old Chinese story of craven transcendence, which seemed to be the genre that I liked best.

The original goes along these lines: Wang is waiting for the results of his public examination. If he passes, he is on the first rung of the imperial service ladder. If he fails, he has nothing, except for a wife who nags and an obliterated future. He is so nervous that all he can do is get drunk. Overcome by liquor, he goes to bed. In rushes a messenger crying out the good news that Wang has passed the exam. Wang tells his wife to give the man some money but his wife says she already has. Along comes another messenger who congratulates Wang: He's passed the highest degree. Wang is puzzled: How can I? he says, I haven't even entered for it. The messenger laughs. You mean you've forgotten. Wang gets up to find a tip for the second messenger but his wife tells him to go back to sleep, she's already paid.

Then a third messenger comes in to say that Wang has been elected to the National Assembly and two official servants are waiting outside to escort him to the capital. Wang is elated now with his success. He calls out for his two official servants to help him dress so he can make his triumphant leave-taking tour of his neighbors. Go back to bed, his wife says. I'll get them. But when the servants come in, they're insolent to Wang, mocking him, his manners, his character, even his success. Wang is furious. He beats them, hitting one on the chest and the other on the head, knocking off his hat. Then Wang falls over.

Shame on you! says his wife, Getting so drunk!

Splayed on the floor, Wang defends himself. He argues with her. I was only punishing the servants as they deserved, he says.

What? The old woman you mean, who cooks our rice and boils the water for your footbath?

Wang begins to sober up now. He realizes he is waking from a dream. He was drunk; he had slept; the news hasn't come yet; his wife still nags him. But later, disconsolately shutting up the house for the night, he finds, rolled behind the door, a tiny official servant's hat, the size of a wine glass.

I cast the story in the modern day. I made Wang an aspiring civil servant, his wife a social climber, their maid a sexy au pair. My first draft filled about twenty pages. Working on the rule of thumb that one page of a script equals one minute of movie time it was clear that I needed to open up the story.

The second draft started the story long before the exam. We meet Wang and his wife at the beginning of their courtship, follow the broadening path of love into marriage and professional difficulty. Then the story goes on much as before, with reality being questioned by playfully unreliable flashbacks. When the third messenger comes, we have a by-election episode, with Wang standing for parliament.

I gave the script to Alice to read. She gave it back to me. She said there was no story. A story, she reminded me, required conflict. And character, she said. Character is action.

The third draft worked up the part of a rival suitor. I made him into a gangster, Wang's wife his former moll, and Wang a morally upright, crimebusting detective with a drink problem studying for his lieutenant exam.

I gave the script to Alice to read. She gave it back to me. She reminded me that Barry had wanted a spiritual element.

The fourth draft played up the spiritual element. Wang and his wife are adepts in the mysteries of Taoist sex, reaching a thousand loving thrusts at will, spiritual even as immortals—until Wang, lured by the sophisticated machinations of the gangster, takes up drinking again.

I gave the script to Alice to read. Alice said it was better but it needed more color. She gave it back to me.

In the fifth draft I made the rival suitor into a psycho. This was the part that particularly pleased me. I gave the script to Alice to read. She gave it back to me. Alice said the script was good enough to give to Barry except for one problem: The psycho's voice. Every speech of his sounded flat. The script was done; the story, said Alice, suitably arced and journeyed; the dialog was acceptable except for the speeches of Wang's bitter, evil, but thoroughly boring rival. I sat in my shed trying to invent colorful movie psycho language. And in rushed Daphne and Chloë and two smaller cousins.

You're a naughty *naughty* little boy, said Chloë.

I not little. I BIG boy! said one of the cousins.

Willy willy willy willy willy willy, said the other.

Hug me Daddy! said Daphne.

And the idea hit me at the same time as Daphne's needy arms and chest that the villain, Wang's mortal enemy, should speak entirely in the language of children. I didn't know how it would play on the screen, but it unnerved me and I thought that was a good start. The perfect movie psycho: driven by immediate need and sensation, utterly oblivious to the inner worlds of others. Your child and mine; and, excuse me, ourselves.

At a long table in the upstairs room of an Earls Court pub called The Captain's Grief, with appropriate pint of Guinness in my hand, I was sitting polite and bored. In the year of my injury my father had taken me to a lot of religious occasions like this one, where devotees debated matters of faith.

Then it had been Marx and Lenin and Stalin, along with a small number of approved commentators. Holy books, holy writ. Passionate adherents in passionate dispute. Here the primary texts were recordings and lyric sheets of Syd Barrett songs; the commentaries were unpublished, but web-posted papers modestly delivered with downcast eyes by the authors themselves; the icons were black and white photographs and album sleeves; the relics were few.

I was waiting to make friends with someone. I had my eyes on a gentle-eyed boy who ran a website devoted to Syd and a green-haired Australian girl who had read out an essay on the symbolic meanings of arms in Syd's solo work.

What's your name? I'm Carlo.

Phillip.

What you do Phil?

The only person who seemed keen on making friends with me was the one in the room I least wanted to be friends with. Everyone here either ignored him or, if that was impossible, deferred to him. He was dressed like a 1950s grease monkey, checked red shirt, oil-discolored jeans and work boots. He had a bony handsome face, long greased hair combed high and back. His eyes were blue and feral.

I work in the movies. I'm a movie producer, I said.

The gentle-eyed boy announced that he'd been offered for sale a lock of Syd's hair, permed. A man who hosted a Syd Barrett bulletin board performed a number of disbelieving snorts and sniffs. Carlo eagerly said he wanted to buy it. The subsequent conversation, like the preceding ones, was far too technical for me to follow. I found myself noticing that the ends of roll-up cigarettes were like the hairs of Barry's nostrils on those rare days when he'd forgotten to pluck or razor.

Eventually, tiring, in desperation, I said,

Can anyone tell me where Syd Barrett lives?

There was a silence. Weak half-stoned eyes made contact, registered something disapproving and absolute.

Finally someone said,

Leave it out.

No. It's all right, I—

Leave Syd alone, man, said the Australian girl. Leave him be.

No. It's all right. There's a friend of mine you see. I mean, I know Syd lives in Cambridge, but I wondered if—

Go away, said the gentle-eyed boy, his eyes no longer gentle.

I was encouraged then to leave. In case I didn't know where it was, two goateed nerdlings showed me the staircase and even helped me down the first few steps by the method of poking me in the back. On my speedy way down I felt closer to my father than I had in some time. I realized how he must have felt when he used to go agitate at Maoist meetings.

I couldn't keep Alice away from the telephone forever. She answered the phone one morning in the bedroom and she kept saying yes yes yes and her face was glowing.

That was Barry. We're going skiing.

I don't think so.

What do you mean? They've invited us and I've said yes.

Then you're going to have to call them back and say no.

I can't believe you. Think of the girls. Remember how good Sean is with them. They loved it last time we went.

Last time we went they paid for just about everything. They bought our air tickets—

That was frequent flyer miles.

They rented the chalet, paid for the hire car—

He claims that all back. Barry's always on per diems.

—and usually picked up the bill in restaurants.

I don't understand why you're making such a fuss. You didn't then. You always got that happy sickly look on your face every time Barry told you to put your wallet away.

I didn't realize then.

Realize what?

I changed tack. I pretended concern.

What about your toe?

What about my toe?

Skiing won't be good for it.

I'll be careful. I'll wrap it up. Look. If you don't want to go we'll go. Me and the girls.

I thought about that.

No, I said. I forbid it.

Forbid it? Who died and left you in charge?

You don't understand what they're trying to do.

What who's trying to do? They want to take us on *holiday*. They're our *friends*. They say it'll be good for you, that you've been moping.

I'm sorry. I'm not going and you're not going and the girls aren't going. Tell them no.

You fucking tell them.

I refused the invitation to go skiing. I refused invitations to weekends in the country. Pressure of manual work was offered as an excuse, family illnesses. The invitations kept coming, more frequently now. I dreaded the ring of the telephone, the knock on the door. I refused to answer either. I was sick with dread. I invented little chores and sudden events to keep Alice out of earshot. Alice simmered, boiled, and burned. I was coldly unbending.

When the phone rang late one Friday I only picked it up because Alice was staring at me to do so. On the line was Sean. With tickets for a play that Dylan had recommended, and a party afterwards, and the great desire for Alice and me to join them there.

Sorry. We can't. My father's just died. We're all in shock.

I dealt courteously with Sean's sympathy and hung up the phone. I outfaced Alice's horror, contempt, and scorn.

Phillip! *What* are you doing?

Just because they've got money doesn't have to mean

they've got power. I'm not going to play into their hands. And you mustn't either.

What do you mean, play into their hands? We're not fighting a war. These are our *friends.*

Are they?

You're going funny in the head. You need some help. I think you need counseling, I really do.

There was a knock on the door.

I wonder who that is? Are you expecting anyone?

Always, I thought but did not say.

Alice went to the door, came back with a bouquet of lilies in her hands and her face rosy with delight.

They're from the boys. Aren't they beautiful? There's a card.

I read it: *So sorry to hear about your father. Shit happens. Viva la revolución! All our love, B&S.*

When Alice said we had to go to the premiere of Dylan's new movie or else she was going to divorce me, I relented.

I felt relatively secure. But then, as I was ironing my best trousers, relocating the creases further into the groin, the thought hit me hard that this could be a ruse. I didn't actually suspect that Dylan had made a movie just so Barry could maneuver me into a party for it, or at least I didn't allow myself to suspect this for long; but what I did suspect was an unavoidable moment afterwards, at the party, champagne crush, photographers, journalists, pony-tailed boys and elegant girls queuing for the toilet in pairs, Barry would clear a space, his fatuous smile, his open arms, *We got something for you* . . . and the terminal gift would be revealed, and we would have walked into the bright trap of their generosity.

I did not go to the premiere. I claimed a sudden bout of 'flu.

You go, I said, I've stopped you from going to so many things. You know how they'll feel if neither of us go. I don't mind.

Are you sure? If you're ill?

I'll be all right. Go.

I made a poor imitation of an influenza cough. I looked brave and forlorn as I waved Alice goodbye.

Daddy? Can we have a baby?

I wish we could, I said.

I read the twins their bedtime stories and, despite their objections, sang them a lullaby, and kissed them on their foreheads, and when I went downstairs again there was nothing to do but worry. Would the rules allow the boys to give their gift without me there? I thought not. I hoped not. But I had created a precedent by giving the rabbits in Barry's absence. But Barry's absence was Barry's fault, not mine. I sat down and stood up again. I weeded the garden by moonlight. I paced the empty rooms of my house. I watched television, I stopped watching television, I put on CDs and took them off again, I tried to do yoga but I couldn't make my breathing steady. In the living room I picked up one of Alice's mother's stray knitting needles and poked a few holes in things, a plaster dividing wall, a portrait of my dead mother, the skin of my hand. Running the taps in the bath I thought of throwing myself out of the window. Lying in the bath, I thought of running far away to an indifferent oblivious place where no one would ever give me anything.

And then I realized. Stupidly, passively, I had been worrying about what they were about to give. For too long I had been reactive. I had to think proactive. All I had to do was reverse the situation: I would hold something in reserve. Agree to meet them the next time an invitation came, and when they said *We got something for you* . . . politely receive the gift, whatever rare precious thing they had found that could tip the scales further in their favor, express my bogus gratitude—and then retaliate with the sucker punch of a return present straight away. Oh here, I would say, suavely, almost absent-mindedly, I almost forgot. *We* have something for *you* . . .

I ran splashing out of the bath, I ran to the shed and found the business card I was looking for in one of my more recent piles of Things To Do, sub-division: Things To Put Away. I called Samantha, Molly's cousin who did very good legs. I invited her to come over straight away. She said that was impossible. I said I would come over straight away. She said that was impossible too, but it wasn't—I showed her what impossible meant: *I* was impossible, impossible to put off, impossible to ignore; I promised her a commission, she hummed and hahed; I promised her money: she said I should come straight away.

I went back into the house, where I got quickly, inefficiently, dressed, bath water on my skin making damp maps of nowhere on my jeans and shirt. I ransacked the chest of drawers in the kitchen, I found the wallet of snapshots that Barry and Sean had sent us from the skiing holiday. I put them in my pocket along with my checkbook. I went to the door. I stopped. My exhilaration drained away. I remembered the twins.

Unless they were ill they almost never woke up during the night, and even if they did the company of her familiar other was usually enough for either, but all the same technically it was illegal what I was doing, leaving two sleeping, underage, unprotected girls alone in the house.

If they should wake crying . . . ? If something should happen . . . If Alice were to come home before me . . . ? It would be a difficult, impossible dereliction to explain away. I ran upstairs. I opened the door of the twins' room, admired them sleeping, marveled—heart-swollen, heart-breaking—that any part of me could have made any part of them. I tucked my daughters back under the duvet covers that had fallen away. I kissed their untroubled brows. I ran downstairs. I picked up the car keys. I was gone.

Molly's cousin lived and worked in a studio in the East End. It was next door to a mosque and above a clothes factory. There was no bell. I stood in the rain on Whitechapel High Road and bellowed *Samantha!* to dark high windows. Passers-by took detours to avoid me. Someone eventually heard me, leaned out of a high window, threw down a bunch of keys wrapped in a sock.

I climbed up cold stairs into an even colder studio. Canvases were turned to the wall. Stones and maps filled shelves that sagged on bricks. Samantha wore a heavy overcoat, she looked cold and thin, there were Braille letters written in acne across her upper lip.

I tried to make conversation. I talked about her legs, about myself, about my friends, about her art. Samantha was not a fluent conversationalist. She stared at me, she silently made a pot of tea.

I work primarily on gesso now, she told me finally, as she sat cross-legged, drinking green tea.

That's great, I said. That's fine.

What I like to do is inscribe something, words, on the gesso, something significant, and then paint the portrait over it. So it's like a secret message.

What? Like, Fuck you?

I don't think that's very nice, is it?

No. I'm sorry. I was joking.

I'd have to meet your friends. I can't paint just anybody. There has to be a feeling between us.

You'll like them. Everyone does. Would they come here or would you go there? It's very cold here.

I'm getting a new heater.

Oh.

I wasn't wearing my watch. There was no clock in Samantha's studio. I thought of my children, the accidents that could obliterate them in my time away, the fire that was consuming them, the bathwater drowning them, the midnight binge alcohol and drain-cleaning fluid ripping apart their insides, the sudden-onset illnesses they were screaming fighting against with no parent to make them safe.

Could I maybe see some of your portraits?

No.

(Daphne and Chloë clinging to each other try to make their voices heard above the crackling of the flames, across miles of sleeping houses and wet roads to their father who has abandoned them.)

How about? I've got some photos here. I don't want to be pushy, but maybe you could have a look at them?

Glumly she accepted the snapshots. Barry and Sean, arms around each other's fleece-padded shoulders at a mid-mountain cafe, smiled into the camera.

What's he got in his hair?

Things. Trinkets, amulets. He wears things in his hair. His newest one's a seashell.

They've got interesting faces.

Yes. I think so too.

She was silent after that. I tried smiling at her but she

didn't notice. She shut her eyes. She might have gone to sleep. (The twins thrash about in black deadly water, their voices plead for Daddy, there is no Daddy.) Samantha's eyelashes were very short. I wondered if they'd been singed. Then she spoke again.

OK. I'll meet them.

That's great. That's terrific.

She reached for stubs of charcoal with each hand. With her eyes half-open she executed a quick sketch. Simultaneously she drew Barry with her left hand and Sean with her right. The likenesses were undeniable albeit peculiar.

You can have that if you like. You probably want a sketch to show them.

I do actually. Yes I do. Thank you.

That'll be a hundred pounds.

Really? I'll give you fifty.

OK.

I should have offered her five. It was too late. The twins were dead, wet, burned, lost; my wife was outside the ruined house pulling at her hair, keening and ululating her grief, sobbing on her knees, unchilded, undone. I wrote the check and gave it to Samantha.

How much for the whole job?

Five thousand pounds.

Really? I'll give you five hundred.

OK.

Samantha closed her eyes. I ran downstairs.

And upstairs again when I discovered that the front door needed to be unlocked before I could get out on to the street.

The house looked intact. No sign of fire or flood or blood. No emergency service flashing lights or police cordon outside, no horrified neighbors hugging themselves for comfort while staring into the carnage. I let myself in. The house felt as I left it. I removed my coat, hung it in the hall, next to the empty hook that my wife would use, leaned against the wall in relief that I had beaten Alice home—and then the thought sickened me, unmanned me, sat me down on the bottom stair, that she had come home, of course she had, she'd entered the house, lightly called my name, *Phillip? Are you awake? How are you feeling? The movie was great, you really missed something* . . . and then up she would have gone to visit the girls' room, discovered them in agony there, dying, in horror, furniture spattered sticky and viscous with death juices, she'd carried them wailing downstairs (which one would she have taken first?), she'd rushed the abandoned girls to hospital. Pointless of course, no hospital could save them now. She'd be beside them still. Tracing their cold dead features with her grieving fingertips.

I ran upstairs. I waited as long as I dared before pushing open the girls' bedroom door. Chloë was as I'd left her. Daphne had pulled herself out of her covers. I tucked her in, kissed her brow and then Chloë's, went into my own room, where I pulled off my clothes and lay beneath the covers, flattened by a sudden and absolute exhaustion.

I couldn't sleep, not until Alice returned home. Twice I got up to check the children again. Twice I fought the temptation to hold on to their narrow shoulders, to whisper apologies to them. The second time I lost. I whispered into their ears and they stirred against the insect trill of my confession. I sang them a lullaby perfectly remembered from years before and they let me.

Finally Alice did come home, a few moments after I was back in bed again. She whistled as she removed her clothes.

How was the premiere?

Good. It was good. Very moving.

Did you speak to Barry?

Of course. I told him you were ill.

She said this quite proudly. As if she expected now to be praised.

Did they offer you anything?

What? Like drugs you mean?

No. Not drugs.

They didn't offer me anything. What are you expecting?

Nothing. I was expecting nothing. Come to bed.

And with that I slept. I neither thrusted nor dreamed.

I couldn't resist. I knew what I had to do—I should wait, in strength and silence, for the inevitable call. Thunder rolls and the wind blows and the superior man endures, unchanging. Not me. I called Barry's mobile. Barry picked it up straight away.

I'm glad you called, said Barry.

Yes. Me too.

That vegan deluxe was good, thank you for it. But I got to tell you something, you're an elusive fuck you know that? We got something—

Let's meet up, I interrupted.

Barry was taken aback by that. He was used to evasion, deferral. I enjoyed the soothing sound of my enemy being puzzled.

Great, he finally said. Just what I was going to suggest.

I've got you, I whispered.

Say what?

Nothing. Your club?

Sure. Tomorrow night? Bring Alice?

She'll be there. Bring Sean?

Of course. See you tomorrow.

Yes. Tomorrow.

Looking forward to it, said Barry.

Me too, I said.

I drove in triumph to Barry's club. A dictator in his staff car gliding through a conquered city would have felt no more pride. I was bursting with the stuff. As I struggled to squeeze the car into a Soho parking place, instead of the silence I usually insisted on when executing this kind of maneuver, I bragged about the portrait, the impending gift.

She's got something this girl, you can tell, did I show you the sketches?

You showed me the sketches.

They're good aren't they? They've got something. You know, inner. That's why a portrait is so good, better than a photograph can ever be, a photograph's only surfaces. The boys're going to love it. And hate it. This gift's— I whispered the word, hissing it out as the car squeezed snugly between a Jaguar and a jeep—*unanswerable*.

Alice shook her head. The folly of her husband was not new to her. She asked me how much the portrait was going to cost. I told her. She shook her head again and said that she was thinking of taking up smoking again.

Anyway, she said, I don't think they, I don't think *Barry*, ought to get anything. He hasn't been behaving very well.

What do you mean?

You know he's having an affair? Everyone's saying so.

No.

It's true. Well it's what people are saying.

That's crazy. I don't believe it.

I only hope Sean doesn't get to hear about it from anyone, you know, vindictive. Everyone's saying that's why he didn't go to his party.

Who's he meant to be having this affair with?

I don't know. His AA sponsor maybe. No one knows.

Barry wouldn't be having an affair with anyone. He wouldn't. They're so, I don't know, settled.

What. Like us, you mean?

Yes. No. I don't think, all the same, I said decisively.

We walked past the beggar wormed inside his sleeping bag by the entrance to Barry's club. I dropped more money into his cap than I usually did. We waited at reception for one of the starlets who worked there to bother with us, before I, confident, bold, seized the members' book and signed in, a message to the future: *Triumph.*

Are you a member, Mr Triumph?

I pulled Alice with me through the double doors. Eyes turned swiftly our way in case we were famous and then left us. I had never been quite so speedily unnoticed before. Ordinarily this might have troubled me, fueled my resentment. Not tonight. I had a script in my left hand, a sketch in my right.

It was a duel. I was a gunslinger, Alice my brothel babe. I saw my opponents, the soon-to-be portraited couple, Barry and Sean, unwarily sitting at a round table near the piano. Their friend the very tall writer was tottering away from their table towards the stairs to the toilets, presumably to snort cocaine or vomit or both.

I approached them swaggering.

The lost boy! We'd given up on you, thought you didn't love us no more.

I stroked the security of Samantha's paper. I was ready. Invulnerable. The superior man. The superior man is steadfast.

How are you Barry. Sean. I'm sorry. It's been a long time.

Too long.

Kisses were exchanged. Murmurs. Hands gripped arms, compliments flickered like lizard tongues. Everything was blue here, and chrome, at Barry's club.

Faces at the bar distracted me. I thought these belonged to friends of mine whose names I unaccountably couldn't remember and for a moment I panicked, thought I might have suffered a stroke in my exaltation, blood clots in my head closing down the memory of old teammates and schoolfriends. Then I realized that these faces had never belonged to me; they were just vaguely recognizable from TV and from Barry's parties, doubly half-familiar which didn't equal familiar. I didn't care. I was about to win.

What will you have?

Whatever you're having.

I'm having water. Sean's drinking wine.

Wine is fine.

The pleasantries lingered on, this was a most amiable interlude, the false innocence in everyone's eyes, Barry's hooded, Sean's blue candor that accessorized well with the velvet furnishings, which was why, Alice had once said, in an early catty moment before we had all become proper friends, why she thought Barry had chosen him. I could not believe that Barry was having an affair, so I decided not to try.

I lifted my fingers away from the sketch, worried I

might smudge the charcoal. I was a chess grandmaster with my fingers about to move the crucial piece, I was a footballer with a clear run on an empty goal. I had gracious smiles for everybody. For Barry, for Sean, for the man at the bar who played a doctor in a TV program, for the stand-up comedians sitting down at the next table, for all the reassuring vaguely famous faces. Alice kept looking at me. She didn't trust my mood. Soon I would make her remember why she married me in the first place. We would end the evening dancing in public like we used to do. I wondered if we could still execute a tango. For the first time in my relationship with Barry and Sean, I felt wordlessly cocky. On top of things. They were talking to me.

Sorry? What?

Don't worry about it.

Phillip!

Alice poked me. Looks were exchanged between Barry and Sean, funny old Phil, funny old ways. I didn't care. I was about to enjoy my triumph. Just wait now, for Barry to speak, to say those predictable braggartly condescending words. I wondered if I would feel any melancholy when the game was over for good. Does the chess champion miss the move that won him the title? Does the player miss the game that won him the cup? I didn't know. I'd never had the opportunity to find out.

Are you OK?

This was Sean.

Yes. Of course I am.

You seem in a funny mood, Barry said.

I *am* in a funny mood. I'd quite like something to happen to me. Something new.

I realized, to my surprise, that what I was saying was true.

Be careful what you wish for in case it comes true, Barry said in his fatuous pompous way. Answered prayers you know.

He shook his shaggy head emphatically. His ridiculous assortment of amulets and trinkets tinkled and chimed. I realized I was holding the sketch in my pocket harder than I would have expected. And then the moment was come: Something changed on Barry's face. He was benevolence, he had become the expression on his face, all-giving. Here it was and I was ready.

I got something for you, Barry said. *We* got something for you.

Yes. I have something for you too. *Two* things.

It was as if I hadn't spoken. My words passed by unnoticed.

Sean?

Barry held out his hands. Sean reached beneath the table. He lifted a plastic bag that he handled with great care, staring at it, unblinking, as if he were wishing for something.

This. This is for you.

Sean passed the bag to Barry who held it out for me.

Be careful. It's quite heavy.

I wondered if the package was a bomb, they were handling it like one.

We hope you like it.

I'm sure I will, I insincerely said. Reluctantly separating my hands from the sketch in my pocket, I held them out to receive the gift.

Be careful. It's quite delicate. It's very old I think.

Complacently, I allowed the bag to fall away from the object in my hands—its warm hard touch had already aroused a small, unnerving suspicion—and I was stunned.

Their gift was gorgeous. Unanswerable. A carving in jade, maybe as recent as Qing. The date didn't matter. What mattered was beauty. This was more than beautiful. A miniature sculpture of three mountains, three peaks, the highest one in the middle with a figure that was part bird and part river curling around it. The carving was so beautiful it made my heart lift and then sink. It made me feel sorry for everything inept I or anyone else had ever done in this or any life. The gift was cruelly perfect.

That is so gorgeous, Alice said.

It's for you. We want you to have it.

Oh we couldn't possibly. It must be very valuable.

No it's for you. You're our friends. Our best friends. Phil?

I was staring speechless at the gift. The carving was a testament to the gifters' good taste and the giftee's; it was something that could only be appreciated by the very sophisticated precisely because it was so beautiful that it would be recognized as such by everybody. It was a perfect object enduring, and—I had no doubt—improving through time. I wanted to weep. I had to fight against the gloomy passionate urge to lie down on the polished wood, yield myself to whatever came, shrink into the floor, bury myself in the sound of other people's footsteps.

I of course had nowhere to put it. All surfaces in my house were reachable by girls' fingers. In my shed was the only place it could go. The window-ledge or the desk. Humiliating me. Tinying me. Reproaching me for not producing great work, proving with its own beauty that all my best efforts weren't worth the labor I spent on producing them, except for the fact that if I wasn't wasting my time doing that I would no doubt be perpetrating something worse in another field.

This gift shames me.

Don't be silly.

We want it to give you pleasure.

How can it?

I detected in their concerned expressions benevolence triumphant. And my own utter servility confirmed and condemned.

Did you say you had something for us?

No. Sorry. You misunderstood.

The game was over. I had lost. I had been defeated utterly. Routed. I tried to think clearly. How could I beat this? I couldn't. I was the inferior man.

Phil?

Do with me what you like . . . I could give myself in return, Alice could help me; her last wifely acts would be to shave and buff and perfume my skin, and then wrap up her fallen husband in ribbons and bows. I wouldn't even take up houseroom, all I'd need was a horse blanket, I could go to sleep in one of the stables they hadn't got round to converting into editing suites yet. I could help out around the house, gather firewood, chop things, wood and weeds and herbs and suchlike. They didn't mind people being there, I would be part of the household, a testament to their largesse and potency and power. I knew how to keep myself to myself, all I had to do was mirror their graciousness back to them. My family would be well rid of me but then a pang of loneliness lowered me even further. Maybe the children of failures still like to have a father to hand. They could always visit. But that might worry them. Here is what your father has become, less than a man. I would grow unhappy and they would become concerned, take it as a failing on their part, they would trouble themselves to come up with a remedy. It was impossible.

To give myself would be too abject. That would be the greatest imposition, giving Barry and Sean the responsibility to house and feed and succor me; I would make everyone uncomfortable, I had noticed recently that my presence often made people feel uncomfortable.

Phil? What's wrong?

In this wild dreamless moment, I conceived of a cruel tableau. I pictured leading my children half-armored, fetishized, with breast plates like jagged teeth, in a solemn parade, elephants somewhere, bugles, red banners and gold, me with a short heavy sword in my hand, walking the now broad boulevard towards the temple of Barry and Sean's house. Vultures or buzzards in the sky. A priestess, my own wife, with her white-robed adepts looking wanton and demure, a brazier of fire, flames licking up. I would solemnly present the girls, who would disrobe, virgin sacrifices to the great shaggy-haired ape god and his smooth-skinned catamite, and then I would rip apart the virgins' flesh with my knife and gouge and sever and tear out two beating hearts, pulsing and pulpy, dripping splashing purple on the light marble floor, the servants' robes.

Phil?

Barry was leaning forward, gruesome sincerity on his triumphant apish face. His stupid hair hanging down, clinking.

I had been destined for grandeur, for immortality. The future's eyes had been upon me. But I had never learned why. That had become an ache. And the ache tumored now into a horrifying realization. That yes my life would have perfect shape. A circle is the only perfect shape of all, nothing to disturb its self-consuming line, an O of surprise, a zero of achievement.

Once upon a time I had believed. *In the future . . .* was

the door I had expected to go through, in adulthood, to glory. But the flat hand of destiny, indifferent as stone, had squashed me and my prospects flat.

Phil?

A mad roar came out of my body. It terrified me and I exulted in it. I became suddenly ferocious. I stood up. I grabbed Barry by his stupid hair, yanked it down, banging his head crashing to the table, there was pleasure in this, I caught some of the delight of being a fighter and a bully, I yanked Barry again by the hair hard down, banging and letting go—Sean was rising, and so was Alice, identical looks of horror on their very different faces, slowly turning celebrities looked my way, television doctors and romantic leads and fat men with power and lively girls who presented morning shows for children—Barry came up, swearing, his face red, so I grabbed his hair again, I could hear yelling behind me and shouts and womanish voices imploring me to stop, and this time I tugged too hard, clumps of hair and a little bronze fish hook came away in my fists, so I clasped my terrible hands over the sides of Barry's face and pulled him down by the ears to slam his face against the table. The experience was so pleasurable, I did it again, and again.

And then I was pulled away. Wrapped inside strong male arms, I was being shoved out of the club. I was outside, harsh night air, my feet scuffing against the pavement, not allowed to find a grip. There were stars in the sky. It had been raining. The beggar's hair and sleeping bag were wetter than they usually were. Someone considerately pushed my head down so it avoided banging against the door arch as I was shoved into a police car.

In a crowded police station I sat squeezed on a wooden bench against a wall that was cold against the back of my head. The bench was clamped to the floor so it could not be used as a weapon, I supposed, or maybe to prevent it being stolen. I had never been in this part of a police station before, where the criminals go.

This was my peer group now, I would have to find my place among them: Loud black girls, sullen menacing black men, brightly clothed European gypsies, weaselly white men, frightened teenagers of all colors. A drunken Geordie with tracks of dried blood interfering with the patterns of the tattoos on his face stood up to shout. The sergeant at the desk, whom I had come to think of as the good policeman, told him to sit down. The Geordie continued to shout. The spiderweb on his throat grew and shrank with every roar. It took four hard-breathing policemen to muscle him away into a cell.

Maybe this was as down as I was going to get. Rock bottom, as Barry would say. I found a coin in my pocket, tossed it up in the air, silently mouthed the word tails. I watched the coin fall to the ground, where I was briefly permitted to see the queen's head before a foot slid it away and a hand gobbled it up and it was gone.

I stood up. The sergeant told me, not ungently, to sit down.

Can I make my phonecall please?

Try to relax son. We'll get to you.

Son? I was hardly any younger than the good policeman.

I don't regret anything, I said.

Right ho. Sit down.

I subsided. The person who shifted up beside me where the Geordie had been looked like a teenager of fifty years ago. Working-man's boots. Black denim trousers with oil stains on them. Red checked shirt. Long greased hair combed high and back. Bony handsome face. He was reading a paperback book, the front cover bent back in his left hand.

Telephones kept ringing. Policemen and policewomen walked briskly through, speaking into radios mounted on lapels, drinking cups of tea, narrowly avoiding collisions. A plump diseased man with a doctor's bag stepped out of one cell and then into the next, where the Geordie was. The men in suits I took to be solicitors. A woman with large glasses on a saggy understanding face came to sit with the gypsies, asked them questions in their language, listened to the complaining jabber of reply, made notes on a clipboard.

In the center of it all, sitting behind his desk about ten feet away from me, was the good policeman. He seemed to understand everything. He answered telephones, filled out forms, joked with other policemen passing through. His face was broad and tired. His eyes were shrewd. Sometimes he yawned and stretched his arms and rubbed the back of his mostly bald head. I liked the good policeman. In other circumstances I would have wanted to become his friend.

The boy beside me flicked over a page of his book. I saw the pale glint of handcuffs clasped around the boy's wrists and this made me inch away. I concentrated again on the good policeman. The good policeman had two pens. One was blue and the other, only occasionally used, was red.

The emperor's red, I said, not realizing I had spoken the words aloud until I saw the handcuffed boy looking at me.

The teenager wasn't a teenager at all. He was at least in his mid-twenties. There were lines at the corners of his eyes, which were blue. He opened his mouth. His teeth were white and crooked. He spoke in a thin arch voice.

Oh. Wotcha, he said.

We had, I realised, met before, in an upstairs room of an Earls Court pub, that I, a heathen, had been thrown out of.

I'm Carlo, he said.

Phillip, I said.

The emperor's red. What's that about?

Red was the color of truth in imperial China. Only emperors were allowed to write in red.

I write in red. I write in red the whole time!

I had the strong feeling that to have attracted this man's attention was the worst manifestation so far of my luck.

What you in for Phil?

Assault.

Me too! Get up.

What?

Get up.

What?

Carlo nudged me with his elbow. At the same time, the turbaned man sitting on my right pushed against me.

Approach the desk, the good policeman was saying with his merciful eyes finally upon me.

I got up. I walked unsteadily, nervous under the scrutiny of Carlo. The desk seemed a long way away. I banged into a cleaner who was slowly walking through with a bucket and a mop, and whose eyes were either very tired or very stoned. The cleaner dropped his mop and I picked it up and handed it back to him and heard Carlo make a mocking sound behind me. I started again for the desk. People kept confusing me, walking obstructive routes. The policeman's encouraging smile pulled me through. I arrived, exhausted, at the desk, and was about to lean on it when the good policeman shook his head to tell me not to. Another policeman was talking to him and the good policeman was nodding and making notes. Then the other policeman left and he began talking and I concentrated very hard but couldn't understand what was being said even though few of the words were new to me. The policeman's lips were thin and pale and hardly moved. The words came out in long uneventful lines like spaghetti out of a machine. His nose was fleshy and there were blackheads on the side of it, which made me sad; the good policeman didn't deserve to have such neglected skin, there should be someone who loved him and groomed him. His eyes were small and brown and clever and tired. A band of paler pinker skin was growing at his top of his forehead where hair no longer did. Hanging from his left nostril was a little droplet of mucus, which, because of the angle of the desk light, refracted a miniature rainbow on to the papers on the desk.

The good policeman was looking at me. His lips had stopped moving and there were no words coming out any more; the machine had stopped, which meant that it was my turn to speak.

I'd like to call my wife.

If you don't want a solicitor you might want to give reasons why you don't want a solicitor.

Get a solicitor! Carlo shouted. The good policeman ignored him so I thought it was best to do the same.

You may exercise your right to call a solicitor at any time while remaining in custody. Do you understand that?

I nodded.

Please say yes or no to indicate understanding or lack of it.

Yes.

If you are asked questions about your suspected offense, you do not have to say anything. But it may harm your defense if you do not mention when questioned something which you later rely on in court. Anything you do say may be given in evidence. Do you understand?

I think so, I said brightly. I'd like to call my wife.

Do you have any reasons why you don't want a solicitor?

I'm glad I'm going to be punished. I deserve it.

What's your wife's name?

Alice.

It was nice saying her name. And it was a relief being subject to official power. I was glad to have no more decisions to make. The good policeman was a sergeant and wore his power lightly, unlike Carlo, who had unnerved me. I tried to remember Alice's face but couldn't, so, instead, I remembered the photograph of Alice that sat on the chest of drawers in the kitchen, but that got pushed aside by the image of the chest of drawers itself, stout, with damaged drawers I had always been promising to fix.

What's your wife's telephone number?

I gave it. I gave my full name and hers and our address

and the telephone numbers of the house and shed. In return I received two printed pieces of paper. I tried to read them and couldn't and felt suddenly abysmal in an enormous world. I put the pages in my pocket. The sergeant asked me for my height and age and date and place of birth and ethnic origin and occupation. I answered all the questions. To the question about my occupation I said I was a manual laborer.

The sergeant paused with his ballpoint just above the paper. He looked sourly at me.

I'm a writer. I write instruction manuals. You see? Manual, laborer? It was a joke.

I couldn't hear what the sergeant said in reply. All the background noise in the room had become foreground. I shrank against telephone trills and mumbled conversations and heavy voices raised in argument and a metal bucket dragged across the floor and ballpoints cutting across vulnerable paper and fingernails scratching previously damaged skin. Carlo gave me the thumbs-up sign with both manacled hands.

What?

Empty your pockets. Place the contents on the table. They will be sealed inside an envelope and returned to you in the event of your release.

I did what I was told to do. I had no other function. The sergeant was painstaking as he wrote his descriptions of my possessions. His tongue was very pink. The tip of it rested on his pale lower lip as he wrote. He took all my things and gave me back the two printed pieces of paper that had the crest of the Metropolitan Police on the top.

Remove your belt.

Why?

Just do it, son. And your shoelaces. Put them with your contents.

I stripped the laces out of my shoes and hung them on top of my contents and felt ashamed for having treated them so badly. They were tattered at the ends and pulled to single-strand breaking point in their middles.

I'm reminding you again you have the right to speak to a solicitor.

I don't want to speak to a solicitor.

Sign here then to indicate that this is an accurate and full account of the contents of your pockets when arrested, and sign here to indicate that you have been informed of your right to speak to a solicitor. And here to indicate that you do not want to speak to a solicitor at this time. And here to indicate that an extract from a notice setting out your rights has been read to you and you have been given a copy and that you have been provided with a written notice setting out your entitlements while in custody.

I had never heard anyone speak words so fast and so clearly. I wrote my name four times. It looked slowly unfamiliar.

The sergeant, whom I was no longer thinking of as the good policeman, whom I was seeing as something grander, maybe diabolical, lost all interest in me. I was issued with a tired formal farewell and the sergeant's attention fell on to the next person, and a policeman with keys came and led me away.

I was taken into a cell. The door closed. The key turned and the latch fell. The jailer went away, footsteps down the corridor. I sat on a hard bed built into the wall.

The cell was cold and damp and smelled of vomit, disinfectant, and urine. There was a toilet bowl at the end of it, which I tried to be sick into but couldn't. I returned to the bunk. I lay upon it. I closed my eyes. I wished for sleep but sleep was as unavailable as vomit. I said my wife's name again but the good effect didn't happen in the cell. I recited the names of the Chinese dynasties. I tried to console myself with the faces of the twins but that just made me sadder. I counted sheep. I remembered the names of all the boys in the London under-twelves team that I had starred in. I did the dynasties backwards. I cursed my bad luck. A quick self-inflicted wound suddenly opened up deep in the core of myself in atonement or at least reaction for the injuries I'd inflicted. I was glad I'd hit Barry. I felt guilty that I felt glad. I felt glad that I felt guilty. The wound opened further. I pushed away images of degradation and pain. And any time I drifted towards sleep, sounds kept jerking me back into this night-time cell, where I slowed down my breathing and imagined circles of different-colored light at my energy centers, and concentrated very hard on keeping my heartbeat regular. I got down to my knees and crawled around the perimeter of the cell and felt for small openings in the walls.

I lay on the bed again. I clasped my hands behind my head. I stared up at the ceiling, wondered how graffiti could be written so high up: Dates of arrival, initials, diagrams of vaginas, cartoon policemen naked under helmets sodomizing prisoners. I wanted to cry. I felt relatively happy. I deserved to be here and this is where I was, and I was being punished, which was good. I understood punishment.

Two

My dreams had begun in enclosed public places—a rain-shelter in the park, a gray field circled by gray clusters of trees, a taxi drivers' cafe on the Embankment—and narrowed, become subterranean—a long empty escalator trundling down (identically suited pinhead commuters on the opposite escalator going up) through the gloom of tube tunnels that stretched to vanishing point, and into the sigh of small windowless rooms.

As I opened my eyes, I was left with three vaporous images: A party room, a generous girl, a tube platform that sucked at my feet with a gloopy concrete kiss. The images evaporated, leaving nothing, not even an afterglow. I was alone with the feeling that nothing was secure. As I waited for my customary life to intervene, my bedroom to wrap itself around me, my wife's legs to weigh upon mine, I reminded myself that dream images mean nothing at all: They're just gaudy stuff without substance pumped out by the sleeping mind—psychic steam, nocturnal emissions, dream drool.

My bedroom did not wrap itself around me. There was no Alice, and maybe never had been. Instead: Footsteps in the corridor, a key rattling in the lock, the metal strain of a door that didn't like to be opened. A man breathed. The squeak of sole against floor. Bad light entered my cell, with the good policeman following after.

Sorry to wake you.

I wasn't sleeping.

How do you feel son?

Cold.

I'd've brought you a cup of tea, but . . .

(But what? Tea doesn't exist in this world for the likes of you? I drank it myself? I just couldn't be arsed?)

. . . but I thought you'd want to get out of here as quick as possible.

I tried to work this sentence out. The meaning of it was unavailable to me.

Sorry?

You're free to go is what I'm saying.

No.

We interviewed everyone who was at your club last night.

It's not my club.

And no one saw a thing. And as for the alleged victim . . .

The good policeman looked at me reproachfully. I could see my own face in the policeman's response to it. The worry lines on his forehead. A weak, puzzled malefactor struggling with understanding.

The victim . . . ?

The one you claimed to have attacked.

Not claimed. I did attack him, I did.

So you say. Mr Silver doesn't.

Barry. How is he?

In hospital. Recovering. Mr Silver has declined to give a statement. Similarly the victim's *friend*. Which means we have no evidence of the assault apart from the would-be assailant's claim and the victim's injuries, which we are not permitted to take into account.

I did attack him, I did.

But no one saw and no one will tell. How do you account for that?

I don't know. I wouldn't. I don't know. But I did it. I need locking up.

The good policeman looked at me severely.

You're free to go.

I protested.

But this is monstrous. I've committed a crime. Please. Let me pay for it.

There's a caff around the corner which should be open this time of day. You might enjoy a cup of tea in there. They do a good buttered bap.

Barry and Sean had finally outdone themselves in malice. Couldn't they have given me—didn't I deserve?—a couple of nights in jail, retribution, suffering, a fine, a criminal record, the balance even, the scales of credit and obligation steady at last, and when I came out we could all get together; at least, I would be able to ruefully say, I paid for it, it was horrible in there, don't ask . . .

But no, again, I had been victimized with benevolence, persecuted with love, diminished with kindness; if I didn't watch out they'd make me into nothing.

The good policeman made a pile of my contents. There was no one else in the station hall. Last night's bustle had left behind only a few dark patches on the floor.

Is everything here?

I think so.

Then take it. And sign your name. Here here here and here.

I signed and sighed and threaded the laces back into my shoes.

I've never really thought about it before, the idea of tying up feet. You'd think they'd have found a better way by now, I suppose they have, Velcro.

159

The policeman made a noise in his throat, which might have signified scorn or uninterest, I couldn't tell.

Did you call my wife?

There was no answer from the number you gave. Feel free to try yourself now.

I tried to call Alice. I wondered if his use of the word free was entirely unmalicious. The telephone rang and no one answered and I eventually tired of holding a receiver to my ear.

I'll. Surprise her. There's been a problem with our phone. Do you know what the time is?

There's a clock over there.

I knew that. But I wanted to prolong this moment, delay my coming freedom. With this man for company I felt safe, if a little high-pitched. But the episode was ending. Our affair was doomed.

I shook the offered hand of the good policeman who said, quite terrifyingly sadly,

Keep out of trouble son. Nose clean.

I started to panic. I looked for something secure to hang onto, the bench, a water pipe, the good policeman himself. NO! I could scream, don't let me out! It's a conspiracy, that bastard Barry is behind it all, don't you see what he's doing to me? And your part in this? You're making his victory absolute. The jade carving was bad enough but this—*this!*—this is fundamental, impossible, a giddying awful defeat. The abyss. There is no coming back from here.

Yes. Let's hope so, I said instead. I mean, I think so, I do. Thank you. Thank you for everything. I appreciate how nice you've been.

All part of the service.

The good policeman looked down, as if allowing me the

privilege of removing myself back to my own life without the shame of being observed. I stayed where I was. The policeman nodded his head. I did not move.

Was there something else?

I tried in vain to think of something.

No, I said. I don't think so.

I must ask you to leave now sir.

That *sir* was unkind, an unnecessary twist of the knife. Whatever happened to *son*? I had no place here, this was no longer my home, the space that had been made for me was gone. My temporary father no longer acknowledged me. I had to go.

Yes, I said bravely. I understand.

Unless, of course, I committed another crime. The return of the prodigal. I approached the good policeman, who was sorting through papers. The good policeman looked alertly up.

Yes?

I took a step back. It would be too humiliating, even for me, to be thrown bodily out of this place. I had to take the journey on my own, as if from choice. I turned around. I made my feet take some steps. I opened a door. I stepped into the morning. The day outside was bright and terrible.

I stood alone, blinking, light-headed, ungrateful for the gift of my freedom. A car shot past. A bird clumsily rose from one tree and flopped, flapping, into another. A bicyclist lifted her hands off her handlebars to adjust her hair and I forgot myself for a moment to marvel at the grace of the movement. And then the gloom lowered again. I was submerged by my knowledge of the misery of things, of my low, fixed place in the universe. I went to the cafe the good policeman had recommended.

Wotcha.

The boy called Carlo came away from the table he had been sitting at and stood beside me.

I'll *stand* you breakfast.

No, there's no need.

I insist. My *shout*.

Carlo said *shout* in the same odd way he'd said *stand*, partly proud, partly awkward. The word was spoken as if it had been taken from a foreign language that he was clever enough to have learned but which his tongue wasn't the right shape to pronounce.

No. It's OK. Thank you. No thanks.

Come on. What are you having? It's on me.

Carlo took my arm. He shook his head, and he kept shaking his head, as if he was trying to make me shake mine too. There was a friendship offered here, two jailbirds in the straight world in the morning of our freedom.

A cup of tea and a buttered bap, I said to the man behind the counter.

Carlo dropped some coins on the counter before I had a chance to. He led me to his corner table.

I thought you'd done an assault, I said.

Mistaken identity. They thought I was someone else. What about you?

The person I beat up won't give a statement.

Again, inadvertently, I had impressed Carlo.

He must be very scared of you.

Hardly.

Are you *horny*? asked Carlo. I'm *horny*. Getting out of jail always makes me *horny*.

No, just thirsty.

I know how to make things occur.

This was dismal bad luck. I should have known. Other

arrested men are sat next to shy bishops, or suicidal deaf-mutes. I had been given Carlo, lascivious, unpredictable, clearly insane, and trying to become friends.

There was a table of office girls next to us. White blouses, short skirts, attractive thighs, mobile telephones on the table next to leatherette handbags. Carlo talked to them all. Carlo was benevolence, he was magnetism. When he laughed they laughed. When he spoke they listened. He admired their mobile telephones and they felt flattered. He persuaded the prettiest one to join our table and her friends giggled and left.

Carlo finished his mug of tea in two gulps; he took hold of the office girl's hand and sketched a pattern on the inside of her lower arm.

I can read your fortune, Carlo said. You're about to have the time of your life.

He then detached himself to attend to his splodge of black pudding, sausage, bacon, baked beans, and fried egg.

The girl was gazing at Carlo over the cafe table. Her hands kept fluttering around sauce bottles as if she needed to touch something.

Is he always like this?

I don't know. I don't really know him.

Oh. I thought you were his probation officer or social worker or something.

The girl had blonde hair, freckles, a hole in the right leg of her tights. Librarian glasses. She kept smiling. Crooked teeth.

You can put food away can't you? Where does it all go?

Carlo just looked back at her with such conviction that whatever message he was sending her she believed it. This is how cults begin. The Manson family, Scientology, all it takes is one charismatic lunatic with a large appetite and an ability to make women feel good about themselves. Carlo leant across the table towards the girl and lifted away the silver M she wore on a silver chain and kissed her throat. When he pulled away she raised a hand to the skin he'd kissed, which was blushing.

Your teeth. They're like a cat's.

She closed her mouth, looked down at the serviette dispenser.

If I had the money I'd get them fixed. Look. I have to go to work now. I'm already in trouble there.

Call in sick then. My friend's a doctor. He'll write you a note. He's a good doctor. What's your name? I'm Carlo.

I know. You told me.

What's your name?

Guess. Guess and I won't go in to work.

Your name's Melinda.

No it's not.

Melissa. Mandy. Mildred. Look at the day outside, Mildred. It's too good to waste.

No one's called Mildred.

Miriam then. Martha. Melody. Your name is Melody. Let's go Melody. The sunlight's good for us.

She didn't say he was right or wrong but docilely she got up, wiped her mouth with a sleeve, took his hand.

Goodbye, she said to me. It was nice meeting you.

I'll be seeing you, Carlo said.

I sipped my tea. I watched them walk out into the high street, where they would be making things occur. Carlo looked back once, gleefully frowning, slowly winking. He scratched a wavy line along the side of a black parked car.

I hoped his last words to me had been the sort of thing people say when they're never going to meet again, and not a threat or a promise.

I walked home, I sweated in the sunshine, I hoped that my return would be honored with kisses, with flowers, six attendant female hands, rich creamy food and vintage wine, cosy endearments, love with the lights on. I expected none of these things to occur. I dreaded the reproachful silence of an empty house, a note on the refrigerator door held up with fruit magnets, Gone to my sister's, you fucker, the absent imprints of my wife and daughters, the way every object would resist me. Mysterious girlish things would trip me up, kitchen knives rip my skin. I delayed my return, because I could.

I made a detour into Clapham Common where I sat achingly cross-legged on damp grass and watched a game of football. Most of the players were black and showed a high level of skill for park football, despite their lack of fitness. I wondered, for the first time in years I wondered, where I might have gone, what I might have become, if the injury hadn't happened, whether there ever had been a possibility of a different life, if there had been no Friendship Games, if Richard hadn't lost the ball, if Doughboy hadn't fouled the Spaniard, if I hadn't been injured, or whether, no matter what, there would have been the same inexorable consequence of me, here, now, sitting at the age of thirty-nine in a

London field with the residue of night sweats on my clothes.

The ball came bouncing towards me, followed by a sweating man in a yellow strip. I got up, I had missed the touch of a ball against my foot. I controlled the ball with my left foot, felt no answering twinge in my knee, flicked the ball into the air and chipped it back with my right foot into the path of the retrieving player. The whole movement was executed with minimum fuss and maximum effect and was acknowledged by a lift of the player's eyebrows, a slight smile, as he let the ball roll between his legs before he turned and ambled back into the game.

The two teams were evenly matched and the players were shouting and swearing and running hard and trying their fanciest moves. I wanted to play too. I stood up to get a better view and I did some stretching exercises stimulated by the sound of ball and boots and cursing, the homesickness smell of mud. I wanted the ball to come towards me again, and I wanted above all an invitation to join the game. There was one player, on the blue team, who reminded me of Doughboy; less talented than some of his teammates, he kept getting the ball through strength of personality and sheer force of verbal abuse. Maybe there was a finite number of character types in a football team, in any group anywhere, and one of them was mine, the one who gets left behind.

I felt suddenly ridiculous, like a new boy in a school playground hoping to be invited into a bigger, more competent world. I walked quickly home through streets charged with energy and anticipation. Brickwork was livid red, shop windows were astonishing, electric ocean and fire. People's faces looked ready to explode from the hidden pressures of hunger and need. Proximity to the unstable passions of Carlo had made me jittery. Confinement had given me energy. Football had given me hope.

The house was empty. The twins would be at school, Alice at work, rebranding. I sidled through to the shed where Alice, I supposed thoughtfully, had put the jade carving on the shelf above my desk. I sat hunched below it, condemned by the impossibility of achieving anything worthwhile with an object that beautiful above me. Green jade, perfect curves, a dead artist's hand turns a chisel, and how I wished some of that perfection, some of that immaculate control, could leak down to me. But I wouldn't know what to do with it if it did, I would be petrified, actionless.

NO! I yelled. I picked up the carving. Ruthlessly I made a fingernail journey along the carved river, up the central peak. And then I let go. I opened my hand, allowed the hateful object to surrender to gravity; it dropped to the rug, it made a little bounce and then lay there, on its side, intact, perfection undisturbed perhaps even improved. It didn't even look ridiculous.

I left it there. Creating the possibility of someone walking in, most likely myself, forgetfully breaking it, a gristly crunch, a snap.

At supper, I tried to explain to Alice what it was like in the police station.

It was fascinating. There was this very nice policeman who I felt quite sorry for. And I met this boy in there, not a boy, man, in his twenties, sometimes looked very young, sometimes very old, he might be dangerous, I think a little cracked, the sort of person I would never meet unless he was mugging me, or—but it was fascinating. Other people's lives.

You should think more about your own.

I know. Yes. But what I'm trying to say, I don't know. I had this thought on my way home, that things could be different—

Have you called Barry yet?

Not as such.

You must. You have to apologize.

You think so?

Of course you do. You beat him up, in a public place.

I should have done it somewhere more private?

The look she gave me was the one she used to wither the twins with when they had done something so stupid that her response was beyond words or threat.

Do you know they take your shoelaces away? I thought that sort of thing only happened in the movies.

You know what I think? I think you're going mad. You should speak to a doctor or take up marathon running or something. Learn to tap dance. Anything. Yoga.

You're right. I know you're right. But I tell you, we have to make something occur.

Occur? Where did that come from?

I don't know, but—

It makes you sound like a bureaucrat. Occur.

I knew where it came from. It came from Carlo; I heard in my head the high mocking voice of the boy I had been too close to. I hoped if I carried on speaking then I wouldn't hear it any more.

And I should get Barry something. Show my gratitude. He refused to give a statement against me, you know.

Stop it stop it stop it stop it! STOP IT! Forget about gifts, all that obsessive nonsense. Think about your family. The people who live with you.

I'm sorry. You're right. I know you are.

169

I bowed my head. I showed contrition, acknowledgement of my wife's superior wisdom, the possibility of, with her help, gaining my own.

You realize what's at stake here, don't you?

Yes. Yes I do.

Nothing more was said. It was beneath her and, it was pretended, me, to talk about this further. Over the next days she watched me for signs of gift-giving. I behaved impeccably.

In a restaurant on Wardour Street, Barry was magnani-
mous, lordly, condescending; I was full of shame. I had
got there twenty-five minutes late, my tiny rebellion,
and found Barry with his Palm Pilot compiling a list of
birthdays of everyone who was about to start work on his
new production, Dylan's latest film. We were having lunch
together, because Alice had told me I had to apologize,
properly, in person, and now here we were, surrounded by
noise, heels on wooden floors, mobile telephone tremolos
and trills, quick-talk of hustler and hustled, trousers rus-
tling as buttocks in cotton struggled to find comfort on
hard chairs.

Barry put his birthday list away.

I never realized how many little things go into making
a movie, I said.

It's not so tough. I just give this list to a woman
who . . .

A woman who what?

It's OK. Nothing. So.

Barry smiled at me.

You said you wanted to talk.

Yes. It's about what happened in the, you know, club.

Barry looked momentarily fearful. I hung my head.

I'm sorry. I don't know what came over me.

Forget about it. It was hilarious. You've given me notoriety.

Thank you. You're being very nice. I don't know what came over me. Alice thinks I'm having a crisis. She's being very nice too.

Please. It was a lark and it's over.

I never hit people. I haven't been in a fight since I was eleven. A fat defender decked me. I'd been making him look silly, nutmegging him and so forth, so he kicked me and I kicked him back and then he punched me on the chin and I fell over. I decided I'd never get involved with that kind of thing again. I don't understand it at all.

I'm not sure what you're talking about but maybe you should get some help?

That's what Alice says.

I could give you the name of a wonderful guy.

Yes.

Give him my name, you could probably jump the queue. He really helped Sean with the parents issue.

You're having a baby?

What? No. My parents. My mother not talking to him and all.

Oh. I see. Sorry. Thank you, I mean.

At an early point, I had started counting the number of times I said, Thank you. I'd lost count long ago. Now I just tapped the table every time I noticed the words leaving my mouth.

You gave me quite a shiner.

Barry's hold on English slang had never quite taken. He meant the bruise on the right side of his forehead, just below the hairline, the purple mound of insulted tissue that I had raised by slamming Barry's head against a table. It looked good on him, piratical. I remembered with some pleasure the pulpy sensation of bone and flesh softening with repeated administrations of wood. Then I felt desperately ashamed again.

I'm sorry. How's Sean?

His head is completely turned. Said he might join us for a drink, you know, afterwards, leave us, discreet, and then come by for a drink. *If* he can spare the time.

Thank you, I said because I had got into the habit of it. I mean for being so decent about it. Thank you.

I hit the side of the table with my knuckles, harder this time. Barry jerked back in his seat.

Hey come on. You're going to get me riled in a moment. Let it rest. And anyway, you know what? (Barry leaned forward and confidentially flicked my arm with a pudding spoon.) I mean it when I say it's not half-bad for my reputation. So come on, let's order another bottle and drink to friendship.

I felt more in Barry's debt than ever. My shoulders fell under the weight of my obligation to my friend. The fact that he was physically frightened to be with me was only slight consolation.

I feel your pain.

Oh?

We're best friends right?

Right, I echoed dismally.

Right. Do something for me?

Of course, yes. Anything.

Bud is going to be in town any day now. It would be great if someone, you know, reliable, could show him around a few places. The countryside for example. And whatnot.

There was no need for me to answer, and anyway

Barry's voice raised now to greet Sean approaching our table.

Hey! Here he is. Hollywood's latest. Read all about it. Golden boy. Soon he won't have any time for the likes of you and me.

Sean sat down. Unlike Barry, he showed no physical fear of his best friend.

Let's all drink drink, Barry said.

We drank drink. Sean and I drank wine and Barry drank fizzy mineral water and Sean asked me what the jail cell was like and I tried to explain but the images in my head became estranged from my words and all that I produced was a pair of empty bored looks in their eyes. I tried to tell them something about the boy I'd met called Carlo (and, as with Alice, I didn't think it appropriate to mention that it was our second meeting) but I conveyed nothing of him, none of the menace, the silly pride, the uniqueness of him; I couldn't make them see the baleful face I still carried around in my mind's eye.

Barry then launched into an anecdote about Dylan, which segued into a digression on the subject of deal-making technique.

The trick you see, the trick, is to know something the other fellow doesn't. So what you got to do is keep in mind something he doesn't know, the color of your underpants, that's the classic, I prefer to think of the shape of Sean's cock or the fact that I've got urine on my hands from going to the loo.

And I, although I'd promised Alice and, to a lesser extent, myself that I wouldn't, said,

I've got something for you.

A look passed between the lovers, it was almost loud enough to hear, *Here we go again . . .*

There's an artist, a young painter. I've asked her to paint your portrait. Portraits. Portrait.

Oh, said Barry.

Thank you, said Sean.

Her name's Samantha. I think she's very good. She likes to paint on gesso. She inscribes secret messages and then paints over them.

The next look they passed between them was unmistakable. *Poor Phillip.* But I wasn't giving up the battle. I gave them Samantha's phone number, directions to her studio in the East End. I extracted from them the promise they would go. Then the conversation returned to its natural place, Barry talking about Dylan, her genius, her enchanting clumsiness in the ordinary world, which I managed, briefly, to interrupt.

And I've got something else too. Here, a script. I wrote it. I'd be interested in your comments.

Barry smiled, took the script, lifted it, pit-pat-patted it towards his chest in a meaningful gesture the meaning of which I couldn't reach.

It's called Wang The Unlucky.

Is it?

It was called Wang The Unlucky Scholar, but then I changed that, because he wasn't a scholar any more.

Oh? That's great, Phil. That's great.

And Barry went back to talking about Dylan again. Barry was peeved with Dylan. Dylan had insisted on an open casting for a minor role in the new film. I put extra sugar in my double espresso, drank more wine, as Barry grouched.

Open castings are trouble. They give directors ideas.

Aren't they meant to have ideas?

Not new ones. We have to go now. It's been great.

Barry rested his hands on mine and looked at me with dreadful sincerity and invited me to a party at his club, to which I had to promise to go.

The reconciliation had been effected.

It was not a simple subject to introduce. I failed several times at the breakfast table, came straight out with it at lunch.

Is there anything, you might like, for an anniversary present?

I had been dreading Alice's response. Generously though, she took the inquiry as due tribute to her, to our marriage, as a signifier of love rather than pathology.

Diamonds and pearls, she said. Always.

Oh. Right. Yes.

Don't look like that. We can just go window-shopping.

Which meant giggling in jewelry shops in Burlington Arcade and New Bond Street, where small men with large black optics screwed into their eye sockets offered us gems for our inspection, and sleek young men in chalk-stripe suits slipped diamond rings on Alice's fingers and hung chains of pearls around her throat and wrists. She dazzled herself in the glass until the sleek young men reproachfully reclaimed their jewels and locked them away beneath security glass.

In St James's Park, on the grass, sheltered by a willow tree and a gaggle of unobservant old men with bags of breadcrumbs who were enjoying intimacy with pigeons, we achieved six hundred discreet thrusts and getting no further was the result of no infirmity of mine, but the advancing threat of two park policemen and a red-faced deckchair attendant coming our way.

We fled the park and went to a movie and kissed in the back row, and walked home after that, across Chelsea Bridge, up past Battersea Park, along Wandsworth Road and up to Bramley Road, entwined.

Alice's mother was our babysitter. The idyll that we had made was broken by the sight of my mother-in-law weeping in the lounge.

I miss your father, she said and it was unclear whether she was saying this to Alice or to me.

I'll give you a lift home, I said.

Alice's mother lived in Fulham, which wasn't far from Earl's Court, The Captain's Grief. I told myself to be strong, that to pursue gifts for Barry would in some way corrupt the day that Alice and I had made.

Would you like to come up? said Alice's mother somewhat skittishly.

No. No thank you. Will you be all right?

She snorted at that.

I hope you don't see me as an old person.

No. I don't. Of course not.

Because I'm not, you know. Not really.

She said this as if she was letting me in on a great, privileged secret, which I honored with solemnity and the chastest of kisses to her pleasantly lined cheek.

I went to the The Captain's Grief. I drove there thinking I might find Carlo inside. I pushed open the door hoping I wouldn't; but there he was, sitting at a dark wooden table in a corner of the saloon bar next to a fruit machine. Newspapers were piled in front of him.

I'm reading newspapers. It's important to *keep up*, isn't it?

It probably is. I suppose I don't keep up as much as I should.

Do you have a subscription to Reader's Digest?

No, I admitted. I don't.

I could get you one.

No. No thank you. How's Melody?

Who?

That girl, in the cafe.

That wasn't her name, would you believe it? She was called Mary in the end. Do you want her phone number?

No thank you. I don't think I'm her type.

She doesn't have types. She just wants someone to be nice to her.

And I said it. I asked what I was here to ask, and I made my voice sound casual and bored.

You wouldn't, I had thought, I don't know, tell me where Syd Barrett lives?

That's fine. We can discuss that. Let's settle up first and then we can move on.

Sorry? Settle?

I bought you breakfast remember? In the caff.

I shook my head. I might have chortled. Was this a joke? A paltry debt echoing everything that had occurred with Barry and Sean? Or maybe this was how the world was organized and I had only recently noticed.

How much do I owe you?

It's not a question of money.

What is it a question of?

Carlo nodded his head. I shook mine. I was beginning to realize that most of Carlo's gestures signified their opposite.

He offered to buy me a drink but I thought it best not to accept. I offered to buy him a drink but he told me, no, all the same, he'd rather buy it himself. We stood at the bar, side by side, making our separate orders.

You said you worked in the movies.

Well yes and no.

You said you were a movie producer.

Did I? Well I'm not really. I've written a script that's all. But I do have this friend, who is a movie producer. He used to know Syd Barrett.

I'd like to meet your friend, Phil.

I don't know if that's going to be possible.

We looked at each other, and I couldn't tell who wanted more from the other and who, therefore, had the power to put the other in his debt.

You introduce me to your friend. And I'll tell you where Syd Barrett lives.

You know where he lives?

Me and some friends sometimes. We go to his house. We knock on the door and he doesn't answer. Then we try to climb into the garden and the police come and chase us away.

What's the point of that?

What's the point of anything? If you put it like that.

After he'd finished scoffing at me, he took out a paperback book. In the inside cover were many names and telephone numbers and addresses.

Where does your friend live, Phil?

I was not going to be giving him that. I did tell him he could meet me outside Barry's club the following night. He wrote down the address in very neat capital letters. There was an agreeable silence after that.

I have to go home now, I said.

I'm going to tell you something.

Home now. To work, I added just in case he was intending to construe this as an invitation.

Yes. You said. Don't tell anyone this. It's kinda a secret. I wanted to be a movie star so I went to Los Angeles. Wasn't even allowed into a carjacking gang. The Yanks don't *get it* do they? Gave them my best, Sal Mineo meets Richard Widmark. And ended up working in a place called Nightmare Circus in a nigger part of town. Abandoned cinema, this place. There was a vampire and a zombie and this werewolf who had cotton wool painted brown stuck all over him. I was Maggot Boy. Had to wear white jeans, white shirt, lie in a coffin in a corner where the screen used to be. Stare at fake cobwebs all day long. Not enough light even to read. When punters came towards me, I was meant to rise up like Bela Lugosi and sort of wiggle. They told me to shriek too but I didn't want to appear ridiculous. It was supposed to be like I was covered with maggots but they didn't have the budget for maggots so I've got this white wedding stuff on top of me instead. What's it called?

What?

That stuff they use at weddings. Throw it over people? Confetti?

Is that an Italian word do you think? What was I talking about?

Maggots.

Yeah maggots but no. Maggot Boy. I got the sack after a few days. Didn't show enough enthusiasm. That's what they said. Enthusiasm. The joke though, what it is is that I'm the only one gets paid. This really pisses everyone else off because the company was going bankrupt and nobody else'd been paid for months. Not even the werewolf who was, I got to say, very good.

I'm going home now.

Cautiously, I separated myself from Carlo's company. He didn't seem offended. He turned his attention back to the newspapers. His focus was narrow and absolute.

Where have you been? Alice asked when I entered, confidently, our bedroom.

Oh. You know, I said.

My mother didn't make you look through photo albums did she?

Yes, I said putting on an air of great nobility. She did.

Poor you, said Alice with feeling.

Trying to push away some of my anxiety about seeing Barry for the first time since I had given him the script of Wang The Unlucky (each day I had waited for the telephone to ring: the telephone had not rung), I showed Alice the chocolate Leaning Tower of Pisa.

They've been so nice I thought we should——, I started to say.

I might have timed it better. We had begun speaking at almost exactly the same time.

I'm so glad you've pushed all that——, she said.

——give them something in return, I said.

——gift nonsense behind you, she said.

I had thought that any sight would be preferable to my wife's face at that moment. The empty black bicycle lock hooked around a parking meter, the broken cassette tape spooling out by the feet of minicab drivers, the dreadlocks of the rickshaw driver pedaling past, the yellow police incident sign, SERIOUS ASSAULT CAN YOU HELP? Even the club beggar, in whose pale watery eyes I could read a sort of compassionate superiority. I was wrong. Alice's face was preferable to most and always to Carlo's.

He stepped forward. Laughter in his eyes, the alchemist's knowledge.

I'm Carlo. I'm a mate of Phil's. You must be his *old lady*.

Alice looked from my face to scowl at Carlo's and then at mine again.

Are we going in? she said in a rather more haughty tone than I would have chosen for her.

I believe the phrase is *pussy whipped*, Carlo said as I followed her and he followed me.

The whisper of Barry's name allowed Alice to lead us up two staircases, through a corridor where mobile telephone users, heads lowered, walked talking in private circles, and up a final staircase into a crowded bar. Fleece-jacketed girls and boys with superior looks and white-dusted nostrils smiled at each other in the rustle of artificial down.

Dylan's new movie was about to go into its first day of filming and everyone was very happy.

Amazing. Studio. Dylan.

Dylan Dylan.

Funny.

So funny.

Genius. Brilliant. Love.

Alice hobbled to fill the empty chair beside Dylan's husband, leaving Carlo and me to fend for ourselves.

Who are you?

Nobody, I'm nothing, I heard myself saying to a stern young man with the same sort of facial hair configuration as myself. I resolved to shave off my beard the first chance I got.

It's a private party. Sorry.

I'm looking for Barry. I'm a friend of Barry. Have you seen him?

The young man had to admit to himself that there was a chance he might have misjudged me. Sternness was replaced by appeasement and then by fear, when I lifted my hand and he flinched from it and a startled recognition came into his eyes.

I think he's with Dylan.

Where is Dylan?

Around, said the young man waving towards heaven and moving fast away from me.

Dylan was a goddess in this world. Omnipresent if not omniscient. I didn't care. I felt tougher than usual. We went to the bar, where Carlo tired of waiting to be served and picked up two pints of Guinness, and walked me away before their owners could complain about their absence. He led me along an airless path between fleecy padded elbows and interrogative noses and cigarettes held at dainty angles.

Carlo found a window bay to lean into and sneer from. He handed me my beer and the blue glare of his eyes diminished the neon lights shining in from across the street.

What are you doing here? You don't belong do you?

Worse than being mocked and threatened, was that Carlo appeared to be genuinely fond of me. He was like a patient older brother who accepted with goodish grace his duty to protect me. I tried to move backwards but the crush of film flunkies kept me where I was.

What's that you got?

A pint of Guinness. You gave it to me. Do I owe you anything for it?

No. In your other hand. Behind your back. What is it?

I kept my hand where it was. It held hidden a chocolate Tower of Pisa, melting.

Stop shaking your head. Show me your hand.

I let the Tower fall. I kicked it away behind me

with the heel of my right foot. I showed my empty hand to Carlo who smiled again and laughed one of his B-movie laughs.

I finally saw Barry at a table beside Dylan. I moved towards them and felt the clench of Carlo's hand on my shoulder. I was regretting this already. Carlo should have fulfilled his side of the bargain first. We should never have made the bargain to begin with. Maybe when we got to the table, then some vigilant fleecy flunky—or a pair of them, probably would need two at least—would take Carlo away, banish the interloper into Soho streets where no membership was required.

Dylan waved towards us. She stood up. She showed us her best smile and an attitude of—and this was truly shocking—humility. As I tried to work out how to react to this improbable event Dylan reached past us to grab in her luminous hands the arms of the boy who had been walking in our footsteps.

Bud. Bud. Bud.

Bud. Bud!

Bud Bud Bud Bud Bud Bud.

Bud.

Bud!

The movie star's eyes were down, his skin was spotted and pocked with adolescent acne. His body, beneath jeans and tattered jumper, looked too slight for this or any world, unready.

Someone get a seat for Bud.

Bud! Sit here.

Come over here, Bud!

Bud!

Bud!

Hello Dylan, Bud said finally. His voice was so soft it

demanded everyone's attention, even the flunkies squeaking around with chairs. Barry. How are you?

We're great, Bud. Cooking. Say Hi to Sean. You remember Sean.

Hi Sean. This is my friend Martha.

Hey! Someone! Get a seat for Martha.

Bud's friend Martha was a stout, glowering, older woman whose hair was dyed black in some places and red in others and was unfetchingly cut into a flapper's bob that jabbed at her cheeks with sharp points.

Bud and Martha sat, and I tried to make myself noticed.

Barry. Sean, I said. Barrysean Barrysean.

Carlo intervened. He walked towards Dylan, hand outstretched, gleam of certainty, salesman of the apocalypse.

I'm Carlo. Who's the kid?

Who?

Why!

That's—

??!

My name's Bud, the movie star said and smiled. His face was transformed and so was, briefly, the world.

Space was made for us to sit down. A flunky fetched a chair for Carlo and me to share. I perched shakily on the edge of it, nervous at the touch of Carlo's hip hard against mine.

Bud's clever frightened eyes followed whoever was speaking. Usually it was Dylan, sometimes Barry. Alice and Mr Dylan disapproved quietly together. Carlo spilled some language over Bud, who didn't seem to mind. Sometimes a flunky or a willowy girl would report news of Dylan's or Barry's glory in another country a long way away. And once, decisively, Carlo said something to Bud, who nodded and then leaned across to whisper to Martha, who sighed.

Bud wants to know if anyone has any drugs.

Flunkies' hands reached into pockets. White envelopes appeared on the table. Carlo said he didn't like cocaine, but he'd take it, unless someone had something stronger—a remark that made Dylan, who did like cocaine, very much, judging by the amount she was sucking into her nostrils, happily laugh. Barry said he didn't like cocaine either, not just because it made him talk nonsense, but because it made him listen to it too.

Both Alice and I were watching Barry. She was watching him for signs of betrayal and deception to his boyfriend. I was waiting for him to say something about my script, or at least refer to it, and in the meantime I was interpreting every action of his for critical meaning. He showed a new hair charm to Bud (neutral). He slammed his hands together and laughed and disagreed with something Dylan had said (good sign). He leaned forward to say something secret to Bud (ambiguous for my purposes, telling for Alice's). He sat back and said to Dylan that Syd Barrett was the only man other than Orson Welles and Roy Cohn that he'd ever unreservedly admired.

Roy Cohn sucked, said Martha in a strong German accent. He was the most evil man who ever loved.

Who's Syd Barrett? Bud said. I think I've heard of him.

He was a pop star, said Sean.

Who stopped being one, said Barry.

Who stopped wanting to be one, said Carlo. That's the point.

Is it? asked Barry annoyed that Carlo knew anything about Syd Barrett.

Yes, said Carlo shaking his head and smiling happily, which probably meant he was equally annoyed. It is.

Make your name like a ghost, said Barry.

When I live I die, said Carlo.

What's happened to them? asked Dylan.

I think they're doing Syd Barrett quotes, said Sean.

I don't get it, said Martha.

There was a personal, chemical rejection between Barry and Carlo, made more antagonistic by their shared devotion. A private pleasure shared is a pleasure threatened.

Where is he now? someone asked.

Cambridge, said Barry. He went back home to live with his mother.

She's dead now, said Carlo.

That's enough of all of that, said Dylan. Let's have another round of that stuff.

I'm going home, Alice said. Are you coming?

I rose dutifully from my chair. Carlo mouthed the words *pussy whipped*.

No, I said and I wasn't sure which of them I was spiting. I think I'm staying.

We'll talk when you get home.

Mr Dylan left shortly after. I was sitting at a glass topped table with Carlo and Dylan and Barry and Sean and Bud and Martha, and three expressionless willowy girls and one boy flunky, who was cutting out lines of cocaine. After another round Carlo became exuberant.

This is it! yelled Carlo. All those geezers, the ancient Greeks and Phil's Chinese, and the Russians, they thought everything was getting better. Next stop God. Plato, Tolstoy, if only they could be here today, man think how pissed off they'd be. America. What's that about? Some fat cunt eating popcorn out of a bucket and fucking his sister up the arse. Look at us! A bunch of wankers stuffing powder up our nostrils. Jesus meet Confucius. Moses, this is

Leonardo da Vinci. Buddha, this is Dostoyevsky. And, and, and, Einstein, hello Einstein, I'm your fucking inheritor! My name's Carlo. I'm a fuck-up and a pervert. Doesn't that make you laugh?

It made Bud laugh, and Dylan.

How do you know Phillip? asked Barry who was not laughing.

I was not enjoying any of this. And it was getting worse: Carlo would now reveal that I wanted him to find Syd Barrett for me and the whole project would be exposed as something unseemly.

We met in jail, Carlo said.

Dylan barked twice and clapped her hands together and held them clasped as if in prayer.

I like this guy! He's great! Isn't he great?!

He's great, said wary Barry.

Are you an actor?

I've done some work in LA, Carlo said off-handedly. I was Maggot Boy.

I think I've seen it. Who's your agent?

For a moment Carlo was puzzled for a response, then, triumphant, pointing to me, he said,

He is!

Oh, Dylan said. Given up being a doctor have you?

After more cocaine, and cocktails the same color we'd served at the twins' birthday party, and dancing, I was still at the club because I couldn't think of how to get anywhere else, and not just because Carlo—who was acting like his own notion of an actor—had asked me to stay.

Carlo was watching Bud and doing what he did, a somewhat fruitless pursuit, because Bud, I noticed, took on the manners and intonation of whoever was speaking to him. Between them they bounced each other back to himself, Bud becoming stranger and Carlo gentler in the process.

One of the willowy girls found the chocolate Tower of Pisa. The foil wrapper was ripped and bruised with footprints, the chocolate was flattened, melted, run.

Look, she said. Doesn't this look like poo?

Everyone had a turn laughing at it except for Carlo, who stared at me, clicking his tongue in disapproval.

Did you hear about Jerry? said Barry.

What about Jerry? said Dylan.

He died, said Sean.

No, said Dylan. Where?

On his exercise bicycle, said Barry. Toodling along and he died. Never smoked or drank, stayed away from dairy and red meat.

He did drugs.

Jerry did not do drugs.

Jerry did drugs.

I'm telling you, Jerry did not do drugs. He was on his exercise bicycle and something popped inside his head and he died. A blood vessel. Popped.

But I saw Jerry last week.

Dylan looked puzzled, as if she couldn't work out how the power of her gaze had failed to keep Jerry alive.

Jerry's dead. That's very strange. Do you think there's any more of that, stuff?

Dylan was looking at the flunky, who quickly pulled out his drugs envelope, peered disappointedly inside it, lifted a little of the remaining powder away with the corner of a supermarket loyalty card.

Do you mind if I have a look at that?

The envelope was passed over. Dylan opened it and a corner ripped, and all the cocaine plumped to the table.

Oh sorry. That was my fault.

The disgruntled flunky chopped more lines into shape. Everyone waited for Bud to go first, but his eyes were closed and he was gently rocking, and there were little bubbles of saliva on his lower lip. Dylan shrugged and took the first line. Other noses followed.

So Jerry's dead. That's very strange. He was quite a young man wasn't he?

Fifty-two Bob told me.

That's quite young.

Carlo had the flunky's rolled twenty-pound note sticking out of his left nostril. He had started laughing, an almost noiseless pantomime panting with his mouth open showing yellow crooked teeth, the banknote in his nostril wagging from side to side. For a moment no one else at the table made a sound. Everyone waited for Dylan or Bud to show a response.

I like this boy! Isn't he great! said Dylan.

He's terrific, said Barry.

Cut me another line, Carlo said. And I'll show you how great I can be.

I did not especially want to be alone with Carlo. When Barry and Sean stood to go I got up with them but Carlo pulled me down again. When Dylan left, with the boy flunky and a silent willowy girl, I got up and Carlo pulled me down again; and when Bud left, supported by Martha, I got up to go but Carlo pulled me down again. When the remaining willowy girl showed her inclination to stay with Carlo, or to go wherever he might take her, he nodded his head.

Take a walk. I have some matters to discuss with my man here.

She showed no disappointment or relief. She got up, she

walked away. I was alone with Carlo. I did not want to be. A waitress was laying down clean ashtrays on empty tables. The barman was performing spin moves with the cocktail shaker for an audience of none.

Carlo speculatively wiped his fingertips across the table-top and stroked them along his upper gum. Then he leaned back in his chair with his hands clasped behind his head. He was waiting for me to say something, to honor him. Carefully, I said,

I think Dylan might give you a part in her film.

Yeah and I might give her a part in mine, if you know what I mean. I've told these *suckers* a few *lines* and they've *swallowed* them and you're the only one that knows any different. Which *ties* us together, doesn't it?

Carlo leaned forward. He took hold of my right hand. He pushed his face into mine. I had to travel closer than I would have chosen to the center of Carlo. The distinctive maybe unique smell of him, leather, sweat, wet cardboard, semen, urine, wood smoke, petrol. I struggled, used all my will and strength not to pull away or flinch. Time slowed. Light dripped through the windows, fell short on the wet floor. Solid shapes had lost their form but were gaining in density. The sound in my ears was devastating, it was like being in a cave behind a waterfall. I wanted release.

But your so-called mates. You shouldn't give them presents.

That's what my wife says.

I like your wife. She's a little bit fat but she's gorgeous.

I tried pretending I'd received a compliment and not an obscure threat of a Carlo occurrence.

But that's not the point here. You see the way they are around me. I'm the *king bee.* I've got that Dylan cunt, I've got her *eating out of my trousers*. Nothing you say could spoil that.

You don't have to worry.

Fucking right I don't.

Carlo blinked twice. The lines on his face disappeared. He looked suddenly very young and for the first time since I had met him, vulnerable.

But I owe you, don't I?

I nodded, trying to disclose no indication of smugness.

You can help me find Syd Barrett, I said. But I'm going home now.

I was greatly saddened by the death of Jerry, the opportunities missed, the life cut short, the laughter that might have been shared, the wisdom that should have been passed on but instead had been lost because Jerry, who may have done drugs but did not do alcohol or red meat, had died one morning on his exercise bicycle.

I had never met Jerry. I had never even known anyone called Jerry. I remembered Dylan at a party having to go talk to someone called Jerry and I assumed that this was the man they had been talking about who had had something pop inside his head.

These are the people I knew who are dead: My mother and my grandparents and two aunts and an uncle; Alice's father, grandmother and aunt; three friends from university and one from school; two coaches and one coach driver on the English Schoolboys training staff; a Korean electronics company man who had commissioned me to write manuals; the old couple two doors away from the house I had lived in as a child; a school boyfriend of my sister's; an Irishman called Connor; my old colleague Nikki; a gossip columnist friend of Alice's; various communists and fellow-travellers of my father's; and several celebrities whom I had never met but had watched so many times on television that I had come to consider them as friends.

The causes of death were as follows: Embolism, stroke, Alzheimer's, cancer, stroke, heart attack, cancer, stroke; Alzheimer's, stroke, run over by a cement mixer; AIDS, AIDS, suicide, a congenital brain disease whose name I could never remember; cirrhosis of the liver, cirrhosis of the liver, prostate cancer; electrocution; heart attack, heart attack; AIDS; car accident; power boat accident; suicide. The communists had died of heart disease or bowel cancer at enviably advanced ages. I didn't remember how most of the famous people, except for a pair of assassinees, had died. It didn't matter. Unlike my relations, I still thought of most of the dead celebrities as being alive.

My mother died years ago. She had fractured her ankle on a fact-finding tour of Cuba, and on the flight back little blood clots sped from the broken bone and grew, circulating around her body and eventually, in her sleep on the night of her return, had visited her lungs and stopped her heart. The expression on her face was one of great surprise.

I was considering matters of mortality late one morning while sitting in my shed with the page proofs of the instruction manual for a dishwasher. The school holidays had begun and Alice had taken the girls to her sister's house, a grueling visit that I had declined to be part of because of, I claimed, and she surprisingly accepted, pressure of work. The manual had been translated from the Japanese into a poetically flamboyant English, ripe with metaphors and neologisms, which I had then translated and condensed into plainer English. Now I was double-checking for spelling mistakes, ambiguities, and the ghosts of the earlier translator's mistakes.

I had been enjoying my solitude and my work. But now I was stuck thinking about the people I knew and speculating how they would die. Barry from a broken neck after finally stringing one too many things into his hair. Sean a heart attack from too many bodybuilding steroids. Dylan, a helicopter crash. Alice and myself cancer, the vigorous fruit of all the rage and bitterness never allowed above ground out of misguided consideration for each other and ourselves. The children I hoped were going to live for ever. And Carlo. Carlo would die in flames, a car accident, a bomb blast, self-immolation. I saw the picture in flaming color on a newspaper front page. Banner headline: MYSTERY YOUTH DIES AS HE LIVED

The telephone was ringing. I was blasted by guilt. Someone had just died. Sympathetic magic, murdered by my thoughts. I picked up the telephone. I hoped my victim was somebody old.

I got something for you, Barry said.

I held the receiver away from my mouth so Barry couldn't hear the sound of my heart being ripped in two. His judgement on the script. Or else. (Or both.) Of course. Here it came. Revenge for the portrait. I hadn't known he was so merciless.

A job, if you'd care to take it.

I have a job.

The dishwasher manual was most enjoyable. Four mad pages of operating instructions had been reduced to two. I had alphabetized and double-checked the index, and now I was about to go through the trouble-shooting guide (Problem: Dishwasher does not operate when start button is depressed. Solution: Switch on dishwasher. Problem: Dishwasher does not operate when start button is depressed and power is connected. Solution: Close dishwasher door. Problem: Dishwasher does not clean dishes.

Solution: Add cleaning tablet). Manuals were sometimes very clear.

What can I tell you? It's your *client* we're talking about here. Agent. What was all that about?

I'm sorry. It wasn't my idea.

Yeah right. The guy's loopy. He was higher than a . . . fucking . . .

Kite?

I didn't know he was Jewish. But that's not really the point is it? Look. I'm trying to talk Dylan out of giving him a screen test but in the meantime he's allowed to be around. Bud's happy tours are on hold for the moment. But we need someone to pick up laughing boy, take him away again. He does not appear to be the most reliable individual. Will you be able to do this thing for me? He said he likes you.

Afraid not. Sorry.

Think of it as a favor to me.

No, I don't think I could.

I'm not saying I don't like your script if you don't help me out here.

I examined this remark from several angles, lacked the necessary high-grade optical equipment to understand what it meant.

What about Alice? Do you think she could do it? He likes her too. He said so.

No Alice certainly can't do it. Can't you get somebody else?

Yeah yeah right. We'll get someone else.

Barry hung up. I felt appalled. For once I had had an opportunity to reduce the weight of my obligation to Barry by giving him something he actually wanted, that he was asking for. But for the moment at least my aversion to

Carlo was stronger than any desire to give a clinching gift to Barry.

It wasn't a very long moment. I called Alice. Hoping for sympathy I told her about Barry's phonecall.

You have to do it.

He gives me the willies, Carlo.

I thought he was all so *fascinating*?

Well yes. That was a while ago. I think I might have had enough of him.

Just do what Barry asks, Alice said very patiently as if she were reading aloud his newspaper horoscope to a retard. Call him up and drive Carlo to the studio if that's what Barry wants. He won't be interested in your script otherwise. You know what he's like.

It's a bit more complicated than that.

Why? What's more complicated? said Alice beginning to become interested.

I had this plan, arrangement.

Yes?

Well, I don't know. I'll tell you about it tonight.

We're sleeping over here tonight. Me and the girls. We'll talk properly tomorrow.

I thought we were going to Lionel's Cuban-Chinese.

He's sold up in that one. He's backing a Scottish-Italian. We'll go there tomorrow if Mum can babysit. Why don't you go out tonight? It'll do you good. Give one of your friends a ring. Go to a football match. Or something.

The football season's over.

Well something then. Call Richard.

I haven't been able to get hold of him. His telephones seem to have been disconnected.

Well if you do get hold of him let me know. Molly says he seems to have gone to ground.

I needed to buy an anniversary gift for Alice. I stared into the imbecilic abyss of an empty building society account. And I still owed Barry and Sean. For everything.

I picked up Carlo from a basement on Saltoun Road. He sat in the passenger seat squashing a recent artwork of the twins.

This car, he observed mildly, is a piece of shit. Did you buy this car, Phil? or do you drive it because you lost a bet? When I'm a movie star I'll have a Mercedes, one of those Nazi staff cars, and me in the back behind tinted windows and my driver's a Hong Kong karate chick with her tongue cut out so she won't be able to tell anyone my secrets.

She can always write them down.

That's true. That's a good point, Phil, I think I'll keep you *on board*, there'll be a place for you on my team, don't you worry about that. I suppose I'll cut her hands off, but that might limit her karate.

And her driving.

That's another good point, said Carlo. You look troubled.

No. Not troubled. I—

I said, You look troubled. I didn't ask you if you *were* troubled. I said, You *look* troubled. You can't say no to that.

Maybe. Maybe I do look troubled.

I'm not surprised. Driving this car.

Maybe I'll write some postcards.

Maybe you should.

He opened the glove compartment and flicked through the CDs, disparaging them.

No. It's a technique. Something Barry told me about once. You write them but you don't send them. You throw them away. You write down everything you want to say, all the things you keep to yourself because you know if you say them the other person wouldn't be able to deal with it. You discover what your secret thoughts are. It's cleansing, it's supposed to be.

Carlo switched off the radio by putting a tape into the player. Syd Barrett blasted out. I turned down the volume and he turned it up again.

Thought you might like to know!
I'm her lorry driver man
She's on the run
Down by the riverside
Feeding ducks in the afternoon ti-i-i-i-de!

Apples and Oranges is an amazing song! It's got everything. What do you think?

What?

WHAT DO YOU THINK??!! OF THE SONG!!!!!

IT'S A BIT OF A MESS!!!

FUCKING RIGHT IT IS!!!! THEY FUCKING RUINED IT!!!!!

Mercifully, Carlo lowered the volume.

Postcards. That's a good idea, Phil. But you've got to take it further. You send the cards, Phil. And you keep sending them. Home truths. Find your man's *trigger*. Postcard him off to his own suicide. And by the end he's thinking that he's the one who decided that the world's a better place without him in it, and you're just there for company. Dostoyevsky could have done it. I bet you that. You might have to use other techniques too.

You can probably get a manual on it.

Yes. You probably can. South American police I'm sure. I don't read Spanish though.

There might be a Civil Service one.

Yeah there might, but to tell you the truth Phil, I don't go by the *book*, I prefer to make my own decisions. Sleep-deprivation is always good, make everything chancy. Do a creepy-crawly or something like that.

What's a creepy-crawly?

It's a mindfuck.

What's a mindfuck?

I seemed to have the knack of being able to amuse Carlo greatly. The boy nodded his head at me. Glee in his blue eyes. Fondness in his narrow face.

Man where was you before I came along? You was lost. A creepy-crawly. You go into someone's house, you move things around. Not in a big way, a little thing here, little thing there, turn a chair the wrong way round, fiddle with the fruit bowl, it messes with their heads. So boring it's really extreme. But let's make a start. Let's write postcards.

I've got to take you to the location.

They can wait. Here. Let's stop here. I'm going to buy some postcards for you right now.

I recognized the aggressive intent.

No, I said. I'll buy them.

Fifty-fifty?

I stopped the car. I parked the Volvo opposite the Tate Gallery. At a fleece-the-tourists shack—London bus paperweights, plastic policeman helmets—Carlo quickly selected a dozen or so of the most boring postcards from a revolving rack. I put my money down before he had a chance to finish the purchase on his own. We squabbled over the extra penny in the change which finally we gave away to a maimed tourist boy who was terrorizing pigeons (Look, *shiny*, Carlo said).

We sat on the edge of a rectangle of grass outside the gallery. The only occupants of the grass were a statue, a pair of purple-haired girls looking at a map, and a security guard in a blue uniform, slicked thinning hair over a bulbous head.

Carlo lit up a pre-rolled joint. He flicked some ash on a picture of Tower Bridge.

Go ahead.

Who are you going to write to?

I'm going to write to all my friends and loved ones. You do the same. You can do your dog if you like.

I don't have a dog.

Well write to your friends and loved ones then, he said impatiently. It's what I suggested in the first place. Have you got a pen? You can use one of mine.

He passed over a stack of cards and a midget pen lifted from a bookie's shop.

You see? Red. Like the emperor.

I sat cross-legged. I put my left arm around the card as I wrote so Carlo wouldn't be able to see.

Dear Barry, You are a cunt. You are obsessed with money and status both of which you have and both of which you abuse under the guise of generosity. Your use of English is preposterous. If people didn't rely on you for work they'd laugh at you. Look after Sean. He humanizes you. Phillip PS. Take those fucking things out of your hair!

Opposite, Carlo was writing with an identical pen and chortling at his own words. My next cards were pictures of the Changing of the Guard at Buckingham Palace.

Dear Sean, If I were a poof I'd make a pass at you. I think you're a lovely boy and you should take as much of Barry's money and power as you can and run away with it. Love, Phillip PS Is there actually anything inside you?

Dear Dylan, You're a pretentious git. Just because there are lots of people saying yes around you and sometimes your films make money you don't realize what a monster you are. Yours, Phillip (the Sinologist)

We've got to destroy them.

Yeah yeah, when we're done we'll make a fire. You written to your wife yet?

Not yet. Who are you writing to?

I've just done this newspaper columnist. He's one of my projects. Want to hear it? *Dear Dead Man Walking. Look behind you. Over your shoulder. I'm going to get you. One of these days when you least expect it you're going to occur brain damage. Signed, A Friend.*

That's not really the rules is it? You're supposed to be expressing honest rage.

Yeah. But this one I'm going to send. Here. This is a good one for your wife. Use this one.

The picture was of a runway at Heathrow Airport. A queue of planes was waiting to take off on a cloudy day. It was a dismal postcard, which fitted the current state of the relationship I supposed.

Dear Alice, I don't love you and I don't remember when I did. If it weren't for the twins and the shortage of money we'd have split up long ago. All the best, Phillip

I stared at what I'd done. I felt exalted and terrified. I wanted to see my wife now. To give her flowers and take her dancing and kiss her in all apology in some place that no one else could possibly understand and woo her all over again.

Let me see it.

I quickly pulled the card away. Carlo's hand clawed at my hand, my arm, my shoulder until I beat it away.

No. No one's going to see this.

I won't show you any of mine, Carlo said coquettishly.

I don't care. Can we burn them now?

Yeah. Suppose.

The Security Guard stared ostentatiously away throughout our ceremony. The map-reading girls applauded when it was done. We gathered twigs and dry leaves, made a little pyre. Carlo fed in his postcards first, then reached for mine. He turned his back on me to arrange the cards and must have smelled my suspicion. He showed me the postcard he was about to put in the flames. Dismal Heathrow, aeroplanes waiting to take off. I wondered if they ever had, if they ever could. I watched it go up in flames.

Ashes man. Let's piss it out.

Carlo unbuttoned the fly of his jeans. I looked away, looked into the camera lens of a Chinese man, or maybe a Korean, to a somber man smoking a cigarette on the steps, to the unending line of cars streaming along the road in front of the river, listened to the extinguishing sizzle of Carlo's jet of urine, which was joined by the rain.

I got him to the set without further incident. He wrote down Syd Barrett's address and gave it to me when a flunky with a walkie-talkie held open a park gate for the putative movie star to enter.

In Regent's Park, sheltering under red and white umbrellas, staring at the rain, technicians in bobble hats stood in small groups cupping gloved hands around Styrofoam cups of tea. Bud was sitting cross-legged on the wet grass meditating alone. Martha was standing behind him, holding an umbrella, keeping Carlo at bay. Carlo was impatient. He had run out of electricians to talk to and now he was practicing leering in shadows, which he seemed to be very good at.

Barry and Dylan, with me only a little below them, stood under the branches of a plane tree.

He might have potential, said Barry reluctantly.

Potential? It's more than that, said Dylan. Klaus Kinski. Richard Attenborough, he could be up there.

I don't think so, said Barry jangling his head for emphasis.

Barry would always argue against anything Dylan said, even if he agreed. It was a matter of policy. In this case I didn't think he agreed.

We don't actually know if he can act.

Oh yes, I think we do, said Dylan and a strange look appeared on her face which her hand couldn't quite brush away.

The wild thought occurred to me that Carlo might be a late, unlikely gift. A surprise star rocketing from nowhere. Barry wasn't always right. He just seemed to be.

Dylan returned to the tent where other, smaller Welsh people were holding clipboards and sitting on canvas chairs peering into a black and white video monitor. I managed to stand in Barry's way as if by accident.

You haven't had a chance, I suppose? The script . . . ?

Barry peered at me.

Oh good. Phil. I was looking for you. How you doing?

Great. Not bored at all.

You wouldn't do me a favor would you?

Sure, yes. Of course.

He thought, like Alice did, that I was doing all this out of greed, for my script to be read and approved of. They didn't seem able to recognize humility. Barry looked at me lasciviously as if trying to get me to acknowledge that my greed and, therefore, generosity timidly aspired to be as big as his own. I had to do something to change his mind. I should never have called the script The Unlucky.

That friend of yours is kinda sucking his claws into Bud, it'd be pleasant if we could have them apart for a while?

I didn't realize you'd started with him.

We're started, we're finished. We'll do his test another day. The weather. Speed home bonny boat now if you like.

Oh. OK. But. I was going to say, going to ask . . .

Barry suddenly became animated.

Oh my God. Fuck. Of course. It's your anniversary isn't it? Man, time flies. Does time not fucking fly? What does—?

It flies.

Damn right. It's soon isn't it?

Yes it's soon.

Great. We'll be there. Hey. Phil? Do something for me?

Yes? I said hopefully.

Treat yourself to lunch. Pick yourself something up from the catering van.

I ate two lasagne croissants and half a chicken tikka masala bagel. Then I drove Carlo away from the set in the Volvo, which felt unfamiliar and heavy, like my heart.

When I'm a movie star, he said, I'm going to collect guns and crossbows and machinery of war and medieval torture devices and things like that. And I'll buy up every scrap of Syd paraphernalia in the world. Who's your hero?

I don't know if I have any, I said wondering if he might be expecting himself to be named. Where do you want me to drop you?

You must do. Go on. Think about it. Well?

I don't know. I can't think of any.

That's sad.

I looked correspondingly sad, and apologetic.

I could take you to a tube station or something.

Do you have any hobbies?

Hobbies? The Chinese stuff I suppose. I like to dance. I still follow football.

I'm not interested in football, Carlo said snobbishly.

No, football's good. I did have football heroes, when I was younger. Through my Dad there was the England World Cup winning side. Some of them at least. The fullbacks. George Cohen he liked. And the other one. Didn't like Martin Peters, thought he was petit bourgeois. He liked Roger Hunt. Bobby Moore of course. And when I got a bit older, I fancied myself as a number ten in the romantic manner. Rodney Marsh, Tony Currie, Pele although he always seemed a bit goody-goody. And Stan Bowles of course. If I had a hero it was Stan Bowles. I had pictures of him on my wall.

What's his name? Who you had on your wall?

Stanley Bowles. They always said about him, if he could pass a betting shop like he could pass a ball, then . . . I'm not sure what the next part is, his life would have turned out different I suppose. Which side of the river do you want to be? Are you going back to Brixton?

You see?! You see!!!???! Syd Barrett. Stan Bowles. SB, same initials. I knew this was going to turn out right. Let's listen to some Syd and then you can tell me something true and I'll tell you something.

He put his tape into the player. A ballad, Syd on quavery voice and unreliable acoustic guitar, struggling to perform a simple, damaged melody.

OK, do it again, Syd says. He starts again, his guitar going faster than his voice with neither quite where they're meant to be; he breaks off, *Again, I'll do it again yeah?*

A pause. I contemplated speaking, decided against it.

There is another man on the tape, speaking from a studio control booth, who seems to think he's being encouraging, when it's only the stone-cold sound of the jailer's voice.

Keep going. Keep going Syd, you're doing very well . . .

See if I can, should we try and sing it, oh it's, it's it's all right, don't worry.

What's it called?

Don't know, says Syd suddenly and inappropriately decisive. *No title. I suppose it's called Dominoes.*

He strums again, takes a deep sigh.

It's an idea some, I (a little gasp of a wail) *It's an ideasomeday. In my tears my dream. Don't you want to see the proof.*

He repeats, strumming mechanically. He pats the strings and trails off.

Decisive again he announces, *Right. Dominoes.*

It's an idea someday.
In my tears my dreams.
Don't you want to see her proof.
Life that comes of no harm,
You and I, you and I and dominoes,
The day goes by . . .

It was a very pretty song, fragile and sad, the guitar strings strummed hard and sometimes mistakenly.

Impossible not to get caught inside the intimate moment of Syd's voice and breath and hands, a desperately short-lived beauty, the passing sound of the singer's surrender.

At the end of the song the guitar dies. Syd says, humbly, *That's all*, which is followed by a nervous cough, and then silence.

Well? What do you reckon Phil? You like this one?

Yes, I said. I like this one.

July Fourteen Nineteen-Seventy.

What?

July Fourteen Nineteen-Seventy.

Bastille Day.

What?

It doesn't matter.

Well shut it then. I'm trying to explain something to you. They'd dragged him into the recording studio, tried to get another solo album out of him again. His so-called mates. He can't do it. It's gone. They're working on this song. And it's time for him to play a lead over it and he can't do it. He tries his best but it's wrong it's all wrong, everything's wrong, from his fingers to his brain, time, space, his body, fucked, then someone comes up with an idea. What he's doing, it sounds backwards, so the next time they play the track to him some clever cunt plays it *backwards* and Syd gets really into it, rips out a guitar solo that sounds so bad, so desperately wrong, and they record it, and play that backwards, and you know what?

It's the best guitar solo he's ever recorded.

You know this story. You've heard this story before.

I could just sort of tell the way it was going.

Oh. Could you?

Flash of menace in Carlo's smile, a warning: Don't ever get to thinking that *you* can be comfortable with *me*.

Sometimes Carlo frightened me. Other times, I couldn't make the imaginative leap into taking him at his own sinister evaluation of himself.

Well it was. The best guitar solo, and the last. Now go on. You first. Tell me something wise and true. What it is. What it is is what?

He was waiting for my answer and he seemed genuinely interested in what I had to say, which was unusual for me.

Come on. Is what?

Well. OK. Here's one. If you want to know. Life's about two things. It comes down to yin and yang. Yin is the female principle. Yang the male. It's all about harmony. That's the point. And that's what sex is for too. Sex restores harmony in the universe and in the individual. That's why cunnilingus is good, the taste of female emission. Yin to the yang.

I'm a *pussy hound* myself, said Carlo.

And it's good for the woman. There's a Chinese expression, Women in their thirties are like wolves, but women in their forties are like tigers. Cunnilingus helps keep them happy. And not emitting yourself, not coming, helps that. Emission weakens the man twice over. It weakens his own chi, and it weakens his ability to pleasure the woman. You see, orgasm isn't necessarily the same thing as ejaculation.

It isn't?

No. It isn't. And then there's afterwards. If you see the woman as a vessel for your semen, as just the means to ejaculation, what happens after you've ejaculated? You don't want her any more. You don't need her. You might find her irritating or even repellent. She's fulfilled her single purpose, so what else is she good for?

Making tea.

I suppose. But anyway. She's made the cup of tea. What then?

You tell her to piss off.

Yes. You might. I wouldn't be able to, but I might want to. But that's really my point. If you don't ejaculate, you don't get into that cycle of male need and male fulfillment and constant female disappointment.

Carlo smiled and nodded his head as he had been doing throughout, which meant that he disagreed with everything I had said.

Man, I'm not even going to *begin* telling you how full of shit you are. You know what it is?

What is it?

Look. Light's changing.

Oh. Thank you.

Dutifully I braked. A pedestrian waiting at the edge of the pavement started across the road in front of us.

My mistake, said Carlo who kicked my foot aside and stamped down hard on the accelerator and the Volvo took off and the pedestrian's mouth gaped open before he remembered that he would have to run if he was going to live. With a leap he flapped past the oncoming wing of the Volvo and got to the opposite pavement, where he stood, shivering. In a flash I saw him—office boy, blue suit, brown shoes, white shirt open at the top button, tie windswept over his left shoulder, thinning pale hair combed back, pitiful life-changing horror on his once smooth face—and then we had shot past and our lives no longer touched. Carlo lifted his boot off the accelerator pedal and the car was under my control again.

Why did you do that! He's done nothing to us!

Exactly, said Carlo.

He stretched out in the seat. He had enjoyed setting me

straight so emphatically. And he was enjoying my response in the aftermath. I shouted in outrage at him. I scratched my face compulsively and changed gear needlessly. I put my foot on the accelerator pedal but that made me shiver so I slowed down again. I told him that people shouldn't do bad things to each other. He waited, with an air of scientific interest, for my gibbering to end.

Random malice, that's what it's all about. If we'd known the target it wouldn't have been such fun. So. What do you want to do now? We can *make a day of it*. Let's find someone and drive them crazy and make them kill themself.

Better to kill somebody with kindness, I would have thought.

That's interesting. What are you talking about?

Nothing. Really. Nothing. I'm dropping you here, I said.

I had passed on to Carlo Chinese wisdom about men and women, their relations. Carlo had told me a Syd Barrett anecdote. He had shown me a nasty way to scare pedestrians. I had taught him an emotional management technique. He had given me Syd Barrett's address. I had been instrumental in giving him a screen test. The balance between us was even. With him at least I could relax. Barry was another matter. It was important for him to understand that I was being servile for the lowly sake of it, and not because I hoped to influence him in Wang's favor. I wanted my script back. I could not ask for it back. He would think that was my pride talking, when in fact it was its opposite.

When I got home Alice was in the kitchen measuring out cups of water and flour. She was wearing the paint-spattered blue dungarees she wore when she was doing odd things to furniture or performing heavy-duty cooking.

What are you up to? I said.

What does it look like?

Like you're making bread.

She pushed back a strand of hair that had fallen in front of her eyes. Her hands were dusted with flour.

That's very good. Well done. Got it in one.

Oh. You got the bread machine to work.

Yes. And now I'm using it. To make bread.

Barry had said that to get ahead in transactions you think of something you know that the other fellow doesn't. The color of your underpants, the shape of Sean's penis, the fact that you've got urine on your hands from when you went to the toilet. I didn't know the shape of Sean's penis and nor did I have urine on my hands. As a result, I kept the fact of the color blue in my head and felt stronger for it. I took a chocolate hobnob from the packet in the refrigerator.

Haven't you got anything to do?

I swung myself back off the work surface I had just decided to sit on. Alice's dungarees were open at the top, showing her cleavage and the inner sides of her breasts. I liked Alice's breasts. They were heavy and pale and marbled with veins. On a disastrous Greek island holiday with Richard and his ex-wife, the local barmen had voted Alice's breasts best breasts on the beach. The breasts of Richard's ex-wife were stringy and brown because of the sunbathing club Richard claimed she belonged to.

Yes. Lots. What sort of bread are you making?

Pumpernickel.

Sounds good.

It's not for you. I've got my reading group coming tomorrow.

Oh. Your book club.

No. My reading group. If you can't think of something to do, why don't you—

I'm halfway through it, I said quick to parry any accusation of husbandly insufficiency.

—call up some of the guests.

Oh. What guests?

No one's RSVPeed, I'm a bit worried. You sent off all the invitations didn't you?

Oh. Right. Yes. Of course I did.

I stroked the hobnob crumbs off my shirt into the cup of my hand and deposited them in the sink. On the refrigerator door, held by magnetic fruit and fish, was an invitation, stiff card, the same cream color as the ones that lay buried in some archaeological level of the table in my shed.

Alice and Phillip Wilson, I read out loud, *invite you to a party on the occasion of their anniversary*. It doesn't say celebrate does it? Or how many years we've been married.

I didn't want to depress anyone.

I lightly kissed her. She lightly kissed me.

I undid a further button on her dungarees, reached a hand down inside, past the horizontal scar on her belly, to the top curls of pubic hair.

I'm a bit busy right now, she said wriggling away.

I think I'm sick at heart, I said.

She nodded, not entirely sympathetically. She offered me the packet of hobnobs as inducement to go into the shed.

And Barry called, said Alice. He left a message. He was calling from the country—or at least he *said* he was, maybe that's the main reason he called, to make an alibi. He wants to arrange a screening for us. Our anniversary present. Says we should decide what our favorite movie is and let him know and he'll arrange everything. Isn't that sweet? I've made a list of possibilities. You can add to it, as long as you don't put Escape To Victory on it.

Uh. No. I'm not having it.

Sorry? Excuse me?

We've got to make a stand somewhere. This is it. Enough

is enough. I'm saying no. He can come to our party, I hope he does. I hope he stuffs himself with our food and drink, and even causes some breakages. But I'm not taking any more presents from him. Enough is enough. Enough is a lot more than enough as it goes.

You're being absurd.

Alice laughed. Perhaps I did sound ridiculous. I didn't care about that. I had grown used to that. What I did care about was that everything was going wrong between me and my wife at this moment that had been meant for wooing, for the obliteration of secret thoughts with consideration and love. This was Barry's fault. Interposing himself between man and wife. Using his generosity as a malicious instrument to drive us apart. And I still hadn't bought an anniversary gift for Alice.

He needs to know what movie we want by tomorrow morning. To make sure he can get it in time. And this was going to be a surprise but I'm telling you anyway. You've got a fitting tomorrow. I'm getting you a made-to-measure suit. Remind me to call Barry before we go to the tailor's tomorrow. It's Barry's tailor actually, so he's very good. He dresses all the stars.

My spirits sank further. I played my last card. It made my heart beat faster and then stutter. Blood thudded in my ears. I felt sick. I tried to say it levelly, matter of fact, hoping my voice didn't rise too shrilly.

If you accept this film show idea of his then our marriage is over.

What?

If you accept this gift, if you accept *any* of their gifts, I'm leaving you.

Alice tried to work out if I was bluffing or not. It was the best kind of bluff—I didn't know the truth of it myself.

218

You're serious. You're actually serious.

I didn't know where I could go. A hotel maybe. Order room service and watch pornography and drink from the mini-bar. And what about Alice? The twins? Maybe they would thrive without me.

Alice wiped a line of flour across her forehead. Her throat struggled on the emotions that I had forced her to feed on raw. I didn't know which was worse for her—the death of our marriage or the humiliation that it was I who was making it occur. I offered her the gift of my touch. She covered her mouth with her hand and refused it.

You know what I think? I think you've gone mad. Where are you going? Where are you going now?

I left the house. I climbed back into the Volvo. I left London. I drove in thoughtless darkness to Norfolk.

I parked the Volvo in an empty pub car park and took a torch from the glove compartment and trudged along a muddy country lane that bent into a village. There was no sign of people, just a stagnant pond, an abandoned post office; a derelict bakery. Then another corner past a clutch of new houses with curtains drawn shivering beneath satellite dishes, garage doors defiantly shut like mouths that won't say aaah, and I had entered the stretch where the rich folks lived, tall trees, garden walls, heavy gates.

Barry's gate was always kept open. I tiptoed between heavy stone gateposts, walked past the plum orchard on the left, the kitchen garden on the right, along the bank above the gravel lane to avoid the sweep of the security lights. My steps made no sound on the damp grass. I stood in front of his house, and then walked down the side of it, crouching beneath hall windows, through the courtyard, past the stables, ducking the light of the laundry room.

They kept their spare key in the outhouse but I wasn't sure where. Blindly, I groped around. Gym equipment cracked at my shins and I tripped over an exercise bicycle that sent me clattering into the chinchillas' traveling cage. My hand became stuck between the bars and when I'd managed to extract it it came out holding a skeleton key, which fitted and unlocked the kitchen door.

No blaring of alarms, no roaring of dogs, no bacchanal interrupted by my uninvited presence. Flagstones beneath my boots. The taste of camomile tea-scented air. On my right was the back hall, ahead of me the scullery, on my left the side stairs that led up to the first floor and then the attic where Alice and I slept when we stayed here as guests. I was not here as a guest.

I knew where the script would be, in Barry's office, a scullery and butler's pantry away, inside the dry fish tank that Barry used to store his slush pile. I took my first steps. I was trembling. My mouth and throat were dry. I couldn't imagine what I might say if Barry or Sean found me here. Dressed in black, skulking through their house. It was unaccountable.

My legs stopped working by the Aga. I leaned against a hot towel rail, experimented with breathing. Everything looked quiet but I couldn't hear much above the thudding of blood in my ears, just a few screams from the animal world outside. There were no sounds or signs of any guests staying, or even the hosts, and maybe the scent of camomile was an olfactory hallucination, purely reflex, a familiar pathway only smelled because I was here and it was night and this was what I always smelled when I was in this house at night, and possibly Alice was right and Barry was in London, on an assignation, and hadn't returned home after all. It was an empty house I was frightening myself inside.

Or, worse, he, or both of them, they, were waiting for me behind the scullery door. Holding weightlifting bars, whistles in their mouths tied to red ribbons around their necks, caps too—Sean's worn low over his eyes, Barry's back to front—their initial relief at seeing it was only me replaced by looks of dreadful suspicion.

Phillip? What—?

And what could I say? *Don't worry about a thing, I'm just picking something up here, it's all a great joke, now go back to bed and pretend you didn't see . . .*

I was terrified of getting caught. I had come this far. I went on.

In the middle of the kitchen I sneezed. An explosion advertising my body and its weakness that backed me recoiling against the larder door. And my terror mounted. Something dark and feral was making ugly sucking noises under the sink. I anticipated bats. Vampires. This would be even more embarrassing, to be found dead in the morning on my friends' kitchen floor with my eyelids wide open, my skin dried white, empty dark tooth holes on my throat. I removed my hand from clamping my nostrils shut to mask the beam of the torch as I swung the light around. Under the sink a chinchilla lapped at its water bowl. Its shoulders shifted as it drank.

I was here. I wiped my nose. I sneezed again. And it came to me what I was here to do.

This was it, what I did; this was my creepy-crawly:

I swapped the contents of the terracotta salt and sugar jars. I placed in the microwave the two copper pans that had been soaking in the sink. Then I stepped back to appraise my work and didn't like it. The chinchilla finished drinking, cast one contemptuous look back and hopped out into the garden through the cat flap. I put the rabbit bowls in the sink and filled them with hot water and washing-up liquid. The copper pans went in the bowls' place under the sink, their handles poking rakishly away from each other.

I moved on into the dining room. I considered breaking one of the antique Wedgwood plates in the glass-fronted cupboard, even took one out, tested its weight, then decided against it. I wasn't here to destroy. This was mindfuck. I didn't lay the table for a formal meal for eight because it might have made too much noise and anyway it was all a bit too creepy-gothic.

There were photographs in silver frames on the sideboard, which I realized I'd seen a thousand times but never looked at before. One was of Barry as a boy, before his teeth and nose had been fixed, but with the same lavish heap of curly hair, sitting on a sledge, wrapped up warm against winter in front of a yellow clapboard house. Another showed Barry and Dylan in evening clothes on a spotlit stage holding up awards. One taken by me of the twins in a previous garden at a previous year's births-day party. Sean in the swimming team at a schoolboy sports event. Barry and Sean bare-chested on a beach with a narrower man in a white shirt hugged between them. Barry and Sean and Dylan and Mr Dylan in skiwear on a mountain. Which then I realized wasn't. That it was me and Alice in skiwear with Barry and Sean on a mountain. My pang of guilt at friendship betrayed ordered my hands to turn all the photographs to face the wall.

In the morning room I moved armchairs around and left the strange metal one upside down. I switched on the TV and retuned some stations to an Egyptian shopping channel and others to a Scandinavian test card. Then I opened the games cabinet and removed a tile from the Scrabble set. I carried the firewood basket from the left hand side of the fireplace to the right. Looking at my work, I thought I might have overdone things; I would be more subtle in the hall. I wondered about the bedroom. I knew I didn't have the guts to go upstairs.

I opened the cupboard doors by the fireplace, winced at the squeak of hinges, turned the volume knob on the stereo as high as it would go and gently closed the doors again. This one assault I allowed myself. I left Barry's office alone. The script was irrelevant now, and the joke shouldn't threaten anyone's livelihood. In the cloakroom by the main door I turned up the corduroy collars of oilskin jackets and switched headgear around on to different pegs.

I went back through the hall and stood by the main staircase. My senses were clear, my legs were strong, I felt giddy and exalted and powerful. I could walk silently up the stone steps if I had the nerve. I walked up the first few stairs, and stopped. What I thought had been the sound of a mobile telephone was an owl's lonely hooting in the trees behind the house. A car was going past on the road. Someone was snoring in the master bedroom. The rest of the rooms tasted empty. I could go now, I should, back down, back out, I had proved my daring, experienced something strange and extreme, performed my function, perpetrated mindfuck. No more risks were necessary. I walked on up the stairs.

At the top of the staircase I went into the library where, very quietly, I shifted books into different positions in the bookcase. I told myself, again, to go. I had braved the first floor; my honor and courage had been proved indisputably. I could picture myself slipping down the stairs now, out through the side door, locking it, pushing the key into the rabbit cage, and running along the grass bank, dodging the light sensors. This was exhilarating. Possibly addictive. I switched off my torch. I tiptoed towards the master bedroom. I wanted to see someone sleeping.

The bedroom door was open. I crept into the room. A floorboard creaked under my foot—answered by a mattress squeak and a change in rhythm of the snoring. I waited, appalled, balancing on one foot, the other poised in the air, aching to be lowered. My eyes adjusted to the darkness. A picture beside me slowly revealed its shape, then its frame, and lastly its shadows. I realized I hadn't taken a breath in some time. I kept my eyes on the picture, made a vow that when it was fully revealed I must act. I saw ticket stubs, holiday snapshots, the collage work of Sean, with trinkets glued to photobooth faces that had been sewn together. I could see them now, and they could see me; a hundred small party eyes followed me in as I walked further, utterly vulnerable, shivering, into the room. I took shelter beside the wardrobe. My body was unreliable; I was not convinced that I was not urinating as I walked.

Moonlight was dripping in through the opened bathroom door, which was on Barry's side of the bed. Barry was wearing striped pajamas. The duvet was pulled up to his stomach, his arms tucked underneath, straight by his sides. Everything seemed now terribly funny. I was in danger of laughing. I tried to think of something mirthless. Carlo. Syd Barrett. Barry's skin disease, which I wondered if I might lower Barry's pajamas to expose.

I approached the four-poster, stepping over a pile of underwear, hiding myself behind velvet drapes. Barry slept on, alone in bed, oblivious of everything, while in the bedroom an intruder stood at his bedside table. On the table was a photograph of Lucifer Sam the dead cat, memorial black and white in a beaten silver frame. Beside the photograph was a glass of water. Next to the water glass was a film award figurine of a golden bear. And beneath, on a subsidiary ledge of the bedside table, was the pale flame of an aromatherapy candle—a perfect Taoist universe in here: Fire and water and rock.

And crouched over the table was funny old Phillip,

dressed in black with a mad keen expression on his face. My knees were shaking, because, ever since a Spanish boot in a Chinese stadium, that's where fear always hits me. I smiled on the sleeping face of my friend.

I was trembling, apologetic, aghast, disgraced, triumphant. And clumsy. A Scrabble tile dropped out of my hand, which, failing to catch it, collided with a corner of the photograph frame, which shifted its position and nudged the glass of water. The glass of water shook away the golden bear. The bear fell against the aromatherapy candle.

The candle in its glass bowl tilted towards Barry.

The disturbed air vibrated the flame.

Liquid wax dripped over the lip towards Barry's skin.

And on to the back of my hand as I reached out to intercept bear in my left hand and hot wax on my right. Fear and eye and hands in perfect understanding, a perfect movement, a moment of grace.

And an excruciating pain which found its only expression in the sound of my feet hopping on the mat.

Barry stopped snoring. He stirred in his sleep.

I put the bear back where it belonged, and pulled away, breathless, stepping slowly backwards.

Barry wiped his hand across his forehead. He muttered something and shifted to his right side and then to his left, pulling the duvet around him. I wondered if he always slept like this, if, nightly, duvetless Sean struggled against the cold.

Then Barry suddenly sat up. He rubbed his thighs. His eyes were open and appeared to be staring straight at me. I couldn't tell what Barry saw, whether he was awake or asleep. I didn't dare look away. Barry got out of bed. He walked to the toilet and I watched him through the moonlit doorway. He pissed, one hand on his penis, the other on his hip. He looked sideways, out of the window, towards the lime trees in his garden, and his mouth reflected in the glass made the shape of his own name or at least its beginning. Then he farted. I felt the overpowering urge to giggle, which I only suppressed by putting a hand over my mouth and pinching my nose hard. Barry walked back to his bed without looking towards me. He swung himself in, gazed with a pleasantly mournful expression at the empty space beside him and tucked the duvet around himself and curled back into sleep. I fled.

I ran down the stairs, I exited Barry's house. Returning the key to its cage, I stepped out of the outhouse, and heavily crunched a rabbit beneath my feet. A pair of solemn ponies watched me over the stable doors as I walked, carrying a gray wet body, a careful route away.

Three

If I could do Barry's by torchlight I should certainly be able to do my own blind. Closed-eyed and silent I turned the key in the door. Closed-eyed and silent, a ghost of myself, I entered the house, took two steps, and barked my shins against a flowerpot that I knew to be large and red-enameled. Closed-eyed and silent I hopped about the hallway, coming finally to rest, clutching my damaged leg, on the penultimate stair.

By touch and scent I hobbled through the house. Fried food smells lingered in the kitchen and hung just outside it, an odor cloud. I went upstairs, where I inhaled the sweet scent of my daughters, the new-paint emptiness of unused rooms, the coconut musk skin of my wife, freshness turning with the night, the slow sound of her breathing. I dropped my clothes where I stood and climbed into bed. I spooned against her; she shifted to accommodate my shape around her. Mandarin Ducks Entwined.

Did she know it was me? Did she want it to be me? I felt I owed it to both of us to invent, or discover, a different man. A dream lover, who had thieved into her bed under cover of the night. I kissed her hand, her shoulder; her face turned to mine. Our teeth touched. Our hands felt each other's skin as if it was new to us. I whispered,

I'm sorry, I—

Uh, she said.

Two, I said.

I alternated my thrusts between the deep and the shallow. I pushed down to the jade substance and pulled up by the gold gully as though slicing off stones. I jabbed my jade peak back and forth in short and slow thrusts like a farmer preparing his land for late planting. Three shallow and one deep. Six shallow and one deep. I tasted the damp skin in the hollow of Alice's throat.

It became crucially important that I, we, reach a thousand loving thrusts. I felt sure that this was understood by us equally, without it needing to be referred to. The counting was silent. Everything could be all right, would be all right, between us, with the world—or our part of it at least, the place where we lived and watched over our children—if we could reach one thousand. Something was going to be proved or disproved here tonight.

Between one-fifty and two-ten, I was wondering who had led this. By two-eleven I no longer cared why or how. Our mouths open, myself upon her, Flying Butterflies. Nine shallow and one deep.

Two hundred and fifteen. Two hundred and twenty.

Alice?

She put a hand to my mouth to stop my words. I kissed her fingers. Phoenix Plays In A Red Cave.

Nothing else existed, the two of us, our bodies, the dimples on her thighs, the silent numbers of my thrusts.

And the twins. They rushed into our room and climbed anxiously into bed as they hardly ever did any more.

We're scared, said Daphne.

We had a bad dream, said Chloë.

Daddy's jade peak wilted in Mummy's jade chamber. Daphne cuddled into me, Chloë tucked herself against Alice. The family together fell asleep.

The doorbell woke me. I blearily went downstairs to open the door to Richard wearing his worst clothes and best smile.

It's coming through, Doughboy, he's the dog's bollocks, but in the meantime I need some cash. Don't ask why.

Why?

You have to help me out here. I've got no one else to ask.

I haven't got any money. I gave it all to you.

Well that's not very clever is it? Why'd you do that?

It was a mistake.

Of course it was a mistake, always keep something in reserve, I'll tell you that for nothing.

I allowed Richard to enjoy patronizing me. When he had finished I invited him to our anniversary party. Richard said he might be able to make it, and with a superior air of purpose he struggled into his junkmobile and puttered off in a cloud of dust and steam.

I sat, wearing Alice's bathrobe, at the kitchen table. Most of the time my tossing away of the building society account had bought me only a dull intimate ache in the belly, the reverse of destiny's throb, not even painful, an only slightly unpleasant reminder that I was still alive. But sometimes, like today, after Richard's performance at the door, I was sweating.

I went through the filing cabinets and removed building society statements and cashbooks (squinting my eyes shut from the sight of lost savings). I intended to bury any evidence that we'd ever had a building society account in unlikely but excusable places. I ended up rummaging through the drawer where Alice kept photographs and sentimental things.

She had more keepsakes than I would have supposed. A brochure for a resort complex in the Caribbean; a program for an England under-fifteen game (Philip Wilson number four) that I thought had been lost; her high school yearbook from the year she had spent in America when her father was working in Washington DC—I found her easily enough, in the back row of the class photograph, bright open face, center parting, fifteen years old, elected Best Organizer by her classmates, and whose declared ambition was to travel the world as a singer-songwriter; the plastic hospital bracelets that had been strapped to the twins' wrists after she had given birth (nothing here of the panicky surgeon who had pulled out the twins, his suave manner left behind in a less bloody room); snapshots of husband and wife in the garden at Barry and Sean's house; the two of us on our honeymoon blinking into the sunlight of a Spanish afternoon; the twins on donkeys; the twins on Barry and Sean's patient backs; the twins dancing in pink ballet skirts at an end of year school concert, with purple ribbons tied to their expressive arms. I had use for them all.

I moved everything into the safety of the newspaper recycling bin when I heard my wife's tread on the stairs. I switched on the kettle.

Sit down, I said. I'll make you some tea.

I busied myself with kettle and teabag and spoon

waiting, anxiously, to discover which world she was going to place us in, the emotional path she had chosen for us to follow—marital ultimatum or marital erotics.

Who was that?

Who was what?

At the door. I couldn't get back to sleep afterwards.

Um, nobody. Richard.

What did he want?

Money.

And?

That's all, he only wanted money.

No. Did you give him some?

Of course not. I thought it would be a bad investment.

Humph, said Alice.

I gave her the tea, Earl Grey, decaffeinated. She blew at it, sipped it, and sniffed. The following conversation, whatever its subject, was beneath her; and before she could pursue it she required me to acknowledge that we both understood she was verbally and emotionally slumming.

Go ahead, I said hoping for expansiveness in my tone. I had won the carefree poise of the condemned man.

Barry's bad enough, but *you*.

She narrowed her eyes. I narrowed mine. I struggled to understand what her accusation was. And then, with a little accompanying chuckle that I awarded myself the right of, I realized.

You don't think I'm having an affair do you?

Yes it does sound ridiculous. But where have you *been*?

Oh, you know, I was not able to say, even airily, *moving things around in Barry's house, that sort of thing*.

And anyway Barry isn't having an affair. I know so.

Of course he is. Don't change the subject.

I was just—

236

I had Sean here last night. He's in torment. Barry had *said* he had to go the country, for stabling or something for the ponies. You know, I'm not so sure there are any such ponies.

Oh there are.

And Sean's desperate about it. He couldn't get hold of Bud last night so I think we can be quite sure who *he* was with.

Can we?

Anyway. You're changing the subject again. Where *were* you? Where were *you*?

I smiled.

Please don't do that. I spoke to my mother last night. She said that you didn't come into her flat after you gave her a lift back that time. So where were you then? At a PTA meeting? I don't think so. What's the matter with you now?

I had been choking at her mention of PTA meetings. She waited for me to work out how to breathe again.

You're very transparent, you know that? The way you've been skulking around doing your hunted gerbil routine. If you've got something to tell me I think this is probably a good time to do it.

I tried some words out in my head: Well, the thing is, what it is is, you know our building society account? Well it's gone, emptied . . . all the money you earned, that you stupidly put into an account under both our names? Well I lost it . . . gave it away, to the dog's supposed bollocks . . .

And what I said was,

I've got some work to do.

She nodded very gravely.

You realize what you're doing don't you?

I hoped a mournful look of infinite wisdom and infinite resignation was answer enough, and wouldn't make me resemble a gerbil.

I've canceled the fitting, she said. I don't think I want to give you a new suit.

You don't? Good.

She stared at me. She turned her back. I sneaked the recycling bin off into the shed and made myself busy with scissors and glue and heavy gauge paper taken from the twins' art cupboard. If Sean could make a sentimental collage so could I.

At first, the collage was very good. I arranged the sentimental items on the paper and then rearranged them and took a step back to approve the emotional map I'd made while stroking the straggly hair on my chin. A guerrilla raid back into the house brought me the prize of Alice's sewing box, but when I experimented with sewing snapshots together the needle kept ripping the photographic paper so I gave up on the procedure as unnecessary adornment.

It was when I started with the glue that things went awry. Big semeny puddles of paste soaked through the paper, dripped around the sides of the photographs, the brochure pictures, completely saturated the scrap of paper with the penciled lyrics of the song that Molly had delivered at our wedding and which, I had never realized before—as the words smearily obliterated—had been written by my wife.

With J-cloth and paper towels I dabbed at the overwhelming glue, rubbed away most of it. The collage was still heavy and wet and all its elements were tilted at angles, often overlapping. It looked as if it had been put together by a chimpanzee with learning difficulties.

While I waited for the collage to dry I called up Barry.

I knew what the expression would be in Barry's eyes

when he read the name on his telephone display, the look of complacency that stretched to disdain; he was so far ahead in the game he might not need to speak to me. He didn't: I was diverted to an answering service.

I spoke wearily. I'd been beaten a long time ago.

Hello Barry. Our anniversary party. Thanks for offering the movie show. But no thanks. The party's on Saturday. Here. At our house. Hope you can still make it. Oh. It's Phillip by the way. Bye.

The collage was still soaked through. I carried it into the house and into the kitchen, where I hid it on the work surface beneath dishcloths so the future surprise of it would not be ruined. I unpacked the bag of vegetables from the organic delivery company. Beetroot, potatoes, onions, three kinds of lettuce, spinach, Chinese cabbage, mushrooms. I still had a pin in my trousers from my attempt to sew snapshots together. I decided to use it.

I passed a very enjoyable hour inscribing love letters to Alice on the heads of mushrooms. By the second mushroom I had learned how to coordinate magnifying glass and a sure hand. By the third, I was able to get seven lines on the mushroom. By the fourth, ten. I wrote tiny memories of happy times on the organic heads of pale chestnuts, and when I was done I put my miniature love offerings in a zip-lock sandwich bag, which I stashed in the freezer between the ice cube tray and a stack of wholemeal pizzas. I felt very proud. On the largest-headed cap I had tinily recollected a football game that Alice had organized as a birthday present to me three years before. Richard had been showing off for one side, me for the other. Alice and Molly barefooted running laughing for the ball even though they were on the same side, pushing and shoving each other away from it until Barry, unskillful but dogged, kicked it away from both of them and went chasing after. Sean was in one goal, my Korean instruction manual employer in the other. The twins had knelt undisturbed in the center circle, plucking daisies and making them into rings. Lionel, Alice's boss, in a Brazilian football strip, had showed some annoyingly quick clever moves, until Richard, as if by accident, crashed into him, and sent him limping, perhaps weeping, to the side where Alice's mother fed him slices of oranges and hot elderflower tea from a thermos flask. I wrote all the players' initials, and the date, and the final score (9–7 to our side) and the venue (Clapham Common) and I signed it with love.

The doorbell rang. Nimbly, I avoided barking my shin on the flowerpot while going to the door.

Oh, Sean said. It's you.

Yes. I live here.

Is Alice in?

It's Friday. She works Fridays.

I need to talk to someone, said Sean.

Come in. I'll make you some tea.

I have to talk to someone.

You can talk to me.

I sat Sean in the kitchen and switched on the kettle. The telephone rang.

Excuse me. I'll just get that.

Phil, hey, what's up? shouted Barry. Is Alice there?

No. She's at work.

It's about Barry, said Sean.

Who's that there with you? said Barry.

No one. The radio. Excuse me, I whispered to Sean. It's a work call.

I took the telephone out into the garden.

I'm sorry, I said.

I also am very sorry. Are you my friend, Phil?

Yes Barry I hope so.

I know so.

There was a silence on the line. Barry on the telephone was seldom silent, he considered it a waste of resources.

Bud has a day off. He's expressed a desire to see some cows. Thought you might enjoy hanging out with him for the day. Martha's not available. She's having a medical procedure. Can you be there?

I'm not sure.

I would like to speak to you also, on a personal matter. We're meeting at the editing room. Corner Old Compton and Frith. You can see some rushes. They might interest you. In your *agent* capacity. Have you got the time?

The tone of his voice was, although loud, respectful. Which meant that he knew he was going to be obeyed.

I'll try. But. Oh. Barry. Before you go on. I left a message for you. I'm hoping you can come to our anniversary party? It's on Saturday. Thanks for the movie idea but I'm afraid it won't work out.

You don't leave me much chance to find an alternative. Please don't do that.

The line went dead. I went back into the kitchen, where Sean had made two mugs of tea and was glumly staring at his.

I'm sorry about that, I said. It was a work call.

Barry, said Sean, is having an affair.

Is he?

Last night he said he had to go home, for the ponies you know. We're getting in a lad.

Oh?

That's what he said. But you know what? Bud wasn't at his hotel last night.

Wasn't he?

No. He was not. And you know where he was.

Where?

With Barry. And I think what hurts the most is that it was in our house. Our bed.

No, I said. Surely not.

There's been all these rumors which I haven't wanted to believe, but when I spoke to Barry today he was like a different man to me. Someone who had secrets to keep. I don't know what to do.

Look, I said. I know, I can't tell you really how I know, but I *know* that Barry wasn't with Bud last night.

Thank you, that's very sweet of you, but how can you know that?

I just do, that's all.

Did you see Bud last night?

No, I had to admit. I did not.

Look. I better be off. I'm useless today. Thanks for the tea and sympathy. I'm going to the gym.

Sean got up. For want of anything better to do I patted him on the shoulder. Sean reached to press my hand and for a moment held it there against his shoulder, lacing his fingers with mine.

Thank you, he said.

He picked up a dishcloth from the table to wipe something away from his eyes.

What's that?

Oh. It's a, collage.

Is it?

I understood his skepticism. Snapshots and sentimental things gluey and awry on super-saturated cartridge paper. After Sean left I put it in the oven to dry.

I went to a building in Soho, where darkness clung lecherously to London brick. Barry was waiting for me outside.

Phil. Phil. May I trust you?

Yes Barry. Yes you may.

Phil. Answer me this. Do you believe in poltergeists?

Poltergeists? I don't think so.

Me neither. So how do you account for this? I went downstairs this morning and all these things were not where they were meant to be. I couldn't remember if I'd moved them and forgotten I'd moved them or if they'd always been in these places all the time and . . . and, there's no and. I don't know.

What does Sean say?

I haven't told Sean. And I'm not going to tell him. He'll worry. And I can't tell Dylan because she'll think I'm not up to speed. You and Alice are the only ones I can trust with this, Phil. Is everything OK with Alice? She's been kind of off with me. And you know what else? Mitzi's missing. Fritzi is desolate.

Who?

Fritzi. The chinchillas.

Oh. Yes. Of course.

It's going to break Sean's heart. He loves those rabbits.

So if we rule out poltergeist then option two, I'm going crazy. Do you think I'm going crazy?

No. I don't think you're going crazy.

I'm having memory leakage. Something's gone wrong with my head. I'm going crazy.

Listen to me, Barry. I know. You're not going crazy.

Then option three then. I'm sick. Which is worse. I'm going to get a CAT scan. And an MRI. And an EEG. And an EKG I guess.

I'm sure, I said, that there's another explanation for this, a perfectly innocent explanation.

Yes? Like what?

Like. I don't know. Maybe you had an intruder?

What? Who came in and moved a few things around and took nothing except maybe a rabbit? Who would do a thing like that? Tell me.

I don't know who.

Thank you, Phil. I appreciate you trying. You're a good friend, a very good friend.

No. I'm not. I'm—

Enough. Let's go downstairs.

He took me down to a viewing room in the basement. Barry sat beside Dylan in the middle row. Carlo was sitting at the back, legs stretched over the seat in front of him, a box of popcorn on his lap. He waved at me and I pretended not to see him. I took a seat in the front row.

Let's get going, said Barry. His voice was louder than it usually was, and consequently less commanding.

An editor ran the footage. The lights dimmed. Carlo took this as his cue to come over to sit next to me. I leaned back in my seat. It was a good seat, the bottom of it pushed forwards when I leaned back; the backrest tilted to accommodate my movement. I was not permitted to concentrate long on the comfort of my seat.

Carlo's hand gripped my thigh.

This is going to be great, said Carlo.

I'm sure it will be, I said.

It was not great. It was terrible. And Carlo was terrible. There was a stiffness in him that was evident on screen if not in life, an artificiality that negated his natural fearsomeness. In company, in the flesh, in a pub or a Volvo, or a police station, or standing outside a private members' club excreting malevolence, he was the perfect B-movie villain, figure of dread. On screen he looked like a very bad actor.

Dylan called a halt to the screening. The lights went on. The image died.

It's no good, she said. You can see that can't you?

See what? Carlo said.

I appreciate the time you've spent, you know, the efforts you've put in but it's no good.

It's only one scene, Barry said. He could improve.

You think so? I don't. Sorry Carlo. You know the expression the camera loves somebody? Well it seems to hate you. Maybe he'd be all right on the stage or somewhere.

It's no good trying, is what you're saying, Carlo said. I understand.

You just don't look good on screen. Most people don't.

As he left, Carlo winked at Dylan, smiled at Barry, and nodded his head very matily at me, which meant that none of us could be guaranteed safe from reprisals.

Barry walked me out to the street. He gave me the directions to Bud's hotel.

I'll see you at the party. I'll do my best to make it.

I—

I might have some people with me. Could I bring people?

Yes. Please. We like people. Bring as many as you like.

I watched him go back into the film building. He looked shrunken. This is how I had repaid him for his generosity over the years, first a physical assault and now a psychic one. I didn't know if even the unlikely gift of Syd Barrett could begin to restore the balance.

The Volvo had a dead rabbit in a bag making a nasty smell in the boot, and a long scratch down the driver's side, which I interpreted as Carlo's calling card, a sign of malicious intent. The garden was empty, the house curtains closed. I went into the shed. Nobody was listening, nobody watching. I waved my hands in the air over jade mountains. I could make as many magical gestures as I liked to banish the bogeyman.

I stood and lifted the jade mountain in my hands. Then I put it on the desk and reached below, through the rubble under my desk, for a silver candlestick. I tested its weight and found it good. I tapped the candlestick very lightly against the central jade peak. I held it higher and brought it down, stopping just before it hit. I lifted it again. I wondered if I could bring myself to break the carving this time. And then I put down the candlestick because I'd noticed the hair scrunchies that surrounded the two lower peaks, put there by the twins, a double signature twisted from their hair, a tender thoughtful touch that maybe used to occur every day but which Daddy was too oblivious to notice.

I sighed. I had to be strong, for their sakes.

The threat of retaliation is retaliation in itself. I could almost convince myself of this. Perhaps anyway it was all pose, ineffectual and pretentious. What could he do? The best mindfuck must be the one that takes a lifetime to occur. Alice? The twins? *The twins?*

The telephone rang. I dreaded who it might be. Carlo, I thought instantly, he had the twins, locked to a radiator pipe and shivering in some hideous room. Girlish eyes round with horror, twin voices muffled by oily scraps of rag tied to their mouths. And advancing upon them Carlo and his cabal of shadowy fiends sniggering at the unspeakable acts they were about to perpetrate upon my daughters' innocent bodies. *About* to perpetrate? Had *already* perpetrated. A lascivious roar, an unearthly laugh, pitiful gagged sobbing. *You hear that? It's the sound of their blood. Dripping.* Or worse.

I didn't want to answer it. I answered it.

Phil.

Barry?

His voice was diminished, plaintive. This was the achievement of my friendship: I had made him furtive and low and frightened of his own perceptions.

Bud's waiting for you. He's at the hotel.

Oh. Sorry. I'll be right there.

I went into the house. The kitchen had a dry parched smell that I put down to Alice's pumpernickel bread. Alice was in the lounge with her book club. They lowered their Virago Classics to glare at me. Alice was the only wife in this collection of frightening prosperous women, divorceds and never-marrieds and one perpetually smiling widow.

Where are the twins?

Kelly's house. One of us'll have to pick them up, she said meaning me.

Despite my fears—which escalated on my breakneck, wild-man-of-the-roads journey to Kelly's house, vicious

249

exchanges with other motorists, no quarter asked and none given, red lights smashed, pavements mounted, bus lanes violated, cyclists shoved whimpering to face their own mortality—the twins were safe. I was only able to remove them from Kelly's house with the promise of a secret, which I told them in the Volvo on the way home.

You're going to boarding school, I told them.

It would cost a lot and we had no money to pay for it, but it would keep them safe from Carlo and I would go begging. I would have to see my father, endure his remarks, borrow money that had been salted away in ethical bank accounts, maybe ask Alice's mother too; she disliked me sufficiently to be quite generous.

The rest of the journey was celebration. When we got back home they danced into the house and they allowed me to dance with them.

Alice came into the hall with a bulging kitchen bin liner.

I agree with you, I said. The twins should go to boarding school.

The twins danced upstairs. Alice encouraged me to find my fun elsewhere and throw out the rubbish on my way.

The secret triumphs, our moments of grace, unapplauded, unrecorded, unobserved except by the athlete himself, such as when he throws out the final rubbish bag on a pre-collection night, tossing it one-handed so expertly that it lumpily arcs over to make a perfect landing on top of the already full bin.

The movie star's hotel was a lowering, glowering old building that looked like an institute of correction. He was in tattered jeans and jumper, grubby white basketball boots, shiny new sunglasses. His short hair was spiky still from sleep. Schoolgirls were besieging him with their attentions, to which he was graciously acquiescing. He stood in a public acclaimed place that I had once expected to be mine.

Hi. How are you? asked Bud over their heads customarily polite.

Not bad, I said lying expansively. Not bad at all.

Bud's hotel was my fourth stop since leaving my house. I had been to my father's flat, and then to my mother-in-law's, to ask them for money, which neither of them gave, even after enjoying watching me perform various exercises in self-abasement, from which I admittedly derived a low, masochistic pleasure. Then I had driven to Richard's house, which was curtainless, empty, up for auction. Which meant, as I should have known, that giving him our money was like dropping it down the saddest of wells.

Bud climbed into the Volvo after signing the autograph books, then the photographs, and finally the breasts that belonged to his female fans. He was polite with them, mild and courteous, and they blinked, giggled, stammered in the golden light of his stardom, their skin rising in goose bumps, their eyes growing wilder. We made our escape. We drove.

I put Carlo's Syd Barrett tape into the stereo. An invoice of sorts.

It's awfully considerate of you to think of me here
And I'm most obliged to you for making it clear that I'm
*   not here*

We drove through an interminable north of London, high streets, train stations, and nightclubs, launderettes and pubs, second-hand car dealers and hairdressing salons, the broken bulbs of belisha beacons, afternoon loungers outside betting shops.

And I never knew the moon could be so big
And I never knew the moon could be so blue

Finally, release. Motorway.

Look. Cows, I said.

I'm not really very interested in cows, Bud said.

No. Me neither. Barry seemed to think you might be.

Barry's very sweet.

Is he? I've never thought of him as sweet.

I tried to think of a smooth casual way to ask him if he was having an affair with Barry.

Everyone seems to think you're having an affair with Barry.

I don't really do sex.

Oh? Don't you?

I don't think I like it. Do you?

Yes. Of course. At least, I think so. Yes. I'm sure I do.

I think Barry might think it's good for business if everyone thinks we're, you know. Barry's very sweet. He worries. I think he worries I might get into trouble if I don't have someone sensible looking after me.

We got to the M25, headed clockwise. I knew now where we were going. I hoped Bud wouldn't mind. I didn't know how sensible it was.

My father, I said, used to ride the Circle Line when he was a boy. Sit and read Marx when he should have been at tech school. Then he'd go to Conway Hall for leftist meetings.

From the polite way that Bud nodded I realized that he had understood none of the nouns I'd just used apart from, presumably, the words father and boy and meetings and school.

The M25 goes around London, I said. It's a circle, you see. Apparently there's people who've been going round and round it for years. Eat at the service stations, pull over to sleep on the hard shoulder. Then carry on their traveling.

That's very interesting, said Bud falling asleep

I was impressed by the movie star's capacity for oblivion. I even experimented in a small way with it myself, closing my eyes, lifting my hands off the wheel, enjoying the small thrill of panic; then I made myself concentrate, allowing the diversion only of looking at other drivers on the motorway—driving with such bad-tempered single-mindedness, or else happily in motion inside their speeding cars, talking on telephones, lighting cigarettes or killing them out of windows, squeezing chin spots in rearview mirrors—and I wondered how many of them were on dopey hopeless quests like mine.

253

At the end of the motorway the road forked. Left to Barry's house. Right to Syd's. I had to resist the urge to drive to Barry's, to sneak into his house to perform a reverse creepy-crawly, picking up objects to return them to where they had once been. But there was an irreversibly dead chinchilla in a bag in the boot of the Volvo. I had to make reparation.

Bud woke when the windscreen started spotting with rain as we slowed down at the outskirts of Cambridge.

I think we're here, I said.

Mmost obliged, he said.

Really, no. It's a pleasure, I don't mind driving you at all.

It's *awufully* considerate of you.

No, you've—Oh I see. That's very good.

I'm still working on it, he said modestly.

It's very good.

Bud's Syd Barrett impression was indeed very good. The Californianness of his voice was gone. It had been replaced by a gentle English manner, slightly arch, quite amused, and desperately sad.

Your friend Carlo, Bud said, knows a lot of information. Showed me all these pictures and things of Syd. Old ones and new ones. It's like religious isn't it?

Yes. I thought that.

The thing I've realized about Syd is that he had no talent at all. I don't mean that in a bad way. I don't have any talent either.

Oh I don't know about that, I said agreeably.

He was just this smart great weird kid from the suburbs. Wild stuff bursting out of his head, and it fitted in for a while and then it didn't. Are we looking for him?

I thought we might. You don't mind do you?

We had reached the dowdy residential area that contained the address that Carlo had given me. Bruised terraced houses with Neighborhood Watch stickers. Garden hedges. Children's bicycles, which made me feel very removed from my own life.

What happens if we do find him?

I'm not entirely sure. Well. I am. I sort of wanted to bring him back to London with us. Barry's a big fan, you see.

I didn't know if the curious look Bud was giving me was a result of my words or my own visible reaction to them. Alone, or in the company of Carlo, the idea had not seemed such a strange one.

Maybe it's better if we don't find him, Bud said in a tentatively stubborn voice that alarmed me all the more when I realized it was an echo of my own.

I'm sure we probably won't, Carlo never did, I said trying to reassure both of us.

Carlo's very sweet, said Bud.

By a high scabby hedge we got out of the car. We stood in front of one of the larger houses, which looked neither abandoned nor lived in. I stretched. I tested my knee because that is what I always do after a long car journey.

That's Syd's house.

It doesn't look as if anyone's in, Bud said.

I don't know if we should be doing this, I said. Maybe if he doesn't want to be found we shouldn't try to find him.

Maybe we should just go to a pub. Have a Guinness in his honor.

Play dominoes.

Eat pork chops. That was his diet wasn't it?

Past the wet little wooden gate were random clumps

of purple flowers lining a path to a tall red door with an ornamental brick archway above it. No sounds came from the house. No curtains flickered at upstairs windows. At the side of the house a narrow passageway led towards a closed wooden garden door, which I would not be creepy-crawlying past.

A pair of yellow-haired Japanese girls in shiny leather boots and miniskirts and rock tour T-shirts stood beside us. At first I thought they wanted directions. They did not want directions. They wanted Bud. They looked at him, at each other, at him. They giggled behind their hands, which extended to touch the movie star. He lightly disentangled himself from his admirers. He submitted to several group shots after the girls had explained to me how to work their camera. We got back into the car.

Does everyone recognize you? I asked Bud. And do they always show you their breasts?

I don't know.

Or maybe it's the same thing that makes you a movie star that makes them respond to you like that. And you do a great Syd Barrett impression. So you can't say you haven't got talent.

I couldn't tell you. I've kind of got to be filming later.

I'll take us home.

Let's find a pub first.

We found a pub. It did not have dominoes or pork chops. It did serve Guinness.

Mmost obliged, murmured Bud when he received his first pint.

We ate bags of roasted peanuts and soggy bacon baguettes in lieu of pork chops. I couldn't keep up with Bud's consumption of beer. His words frayed at the edges, his politeness became more courtly. His slowness got slower. When I fell off my chair a second time we agreed that it was time to go home.

I drove the car very carefully away from the pub. I rolled down the windows and switched on the windscreen wipers to provide some amusement.

Look! said Bud.

Yes. That's lovely wisteria.

No. There. At the side of the road.

The man Bud was pointing to was waiting to cross a wide residential avenue. He was probably somewhere in his mid to late fifties, wearing clothes that were far too warm for the weather. His right hand was tucked into a pocket of his green oilskin jacket. In his left hand he carried a red string shopping basket that reminded me of my grandmother.

That's him, said Bud.

I thought he'd be younger.

I think that's him, I'm sure of it.

I stopped the car. We stood next to the man at the pedestrian crossing.

The collar flaps of Syd's shirt were neatly tucked over the top of his thick jumper. The jacket he wore was just like the ones hanging in Barry and Sean's cloakroom, except that it was bulging at the pockets and rolled up at the cuffs as if someone had convinced him he would one day grow into it. There were no cars coming along, but he was waiting for the green man to show on the crossing light. His hair was cropped very short and his head was shiny in the patches where no hair grew. His face was heavy and timid.

Hello, said Bud.

The man nodded, returned his attention to the pedestrian crossing light. His eyes were a shade of blue that might be considered violet.

My name's Bud and this is my friend Phillip.

Syd, if that was who it was, nodded again but showed no inclination to be deflected from his aim of crossing the road. The standing red man changed to a walking green man and Syd started across and Bud and I walked with him. When we had got to the other side, the strength of Bud's attention made Syd look at him.

We want you to come to London with us, said Bud with great conviction and sympathy and sounding just like Barry. We'll look after you.

I felt very proud of Bud. I also wanted to sit down.

I'm going to the shops, Syd said. His voice was light and a little breathless and surprisingly young. He sounded like an asthmatic schoolboy who something wrong had happened to. He showed us a list of things written on the back of a grubby envelope as if it was his credentials. Bud looked at me. He was used to acting in short bursts, three-second scenes. I could see that his energy was close to spent. It was time for me to make a move. I balanced myself carefully on my feet.

I'll make sure you get these things. OK?

Syd anxiously nodded. I took the list. I felt sure it had been written by someone else, probably a woman. Underneath the sedimented smears of dirt and thumbprints the words were very neat and assiduously formed, like the twins' handwriting. Milk, two pints. Cheddar cheese, mild. Orange juice without bits. Hovis, medium slice. Bacon, unsmoked, streaky. Six new potatoes. One bunch broccoli. Three parsnips. Two pork chops. <u>No sweets</u>!! I put the list in my jacket pocket but when I saw the panic on Syd's face I returned it to him and he sighed with relief to have it back. He looked at it very carefully front and back as if making sure that it hadn't been spoiled in the time away from his possession. Then he pushed it into a pocket of his jeans, which hung loosely around his hips.

We'd be most obliged, said Bud shyly.

I have to be sick now, I said.

And I was. I bent down, with my hands on my knees. Waves of rejected Guinness rolled high up into my throat and gushed out into a hedge. Pub peanuts. Streaky globs of bacon still clinging to muddy shreds of baguette. The vomit ripped painfully out of me, scarring my throat with the taste of bile.

When I lifted my head again, after I had survived the after-rush of fluidless heaves, after I had won the battle against letting myself go—my body, my future, just to lie in the dubious warmth of a hedge—after I had wiped my mouth with my sleeve and inspected the bright regurgitated flecks and grains that were clinging to my shirt, I saw Syd looking at me with some alarm but at the same time evident enjoyment.

He consented to come with us to London. Our wills were stronger than his, or it was the magnetism of Bud that pulled him along with us, or he was just hoping for more bodily fluid entertainment to be provided by me.

I'm hungry, Syd announced, his first spontaneous remark, made somewhat querulously, as we were teetering south along the motorway.

We stopped at a cafe. Sitting at a blue Formica table, with large jeering men around us, Syd fastidiously tucked his paper napkin into the top of his sweater. He ate with gusto. All attention on his plate, an efficient shoveling action with his fork, only a few stains of baked bean juice dripping to his bib. He made the same little noise of satisfaction after every third swallow. Bud closely watched the lorry drivers surrounding us. Consciously or unconsciously he mimicked the way they sat with legs out wide, with elbows on the table. He protruded his belly to make it look fatter.

When the mugs of tea arrived Bud winked at the waitress, which made her flutter and sigh and cause a very loud kitchen accident after she reluctantly departed. Syd inspected his mug inside and out, then stirred in three large spoonfuls of sugar. He finished his tea and cleared up the stains of egg with shreds of toast.

That was good, I liked it, Syd said, his second spontaneous remark.

Bud smiled. It felt good to us both that we had given Syd some pleasure. The living star patted the dead one on the arm and he didn't shrink against the contact.

Would you like some more?

Bud offered his plate, his own splatter of beans and triangles of toast and hard-luck egg. Syd shook his head. He probably didn't trust other people's things. A protective mother's warning.

Bud went back to inspecting the lorry drivers. He sat back in his chair. He opened a low button on his shirt. He scratched his belly button. He belched.

'Ere. Mate, he said. Mind if I ponce a fag?

As he reached for the cigarette packet on our neighbors' table his truck driver manners were impeccable.

Are you taking the piss?

Bud frowned. I felt his disappointment that he had failed to strike the right note. He tried again.

Who you calling pissed? he said.

I think maybe we should be on our way, I said.

Syd was looking unhappy. He was clenching his hands into fists and putting them into his jacket pockets and taking them out again. Bud noticed this too.

Look! You've upset Syd!

What are you going to do about it? asked a lorry driver.

Bud frowned again. He shut his eyes and when he opened them he had taken on a tough guy persona that made Syd jerk away from him and convinced me almost entirely.

I think you and I, gentlemen, might choose to settle this outside, Bud said.

Four lorry drivers took Bud outside the cafe, on to the oily tarmac between diesel tankers. Syd and I were not permitted to follow. Bud told us to wait for him in the jeep. As we got into the Volvo I wondered if the idea of jeep was somehow part of Bud's streetfighter fantasy or whether he thought that was what all cars were called.

Syd sat in the back seat with his hands squeezed between his closed thighs. He stared straight ahead at the seat in front of him and rocked only slightly. I tried to make conversation. Syd didn't respond. I wanted to block out the sounds I could hear, feet scuffing on tarmac, the soft thuds of male flesh, low pleasured grunts, as cars flashed past on the motorway.

It smells in here, said Syd making his third spontaneous remark, which was quickly followed by his fourth.

I want to go home.

Me too.

Our conversation was interrupted by Bud limping back into the Volvo. He looked triumphant, despite the blood and injuries on his face, his part-closed right eye, his swollen ripped mouth, the odd angle of his nose.

Octopus rides, he said obscurely. I clattered the Volvo into gear and drove us back to London. Syd stayed gently rocking throughout, his heavy, quite handsome features perfectly still.

We reached the location. Flunkies with walkie-talkies and puffy fleece jackets guarded the entrance to the park that the film crew had taken over. Joggers and dog walkers and parents with buggies and boys on skateboards were being turned away. Most were looking very gratified to be treated so shabbily by glamorous filmmakers.

I had been dreading this. I felt craven and drunk and degraded, and even worse when a flunky smiled to see the Volvo, spoke into his phone while waving at the car. Bud and I got out. Syd stayed where he was. He didn't seem to be noticing anything.

The flunky stopped smiling when he saw the damage to Bud. The hand holding the telephone dropped to his side. The telephone fell into a rose bush. Barry came bustling through the park gates, still talking to the phone pressed to his ear.

They here? He here? Where are they he here?

And then Barry saw Bud and Barry's face imploded.

Oh my God. Oh my God. Oh my God, said Barry.

Dylan followed shortly after, and flunkies attending.

Look at the state of him! said Barry. His *face*!

It was like a funeral party that was gathered respectfully a little away from the Volvo. A small elite of the British film industry mourned at the ruins of the American star's face.

We should see the other guys, right? said Barry disconsolately.

Not a mark on them, said Bud merrily through thickened lips.

There were four of them, I said.

I bet there were, said Dylan.

Barry hugged Bud and then held the star's face between both hands for Dylan to inspect.

Maybe this is superficial damage, said Dylan without much conviction.

Yeah right maybe.

Dylan put maternal arms around Bud and steered him slowly towards the set.

Barry stared at me, then at the Volvo, then at me again.

Who's that in there? He smells pretty rank doesn't he?

Oh that's not because of him. That's—

I hung my head. This was not how I'd pictured it. My triumphant, clinching gift.

Syd Barrett, I finally said. For you.

Barry shook his head. I nodded mine, unable to echo the sound his hair made of a faraway beach.

Yeah right.

No. It is. He is.

Look. Phil. Firstly, number one, I got to hear what the doctor says about Bud. This whole movie might be dead. But, B, do something for me. Go get yourself a cup of coffee or something.

I've got to go to the supermarket first. Syd needs to go to the supermarket. He's got a list.

The supermarket. Yeah right. Jesus.

Barry walked wearily away. I got back into the Volvo and drove to the nearest supermarket.

Syd perked up in the car park. The familiar universal sights woke him from deep inside himself. He looked worriedly through his pockets and found his shopping list in a back pocket of his jeans. His walk was almost jaunty as we went inside and he gave me a very nice smile when I didn't take the shopping trolley away from him even when he banged it into other people's because signs announcing *Special Offers!* and *New Products!* had attracted his attention. I held on to the list for him and lifted it close to his face when he needed to refer to it to make sure that he was putting things into the trolley in the order they were written on the list. Twice he surreptitiously put in items (chocolate ginger biscuits, a can of fizzy orange drink) that weren't on the list, and I pretended I didn't see, and his resulting expression reminded me of a photograph of a beautiful pop star from the 1960s. Maybe, I thought, I could bring Barry with us next time and next time Barry would believe me.

A woman in white carried a tray of red cheese chunks speared with toothpicks. Syd ate two and told her they were very nice and that he was going to buy some. He then scrupulously wanted to return the packet of mild Cheddar to the chill cabinet he'd picked it up from, but he couldn't remember which direction to go.

It's this way Syd, I said.

My name's Roger.

Oh. Sorry.

I was surprised by the extent of the disappointment I felt. I had grown accustomed to being with a living dead pop star. I had even quite liked it. Instead I was with a taciturn defective who I had transported a hundred miles away from the supermarket of his choice. I felt disgusted. At myself, at my works, at the world. I couldn't look directly at him. Wrinkled skin around tired violet eyes. The sad bulk of a person who did not cohere. The shyness of a man who expects nothing from the world except threat and confusion and irritation.

It's over here. Roger.

I tried to pay for his shopping but he wouldn't let me. After we got into the car I drove him back to Cambridge. The journey was silent. I deposited Roger and his shopping on what I hoped was the same street corner we'd taken him from. I watched him wave goodbye until he had shrunk out of sight of the rearview mirror.

I spent the night, and much of the morning, dreaming of mushrooms and dolls' houses and cracks in pillows in a lay-by in Essex. I drove back to London sighing in sunshine, and when the car broke down on the north side of Lambeth Bridge I left it there and walked the rest of the way home.

I sat for a while, because I was invited to, with the Clapham Common drunks on their clump of benches by the dead fountain donated by a temperance society a century ago. They lost all interest in my society after they realized that I had given them the last of my money and that my acceptance of a couple of sips of warm hyper-strength cider was an indication of politeness rather than need. I wandered across to the fields where men play football. The first group I asked to play with told me to fuck off. The second group shrugged shoulders and let me. I played football and things were good again. I scored goals, I helped out weaker players, I executed reckless tackles with my uncomplaining left leg. The game was savage and bloodying and glorious. I lacked only the roar of a crowd to make my happiness complete.

And when I got to Bramley Road and saw the off-license delivery van parked outside our house, and the driver glaring through his open side door at the cases of wine and boxes of glasses stacked inside, I understood with a twin surge of pity and pleasure that today was the day of our anniversary party. I didn't understand the For Sale sign planted in our front garden.

My father was in the lounge scowling at the television. I went to the kitchen where I could hear the low bird-call of my wife's voice.

Alice was dolloping dips into colored glass bowls. Molly was cutting pitta bread into slices. Both of them were wearing pink T-shirts and wraparound skirts.

They say that food is the new politics, Molly was saying. Who's they?

Or maybe it's the new pornography, I don't remember.

This was where I belonged. I wrapped myself around my wife. These were the people who belonged here with me, my girls, my father, my wife, my wife's friend, all of whom (except for perhaps Molly) I loved and all of whom (except for Molly), despite everything, every fault of mine, inexplicably loved me.

Alice battled away from my grip so I held her tighter.

Let me go please, she said.

I think you should let her go, said Molly.

I let her go, pretending that all this was playful.

It was time to cut away now from Barry and Sean, sever all bonds except for the most distant ones, Christmas cards, birthdays; I would send a note: I'm back to my life now, reconciled, I'm going to concentrate on that, thank you thank you for your generosity over the years but it was a mistake to think I could ever thrive in your world. I don't belong to it and I never will. I know that now. Sorry for everything.

I reached for Alice again. She backed away to stand in front of the refrigerator.

Your dad's here, she said.

Yes I know. I saw him.

Alice has packed you a bag, which has been acknowledged as your personal property, said Molly.

You can put anything else in it you want, said Alice.

But itemize it first, said Molly. There's a list in Alice's bedroom.

The doorbell rang.

I don't quite understand, I said.

I looked at Alice but she wasn't looking at me. She had moved away from the refrigerator to busy herself at the work surface laying strips of anchovy along the hillsides of Caesar's salads. Something about the refrigerator bothered me but I couldn't work out what it was—nothing seemed out of place, postcards and photos and invitations and school timetables held in place by magnets as they always were, wherever we were living.

It's really very simple, said Molly. You are making a full admission that because of your unreasonable and erratic and negligent behavior and your dangerous violent tendencies you have disqualified yourself from your rights as a father and husband and disavowed Alice from any obligation towards you, without of course prejudice to claims now or in the future on any of your income and property.

The doorbell rang again.

If you ever have any, that is, concluded Molly.

That'll be my mother, Alice said. She always arrives too early.

I really don't know what you're talking about, I said. But it might be Barry. I better get my father to hide.

I ran back into the lounge.

Sorry Dad.

My father looked surprised on two counts. Surprised that I had used the word Dad, which I ordinarily went to elaborate conversational lengths to avoid, and even greater surprise that I'd lifted him away from his chair and was now pushing him down behind the settee.

Just stay there for a moment. Keep out of sight.

Phil! said my father more weakly than usual.

Sorry. You've got to be quiet as well.

I didn't consider explaining to my father that he was meant to be dead in certain people's worlds. Partly I was being considerate of my parent's unreliable heart, but also I didn't have the time for explanations, already footsteps were approaching the living room.

Into the room came something large and flat and bubble-wrapped. Holding it was a dark-haired young woman with a pretty, lightly acned face. She shakily put it down and rubbed circulation back into her hands.

Hello? Can I help you?

This is yours, she said.

Is it?

I was wary now. This had all the hallmarks of a gift, delivered on behalf of Barry and Sean.

You owe me five hundred pounds.

Do I? I do? Oh. Samantha?

The artist, Molly's cousin, acknowledged that this was her name.

Is that the portrait? Great.

Behind the bubble wrap, which I looked forward to offering to the twins for a marathon popping session, the faces of Barry and Sean benevolently smiled in shades of blue and gray. My vows were threatened, then reconfirmed. This was the final gift: *Happy something-or-other*, I would say, when they arrived late for the party. *Here, for you, a portrait, now let's stop it please.*

It's not framed, Samantha said. Framing would have been extra.

That's OK. I can get it framed. Would you like a drink or a canapé or something?

I want my money please.

Oh. Right. Yes. Can I write you a check?

She allowed me, with a consequent increase in the price (for administrative charges, she said) to write her a check. I reached hopefully into my back trouser pocket but pulled out only Roger's shopping list. Alice's handbag was on the armchair. I expertly found her checkbook inside it and wrote a check to Samantha.

Kiss me, she said.

What?

I had been backing away from her. Obediently I overcame my reluctance and advanced upon the artist, whose eyes were not half-closed, her lips neither sensuous nor parted, her face not yieldingly inclined; instead she was looking at me more disapprovingly than I had ever been looked at, even by my wife.

That's the secret message, she said.

What secret message?

I told you. I write secret messages on the gesso and paint the portrait over it. That's the secret message they wanted on their picture. You've paid for it. You've probably got a right to know.

Oh I *see*. Great. Terrific. Kiss me. That's very, romantic. Thank you. Would you like to stay? We're having a party.

Samantha folded the check away inside her jeans and left.

Can I come out now? my father said.

Not just yet. Sorry.

I want to come out now. *Phil*!?

My father nervously peeped up from behind the settee so I pushed him down again. The top of his head was warm and scaly and pleasant to the touch, like a practice football.

No. Best not. I'll bring you a drink. And a cushion maybe.

I carried the portrait through to the kitchen, where my wife's legal representative was squirting little dishes of chocolate mousse with curly lines of red essence from a tube. My wife was heating up baguettes over the gas hob.

Why don't you use the oven for that? I asked.

The oven doesn't work, she told me. Some idiot started a fire in the oven.

Oh. Did he?

Yes. He did.

I was shocked by my reflection in the oven door—mud and blood and beard, my hair poking up in random spikes, an utter exhaustion around my eyes. Still in the oven was the burnt offering of my collage. Opening the oven door disturbed the charred fragments, snapshots turned to dust, a swirling cloud of charcoal flakes of the twins' art paper. I shut the oven door again.

I'm sorry about that. It was meant to be a gift but it went a bit wrong.

The police just called. They found our car. Did you know there was a dead rabbit in the car? Did you put it there? Were you making a *statement* of some kind?

The doorbell rang again.

Would someone get that please, said Alice shaking her head, a gesture that pleased me until I remembered that it was in Carlo's world not ours where things meant their opposite.

I let in Alice's mother and hung her coat on the banister and put her customary box of bath soaps and salts on the hall table and led her apprehensively into the lounge where

I placed her beside my father in his nest behind the settee. I gave them champagne and North Korean wine. They cast nervous looks at anything but me until I showed mercy and left the room.

Alice was no longer in the kitchen. Molly barred my way to the staircase.

She says she doesn't know why no one's turned up, said Molly.

I think there might have been a cock-up in the invitations, I said. Do you mind letting me through? I want to have a shave.

Molly didn't shift from her position. Standing on the bottom stair, one hand on the banister post, the other against the wall, her legs were apart as if she was daring me to try crawling through.

I think it was probably my fault. A few of the invitations might have gone astray. Bit of a cock-up. Do you remember when you first discovered that word? Cock-up. It was a great discovery. Here's a word that sounded like a swear word but you were allowed to use it almost as much as you liked. Do you remember?

No, said Molly coldly. I don't.

Is Alice really that upset with me?

This question interested Molly. If only as a specimen remark made by a defendant.

Are you saying you don't think you've done anything wrong?

Well it depends on what you mean by wrong. I mean you said before I had violent tendencies, well I don't think I do really. I know there was that time with Barry but that was a special case. I'd never hit Alice. I've never thought—never *dreamt*—about hitting the children. Where *are* the twins? It's not like them to miss a party.

Normally, at social events, they would be delighting themselves with hostessy tasks, handing out dips and olives, taking new visitors on a solemn tour of the house, suffocating under guests' coats, or just performing some casual display by the bay window.

So you're admitting you have thought about hitting your wife. *And* dreamt about it. On how many occasions? Five to ten? Ten to twenty? Or so many that you've lost count?

No, of course not, nothing like that. I'm not a violent man.

There are many types of violence, Molly gravely said.

Well obviously yes, of course. But I don't think . . . and you said I was negligent. And what else?

Unreasonable and erratic.

Who isn't if it comes to that? Isn't it a question of interpretation?

Alice has been frantic.

Really? Has she?

Really, yes. You just keep disappearing.

It's nothing sinister. I've been busy.

Doing what?

Looking for gifts really, amongst other things, I said and it sounded hollow even to my ears.

And then of course there's the question of the money. I think you ought to know that Alice hasn't ruled out criminal proceedings against you.

Oh. The building society.

Yes. The building society.

Look. I'm sure if I could just see Alice then we could thrash things out.

Are you making a threat of physical violence against your wife?

No of course I'm not.

Because it would be very easy to take a court order out

against you. It would be the easiest thing in the world.

She was, I realized just in time, making me angry on purpose. A lawyer's trick. A wife's best friend's sensible mischief.

It certainly would have been done if the twins were still here. To protect them.

Where *are* the twins? And why is there a For Sale sign outside the house?

It's a little too big for just one person, don't you think? The twins are at boarding school. Alice took them down yesterday.

Oh.

They're doing a holiday term there, to get them acclimatized. Your friend Barry paid the fees.

I stopped myself doing what I wanted to do, which was to make a rush up the stairs to my wife, swatting or swiping or shoulder-charging Molly to get past and perhaps even trampling her on my way up. Instead, I rubbed the side of my nose quite vigorously.

I think I'm going to check on the food, I said.

Brightly colored Italian dishes covered every flat surface in the kitchen, all piled high, wet food, dry food, finger food, and two-handed food. Soups and dips and dainties. Bowls of borscht and vichyssoise decorated with swirls of crème fraîche. Wooden dishes of Caesar's salad. A Basque-style sausage stew simmered on the hob. A Moroccan mushroom salad, oily-brown, green-flecked with spicy pepper and mint, was waiting on the countertop. There was something recognizable about the salad, and a difficult feeling hit me, achingly confirmed when I searched through the freezer and found nothing between frozen pizzas and ice cube tray, no miniature testaments of love in a zip-locked sandwich bag.

I cursed the mushroom salad. There had been memories in there, anniversary weekends, moments of love, football matches with friends. All of it gone, peeled away, written out by the cook's careless hands. In my disappointment I dipped my finger in a bowl of borscht and watched the way the beetroot soup clung in strands to my skin like drying tracks of blood.

And I had a revelation.

In this room that I had been in a hundred times before, prepared for a party that hardly anyone would come to, I saw things in a different way. Borscht like blood, vichyssoise like semen, Basque-style sausage stew, little round penile sections of meat floating in gut juice.

I would give of myself. Like my mushroom memories made into party food, I would donate myself anonymously, expecting nothing in return. All of it before had been instrumental, the giving. Gifts of retaliation offered, gifts of obligation received. Every present had come with its own invisible invoice attached. But now I would give of myself freely.

I cut the ball of my thumb with a kitchen knife and squeezed blood into the borscht. I grated skin from the inside of my arm into the shavings of Parmesan cheese on the pyramid mounds of Caesar's salad. I squeezed more blood. When the blood was harder to squeeze out of my left thumb, I used my right.

But Barry would be on a diet. He might ingest none of me.

I winced as I stirred the sausage stew. I rejected joining with the stew as being in bad taste, unnecessarily brutal both to my guests and myself. I didn't want to put anything unpleasant into the food until it was absolutely necessary. Barry ate bread. I wiped sweat from my forehead into the glistening pool of garlic butter. He drank fizzy Italian water and camomile tea. He usually opened a fresh bottle of water himself and carried it with him as he went. For the moment blood and sweat would have to do. Later, if I wept, I could add tears to Barry's tea.

I carried bowls of borscht on a tray into the lounge. Alice's business partner Lionel, dapper in a black linen suit and open-toed sandals, was the latest, disconsolate, guest, sitting on the arm of a chair. I was disappointed to see my father on the settee instead of behind it. I stared disapprovingly at him and he flinched but defied me. I remembered my duties of hospitality.

Borscht anyone?!

My reputation went before me. No one dared refuse. Molly and Alice's mother and my father and Lionel all took a bowl.

Aren't you having any? asked Molly suspiciously.

In a moment. Try it. How is it?

Everyone tasted the soup and made flattering noises praising its deliciousness. They continued to sip, to please me, and because they had run out of other conversation, and because the soup was no doubt delicious, swirls of cream, lemon juice and pepper, beetroot from an organic farm and blood from their host.

When the doorbell rang, my father, without needing to be reminded, dutifully put down his soup bowl and obligingly went to crouch behind the settee. Alice's mother went with him.

I released them when I came back into the room.

It's OK, I said. It's only Richard.

The parents warily took their seats again. Richard was more prosperously dressed than I had been accustomed to see—new trainers with flashing lights on their heels, black silk trousers, some lavish hood and sweatshirt number with sponsors' names printed huge on the front. He kissed Molly, he glared at Lionel, because Richard seemed to be resuming an alpha-male fantasy lost a long time ago. I went into the kitchen to fetch more borscht and Richard followed me in.

You look crap, Richard amiably told me.

Yes. I know. I meant to have a wash and a shave, but— what's that?

A wad. *Your* wad.

He was offering me an enormous pile of magnificently crumpled and creased banknotes. I took it.

Thank you.

Flicking through the pile, I could only see fifty-pound notes.

There's a lot of money here isn't there?

Everyone says you've gone potty.

People seem to think that. I've just been quite busy.

I was going to give this to Alice. Doughboy came good. We're in the gravy. Do you know how many Balkan FAs he controls? Kickbacks from every direction, advertisers, TV companies, airlines. He says he might let us in for some more business with him. But I'm going to talk to the ladies now. Alice isn't available is she? I've been hearing rumors.

No. She's not.

Never mind. I can make do with Molly.

Magical. The offering of my blood had transformed Richard, his and my finances, and therefore, I had to conclude, the world. A moment before he would have been tattered, in rags, pushing his junkmobile up the hill. I had no doubt that if I looked out of the window there would be a gleaming studwagon parked outside.

I put the wad in a front trouser pocket and liked the bulge

it offered to the world. I went back, optimistic now, into the lounge.

Alice had come downstairs. She was talking to Lionel. Molly was talking to Richard. My father was talking to Alice's mother. I smiled upon them all. Silently I bestowed my blessing. Chattily I passed out plates of Moroccan mushroom salad. This was a day for giving.

My presence quietened things. Everyone, except for Alice, looked my way.

Isn't there anyone else coming? Richard asked.

I don't know. There was a bit of a cock-up in the invitations. But Barry said he might bring some people.

Oh great, said Alice. We can make a party of it.

I wondered if Alice and Lionel had ever had an affair or ever would. Lionel looked especially uncomfortable and when he expressed his intention to leave, Alice supported him. I did not. I bullied him into eating some Caesar's salad.

And as soon as Lionel took his first mouthful more guests arrived, as I had been sure they would.

Alice let in Sean and a crowd of movie friends. She apologetically led them into the lounge.

Sorry so many of our friends seem to be here, said Sean.

That's OK. If it wasn't for them there'd be no one here. I made a bit of a cock-up with the invitations.

You look terrible, Barry said to me not without pleasure. My God. You've cut your hair.

I hadn't recognized him at first. He looked bad too, not as bad as me I was sure, but bad. Older and shrunken in a riverboat gambler's frock coat and floppy tie.

It makes you look much younger, I lied.

Barry stroked the silent, ornament-free stubble of his hair. He was momentarily appeased.

That isn't your father is it? said Sean.

I had forgotten to hide him and he, irritatingly, hadn't thought to act on his own initiative this time. Instead he was still talking to Alice's mother. I wondered what they were talking about with such enthusiasm. Me, I supposed.

My uncle, I said swiftly and suavely. He's called Len. My Uncle Len. My father's brother. They look very much alike don't they? Len's a couple of years older than my late father. But tell me. How's Bud? Is the movie OK?

The movie is not OK is the movie. Bud's gone back to the States. The movie's dead is how the movie is.

Oh.

Yes, oh.

I performed a series of mental calculations. The table of obligation would now look like this:

Poster	3	97	Bottle opener	9	106
Kaleidoscope	5	101	Skiing holiday	15	116
Rose bush	7	109	Football tickets	5	114
Rabbits	15	99	Muffins	2	101
			Flowerpot	3	104
			Ponies	25	129
Picnic hamper	-1	130	Chinese carving	50	180
Vegan deluxe hamper	3	177	Freedom	100	277
Creepy-crawly	-100	377			
Killing Mitzi	-7½	384½			
Bud's injuries	-200	584½			
			Twins' school fees	30	614½

The twins' school fees could be immediately recouped. I had the wad for that. I also had Samantha's portrait, which would count for something. If only Syd had been Syd and not turned out to be someone called Roger, I might still have been in the game. That would have balanced out the creepy-crawly at least. But even then, Bud's injuries and the cancelation of the movie would have left an overpowering debt. I worried too that I was shortchanging Barry for the death of Mitzi. She would have come to be worth much more than just half the sum of the initial gift. Value would have been added in the time that she had lived and flourished with Barry and Sean, the devotion she had received, their pleasure in her fur, the accumulating nature of love.

I'm terribly sorry, I said.

Yes. Me too. I also am terribly sorry.

Let me get you something. Would you like some borscht? Moroccan mushrooms? Alice has made a very good Caesar's salad.

I didn't stay to hear the whole of his answer, which began with a snort.

I went into the kitchen and loaded up bowls of soup on a tray. I grated some arm skin on top and dropped an ice cube in each and pulled my sleeves down to cover my wounds. I went around the guests, offering myself. It was the least I could do.

Would you like some borscht?

Yes thank you, said a pleasant-faced woman in a floral print dress.

She took a bowl and sipped from the side of it because I had forgotten the spoons.

Umm. It's good.

It's a special recipe.

It's very good. Oh hello. I remember you. You're the garden man.

Oh, yes, right.

Have you just come in from work? I envy artists, the way you don't have to care about things like mud and stuff. Although, I'm sorry to tell you this, I think your show's gone downhill. It's not half as good as it used to be.

Yes, well, sorry about that. Would you mind holding this for me for a moment?

She took the tray. I went to the wall and picked up Samantha's portrait.

I had caught sight of Barry near the doorway talking to Alice and started toward them but I had to give up because I was pushing the wrong way against the maul. Otherwise, things were working well. Our borrowed guests were eating and drinking with Roger-like gusto. I went back to the woman in the floral dress. She had passed the tray on to a woman beside her, who was passing it on to the person beside her.

Speech! Speech!

Barry, as if bashfully, raised his arms to wing height; he silenced his crowd with a couple of flaps of his hands.

Friends, he said.

He's changed hasn't he? said the woman taking another mouthful of the gift of my skin and blood. She then reached for a piece of baguette dressed with garlic butter and sweat.

What's that?

It's bread.

No. That.

A portrait. I just bought it.

Did you get it from a gallery or an agency?

No. An artist.

Oh, you went straight to the artist.

Is there something wrong with that?

No, of course not, you might have done all right this time. It's just not what I'd suggest, for the layman.

Layman?

The woman who thought I made Chinese gardens on TV took another sip of borscht and smoothed out her dress. She talked to me very clearly and sensibly.

Look. If someone came to you saying they wanted to improve their garden you wouldn't just suggest they buy some flowers would you?

Well, I might.

Oh you!

She wagged a playful finger at me.

You're just being naughty aren't you?

Well maybe a little, I conceded.

I'm going to have to watch you. You're naughty. But seriously, you'd say bring in a professional. A specialist. Let them have a look at it. Pay money to someone who knows what to do. That's what you'd say, isn't it?

Maybe. Maybe that's what I'd say.

Of course it is. Because you *know*. And that's what I do.

What, know things?

Exactly.

She looked very pleased with herself in a generous way that didn't exclude me.

I'll give you my card. I'm a saucer.

What? People put teacups on you?

Oh you're *so* naughty! No, *sourcer*, I *source* things. I get things for people who want them for other people.

What sort of things?

Birthday presents, gifts for cast and crew. There are so many *things* out there. You'd be surprised how confusing it all is.

I wouldn't actually. I know all about it. It's the trickiest thing in the world. You might be able to help me.

Of course I can. That's my job.

There was a reassurance in talking to her. A professional who cared. A woman who knew things and had an understanding heart.

There are so many things, my wife for one. I have to get her a present. It's our anniversary today, you know. I tried making a collage but that, that didn't really work out. I did do something with mushrooms but that went wrong too. It's very short notice I know but any ideas you have would be gratefully, and there's also—hold on. You don't do any work for Barry do you?

Oh all the time. You should see what's waiting for Bud in LA.

No, I don't mean just business. Personal. Friends for example.

Friends don't really apply in the film world. Everything's work. Except actually there is one. There's one friend of his—Look. Is Barry crying?

I don't know. You were saying. There's a friend of his.

No no. Look.

With poor grace I looked. Barry in the center of the room was in his Oscar-receiving posture: Hands together suggesting prayer, head slightly lowered, looking at the crowd from under damp eyelashes.

Yes, it's very nice. Now about this friend.

Sssh, said the sourcer.

Barry looked at me, as did some of his friends, because I was the only person speaking in the room. I recognized famous people who had been rude to me and famous people who had been nice. I did not at first recognize the approaching woman dressed very simply in a brown hooded dress. She spoke to me, by name, astonishingly mine. She nodded her head very sincerely and took me by both my wrists and looked at me perhaps even repentantly in the eyes and whispered,

Yes. China. I know. China. Yes. Yes. Yes.

She smiled upon me most dotingly. It was Dylan, transformed, exuding humility and love.

What's the matter with Barry? I asked.

He was trying to make his announcement or speech but the words wouldn't come out no matter how hard he jerked his head to shake them from his mouth.

He and Sean are sundering, Dylan said.

Sundering?

Splitting up, she said without any hint of patronizing me.

Oh. That's terrible.

Barry made another failed attempt to speak. Then he blew his nose with a handkerchief decorated with nautical motifs; and he left the room, shrugging away the attempts of first Sean and then Alice to hold on to him.

They're sundering, I told the sourcer who spread the news with the same efficiency she'd shown passing on the borscht. I walked through the subsequent gossip to Alice, but by the time I had reached the lounge door she was in the hall, and by the time I was in the hall she was on the stairs, and by the time I had got to the top of the stairs she was nowhere to be seen.

I walked into empty bathrooms and WCs, wandered through empty rooms, avoiding the twins' room because that would have made me feel sadder. I expected to find my wife in our bedroom. She was not in our bedroom. Our bedroom was empty.

I needed to talk to Alice, but Alice was showing no desire to talk to me. Even without her legal advisor she was unreachable. I caught her outside the first floor toilet and I chased her down the stairs, waving my wad of money at her—*Look here it is! Look! I didn't lose it!*—and I lost her in the lounge, where my father and Alice's mother had resumed residence behind the settee, and a nice flunky had joined them and the three of them were playing cards.

I'd like another bowl of that delicious soup please, said the sourcer.

Oh would you? Oh.

I went into the kitchen and walked unnoticed past Richard and Molly kissing, and out into the garden. Looking for Alice I had found Barry. He was sitting against the artificial mountain tossing little shards of slate into the paddling pool. I ran back into the kitchen, loaded up a tray with soup and spoon and two types of salad and bread. I sat next to Barry and joined him in his sport.

Eat, please. Eat.

I'm not hungry.

Barry threw another piece of slate into the paddling pool and I pushed the spoon into his hand.

Try the soup at least. Everyone says how good it is.

Barry took a slurp of borscht, and picked at a couple of mushrooms and chewed on some bread. Breaking his vegetarian diet with blood, memory, sweat. He eschewed the Caesar's salad. I didn't blame him for that. My skin had wrinkled and wilted on top.

Something sinister appeared on his face.

I got—

Are you really sundering?

Really yes. We are.

That's very sad. That's terrible.

Maybe it is. I guess so. But listen. I got something—

Sad or not, he was persistent, he always had been. He

must be a demon negotiator, always seizing the rhythm of events: Dance-master, fairground-barker, gift-giver. But I was not giving up without a fight.

Barry? You know when I hit you that time? You should never have let me out after I hit you. You shouldn't have been so nice about that. So *generous*. I think that's where everything went a bit wrong.

Barry ate another mushroom and took in a big gulp of air and let it out in a slow squeak from the corner of his mouth. He threw another piece of slate into the paddling pool.

You should have made me pay for what I did.

He looked up sharply, there was no consequent jingle from his naked head.

Don't take everything so fucking personal. I'm telling you this because it's true. I thought you should stay in jail. But the fuzz would have got my medical records when I pressed charges. They're worse gossips than actors. I've got this thing, skin disease, it's to do with capillaries. Do you want to see it?

No. No thank you.

He relented in the unbuttoning of his waistcoat.

People should think I'm impregnable. You want to know the point? This is the point. It had nothing to do with you.

This is the point, what it is is. In some ways he was just like Carlo. Maybe that's why they never got along.

You *wanted* to keep me in jail?

For your own good, you understand. I thought—

Yes. I understand.

Broadly smiling, I could feel unfamiliar muscles doing happy things. The balance had been altered. Strike another one off the list. There was never anything kind about that. It was no gift of freedom, I was merely the unlucky beneficiary of Barry's unsightly medical condition. Take away too all those seemingly thoughtful gifts that the sourcer had chosen—flowerpot, carving, maybe even the bottle opener. The game was never lost and it wasn't too late to win it now.

You don't find that preposterous I hope?

Preposterous? No, of course not. That's an odd thing to say.

Is it? Really? And Sean and I are going through some changes and look at me, you asshole. I'll tell you when everything went a *bit wrong*. Everything's been on the slide since that morning I woke up and everything was weird. Bud getting hurt, and Dylan doing her Saint Veronica I'm-Jesus's-sunbeam, and Sean. We had a fight about Scrabble. How many ees there are in the set. I told Sean there was something missing and Sean said I was a, and I called him a—it doesn't matter what I called him, the point is this, we had this stupid, dumb, fucking . . .

Argument?

Yes argument. And the next morning I found the missing letter in my underwear. Can you believe it? Does that sound pathetic or what?

You're sundering because you had a fight over Scrabble?

Partly that. Partly other things. There were these rumors going around, Bud and I. That kind of destabilized things.

But that wasn't true.

Barry switched from his mood of wistful pride to look at me suspiciously.

No it wasn't true. But can anyone know that for sure?

Yes. No, I mean. That's right.

I ended up making money on the deal. The compensation I got from the movie being canceled was something quite good. So maybe it wasn't all bad. But while we're on the subject, I got something for you.

Yes. I have something for you too.

I showed him the portrait, still bubble-wrapped. He nodded and ignored it.

And we brought the rabbit back. Fritzi. She's been kind of down ever since Mitzi went missing, pining, and we're closing up the house for a while. I'm going to the States. I don't think Sean's coming with me. Maybe he will, who knows, but this is what I got for you. Some news. We want to do your movie. Bud read the script. He considers it very spiritual.

Wang?

Yeah we'd have to do something about the name. I don't know how it would play in Topeka if you know what I'm saying. You should get yourself an agent. I recommend mine. There might be some good money for you.

I'd rather give *you* money. Would you like some more money? I've got quite a lot. And the money for the school fees. I've got that for you too.

Trying to copy Dylan I smiled beatifically at Barry. I waved notes from my wad in front of his face. I peeled off a bundle and pushed them into his breast pocket between the wings of his handkerchief.

Barry sighed. Reaching for his handkerchief he wiped his reddened mouth with a banknote.

Phil? You understand what I'm telling you?

Yes. Absolutely. Don't take things personally. Bud, spiritual, Wang, new name, movie, Topeka. That's great.

Jesus. I'm going to circulate. Or kill myself. One more thing. Do something for me, will you?

Yes. Of course.

Make things good with Alice. If you two can get it right maybe there's hope for all of us.

We tossed a last couple of stones into the paddling pool.

His, I was pleased to see, went further than mine. After a final exchange on the subject of the weather, which was, as Barry said and I agreed, glorious, we went back into the house.

Sean I dealt with in a matter of minutes.

Look, I said. We've sort of spoken about this before, but I know. I *know*. I know know know *know*, that Barry hasn't been having an affair with Bud.

But he wanted to, Sean said. Even if you're right, and—

I am right. I am. Am am.

OK. I believe you. But even so, he *wanted to*, and how do you recover from that?

With the greatest of ease. People want to have affairs with people all the time. They commit adultery in the heart all the time. I know I do—(I realized as I said it that at this moment at least the only person I wanted to commit adultery with was my wife, but I needed to add testimonial weight to my argument so I brought the image of the school liaison officer to mind and that aroused a guilty blush)—but it doesn't matter what anyone *thinks*. It's what you *do* that matters. I tell you, if there's one thing I know, it's that.

I always thought faithful was a kind of heart thing.

That's a very sweet thing to say and in a way you're right, but there's room for lots of things in the heart and just because there's one bad thing that doesn't mean it should cancel out all the good things.

Sean stared at me somewhat agog.

I think you're right, he said surprised it seemed not so much at the wisdom as that it was coming from me.

So give it another go, all right?

Yes. Maybe. All right.

He patted my shoulder and I patted his, and then we hugged and then we performed a sort of little dance which ended up with us like a pair of boxers playfully throwing punches, and I broke this up because I had seen Alice watching us in the kitchen doorway and I knew as I walked towards her that my face outsunned the sun.

Hold on, I said.

Yes?

This time she waited for me, to inflict upon her whatever tiresome thing I had to do or say, and I was suddenly shy. I went to the refrigerator to fetch out ice for the sourcer's borscht. I opened the freezer compartment and I shut it again when I realized what I had just seen. If I didn't see it then it might not exist. Reluctantly I opened my eyes again.

Fruit magnets holding a postcard to the refrigerator door. A postcard of Heathrow Airport on a dismal day, aeroplanes about to take off, I wondered if they ever had, if they ever could. I flicked a corner of the card, this evidence of my thought crime, monument of perfidy, the emperor's red.

I thought he'd burned. He'd showed me he'd burned . . .

What? Who showed you who burned what?

You don't understand.

What don't I understand?

It's a mindfuck.

Isn't it just?

I lost her again, between kitchen and hall and stairs and upstairs corridor. I went to the only part of the house that could offer me consolation, the twins' bedroom. Everything had been neatly tidied away in there, except for a few objects scattered as if randomly across the floor, a glass tiara, a couple of CDs, a pony-care manual, as if life still went carelessly on in this room. I lay on my stomach on the floor and opened the front wall flaps and moved things around in the dolls' house.

I was making a second bathroom out of the library when Alice came into the room and nudged me with her good foot. Jealous of the room, she was intending to drive away intruders.

Oh, she said. It's you.

I got up. I nimbly blocked her way to the door.

Barry says we should make things right between us.

When were things right between us?

I wouldn't let her out of the room, so she went to the window and I joined her there. A light rain was coming down. A woman was setting off fireworks from the lawn. Celebration, commemoration of Barry and Sean's sundering, which made every other couple, or at least this one, think of its own. Pairs stood together, showing in the explosive flashes of light the same expression that was on Alice's face and maybe my own, a little aloof, quite sad, a civilized attempt to show some amusement too. The visual equivalent of Syd Barrett's voice.

And the last image of Roger came back into my head, stomach-churning and clear and with an entirely new meaning attached: The man waving on a street corner at a departing Volvo estate wasn't waving goodbye: I had forgotten to return his shopping list and he wanted it back. He was waving very hard because he wanted it back very much. I wanted Roger to have his shopping list back. I wanted Alice to have me back.

I miss the twins, I said.

I miss them too, she said.

She moved her face so I couldn't kiss her mouth. I was allowed to graze her cheek with my lips. Tears weren't far away. For bad choices made in former times.

Things haven't been so bad, I said.

Really?

We had some good anniversary weekends.

Yes we did, didn't we? So what?

And birthdays. Do you remember that football match we had?

The memory didn't make her, or me, any happier. Apologies offered to the past, promises made to the future, and broken.

In the garden other couples were moving deep into words or embraces. The end of Barry and Sean was giving a delightful flavor to everyone else's beginnings.

We don't have to sell this house you know. I've got all that money back and a lot more. Look.

I showed her my wad. I tried to give it to her and it fell, fanning, to the floor.

No one ever liked it here did they?

You did. Or if you want a new one we can do that too.

She shrugged. I led her, without much protest, to Chloë's bed. I was allowed this last intimacy. Soon—in a day, an hour, less—this too would be denied me, to place my hands where I cared to on the body of my wife, to lift away her T-shirt, to unwrap her wraparound skirt, to expose myself in nakedness to her. A valedictory moment, for us to make our final assault on the highest peak.

We began as Loving Swallows, me on top, Alice grasping my waist, my hands at her neck.

Would it count if we picked up from where we left off before? Four hundred and fifty something?

Of course not, no, she said.

A shallow stroke of my jade peak into her lute string—
One, I whispered—and then a deeper one, black pearl. *Two*,

I said. And again. *Three*, in unison.

Irritated Swallow Pecks Rat.

By the way, it was four hundred and two. Actually.

Actually.

Three shallow thrusts, one deep. Five shallow, one deep. *Nine* shallow, one deep. One hundred and one. Dark Cicada Clings To A Branch. One hundred and two. A short thrust that resembles the jerking movement of a carp toying with the hook. One hundred and three, a snake enters his hole to hibernate.

One hundred and four, the stroke is deep, eagle catches elusive hare.

I stroked her arms, her shoulders, her breasts, remembering to keep my hands in motion caressing her body throughout, as my teacher Ken taught me. We moved into Dwarfed Pine Tree as her legs surrounded mine. That became Giant Bird Soaring Over Dark Sky, as I lifted her legs with my upper arms and held on to her waist. The Dance of the Two Phoenix, we rolled over so Alice was on top. We were Cat And Mouse Sharing A Hole.

Four hundred and two. Singing Monkey Holds A Tree. I sat up, she upon me facing, I had one hand behind my back supporting our weight, the other clasped to her buttocks.

Four oh three. Four oh four. Four oh five.

If we get to a thousand do we stay together? I asked.

Men, she thought, spoil every thing, even the smallest. It is not even my own deformity, any man is capable of exactly the same thing. Monkey Crushed By Tree.

Four ten.

Well, do we?

It's a test, it's NOT A TEST!

I can't begin to understand that, I said.

Four twenty. We moved back into a rhythm. Four

twenty-one, twenty-two. Four two three. Four two four. Lizard Basks On Rock.

Four thirty—four forty—

What's that? she said.

What?

Your arms. Those cuts.

Nothing. Just some grazes. Caesar's salad.

What? she said.

Mushrooms, I said.

What? she said.

Four fifty. Turning Dragon.

Five hundred. Five twenty. Five fifty.

I pushed in slowly as a snake entering a hole to hibernate. I thrust swiftly as a frightened rat rushes into a hole. I thrust my jade peak inside the examination chamber short and slow like a farmer preparing his land for late planting. I thrust down and then pulled up by the gold gully as though slicing off stones to find beautiful jade. A short thrust that resembles the jerking movement of a carp toying with the hook. A swift thrust like a flight of birds against the wind.

A knock on the door thundered like a cloudburst. I could take the interruption; somewhere inside us I had been about to be overwhelmed.

We hid under Chloë's duvet. Someone giggled. It might have been me.

Hold on! I shouted. We'll be coming in a minute!

We peeped above the duvet cover: The door to the room was ajar, but the invaders had retreated. We resumed as if anew. Rebranding. Everything can always start again.

A switch. The difference between zero and one.

The touch of her arm, the curve of her shoulder, the shadows on her throat. Hair fell in front of the smile her mouth made. Mandarin Ducks Sleekly Entwined. Her body stretched, lifted towards me. Silkworm Spinning A Cocoon.

This was indisputably a time when we had no need of a triangulated other. It was just her and me, our bodies, our selves, the grace of her skin, the scent of her flesh, the touch of her fingers upon me. We might even be heading for Autumn Dog.

What was that?

Nothing (eight hundred) . . . I don't (eight oh one) hear (eight oh two) . . . The rabbit maybe (eight oh three) . . . Barry (eight oh four) brought (eight oh five) Fritzi back (eight oh six).

It wasn't the rabbit because if it was I would have been sneezing. I didn't care what it was. I was past that and I thought she was too.

Cover my disappointment that she is capable of listening to extraneous noises. Return to the world that the two of us made. Leaping Wild Horses, Alice on her back on the bed, her legs up, feet on my shoulders. Her mouth, wide, ready to smile, hoping to, the beauty of her arms rising, a smiling crease at the nape of her neck.

Eight sev eight.

Nine.

Eight . . . eighty!

The deepest thrust so far, through the deep chamber, plunging low like a sailing boat braving the gale.

She flinched, muscles tensed, eyes focused—I could hear her telling herself to relax. The thought is single parent to the deed. A floorboard creaked. She stared past my right shoulder, stiffened, closed her eyes, and relaxed. We resumed. Nine hundred. Nine fifty. Tyrannies crumbled around our bed.

Nine hundred and ninety-nine! I roared.

For a moment, a pause. The heaviness of breathing. Then: Silence. I made the deepest thrust all the way to the Inner Door, the North Pole.

ONE! shouted Alice.

THOU—! I yelled.

—*SAND!* applauded the crowd of partygoers standing in the twins' room.

When we finally went downstairs no one met our eyes. Amusement flickered in party faces as the guests made their satisfied exits. My father and Alice's mother were the last to go. They had been having an argument, presumably political, which had put color into her cheeks and lasciviousness into his veins; I recognized the look he had shown in black and white photographs when he was courting my mother and fighting the class war across sexual barricades.

We'll have to agree to disagree, said Alice's mother gaily as she waited for my father to open the front door for her, an act which he had been previously incapable of and not just for political reasons.

Alice and I quietly cleared up the party remains, which took less time than she would have budgeted for.

Well, she said tossing her rubber gloves into the sink. That was eventful. I think I'm going to bed now.

This was not an invitation.

At the wedding of my father to Alice's mother, the bride wore white, the groom a tight-fitting flared denim suit, splashed with antique red paint from long-ago graffiti campaigns. The ceremony took place in a registry office, gilt chairs, flock wallpaper, swirls of dust in the sleepy air, to a small audience of family, friends, and fellow-travelers. I was, by default I supposed, best man. Alice, matron of honor. The twins were bridesmaids in yellow silk. They carried the wedding rings on little plush cushions alongside the groom's spectacle case and the bride's hearing aid.

Boarding school had not lived up to the twins' expectations. There was no lacrosse, a game that had been heard of by few of their dormitory mates, even the older ones, who anyway seemed to prefer sex and drugs with local boys to eating midnight feasts. It had been easy to convince Alice to bring the girls back home. I had not convinced Alice to allow me to continue to live with them. But I was permitted to visit, making the short walk over from my room in Richard's grand new house to deliver the girls from school, to sit with them while they watched TV and I stared at their homework books, to share my Doughboy and Wang Hollywood money, to perform little tasks of domestic ineptitude, and to achieve, quite regularly, and in applause-free private, a thousand loving thrusts with Alice.

We could get divorced couldn't we? Alice said in the tone she had formerly used to make suggestions for weekends away.

I suppose so, yes. I don't want to.

Alice was wearing a new dress, bought for the occasion, figure-hugging blue silk that I couldn't avoid touching.

I have to make my speech now.

What are you going to say?

What can you say?

She had treated the whole thing up till now as an embarrassing joke, senile romance, cankered satyr meets demented widow, a distasteful display whose small physical details she found unimaginable. But now, here, standing beside the aged couple, facing the guests in a dress the same color as her eyes, she spoke of love, to the accompaniment of the assistant registrar's impatiently tapping pen.

The day before, clearing, more slowly than Alice would have liked, traces of myself in the debris of what used to be my shed, I had been practicing my toss by the front door just before delivering a black bin liner full of unnecessary things to the rubbish bin, when Carlo came in through the gate with the nozzle of an industrial leaf blower in his hands.

Nice gaff, said Carlo.

His face was smiling, his skin was washed, his hair and clothes free of grease, all of which made his appearance more troubling. If, ten years before, we had adopted a thirteen-year-old with a borderline personality disorder, I could have called this man or someone damaged like him by the name the good policeman had used for me. I wondered if the ensuing ten years would have changed us both. I didn't know the answer. Alice would have said yes.

Yes, I said.

I blagged this off a parkie. Told him I was on work experience. Do you want a go?

He flicked a switch on the engine that was strapped to his back. He aimed the nozzle into the front garden: Flowers bowed screeching before his power, stones skittered across the lawn. He playfully aimed it at me for a moment and I was shoved painfully hard against a patio post. Then he gave me a leer and switched off the machine and offered it to me.

Here. Have a go.

No. No thank you. Thanks anyway.

I'd have come round before but I was detained.

Oh?

One of my projects went a bit wrong. The newspaper columnist. Went a bit wrong. But I'm back now. Let's go down the pub. Catch up on things. I'll *stand* you a pint.

I'm a bit busy right now. And I've given up drinking. So, no. No thank you.

How are your mates?

Barry and Sean? They're in America now. LA. They're fine. As ever really. I'm sorry about your screen test. It was a shame.

I don't really *give two monkeys* to be honest. Dylan wears red trousers. Never trust anyone who wears red trousers. They're a tosser.

But you shouldn't have sent those postcards.

Shouldn't I?

Carlo sneered at me with maximum malevolence, which meant that he was feeling at his fondest.

No. I don't think you should have. You burnt blank ones didn't you and sent the real ones. It was a horrible thing to do.

Thank you. I'm glad you appreciate it. Tell me about Syd. Bud said you found Syd and brought him to London.

Not really.

What's that supposed to mean?

I took him back home.

Carlo nodded his head.

Do you know how many times I've looked for him? You found him. And you took him home. What's his house like?

I took him back to the corner we found him at. I thought it was only fair. He's not Syd. We thought he was Syd but he's not. He's not who we thought he was.

Carlo gave me a very pleasant smile, which made me take a step back towards the putative safety of the house.

I liked him. He seemed very, gentle. I took him to the supermarket. He liked that. He cheered up in there. But he's not Syd. His name's Roger.

And you know what your name is? Fucking Moron.

His name's Roger. He said so.

What's my name?

Carlo. You're Carlo.

No you fuckwit. I'm doing a game-show format. Understand? Wait for me to finish the question. Don't buzz in. All right?

All right.

What's my name? I am a lost genius born in Cambridge in nineteen forty-six. My father is a doctor. He dies when I am fifteen. Early on I show a talent for painting as well as music. I'm the most popular boy in school. Do you want more clues?

I don't think so.

Let's have your answer then. You're in the four-zone. What's my name?

Syd Barrett.

Uh-*uh*. Wrong! Do you want more clues? That'll take you into the three-zone. Some of my early bands include Geoff Mott and the Mottoes, The Hollering Blues, Those Without. I play guitar and sing. I take acid for the first time. No? You're in the two-zone now. I move to London in nineteen sixty-five. I'm a student at Camberwell Art School. I join a band with a bunch of stupid wankers studying architecture. I play guitar and sing. The one-zone. I change my band's name to The Pink Floyd Sound. I'm the man. I write all the songs. I'm a star. I have to ask you now. What's my name?

Syd Barrett.

Correct for one point.

But that's what I said before.

But you were wrong before.

I sneezed. Once twice, three times. A gray chinchilla rabbit hopped around the side of the house, glared at me, and hopped away again.

You don't get it, do you?

I tried, very hard, to get it.

I'm sorry.

I'll have to tell you then. Syd Barrett wasn't called Syd. That's not his real name. You with me? When he was a teenager him and his mates used to go see crap jazz bands play. There was a bass player called Sid Barrett. Sid with an *i*, old bloke, and everyone thought it was really funny that he had the same last name as this kid. So they called the kid Syd, with a *y*. Funny joke yeah? And it stuck. That became his name. When he was a singer, when he was a *star*, his name was Syd Barrett. Later when it's all over, after it's left him, he changes his name back to what it used to be. Lives in his mother's place. Same name, same bedroom. As if the last eight years never happened. You're with me now aren't you? He had a star's name and then he wasn't and so he didn't. It's Roger. His name's Roger Keith Barrett. You fucking fuckhead. That was him.

I've got urine on my hands, I said. Excuse me a moment.

I dropped the rubbish bag and ran into the house and through into the back garden and the shed. The dust was gone. On the desk, which had been disinfected and wax-polished, were the few things I hadn't been able to throw away yet. Still there, under the jade carving, was a creased fold of paper. A shopping list, time-smeared. I took that, and I slipped over my wrists the twins' hair scrunchies that surrounded the two inferior peaks of the jade carving, and then I took the jade carving itself. I went back to Carlo. I gave him the list.

Here, I said. This is Syd's. If you find him you can give it back to him.

Carlo held the relic with great care and read the items over and over and emphatically shook his head in a way that implied gentleness.

Thank you, he said.

I hoped we understood equally that a debt had been discharged, with nothing owing on either side. I showed him the carving.

You're welcome. You wouldn't like this as well I suppose?

No, he said. I wouldn't.

He was probably right, and I was ashamed of myself as well as feeling relieved. Worse than owing something to Carlo would be being owed to by Carlo.

I had watched him walk away, blasting at things with his leaf blower—a garden hedge, a pair of pigeons that had previously been nestling in a peaceful tree sent into mad flight, a Jack Russell terrier goofily yapping, terrified to find its belly on the pavement and its legs splayed either side. When I was sure Carlo had gone, I threw the rubbish bag into the bin, and wrote off all debts, except for the inescapable ones.

Alice was finishing her speech. Unrepentant Stalinists wiped tears away from rheumy eyes; pink-, white-, and blue-haired women looked sadly at the empty seats beside them. The groom stroked the bride's hand. They gently clinked together wedding rings.

An accordionist brought the party to its feet with the Internationale and played us out with Some Enchanted Evening. Richard and I carried the wedding gifts, making a pile of them outside the door, while a tired photographer, who had recently resigned from the *Hendon Times* for political reasons, organized us into a square on the town hall steps.

Smile please. Everybody.

I'm going to push aside tiny things, I said to Alice, husbandly and almost irreproachably gripping her by the waist on the top-most step.

I don't know what you are talking about.

Perhaps she was right to doubt. Perhaps, no matter how hard I might try for the large, for the unmistakably immense, my inclinations or something stronger would always lead me back to the small, the almost absent— like the envelope which contained my gift to the newly-weds, their traveling tickets and hotel reservations for a world tour taking in the capital city and principal resort of every state with a Marxist-based ideology, which I had foolishly and vaingloriously placed on top of a scatter of presents, weighed down only by the flowers that the tails of Alice's mysterious uncle's frock-coat had just knocked away.

And I've dealt with all that gift stuff.

Really? Have you?

Yes. Everything's straightforward now. I mean it. I know what it's all about. I appreciate things the right way now. By the way though, what have you got them?

The glare she then gave me went so far beyond suspicion and reproach that it came close to swinging back into love again.

The envelope was caught by an indecisive wind. It drifted away from the steps and towards the door and back among the guests and hung for a moment above the wig of my father's great rival, the retired Party Co-Coordinator, South London, and rested there.

Smile. Please. Everybody!

Something for the house, she said.

Her public magnanimity towards the nuptials may have been enlarging her heart, but it was costing her in little twitches of her upper lip that she suppressed by clamping her mouth shut. In the skin beneath her eyes were the lines of faint stars that might one day equal the constellations of her mother's.

The Co-Coordinator, who suffered from a medical condition that wasn't Parkinson's, but involved making lots of involuntary jerks, jerked; the envelope slipped off his head, hung for a moment on the corduroy slope of his shoulders, and slid out of sight.

Bedside tables, she said. For reading, she added severely.

Everybody! the photographer pleaded.

My father whipped off his cap in response and, alarmingly, started to sing. By the third line his few old

comrades had joined in. His new wife loyally mouthed
an approximation of the words.

> *The people's flag is deepest red*
> *It shrouded oft our martyred dead*
> *And ere their limbs grew stiff and cold*
> *Their hearts' blood dyed its every fold*
>
> *(chorus)*
> *Then raise the scarlet standard high*
> *Within its shade we'll live and die*
> *Though cowards flinch and traitors sneer*
> *We'll keep the red flag flying here*

Alice and I led the applause. My father and the Co-
Coordinator angrily waved us quiet.

> *Look round! the Frenchman loves its blaze*
> *The sturdy German chants its praise*
> *In Moscow's vaults its hymns are sung*
> *Chicago swells the surging throng*
>
> *It waved above our infant might*
> *When all ahead seemed dark as night*
> *It witnessed many a deed and vow*
> *We must not change its color now*
>
> *Then raise the scarlet standard high*
> *Within its shade we'll live and die*
> *Though cowards flinch and traitors sneer*
> *We'll keep the red flag flying here!*

It's sweet isn't it? said Alice.

It's not over yet. You don't think they've finished, do you?

You probably know all the words.

Doubt it, I muttered apologetically because I had bumped her bottom with the top of my head retrieving my gift envelope from the step below and also because, of course, she was right.

> *It well recalls the triumphs past*
> *It gives the hope of peace at last*
> *The banner bright, the symbol plain*
> *Of human right and human gain*
>
> *It suits today the weak and base*
> *Whose minds are fixed on pelf and place*
> *To cringe before the rich man's frown*
> *And haul the sacred emblem down*

Some of them, his mates, his comrades, made fortunes in advertising, you know.

So? That doesn't matter. It's very nice to believe in something.

On this bright autumn day, we had acquired a crowd. Shoppers had stopped to listen. Three small girls chased each other in a circle. A young man in a leather coat was pacing the pavement, slapping a bible and yelling hoarsely. A *Big Issue* seller smoking a roll-up was offering his magazines. Two dark-haired women had set up a table from which they were doing good trade selling duvet covers.

> *With heads uncovered swear we all*
> *To bear it onward till we fall*
> *Come dungeons dark or gallows grim*
> *This song shall be our parting hymn*

Then raise the scarlet standard high!
Within its shade we'll live and die!
Though cowards flinch and traitors sneer
We'll keep the red flag flying here!

Watching shoppers applauded. A collective coughing fit broke the singers' defiant erect postures. A small girl burst into tears, and the twins helped to comfort her but were called away by the rejuvenated ex-*Hendon Times* photographer, who speedily filled two rolls of film of the wedding party. Alice was smiling and so was I. For the final verse and chorus I had even joined in, slipping in some of Syd Barrett's words along the way.

We waved our parents off in the Co-Coordinator's taxi, and waited at the kerb, puzzled about what to do next.

Do you think those duvet covers are linen?

Doubt it, I said. Probably polyester.

They were, in fact, cotton. We bought two for the house, and drove home in the new Volvo.

And so we sit, hearts beating, chests rising, hormones issuing wet instructions, our private dreams locked behind bone. The twins—our obligations of flesh, made flesh—chatter in the back seat. My hand rests on the gear stick, and Alice's hand moves to rest upon mine.

90 DAYS, ONE DAY AT A TIME

A New Beginning for People in Recovery

by
John Behnke, C.S.P.

PAULIST PRESS
New York/Mahwah, N.J.

Book design by Theresa M. Sparacio

Cover design by James F. Brisson

Copyright © 1999 by Paulist Press, Inc.

ISBN: 0-8091-3881-6

Published by Paulist Press
997 Macarthur Boulevard
Mahwah, New Jersey 07430

www.paulistpress.com

Printed and bound in the
United States of America

PREFACE

This book of meditations is meant for the recovering person who is ready to start/continue on a journey of daily reflective prayer.

The style of the text is tailored for the recovering person who needs to keep it clear and simple.

Hopefully, the thoughts in each section will be used as grist material and as a jumping-off point to be followed up with a quiet period of time in conversation (prayer) with one's Higher Power (God).

The unfinished prayer at the end of each meditation is a further aid in achieving some quality prayer time. The users of this meditation book are encouraged to complete these unfinished prayers in their own words, searching the depths of their hearts for the prayers they would like to express to the loving God we worship.

Prayer (deciphering God's will for us) should lead us to action. The phrase, "Today I will...," has been left open-ended so that the reader can choose an appropriate action suited to his or her own situation.

The blank spaces might be used to finish writing the prayer or could be used for the recording of one's daily personal journal that is inspired by the use of this prayer aid.

THE TWELVE STEPS OF ALCOHOLICS ANONYMOUS

1. We admitted we were powerless over alcohol—that our lives had become unmanageable.

2. Came to believe that a Power greater than ourselves could restore us to sanity.

3. Made a decision to turn our will and our lives over to the care of God *as we understood Him.*

4. Made a searching and fearless moral inventory of ourselves.

5. Admitted to God, to ourselves and to another human being the exact nature of our wrongs.

6. Were entirely ready to have God remove all these defects of character.

7. Humbly ask Him to remove our shortcomings.

8. Made a list of all persons we had harmed, and became willing to make amends to them all.

9. Made direct amends to such people wherever possible, except when to do so would injure them or others.

10. Continued to take personal inventory and when we were wrong promptly admitted it.

11. Sought through prayer and meditation to improve our conscious contact with God, *as we understood Him,* praying only for knowledge of His will for us and the power to carry that out.

12. Having had a spiritual awakening as the result of these steps, we tried to carry this message to alcoholics, and to practice these principles in all our affairs.

THE TWELVE TRADITIONS OF ALCOHOLICS ANONYMOUS

1. Our common welfare should come first; personal recovery depends upon A.A. unity.

2. For our group purpose, there is but one ultimate authority—a loving God as He may express Himself in our group conscience. Our leaders are but trusted servants; they do not govern.

3. The only requirement for A.A. membership is a desire to stop drinking.

4. Each group should be autonomous except in matters affecting other groups or A.A. as a whole.

5. Each group has but one primary purpose—to carry its message to the alcoholic who still suffers.

6. An A.A. group ought never endorse, finance, or lend the A.A. name to any related facility or outside enterprise, lest problems of money, property, and prestige divert us from our primary purpose.

7. Every A.A. group ought to be fully self-supporting, declining outside contributions.

8. Alcoholics Anonymous should remain forever non-professional, but our service centers may employ special workers.

9. A.A., as such, ought never be organized; but we may create service boards or committees directly responsible to those they serve.

10. Alcoholics Anonymous has no opinion on outside issues; hence the A.A. name ought never be drawn into public controversy.

11. Our public relations policy is based on attraction rather than promotion; we need always maintain personal anonymity at the level of press, radio, and films.

12. Anonymity is the spiritual foundation of all our traditions, ever reminding us to place principles before personalities.

DAY 1

I admitted that I was powerless over alcohol.

I'll never become like they are. I'll never touch a drop of that stuff. I see what it has done to the lives of the adults in my family. And if I do/when I do, I'll never drink to excess like "they" do.

In the program we're told if you think that you may have a problem with drinking and drugs, you probably *do* have a problem. Even before we are well into our active addiction of drinking, we unknowingly have a sense that there is a problem abrew. *I'll never drink like that.*

Our first alcoholic drink should give most of us alcoholics the proof we need never to lift another drink to our lips. The first legal drink I remember was innocently given to me by a close relative. It was a gin and tonic. It was the most awful taste I had ever experienced. It took close to an hour to get the bitter-tasting elixir down. And yet, when it was finished and I was offered another of the same, I immediately took it. An insane gesture on my part to drink a second one of something that seemed so vile. It wasn't the taste that I found attractive but the immediate results of light-headedness and euphoria. In the last twenty years of drinking as an adult I have no recollection of having a drink or two and stopping. I started early and drank well into the night, yet never missed a day of work. Groggy, maybe, and ill-tempered, but up and doing a full day's work and often more. I can handle my drinks. I can even drink more than the others and still stand on my feet. It helps me to be more relaxed and makes it easier to carry on conversations.

A friend came into the living room one afternoon, almost precisely at 5:00 P.M., poured himself a nice glass of scotch and said, "Lord knows we deserve this." It clicked. I never needed another excuse to drink. *I deserved it after all the hard work I put in.*

I would drink to calm my nerves, to celebrate, to drown my sorrows, to forget, because I worked too hard, but if the excuse was not immediately forthcoming, I needed no other than it was my right as an adult. *I deserved it.*

What insane thinking that governed my every waking moment and often my dreams. Late one night, well into my addiction, I will never forget the conversation I had with myself: *Well you might as well admit it, you're never going to stop drinking for the rest of your life.* What a feeling of despair. What a sense of futility.

Thank God the day of intervention came when I was told that although I may not be sick and tired of my drinking, those around me were, and a program of intervention was to be prescribed.

What a relief to be given the opportunity to deal with the monkey that had taken up residence on my back. What a life-giving blessing to finally be able to admit that I was powerless over alcohol.

Prayer and Action

God give me the grace never to forget where I came from and how quickly one drink will take me back to the brink of that living hell. Just for today help me to....

Today I will....

_____

_____

_____

_____

_____

_____

_____

_____

_____

_____

_____

_____

_____

_____

_____

DAY 2

My life had become unmanageable.

Alcoholic drunks and addicts were unreliable, had sporadic work habits, usually lived in the gutters and drank before noon. Each of us alcoholics had certain standards by which, in our own minds, we were able to keep the dreaded word *alcoholic* out of the description of who we were. *Me an alcoholic? Never! I not only worked every day, but I always had a roof over my head, and I never drank before noon, even when I was on vacation.*

Manage my life? Sure, I worked hard at that. So often I wished I had more time to do the work I had to do. Often I wished people would leave me alone so I could do the work I needed to do. I wished other people would have done their jobs better so I wouldn't have to pick up their slack all the time. If there hadn't been so many demands on my time, I would have been able to do the things I really wanted to do. At work I had to do all the thinking. Everything had to get my approval. I knew how everything should work. I knew all the answers. I knew what other people should be thinking and doing. And when it didn't work out the way I thought it should, it frustrated me. The only real friend I could talk to was a bottle. The only solace and peace I had was when I had some drinks in me. No wonder I drank. But the more I drank, the more that the problems at work and in the world bothered me. If only they would leave me alone, just for a while. No wonder I had to drink.

Keeping it all straight, wondering whom I told what to, if they ever found out how inadequate and insecure I felt most of the time, if I could only keep it all balanced, and if they would only leave me alone for a little while, then I knew everything would be all right.

What pure blessing it was to come to that point in my life to be able to admit that my life had truly become unmanageable and that I didn't have to play the charade any longer. It was all right to be human and to make mistakes and not have to be perfect.

Prayer and Action

God, today I know that you give me the grace that is sufficient enough to do that which I need to do today. If I don't pick up and *use* today, I'm a winner already. Give me the strength to use this day in doing your will rather than worrying about how to control and manage every moment of the day. Just for today help me to....

Today I will....

_____

_____

_____

_____

_____

_____

DAY 3

I came to believe that a power greater than myself could restore me to sanity.

After years of believing that I was insignificant, that God had a lot more important things to be dealing with, that I had breached his ways one too many times with my uncontrollable drinking, it was a long, hard step to acknowledge that my life was worth being reclaimed by a loving God.

To acknowledge and admit that God could restore me to sanity meant that I would have to shut the door to drinking and using. Those were two friends I had had a long relationship with. I was comfortable in their presence. I knew how life worked when I had them flowing through my body. I may have hated myself and the hand I was dealt, but in a weird way it was comfortable, and I was used to the way things were in my addiction. I wasn't so sure I wanted to have the drastic change in my life that not using would bring. It was all too frightening, that future without using.

In my active using I had grown so far away from God. I wasn't sure that living clean and sober would be all that much fun. Without drink life seemed so boring. The real crux of the problem was that allowing God into my life would force me to change my ways. I'd have to change the way I looked at life, the way I felt about life and living. I'd have to deal with my feelings and relate to people in a new way. The thought of change was scary. The unknown future seemed like unsafe territory to trod upon.

Believing that a power greater than I could restore me to sanity meant saying good-bye to some longtime friends: drinking and drugging. In the beginning it took an unwilling leap of faith that my life would be better without drink constantly in my body.

It took a leap of faith to allow the saving power of an all-loving God to restore my life that had strayed so far from the path of light and truth. What a blessed day it was when, with one eyed closed, I put one foot in front of the other and jumped into the arms of a loving Higher Power.

Prayer and Action

God, it is such a wonderful feeling to sense your loving presence in my life. Let me always feel your presence so that I may never sink to the depths I once did. Just for today help me to....

Today I will....

_____

_____

_____

_____

_____

_____

DAY 4

I made a decision to turn my will and my life over to the care of God.

It was my way or no way at all. After all, I knew best. I knew how and why everything should be functioning. I knew the name of the game and how and what every player should be doing. I was given many talents and abilities by that God of ours. It was my duty to use them. I was the master of my destiny, the captain of my ship. You'd play by my rules, or I'd take the ball and go home.

Underlying this sense of inflated self-worth was also a Jeffersonian Deist belief in God, induced by the numbing of the sensitivities that comes from excessive use of drink and drugs. Although outwardly a Trinitarian, inwardly, because of the feeling of separation that drinking can bring about, I sensed God was more a God who got the whole thing going and then went on to other more important endeavors, leaving us to fend for ourselves. Alone and adrift to figure things out for ourselves.

Turn my will and my life over to God? Why? After all, we were made in the image and likeness of God. We were given a brain to figure things out. We were given the commission to master the world and to create a new and better environment in which to live. Turn my will and my life over to a God who had more important things to do? Turning my will and my life back over to a God who had given me so many talents and abilities would seem to me that I was giving up, calling it quits. I would be a loser if I had to depend on anyone, even God.

What a blessed day it was when I finally decided to turn my will and my life over to the care of God. I could stop playing God and be what I really was, a loved child of a God who knew best what I needed for the day and graced me with all that I needed. How blessed to be in the loving care and arms of my Higher Power and not have to fend for myself.

Prayer and Action

God, your will, not mine. Just for today help me to....

Today I will....

_____

_____

_____

_____

_____

_____

_____

_____

_____

DAY 5
God as I understand God...

We alcoholics and addicted persons have a hard time accepting any type of authority in our lives. All that God stuff that we were brought up on is hard stuff to take. In the scriptures we read that we can't serve two masters. In our active addiction we had certainly made a choice. Our every waking moment was spent thinking about using. Did we have enough on hand? Where were we going to buy the stuff today? Would we run out too soon? When could we start? What did we have to get done before we could really do what we wanted to do—drink?

We had long since stopped praying to that God of our ancestors, a vengeful God who was going to punish us for something we had little control over, a God who obviously wasn't interested in us or we wouldn't be in these circumstances. We'd fallen through the cracks. We were left to drift aimlessly through this bleak existence with only one "friend" we could trust. And what a "friend" at that. A "friend" who would turn on us, change our personalities and cause us to be delusional and paranoid. Who needed a God who would tell us lots of things we shouldn't be doing, who would abandon us when things got tough and punish us when it was all over? We existed in a living hell and roamed through life as if we were the living dead. And we were supposed to turn with complete abandon to this God we were brought up on?

Probably, if the truth be known, we couldn't use the way we needed to if we allowed God to direct our lives. We needed to be far away from *any* type of God to live the way we needed in order to feed our addictions. God and excessive drinking don't mix.

What a blessing in my life that there is an organization like A.A.—an accepting group of people who don't tell me what and how I must believe, only that I need some kind of higher strength in my life. I obviously was not able to do it on my own. What a blessing to have an organization in my life that allows me to grow spiritually at my own pace, that allows me to renew my friendship with God gradually, that teaches me that I'm a child of God, loved with all my imperfections and defects. Today I can get down on my knees and pray with all my heart to the God of my understanding and feel that presence in my life. What a wonderfully new experience it is to know that I am never alone.

Prayer and Action

God, life had become so meaningless and unfulfilling when I had drifted far from you to worship that spirit in the bottle. Thank you for allowing the fog to lift from around my head so that I can see more clearly the path that leads to you. Just for today help me to....

Today I will....

_____

_____

_____

_____

DAY 6

I made a searching and fearless moral inventory of myself.

Don't tell anyone anything, or they will use it against you. I remember that a supervisor once asked me how much I drank in a day. Thinking that sixteen or eighteen beers a day was a tad too much to admit openly to anyone, I said, "... somewhere around six or eight." His eyes lit up in astonishment. To me at that time "six or eight" meant just getting started. I felt relieved that I had not told the truth. I didn't even want to think what the consequences might have been if I had. The truth would have been used to prevent me from doing what I really wanted to do—drink.

The active alcoholic and user's life is one of secrecy and duplicity. Keep the cards close to the vest. Don't let anyone know, because if "they" found out what we were really like, they wouldn't understand, they'd try to make us change, they'd be repulsed and probably even hate us. Keep "it" a secret.

The disease of alcoholism is cunning and baffling. It knows that if we don't have a good self-image, if we hate ourselves and are paranoid enough to keep everything a secret, then we will continue to drink and use to cover "it" up. The only way out is a total and complete disclosure of who we are and what we've done. Total. We can't keep one secret, or the disease will use it as a wedge to get us back in its clutches.

And what we discover when we are completely honest about inventorying our lives is that the truth really can set us free. The secrets are all human errors and defects. We discover that we have lied, stolen, cheated, abused ourselves and were abusive to those around us. We may have committed serious breeches but they are forgivable.

Prayer and Action

God, it's frightening to think about all the things I've done wrong in my life. I know if I am to have a new life, clean and be sober, I have to rid myself of those skeletons and cobwebs that hinder my thinking and my ability to live honestly and uprightly. Help me to be thorough and complete in my inventory of who I am and what I've done. Just for today help me to....

Today I will....

_____

_____

_____

_____

_____

_____

_____

_____

DAY 7

I openly admitted to God, myself and another human being the exact nature of my wrongs.

Now that was a scary thing to do—to be open and completely honest about who I was and what I had done, especially the wrong things, in my lifetime: lying, cheating, stealing, being abusive toward the people around me, not to mention the total lack of concern I had for my own body and spirituality. If I could only live my life over and not do any of those awful things again.

There is something extremely mystical (not magical) about speaking out loud to another human being the things we have done in our lifetime. In that one act we end up doing two things. We, probably for the first time, take ownership of our life and our actions. This is who I am and this is what I've done. It may well be the first time we ever spoke about some of the terrible things we committed.

Besides taking ownership, we also discard those things. In a spiritual way we expel those demons and wrongs from our bodies. The Hebrew Bible describes a wonderful ceremony that happened yearly. Once a year the people would gather together for a time of prayer and penance. They would put a goat in their midst and everyone would come forward and place their hands on the goat. It symbolized that they were transferring their sins onto the goat. When everyone was finished they would chase the goat out into the desert to die with their sins on his back. In a sense that is what we have done when we tell another our life story with all its sins and imperfections. We are symbolically transferring those defects of our character on to another human being. We expel them from our body. They don't have to return to us. We are freed of the horrible past with all its secrets.

In the process we can learn from the past and use it to better ourselves in the now of today. The past doesn't have to be a huge millstone around our neck, pulling us further and further down that bottomless pit of self-destruction.

Free of the past, I can concentrate on living today, unafraid of the past catching up with me.

Prayer and Action

God, what a wonderful feeling to finally confront the past and put it behind me once and for all. Help me to learn the lessons I need to learn from my past actions and not wallow in the guilt I have for doing many of the things I did. Just for today help me to....

Today I will....

_____

_____

_____

_____

_____

DAY 8

I was entirely ready to have God remove all these defects of character.

What a great feeling to have all those hidden secrets out in the open. What a cleansing feeling it was to have all these monkeys lifted from my back. The millstone was loosened. The baggage of a lifetime was shed. The weight, more than one could bear, was unburdened. Cleansed in a way I had never felt before, I could now truly pray to that Higher Power with head held fairly high. A spark of worthiness was ignited in that time of honestly and openly taking my fifth step. The tune of the "Ode to Joy" readily replaced the more somber tune of Peggy Lee's "Is That All There Is?"

In the quiet of my room I boldly and happily asked God with all my heart to remove any defects that would keep me from doing his will in my life.

Uplifted and freed, I felt joy in the knowledge that God does hear our prayers. It was a joyous moment to know that I stood in the presence of God as one who is loved and worthy of forgiveness.

Prayer and Action

God, I am so grateful that I am an alcoholic. Thank you for the crooked road of my life, which finally brought me to face your light and countenance. May I always be

ready to do your will in my life and serve you with all
that I am and have. Just for today help me to....

Today I will....

_____

_____

_____

_____

_____

_____

_____

_____

_____

_____

_____

_____

_____

DAY 9

I humbly asked my Higher Power to remove all my shortcomings.

What a great feeling to get all those hidden secrets out in the open. What a great feeling not to worry about the past catching up and dashing everything to pieces. Take all those defects of character, take all those shortcomings right here and now, so I won't have to worry about them anymore. They brought too much pain and suffering to those around me and to myself. One lie led to so many more. One act of deceit led to so many more cover-ups. To be freed of all those crazy and bizarre patterns in my life, to be able to be open and honest with all that I deal with, what a "heaven on earth" kind of existence I can have just by handing over all my character defects and shortcomings to my Higher Power once and for all.

What a temporary letdown when it all didn't happen the way I knew it was supposed to happen. What a temporary letdown when I started to make mistakes and when my actions toward others were less than admirable. The imperfections started to reappear again, in fact, had never really left. I couldn't have prayed harder or been more sincere about removing the shortcomings in my life, and yet there they were, rearing their ugly heads as if nothing had changed—except that I wasn't using anymore.

I have to remember that the program is not a magic elixir that, once taken, solves all my problems forever and ever. The program is just that, a program, a way of life that must be followed on a daily basis, sometimes on an hour-to-hour, minute-to-minute basis, in order for any real and significant change to happen in my life.

I have to continue to believe that my Higher Power will give me all the strength (grace) I need to get through the day and to change the things that need to be changed in my life today. I have to humbly accept the fact that I am human, imperfect. I am not God, who is all-perfect.

Humility and this step allow me to seek God's help on a daily basis, to change what I can and to accept what I can't.

Prayer and Action

God, help me not only not to use but to continue to change my life and my actions so that I can be pleasing to you and happily do your will in all things. Take my imperfections as an offering to you. Replace them with virtues that I can use for the betterment not only of my life, but of the lives of those I will meet today. Just for today, help me to....

Today I will....

_____

_____

_____

_____

_____

DAY 10

I made a list of the persons I had harmed.

That seemed simple enough. Starting from the beginning, there were only a few classmates and playmates through grade school that I could even remember with full names, but the list was to be as complete as I could honestly make, so in some instances, the simple recollections of shameful events in which I remember inflicting harm on vague persons in my past had to suffice. But in the more recent years, as the drinking increased, the memories of some situations were blurred, but, for the most part, I still felt the intensity of the harm I had done and remembered the names of those harmed. Family members, friends, coworkers, business associates, acquaintances, drinking partners—anyone who had had a relationship with me—all were affected and harmed by the disease that fomented within me. And somewhere amongst the carnage was my own self, in need of forgiveness for the harm I had inflicted. This takes the form of a mini-fourth step with names put to the events of the harms I inflicted. This is yet another step in the healing process along the road to daily recovery.

Prayer and Action

God, how provocative is my disease. It not only had a death hold on my own life, but it had a disproportionate effect on those that had even a passing acquaintance with me. Help me always to be aware of the effect I may

have on the people who come into relationships with
me. Let your grace guide my every step. Just for today
help me to....

Today I will....

_____

_____

_____

_____

_____

_____

_____

_____

_____

_____

_____

_____

DAY 11

I became willing to make amends to all I had harmed.

Why should I have to dig up the past and put my self-esteem at risk? Why should I risk being humiliated or even rejected by people, some of whom still hold grudges against me?

It becomes plain and simple. If I don't deal with and face the past and those who have been part of my story, if I am always holding on to the bitterness I have for some of the people in my life, then I can't adequately leave the past behind and live in the present. I have to clear the slate and acknowledge the harm I have done to the people I have wronged in order to start new and fresh. It's ownership. I have to own up to what I've done in my lifetime, and to whom.

I don't really have to worry about the reaction of the one I ask forgiveness from. Whether the person forgives or not doesn't really matter; the point is that I do the right thing no matter what the result. The step is not to win friends, but to do my part in mending my fences and bridging the enormous gaps that I have created. I can't control or orchestrate the response of the person from whom I seek forgiveness. I can only do what I need to do so that I can look into the mirror and be comfortable with the image I see.

Prayer and Action

God, would that things had been different, I wouldn't have to go through this process of admitting my mistakes to those whom I have wronged. Would that I had been perfect. Help me to admit my failings not only to myself but also to those I have harmed. Help me to grow from this experience. Just for today help me to....

Today I will....

_____

_____

_____

_____

_____

_____

_____

_____

_____

_____

_____

DAY 12

I made amends directly to the people I harmed.

What a scary thought—to put into action a list of things to do that involves eating humble pie and asking another person for forgiveness. Sometimes it's hard just to put one foot in front of the other, to do the regular things I need to do in a day. To actually go up to another person whom I have harmed and ask/beg forgiveness for past transgressions seems like an incomprehensible task to undertake. And yet I know that regardless of what I need to do today, my Higher Power will give me the strength (grace) to do it.

Asking forgiveness, in a sense, is really a survival tactic. Many of the wrongs I did to other people were done out of resentment for who the other person was, or what they had that I didn't. We know from the program that holding onto resentments is one of the quickest ways of getting back into active using. Resentments foment and boil within us. They consume our every waking moment, and oftentimes even find their ways into our dreams at night. We can only continue on our road to recovery by letting go of those past hurts, by confronting them straight on, and by seeking to make amends wherever humanly possible. We do this with only one caution: that making the amends causes no further injury.

Prayer and Action

God, the list seems so long, the wrongs so many. It will take a lifetime to make amends and ask forgiveness for all the trouble I have caused. Help me not to be overwhelmed with the formidable task ahead of me. Help me to do this as I must do all of my responsibilities, one day at a time. Just for today help me to....

Today I will....

_____

_____

_____

_____

_____

_____

_____

_____

_____

_____

_____

DAY 13

I will continue to take a personal inventory.

Would that there was a magical pill that I could take once and for all and cure all the problems in my life. Would that once I willingly handed over all my defects to my Higher Power that they would not return and actually reoccur sometimes in multiplicity of forms even uglier than old ones I was so comfortable with. Would that I was able to purge myself of all that was loathsome and repugnant in my personality.

There may not be a magical pill to do all this once and for all, but there is a tried and true formula that can work on a daily basis. In my daily prayer and reflective moments, if I honestly take a careful inventory of my actions for the day, I have the opportunity to see patterns and areas of my life in need of change. And if I do that on a daily basis instead of sweeping those harmful actions under the rug, then they won't pile up on my shoulders, weighing me down as they did in my past addictive life.

In my fourth and fifth steps I cleared the skeletons and cobwebs out of my life. By continuing to take an honest inventory of my life on a daily basis, I can continue to change and grow in small ways rather than waiting for the ax to fall and have to undergo major reconstructive surgery.

Prayer and Action

God, help me to stay close to the program and to work the steps. My life is so much simpler when I do just that. To spend a few minutes every day focusing on what I've done or haven't done helps me to be of single purpose: to do your will in everything. Help me not to be afraid to honestly review my day's actions. It is only when I can be honest and open with myself that I can change and grow for the better. Just for today help me to....

Today I will....

_____

_____

_____

_____

_____

_____

_____

_____

_____

_____

DAY 14

When I was wrong I promptly admitted it.

A good friend in the program indicated that there were three words he never heard when he was growing up from the adults in his family: I was wrong. Many of us in recovery have a hard time vocalizing those three little powerful words. They point to our humanness and our frailty. We make mistakes, but we don't like to admit to them because it is a blatant reminder that we aren't perfect. We always knew the way things should go. We always knew how everything should be played out. How could we ever admit to making mistakes? That would make us lose face. We wouldn't be in total control. The chink in our armor would be a sign of imperfection.

To promptly admit we are wrong when we *are* wrong is actually the normal way to act. It's the way things are supposed to be handled. To admit one's frailties, to seek forgiveness and to learn from one's mistakes—this is the way normal people try to live their lives. We need to do it because that's the way we're supposed to do things. We are simply getting in sync with the way things are normally done. Why were we always a little out of step with the rest of humanity? Why did we always have to keep everything a secret? It's so much simpler to do things like everyone else!

Doing things promptly is a nice new experience too. We had put off everything we possibly could in our lives. We procrastinated to the point of inaction. How nice not to agonize over every little detail and stand up and take ownership for what we've done.

Prayer and Action

God, it's such a nice feeling to be up front and open about the things I have done in my life, even the wrongs I've committed. Give me the strength to let my life be an open book. Give me the strength to attempt to do things correctly the first time so I don't have to spend a lot of my time apologizing. Just for today help me to....

Today I will....

_____

_____

_____

_____

_____

_____

_____

_____

_____

DAY 15

I sought through prayer and meditation to improve my conscious contact with my Higher Power.

For most of us, in our active using days there was little time for prayer or reflection. The most we could muster was the occasional prayer of remorse never to do "that" again or the feeble plea to die quickly in our sleep. Most of us had become Deists at best. To pray to a loving God meant we had to have a relationship to that deity. We had to acknowledge our finiteness and our dependency on that Power greater than we. We already did that with our drug of choice. We spent our waking moments thinking about using. Did we have enough? Where were we going to get some, if we didn't? When could we get away from work so we could do what we really wanted to do? Total concentration and dependence upon something greater than ourselves. Isn't that worship? Why did we need to pray to God? We already had a God of our choice: the almighty alcohol and drugs.

Today it is so nice to be able to kneel down and acknowledge in prayer that there is a loving Higher Power who has always been there, even in our darkest moments. It is so nice to acknowledge that there is a God who is in charge, and that we don't have to be. It is so nice to be able to ask a Strength greater than we are for help and not have to do everything by ourselves.

Prayer and Action

God, thank you for being there—supporting, loving and gracing me. It is so nice to have a true relationship with you in prayer. I am so grateful that there is a loving God like you and that I don't have to flounder out here by myself. Just for today help me to....

Today I will....

_____

_____

_____

_____

_____

_____

_____

_____

_____

_____

_____

_____

DAY 16

...with a God as I understood Him...

What an interesting concept—to pray to a God as I have to understand that God in my life. I am to make that God mine. My own personal God. I am not to pray to the God of my parents. I am not to pray to the God I was told about by other people. So often, we addictive people have a vision of a vengeful, destructive God who metes out justice with an iron fist.

The program teaches us that we are children of a loving Higher Power. We're told that God doesn't make junk. We're given a few principles to use to formulate our own concept of what God is like. We're given the go-ahead to develop our own relationship with that God based on our own standards. We're encouraged not just to mumble rote prayers to a distant God, but to take the time and effort to foster a deep and lasting relationship with a Higher Power, who has always been there loving us and gracing us, even in our darkest and loneliest moments.

What I have come to discover is that the God of my parents and of my tradition was really my own God too. I just had to take ownership and truly work on the relationship that I had ignored for so long a time.

Prayer and Action

God, I pray to you not because my parents told me to. I pray to you not because I have some fear of going to hell. I pray to you because I have come to realize you are the source of my strength. You are the one that I can turn to no matter what the problem, no matter what the situation. I have come to believe that only when I stay close to the program and to you, my life has a peacefulness to it. Just for today help me to....

Today I will....

_____

_____

_____

_____

_____

_____

_____

_____

_____

_____

DAY 17

I pray for knowledge of God's will and the power to do it.

Your will, not mine. What an interesting concept. For so much of our life in active addiction we spent all our time wondering what's in it for us. What do *we* get out of whatever's going on? *I want it. I want it all, and I want it now. So stay out of my way, or be sorry.* As alcoholics, in one sense, we fit in so well. *Give me, give me, give me.*

Your will, not mine. What an interesting way to live out one's life. It's so much more rewarding to reach out to another in forming a relationship. It's so gratifying to try to be pleasing to another. It just seems like the right thing to do when we seriously look at all God has done for us. We have been given our lives back in recovery. There is not a thing we could do without God's support and help. We couldn't even breathe in and out without God's grace to do it. It just makes sense to attempt to do God's will, to do it God's way.

And what is it that God wants of us? We don't have to sit around pondering a great deal to figure that one out. We're called to live soberly and reach out to those around us in love and concern.

We're not called to do heroic deeds, so that some day a great building will be named after us. We're called to be of service to those around us. We're called to show to others some of the love that has been so graciously bestowed on us.

Pretty simple stuff: to do the will of the one who created us out of love, because the one who caused us into being will also be there at our side showering us with the power to do his will.

Prayer and Action

God, your will, not mine. My words and prayers could be longer but the plea would be no different. Just for today help me to....

Today I will....

_____

_____

_____

_____

_____

_____

_____

_____

_____

_____

DAY 18

I had a spiritual awakening because of these steps.

It's not crystal clear, but it's so much clearer than it was before. These steps call us to get out of our selfishness. They give us guidelines to live life the way most "normal" people lead their lives—reaching out not only to other people for help and support, but also recognizing the importance that God plays in our lives. So this is what it's all about. It's all right to be human, with all the foibles and imperfections that our nature brings with it. We have a loving God who puts loving people in our path to help and direct us. No matter what we have to go through today, we can handle it because our Higher Power is there helping, supporting, guiding and pointing the way. We don't have to fortify ourselves with mind-altering substances, for God gives us all the fortification we will ever need.

Prayer and Action

God, never be far from me, for all that I need is pure gift from you, for me to use without fear of running short. Just for today help me to....

Today I will....

_____

_____

DAY 19

I try to carry this message to other alcoholics.

What is gift, I must give to others, for it is in giving that I receive. What a blessed gift I have in this fellowship. On any given day, at any given moment of that day I can call upon another person in recovery for the help and support I need to not use, just for today. They are there for my asking. What I have been blessed with is not just for my own gratification. I can't just use it all up for myself. I have been blessed with sobriety so that I can do the will of the one who created me. I must be of service to others, especially of those most in need. When I cried out for help, the hand of A.A. was there to hold and comfort me. My arms and my hands and my whole being must be there to help boost up those who have finally reached their bottom, who have gone as low as they can go in their active addiction. It is only by banding and bonding together that we will collectively have the strength to not "pick up" just for today. I must carry the message to other alcoholics for it is the only way that I can live in sobriety—by reaching out and not turning in upon myself and my addictions.

Prayer and Action

God, some days I just don't feel like reaching out and being of service. Some days I just feel like rolling up into a ball and shunning the rest of the world. Help me to remember that when I was in desperate need, the hand of A.A. was there to give me the support I needed. Just for today help me to....

Today I will....

_____

_____

_____

_____

_____

_____

_____

_____

_____

_____

_____

_____

_____

_____

DAY 20

I must practice these principles in all my affairs.

There's one thing I know: When I was out there drinking and using, nothing went my way. My life was in constant upheaval. I had no control. I hated myself and wanted it all to end. I saw no way out. Today, in sobriety, my life is going a lot better than I could ever have imagined. I would rather have one day in sobriety than a thousand years drunk.

The formula for daily success seems to be: Don't pick up; pray and follow the steps. Every day that I have done those three little things, the day has been great. It may not always go the way I want, but the day is great and I get through it. I have no desire to mess with the formula.

There's a saying in the program: If you keep doing the same thing over and over again, you're going to get the same results. I like the results I get from doing these three things over and over again, so I'm going to keep doing them. And I've learned that they have the same wonderful effect when I work them in all my affairs.

Prayer and Action

God, what a blessing to have a program and the fellowship to fall back on. They are just examples of the many ways you love and support me. May I never forget where I came from. May I never forget how rewarding

my life is when I practice these principles in all that I do.
Just for today help me to....

Today I will....

_____

_____

_____

_____

_____

_____

_____

_____

_____

_____

_____

_____

_____

_____

_____

DAY 21
The Twelve Steps...

In my active drinking and addictions I hated rules and regulations. I hated being told what to do. Rules were to be broken. They were meant for everyone else but not for me. The ten commandments seemed so archaic. They might have been good for the time and culture for which they were designed, but they certainly were too outmoded for me and my libertine way of living. And what did bosses know? They were from another generation, from an outmoded era.

The only good rule I knew was that I deserved a drink and nobody was going to take that right from me.

Even in recovery, I'm not all that gung ho on lots of rules and regulations. Why then twelve more steps to follow?

I try not to look at them as rules or regulations but as a way of life. They are a gentle guide that points the direction in which I need to be going. I often think of the steps as fence posts that surround a forty-acre plot of land out back. I can roam all around the forty acres as long as I keep within the twelve posts. And if the forty acres aren't enough, it can be a thousand-acre parcel of land that I roam in, being always conscious of the twelve posts within which I must stay.

Within the program I have guides and I have freedoms. And the way to keep both in balance is, just for today, not to pick up.

Prayer and Action

God, when I look carefully at the ten commandments
that you crafted so beautifully and gave to our spiritual
ancestors, and when I honestly look at the twelve steps
that the program offers me as a way of life, I discover
that they are almost identical paths leading us to your
doorstep. Help me not to stray past these guides to life.
Just for today help me to....

Today I will....

_____

_____

_____

_____

_____

_____

_____

_____

_____

_____

_____

_____

DAY 22
The sleeping tiger...

Our disease is cunning and baffling. It's hard to get a handle on it. We want it cured once and for all. But just when we think we have it under control and we understand the ins and outs of the problem, it rears its ugly head. Sometimes it reappears in its old familiar forms of persons, places and things. Sometimes it sneaks its way in through a back door disguised and thinly veiled in new forms and shapes.

In recovery, our disease is often described as a sleeping tiger. A wild, untamed, crafty, unpredictable animal who is resting, gaining strength, plotting and planning for the next violent assault on our sober and clean recovery. An animal, who, if we slacken our vigilance and let our guard down, will massacre and devour the fledgling remnants of sanity that we have left.

For the most part, our real line of defense is gathering together in a fellowship of strength with others susceptible to the periodic onslaughts of possible relapse.

Prayer and Action

God, I pray you, keep the tiger sleeping. Help me to be daily ever vigilant lest I fall prey to a surprise attack or lulled into a nonnegotiable surrender, a seduction by the disease. Just for today help me to....

Today I will....

_____

_____

_____

_____

_____

_____

_____

_____

_____

_____

_____

_____

_____

_____

_____

_____

_____

DAY 23

Getting into the program (whatever it takes)...

Many of us catch on and get into the program when we have hit bottom. We can't take the pain and the destructive nature of our lives, and we seek treatment and/or A.A. fellowship and the program it offers.

Some of us need the direct intervention of concerned and worried people around us to tell us that, though we may not be sick and tired of the way we are living and affecting the people around us, they are. Some of us need to be told in no uncertain words that we need help and we are going to get it no matter what.

Our life and our actions have become unacceptable. Our addiction to alcohol and drugs has become life threatening, not only to ourselves but also to others who have to live and work with us.

For most of us, there then comes such a great sense of relief in the knowledge that finally we can openly deal with that awful monkey on our back that had a death hold on our lives. What a wonderful (and scary) feeling it is to talk about the disease that always wanted everything to be kept a secret so that our shame and guilt would be just one more good excuse to drink and use more, to cover up more and more and to deaden the pain more and more.

On our own, by intervention or just by accident, after only a few days in the program, we know that it was worth it.

Prayer and Action

God, help me to always remember what it was really
like out there, drinking and using. I don't want to lose
the serenity and peace I have been offered in recovery.
It is a most precious gift you have graced me with. Just
for today help me to....

Today I will....

_____

_____

_____

_____

_____

_____

_____

_____

_____

_____

_____

_____

DAY 24

Getting a friend into the program...

Sobriety came to me through a direct intervention by people who loved me and were concerned about me more than I was about myself. In fact, I had long before reconciled myself to the fact that I would drink myself to death.

While I was in a lengthy recovery/treatment program at an in-patient center, a good friend and drinking partner convinced herself that upon my immediate reentry into society, I would whisk her off to an A.A. meeting and thus save her from her own pain- and suffering-filled life. Her use escalated over the time of my in-patient treatment. An overshadowing fear of that fatal day when she could never drink again loomed over her. She dreaded the thought of changing her life forever.

The day I returned from treatment she was sure her drinking days were over because she presumed that I would drag her to a meeting. Actually a good month passed and I never once suggested or demanded that she follow me to a meeting. (Imposed abstinence seldom produces anything more than a frustrated and embittered dry drunk.)

One morning around 3 A.M., she reached her bottom and phoned, begging for help out of the bottomless pit we alcoholics all find ourselves in one day. The next day the walls of the pit were scaled with the loving hands that reached out to her from the fellowship of A.A. Together we went to her first A.A. meeting. She wasn't kicking and fighting. She went timidly, hoping that the monkey would loosen its death hold from around her life. It did.

In our own time. At our own pace. The program works only for those who want it, and not for all who need it.

Prayer and Action

God, why was *I* gifted with sobriety today and not others? Although I don't really want the answer to that question, I don't want to lose your precious gift. May I never forget the bottomless pit whence I came. Just for today help me to....

Today I will....

_____

_____

_____

_____

_____

_____

_____

_____

DAY 25

Thinking too much and not working the program (a friend who died)...

The first person I ever sponsored was a young, intelligent man who was a computer genius and had had a few years of college. He had a probing mind. Why did we do it this way? Why were there twelve steps and not another number? Why were some people addicted and others not? Why, why, why?

He wanted answers to everything and seemed to want scientific proof before he was willing to accept things on their face value. Oftentimes he would even indicate he had a better way to deal with his disease. He drifted in and out of the program, never staying all that long. Wanting it but never quite getting it.

One morning, while reading the local paper, I noticed an article about a young, nameless man the police had found shot to death just outside a bar, where he had last been seen alive. It was the young man who had once asked me to be his sponsor.

We have to keep our program simple. Some questions will never be fully answered. But we know that the program does work, if *we* work it.

Prayer and Action

God, I pray for those who are still out there. I pray for those who have gone out and not come back. I pray for those who have died as a direct result of this all-consuming disease we have. May I never forget the hard lessons I have learned. Just for today help me to....

Today I will....

_____

_____

_____

_____

_____

_____

_____

_____

_____

_____

_____

_____

_____

_____

DAY 26

I know what I have to do!
(a friend who's still out there)...

I have a friend who has been around the program longer than I. He comes in, surrenders, stays around for a few months and then goes back out. "I know what I have to do," he tells me. And he does. He's got the jargon down cold. He even throws in a lot of stuff about how his Higher Power is in his life.

Every time he disappears, I want to search him out and shake some sense into him, because I know what's best for him. I want to save him because I see what great potential he has. I know what he has to do, and I want to make him do it for his own good.

The program has taught me that I can't fix everything and everyone. The only one I can do anything about is myself. I need to be single-minded in my own recovery program and not allow extraneous frustrations and disappointments to get in the way of my own sobriety. I can be there, but I can't save. I don't like that, but that's the way real life is played out. Part of my program is to accept the way things are—the things I have no control over.

Prayer and Action

God, help me to remain focused on my own recovery and not fret about what is really not my concern. I need to be single-minded, for my own relapse is but a drink away. I place in your hands all those who need this program but don't really want it. Just for today help me to....

Today I will....

_____

_____

_____

_____

_____

_____

_____

_____

_____

_____

_____

_____

DAY 27
Staying in today...

One of the great gifts the program has given to me is the possibility of staying in the present. Until I started working the steps I spent a lot of time and energy worrying about the past and when it would catch up with me. I was always looking over my shoulder, fearful my misdeeds would eventually be brought to light and my past would do me in. Don't tell anyone anything, or they might use it against you, said the constant voice whispering in my ears. I spent a lot of time covering up the past.

I spent a lot of time thinking about the future, wondering and worrying about how I was going to balance everything, so my house of cards wouldn't fall, leaving me with a huge mess on my hands. In my mind I would have long and detailed discussions with myself, choreographing conversations I would have with people: what I would say, what they would say, what I would say in retort. Conversations that would never take place in reality...ever.

Worrying about the past catching up, plotting out future fictitious events, never living or dealing with the present—it was a futile balancing act that became more and more immersed in the intricacies of deceit and cover-up, fear and paranoia.

Thank God, through the program I can put the past to rest and not concern myself with anything beyond today. It's nice to live in today and savor all the events as they unfold before me, minute by minute.

Prayer and Action

God, thank you for giving me the program that teaches me to live in the present and not fear the past or worry about the future. The past cannot be changed. The future may never be. The present is gift itself to be savored and relished. Just for today help me to....

Today I will....

_____

_____

_____

_____

_____

_____

_____

_____

_____

_____

_____

_____

_____

DAY 28

Thankfulness
(I'm glad I'm an alcoholic. It answers a lot of questions.)

There are lots of things I am grateful for in my life. The program itself is pure gift. It has enabled me to have close contact with my Higher Power. I have been given my life back, sober and clean, with all the wonderful opportunities it offers me on a daily basis.

If I were to single out one thing I was particularly grateful about, it would be the fact that I am an alcoholic. I have been called a lot of things in my life, some good, some bad. I have, from earliest recollection, felt out of step, out of sync, with the rest of the world. The term *alcoholic* seems to fit like an old comfortable shoe. It answers a lot of the questions and fills in a lot of the gaps. Finally I know why my crazy past was just that—crazy. I am an alcoholic, plain and simple. It all finally makes sense. It doesn't solve the problems, but it at least points me in the right direction.

On a daily basis, I can do something about the problem by not picking up, working the steps, staying close to the fellowship and praying.

Prayer and Action

God, I never wanted to be one, but I sure am glad that's precisely what I am today. Today, knowing why I did the crazy things I did, is all right. Being an alcoholic means I have a terrific support system at my fingertips. It means I have a program that offers me a way of life free from any mind-altering substances. I am free to do your will without reserve. Just for today help me to....

Today I will....

_____

_____

_____

_____

_____

_____

_____

_____

_____

_____

_____

_____

_____

DAY 29
I knew he was an alcoholic.

Back in the late '60s, during my postgraduate days of theological study, we were allowed off-campus, but there was a curfew. As I recall, every Friday night five or six of us would sneak off from our dorm via an outdoor fire escape. Dressed in dark-colored clothing so as not to be easily observed, we would traipse through the cemetery that surrounded our seminary and arrive at a pub located conveniently behind a gas station. There, crouched down in the booth farthest from any window, we would down pitchers of beer one after another. Every time a car would pull into the parking lot of the bar we would slink down even further into the recesses of our booth, fearing that our school authorities had caught on to our antics.

When our money ran out we would meander back through the cemetery, tripping and falling over the tombstones that seemed to barricade easy access back to school. One guy in our group would eventually fall down on the ground. Rolling around, he would quote verses from Shakespeare. I knew he had a problem. It never occurred to me that I might have a problem too. After all, I could hold my liquor. I didn't quote poetry while rolling all over the ground. I could still mostly stand on my own.

How cunning and baffling the disease is that it only lets us see what it wants us to see. We see a problem, but it is always in someone else. I knew he had a problem, but it took twenty-five more years for me to see that I was an alcoholic.

Prayer and Action

God, keep my head clear and my eyes open that I may always see and be able to deal with the truth in my life. Please don't let me cloak things over in secrecy, for that is usually the path back to active using. Just for today help me to....

Today I will....

_____

_____

_____

_____

_____

_____

_____

_____

_____

_____

_____

_____

_____

DAY 30

G.O.D.
(Good Orderly Direction)

For many years of my active addiction, only the most formal prayers of my faith could be recited. Any thought of a personalized prayer to a loving God had been obliterated by the need to worship wholeheartedly the spirit within the bottle of the day. My days and my life had turned into chaos, totally disrupted by the primary need to have a drink.

What a blessing to become sober and discover a Higher Power concerned about my well-being and offering me, through the program of A.A., the opportunity to lead a life filled with Good Orderly Direction. Not a vengeful, hateful, punitive God, but a God offering a way to peace and happiness with a few helpful guideposts set up to show us the way and point the direction.

I find that when I allow this God into my life and want to please him with the way I live my life, I have Good Orderly Direction. And I find the opposite to be true too. When I have Good Orderly Direction in my life, I find I then have God close by my side. And isn't that what I've always wanted? Some stability. Some balance. Some normalcy. Some intimacy with the creator of the big picture. Some direction.

Prayer and Action

God, take me, mold me, form me, shape me, direct me and I shall want for nothing. Just for today help me to....

Today I will....

_____

_____

_____

_____

_____

_____

_____

_____

_____

_____

_____

_____

_____

DAY 31
Pointing the finger...

It wasn't my fault. They made me do it. He talked me into it. I was tricked into it. I never had a chance. It was my circumstances that were against me. No one gave me a chance. The odds were always against me. My genes weren't the right mix. My family was never supportive. No one really understood the troubles I had. I never had a break. They were always picking on me. I never got a fair shake. If only things had been different. If only someone believed in me.

Since joining A.A. I have discovered that whenever I point the finger there are always three other fingers pointing back in my direction.

Prayer and Action

God, help me to take responsibility for my life and not always find a scapegoat for my troubles and circumstances. Just for today help me to....

Today I will....

_____

_____

_____

_____

DAY 32
This too shall pass.

Sometimes it's a commercial on TV that does it. Sometimes it's an outside billboard. Sometimes it's being too close to the old, familiar people, places and things. Sometimes it's because I worked too hard, or I'm too tired, or because I feel frustrated over being between a rock and a hard place. Sometimes it's because it's a happy day, or a particularly sad day, or any of the other old excuses. Sometimes it's just because something inside tells me I can handle it now. Every once in a while I get this undying urge to take a drink. Not lots of drinks...just a drink.

Two things usually cross my mind when I'm in that pre-using mood. They are things I learned early on in recovery. First, I never had just a drink. Second, an undying urge usually lasts about ten seconds. If I use that time to stall by praying or calling another person in recovery, it will pass as quickly as it appeared.

I have to be vigilant of the triggers that, once pulled, would always result in a day, or even days, of uncontrolled, excessive drinking.

Prayer and Action

God, one is too many, and a thousand not enough. I never had just one drink. Help me to resist this urge, for I know that it, too, will pass. Just for today help me to....

Today I will....

_____

_____

_____

_____

_____

_____

_____

_____

_____

_____

_____

_____

_____

_____

_____

_____

_____

_____

DAY 33
Dangling over the edge...

I loved living on the fringe. I loved dangling over the edge. There was a real exhilaration in living dangerously. Life was so boring. A few drinks got some life back into what was usually a pretty dull existence. The more absurd, the more outlandish, the better. It seemed as if all the stops had been pulled out. Each new day called for new and more inventively bizarre ploys to keep from becoming bored to death. Drinking loosened things up. Drinking put a little zip into what was usually the humdrum. Drinking gave a rose tint and a sweet taste to things.

Recovery brought some welcome changes. Perceptions changed. Taking life on life's terms became exciting. Dangling over the edge became downright dangerous. The conversations of drunks seemed inane. The antics of the drinking-impaired were ludicrous and stupid. Recovery enhanced and heightened the experiences found naturally in reality.

Prayer and Action

God, thank you for giving me the eyes to see sunsets as you designed them. Thank you for the beauty of a smiling face. Thank you for intimate conversations full of laughter and tender moments of exchange. Thank you for allowing me to see your creation with sober, clear eyes free of the blurring that drinking always brought me. Just for today help me to....

Today I will....

_____

_____

_____

_____

_____

_____

_____

_____

_____

_____

_____

_____

_____

_____

_____

_____

_____

DAY 34
Be good to yourself.

Somewhere, sometime we crossed over that imaginary line and became in our own mind's eye the worst of the worst. At some point in our alcoholic drinking we stopped really looking into the mirror, afraid of and revolted by the face and the person behind the face that was staring back at us. At some point in our drinking career our actions disgusted and repulsed even ourselves.

Being our own worst enemy, we judged and condemned ourselves to a living hell where the past goes unforgiven. Unredeemable, we wandered aimlessly through the present, knowing that the future held nothing but despair.

Recovery lifts the veil of secrecy and gloom. We discover that we are good and lovable. We rejoice that God didn't make any junk. Our actions may have been repugnant, but we ourselves aren't. We are worthy of some joy, peace and happiness in our lives.

In recovery we have an obligation to be good to ourselves lest we fall prey to demons of despair that the spirits of our alcoholic drinking unleashed.

Prayer and Action

God, for so many years in my active using I prayed that I would die in my sleep. Thank you for my days in recovery. Now I can't wait to see what wonderful experiences each new day will bring. Just for today help me to....

Today I will....

_____

_____

_____

_____

_____

_____

_____

_____

_____

_____

_____

_____

_____

_____

_____

DAY 35
It's a disease.

During the first weeks of recovery it was difficult to accept the fact that I was an alcoholic. It seemed like a shameful lack of moral fiber that stigmatized me.

One day I was in the doctor's office getting some sort of checkup. The doctor had a soft-spoken, kindly way about him. He may have detected my apprehension during this procedure. Reassuringly he said to me, "You know you've got a disease. It's alcoholism. It's not your fault that you have this disease. But now that you know you've got it, you've got a responsibility to do something about it."

Those soft-spoken words made all the difference. It's a disease, not a moral problem. And the nice thing about this disease is that I don't have to take pills for the rest of my life to counteract it. I just don't need to put any type of mind-altering substances in my body.

I'm glad I'm an alcoholic.

Prayer and Action

God, thank you for putting people like that doctor in my life to help point the way. Just for today help me to....

Today I will....

_____

_____

_____

_____

_____

_____

_____

_____

_____

_____

_____

_____

_____

_____

_____

_____

DAY 36
One day at a time...

I want it. I want it all, and I want it right now.

I want to be free of this disease. I want the sobriety of a thirty-year veteran. I want happiness and total peace. I want everyone to like me. I want things to go my way. I want these defects in my life to go away right now. I want balance and tranquility. I don't want to wait. A lot of things come too slowly. Some don't seem to come at all.

One step at a time. One day at a time. In God's time. In God's way. According to God's plan.

Prayer and Action

God, so often I get antsy and want everything to be perfect all the time. Sometimes I forget that the program doesn't promise me an idyllic life, only a chance to do the best I can soberly. Just for today help me to....

Today I will....

_____

_____

_____

_____

DAY 37
Being apart from...

When I was out there actively drinking and using I felt a disconnectedness in my life. Sometimes I felt like two different people, a good person and a bad person. There was a public side to me as well as a secret side of me. There was a me who functioned in the light of day and a me who roamed around in the shadows of the dark side. I couldn't look at myself in the mirror. There were times when I felt like ripping my chest open and climbing out of the person I had become. I didn't want to spend time with myself.

When I was out there actively drinking and drugging, I began not wanting to be around people. They asked too many questions. They got into too much of my business. They took up too much of my time. I even stopped wanting to be around the people I drank and drugged with. They used too much of the stuff I had stored up for my own consumption.

When I was out there drinking and drugging I stopped praying to God. My rationalization was that I was not good enough and that God really wasn't interested in me anyway.

Alone and apart from. Not feeling I had my act together. Not even liking myself. Not at all comfortable with who I was. Not wanting to be around people for fear they would find out what I was really like. Not wanting to be around other addictive people because they wanted what I needed for myself. Not wanting a relationship with God, for I already had the spirit I adored with all my energy and being.

Thank God for recovery—the loneliness abates.

Prayer and Action

God, let me never be separated from you again. I rely on you for support and guidance and succor and grace. Help me never to drift apart from you again. Just for today help me to....

Today I will....

_____

_____

_____

_____

_____

_____

_____

_____

_____

_____

DAY 38
Being a part of...

Deep down in my being I think I have always longed to be a part of whatever was going on. In my active addiction the feeling of separation seems to have been a dominant perception and experience. I felt out of step with everyone else. I didn't even feel much like being with myself. God seemed so distant and unapproachable that I felt totally separated from him. I longed to be whole, to be a part of, and all I experienced was separation and aloneness.

Thank God for these sobering days in recovery. Today I can look into the mirror and like the person who is looking back. I don't mind being with myself in quiet moments of reflection and relaxation. Today I like being with people. I like having them around, and I enjoy the support and friendship I can share with them. Today I can be in relationship and feel connected to that which is bigger than I am. Today I feel part of the bigger picture. I sense a connectedness with the universe and the Higher Power who created and sustains it all. Today I can pray to the God of my choosing and feel his loving presence gracing my life.

Today I am *a part of* instead of *apart from.*

Prayer and Action

God, one day sober is of more value than a lifetime drunk. I relish feeling good about myself. I am grateful that I have people in my life to share the beauty of the day. Being able to hand my day over to you is a blessing in itself. Just for today help me to....

Today I will....

_____

_____

_____

_____

_____

_____

_____

_____

_____

_____

_____

_____

_____

_____

DAY 39

H.A.L.T.
(Hungry, Angry, Lonely, Tired)

I don't have them often, but there are some days when absolutely nothing seems to be going right no matter what I do. Nothing goes the way it should. There are pitfalls every step of the way. On those days I seem to be edgy, moody, easily bothered. It is at those times that my program teaches me to stop and evaluate what's going on. H.A.L.T. Usually when I step back for a moment to review the day thus far, it happens that I'm not taking care of myself as I should be. Most of those times I'm either hungry, angry, lonely or tired. And I discover that when I address those issues in my life, the rest of the day goes far better.

Prayer and Action

God, why didn't I think of that simple stuff before? I could have saved myself a whole lot of trouble. Thanks for the simple aids I learn by regularly going to my meetings and staying close to other people who are in quality recovery. Just for today help me to....

Today I will....

_____

_____

DAY 40
Thankfulness

I am thankful to be alive, sober and relatively well. I am thankful I have a program to fall back upon. I am grateful I am an alcoholic and that I have an understanding of what all that craziness was about when I was out there actively using. I am grateful for the friends and family who continue to love and support me. I am grateful that I can pray and feel my Higher Power's presence in my life. I am so grateful that on a daily basis I can get through a day without using any mind-altering substance. I am grateful for my senses and emotions, for my breath and heartbeats. I am grateful for every experience and sensation I have. I am grateful for the growth and changes occurring in my life. I am grateful for who I am now and who I will become in the future. I am grateful for every moment I have been blessed with, for they are all pure gift from a loving and concerned God.

Prayer and Action

God, thank you for every sober breath I take. It has made all the difference. Just for today help me to....

Today I will....

_____

_____

DAY 41
Resentments

They say we are as healthy as our deepest resentment. They tell us that holding onto resentments is the quickest way back to using actively.

Holding on to resentments sure does cause a lot of havoc and upheaval in my life. When I hold on to a resentment it festers and foments and consumes a lot of the time and energy that I could be using for more productive purposes.

When I look at the resentments I've had/have, I find they usually eat away at my insides and ruin my day, and sometimes even weeks on end. They seldom have an effect on the people I'm having such hateful thoughts about. Oftentimes they don't even have a clue about the vicious thoughts I'm harboring for them, and if they did know, it probably would cause them to lose little, if any, sleep.

Resentments are a form of self-indulgence. I spend an inordinate amount of time licking my exaggerated wounds and feeling sorry for myself. They cause me to live in a fantasy rather than the here and now, doing what I really should be doing—changing and growing rather than reverting to infantile overreactions.

Prayer and Action

God, resentments are hard things to hand over and give up. They were such constant companions for the many years I was out there drinking and using. They were wonderful reasons for drinking—being so misunderstood and sometimes even hated. Give me the strength to hand them over quickly so that they don't fester and boil over and bring me one step closer to a relapse. Just for today help me to....

Today I will....

_____

_____

_____

_____

_____

_____

_____

_____

_____

_____

_____

_____

DAY 42

The common welfare of all should come first.

Traditions form an important part of our lives. They help guide us in our interactions with one another. They set up principles that help us to interact more easily without stepping on one another's toes. They allow us to spend more time and energy doing what we should be doing rather than worrying about who's doing what and why.

This first tradition is extremely important. This is a program of mutual support. We know we can't lick this disease by ourselves. Each of us tried that for so many years, vowing never again, only to repeatedly break that promise, sometimes in the same breath. Together, we can stand tall and sober. Divided, we only wallow in the misery of one broken promise after another.

Let the outreached hand of A.A. be there to help the next one in need. It was there for me. It will only work if I am there stretching my hand in support, too. Together we can, apart we die.

Prayer and Action

God, sometimes I am so tired and don't feel like going out at night for a meeting and fellowship. Sometimes I don't feel like reaching out to one more newcomer. On those occasions help me to remember how important it is for me to have the group for my support and sobriety.

The group's well-being means my well-being. Just for today help me to....

Today I will....

_____

_____

_____

_____

_____

_____

_____

_____

_____

_____

_____

_____

_____

DAY 43

My personal recovery depends upon A.A. unity.

From time to time one hears about splinter groups forming with new approaches to handle the disease we have. Some less daring groups want to totally revamp the program from within.

What we have discovered in the more than sixty years of its existence is that the program works. We have a common problem; we're united in it. We are cautioned to have a singleness of purpose. When we are united on that front there is little that can whittle away at our resolve. Oneness in thought, action and fellowship keeps us centered on the problem and the solution instead of being sidetracked with nit-picking incidentals that can erode our purpose from within.

Being a part of anything is an important need of the human psyche. Maintaining unity with other people facing similar problems is a tried and true method to find support and strength in dealing honestly with what, when experienced alone, seem like insurmountable obstacles.

Prayer and Action

God, keep me centered on dealing with changing my *life,* not the *program,* to suit my ways. Unity, oneness, singleness of purpose bring stability into my life. One of the few places I experience that is at the meetings I attend in A.A. May it always be that way for me and for others in need of its help. Just for today help me to....

Today I will....

_____

_____

_____

_____

_____

_____

_____

_____

_____

_____

_____

_____

_____

_____

DAY 44

There is but one ultimate authority—a loving God.

We aren't very good at accepting authority, no matter who assumes that role. We aren't very good at dishing it out, and we're not at all interested in kowtowing to Napoleonic personalities similar to our own. No one is ultimately in charge but a loving God—wise words from those obviously wise people who formulated these traditions.

We spent a lot of our active drinking days playing God. We knew all the answers. We knew what everyone else should be doing. It was a hard balancing act to keep up. Thank goodness the program puts things back the way they should be in life's natural scheme. There is a God who is loving and concerned, who created and set in motion the rules of the universe. It seems logical that God be the ultimate authority. It seems logical that we attempt to do God's will rather than impose our ill-contrived will on others.

Prayer and Action

God, thank you for being you and doing your job. Help me to be who I am and to do my job, which is to carry out your will the best that I can. Just for today help me to....

Today I will....

_____

_____

_____

_____

_____

_____

_____

_____

_____

_____

_____

_____

_____

_____

_____

_____

_____

DAY 45

The group conscience...

We have the Big Book, the twelve steps and traditions that help guide us in our program of recovery. We acquiesce only to the authority of a loving God.

The question comes up though—how do we resolve dilemmas that eventually arise in a grouping of people no matter how like-minded they may be? We claim an ultimate authority (a loving God), but how do we ascertain what that God wants for us? Each of us has his or her own ideas on that question. If one was to purport knowing God's will better than the next, we surely would ignore such ideas as rantings.

Being, as it were, leaderless by intent, we rely on a process of group conscience. Respecting the opinions of all, we can only function when we have a consensus of the majority. We recognize that there is actually more wisdom in the agreement of the whole than in the sum of all the individual views involved. In fact, if we are seriously concerned with the well-being of the people in the group rather than with foisting our own agenda upon them, we demonstrate our belief that the hand of a loving God is intricately involved in our decision making.

Prayer and Action

God, be present with us whenever we have to make decisions for the good of the group. Help us not to be caught up in our own egotistical ways, but to always want what is best to keep us single-minded in purpose. Give us your strength and your wisdom whenever we have to make a decision that affects other people in recovery. Just for today help me to....

Today I will....

_____

_____

_____

_____

_____

_____

_____

_____

_____

_____

_____

_____

_____

DAY 46
To lead is to serve.

Although we don't have people who have positions of authority over us, we do have people who help lead us, as a group, through the structures and formats that we have decided upon. In fact, leading carries with it responsibilities, not power. Our leaders are called upon to facilitate and to be of service. When they do the job to the best of their abilities, they may gain our adulation. When they use their positions to lord it over us, they are, for the most part, ignored.

To lead is to serve. That statement might make a good poster to hang up in many an A.A. meeting room.

Prayer and Action

God, when I am called upon or when I volunteer to do a specific job in the fellowship, help me to do it for the good of the group and not for any self-serving purpose. I know what lording it over another feels like. Help me not to do it to others. Just for today help me to....

Today I will....

_____

_____

_____

DAY 47
Our leaders do not govern.

1. *No one is going to tell me what to do. I don't care who they are, they don't have the right to even think they know better than I what should be done. I've had it up to here with people trying to foist their will on me. I don't have to put up with this.*

2. *I know what's best. I've put my heart and soul into this. I didn't end up in this position for nothing; when I say something, I want it followed. If it isn't done my way, I can take my ball back and go home.*

Two scenarios, one same person—a drunk, dry or sober. Is it any wonder we won't let our leaders govern?

Prayer and Action

God, help me to keep my sense of humor, especially when I am at a meeting that's not going my way. Just for today help me to....

Today I will....

_____

_____

_____

_____

DAY 48

I only need a desire to stop drinking.

Every organization I belong to has rules and regulations, constitutions and bylaws, mission statements and five-year projection plans for development. They have boards and chairs, presidents and treasurers, some even have sergeants-at-arms. In some groups, meetings are obligatory and dues must be paid in advance. In others, special garb is mandatory and the protocol followed goes unquestioned.

What a blessing and a refreshing difference A.A. is. I don't have to conform to the way they've always done it. I don't have to pay dues. I don't have to wear special clothes or show up at the same time and place week after week. No one takes attendance or looks askance as to why I'm there in the first place.

No dues or fees, no rules or regulations. Just a desire to stop drinking. I can do that one day at a time.

Prayer and Action

God, we're an unlikely group of people to be seen together. We probably wouldn't socialize with one another in other circumstances, but thank you that in your divine wisdom you put us together for mutual support in combating our common disease. Just for today help me to....

Today I will....

_____

_____

_____

_____

_____

_____

_____

_____

_____

_____

_____

_____

_____

_____

_____

_____

DAY 49

Our groups are autonomous, except...

Imagine gathering a group of drunks together from all over the country and getting them to agree on how to do everything uniformly. The police would probably have to be called in. Solomon in all his splendor and wisdom would be scratching his head in disbelief, unable to help them come to an amiable accord.

It is wise to let individual groups form and grow and split and even disband autonomously. Self-help groups, especially those saturated with drunks in recovery, are best left uninhibited to work out for themselves the most practical ways to support one another, except (and isn't there always an *except?*) when a certain matter has a direct effect on another group or A.A. as a whole. It rarely comes up, but that's a good *except.*

Prayer and Action

God, I like the idea of handling things on the local level, if at all possible. We would have had to invent the principle for A.A. if no one had thought of it before. Centralization might be good to keep people in check or to cut costs, but not to keep people sober. Just for today help me to....

Today I will....

_____

_____

_____

_____

_____

_____

_____

_____

_____

_____

_____

_____

_____

_____

_____

_____

_____

DAY 50

Our reason for being:
to carry the message...

What's in it for me? What do I get out of this? What about me?

The only way to keep it is to give it away. In all that we do, in all that we say, in all that we are, we must carry the message to those who still suffer. Give selflessly, not take selfishly.

Prayer and Action

God, let me be aware of the needs of others. You have already sated me. Help me to reach out, that what I have, others might benefit from. Just for today help me to....

Today I will....

_____

_____

_____

_____

_____

DAY 51

Problems of money, property and prestige...

Money, property, prestige have always been problematic for me. The more I have, the more I want. The more I have, the more egocentric I become.

Most family fights and jealousies center around these three words. In some families, members stop speaking to one another over just one of these issues.

Is it any wonder that we in A.A. are cautioned to stay away from these matters, lest we become so embroiled in their governance that we forget what our primary purpose is?

Prayer and Action

God, help me to value the life-giving qualities that the program offers me and not lust after the fleeting allurements that distract me from my primary purpose. Just for today help me to....

Today I will....

_____

_____

_____

DAY 52
Pull your own weight.

We're a self-help group. We never really like to depend on anyone for anything. Sometimes though, we like to try to get things for little more than nothing. When we first surrendered to this disease, we indicated we would do anything to keep the monkey off our backs. Then, at some point, we get comfortable in the program and we stop pulling our own weight. We don't contribute when the basket is passed. We don't volunteer when a need arises. We refuse when asked to do something. If we are going to be a single-minded group beholden to no one and swayed by no outside influence, then we must be fully self-supporting. No matter how one looks at that, it means I have to pull my own weight.

Prayer and Action

God, they say you help those who help themselves. Help me to do my part. Just for today help me to....

Today I will....

_____

_____

_____

_____

DAY 53

Never be more than a self-help group.

Every so often we get these crazy ideas that we could make the program so much better if we did this or that to it. If we revamped it, got some professionals in to spruce the terminology up and make the meetings run more smoothly, then the quality of our sobriety might be all the more enhanced.

When it comes down to the bottom line, either we want the sobriety that A.A. offers and are willing to work for it, or we don't. The tried-and-proved process is that we speak and work from our own experience, strength and hope. "Book-smarts" and knowing all the terminology and definitions don't make a person sober. We have to hear how others of like mind have done it and keep doing it. We're a hardheaded group of people. We don't listen to the ones who have the polished answers. We follow the ones who have lived them.

Prayer and Action

God, the program works when I work it. Help me to keep it simple. Just for today help me to....

Today I will....

_____

_____

DAY 54
Don't make a business out of it.

Wouldn't it be great if we got this thing organized? We could spiff it up a bit, get an ad agency and franchise it. Think of the money we could make. Think of the fancy meeting rooms and upscale coffees we could offer. Think of how much more attractive the whole thing would be. We would have people flocking in to be part of it.

How easily we fantasize and get sidetracked. Organizing and running a well-honed operation takes time, effort and energy that could be much better utilized in keeping our disease in check.

Prayer and Action

God, sometimes I get too caught up in the "what ifs" rather than doing what I need to be doing. Help me to keep my life centered. Just for today help me to....

Today I will....

_____

_____

_____

_____

_____

DAY 55

We have no opinion on any other issue.

I pretty much know it all. I can speak on almost any subject. If I don't know something, I can still make it sound like I do.

I have pretty set opinions on everything. I know how everything's supposed to work and what everybody's supposed to be doing with their lives.

I don't stand alone. We alcoholics think pretty much alike. We know just about everything. We have an opinion for every situation. We like to voice our opinions. We've learned, though, that we can't speak for any other person.

Actually, to have an opinion demands conversation and discussion. By voicing our opinions, we put them on the table to have others debate and help us hone our ideas. In A.A. meetings we express our experiences, strengths and hopes. There is no cross talking. There is no discussion. People express what they're feeling and thinking and hoping concerning the disease we have in common. If what one person says is helpful, we take it to heart. If not, we forget about it. Any discussion about anything other than alcoholism and our sobriety has no place within our meeting rooms, within our literature.

We need to stick to our recovery, and keep A.A. out of any affairs that are not consistent with our singleness of purpose. We can't be sidetracked nor allow the program to be.

Prayer and Action

God, I can use all kinds of diversions, even controversy, to keep me from doing what I should be doing. Help me to be single-minded when it comes to my sobriety and recovery program. Just for today help me to....

Today I will....

_____

_____

_____

_____

_____

_____

_____

_____

_____

_____

_____

_____

DAY 56

We're not even interested in public controversy.

We have our own opinions, but we're not a debating club. We like a good lively, spirited conversation, but we're not interested in foisting our ideas or opinions on anyone. We're a self-help group intent on helping our members find peace and sobriety within themselves.

In a real sense, we are not a public entity. We don't care what other people think or think about us. We are not interested in proving anything or defending anything in the public forum. The program works for those who work it.

Within our own meetings, we don't allow for cross talking. Since controversy within our ranks is not allowed to be directly aired in our formal meetings lest we be sidetracked, then surely it shouldn't be dragged out into a public forum for the very same reasons.

Prayer and Action

God, I like the excitement and the feel of adrenaline flowing through my veins when I animatedly try to make a point in a conversation. I love trying to make someone agree with my side of an argument. There is nothing like getting on one side or the other of a heated controversy. But, in my recovery help me to be single-minded and keep controversy out of A.A. and vice versa. Just for today help me to....

Today I will....

_____

_____

_____

_____

_____

_____

_____

_____

_____

_____

_____

_____

_____

_____

_____

_____

_____

DAY 57

We attract rather than promote.

We're the best. We've got the most. We have the latest. You've got to have what we've got to be happy, popular and loved. That might sell cars and deodorant but you can't tout and promote a way of life and have people buy into it. It has to be a way of life that people see working in those who are participating in it.

We attract people to the program by the way the program seems to be working in our lives. They see what we do, how we act, how happy and fulfilled we appear. They see the kind of life we live and want some of that quality in their own.

Actions have always spoken louder than words.

Prayer and Action

God, *I* may be the only Big Book a person in need today "reads." May the words I say be only a reflection of the way I live. Just for today help me to....

Today I will....

_____

_____

_____

DAY 58

Principles ever before personalities...

We hear people say that all the real characters are gone. One only needs to spend a little time in an A.A. meeting to know that's not true. Characters and personalities abound. Some people have wonderful, attractive personalities. Many people gravitate toward those with such winning personalities and are drawn to what they have to say. Some of our "characters" even attract, in other spheres, what one might call groupies.

Charismatic people come and go, and with them usually the people who enthusiastically followed the program because of them. Some people attract cliques. They can, at the least, be divisive.

We need to keep the program simple and open to all. We can't cater to one group or even be selective. Our doors are open to anyone who has a desire to stop drinking.

Following principles is what keeps us sober, not cottoning up to a flamboyant personality that may be here today and out using tomorrow.

Prayer and Action

God, I just enjoy being around some people more than others. I go to meetings not really to be in the company of someone I like, but to get a morsel of truth by which I can live my life today without having to use. Just for today help me to....

Today I will....

_____

_____

_____

_____

_____

_____

_____

_____

_____

_____

_____

_____

_____

_____

DAY 59

Some of the best advice I ever received...

A few weeks before I was to leave my treatment center, one of the counselors came up to me while I was reading the newspaper in the living room and said in a soft whisper, "Do what you have to do and stay out of their business." As she left the room, obviously not interested in carrying the conversation any further, I asked, "Who are *they?*" She only smiled and kept going.

A few days later the scenario was repeated. My recollection is that this happened one more time before my departure.

She never did tell me who *"they"* are.

I have long since discovered on my own that *"they"* is anyone but me. And I have learned that when I stay out of *"their"* business and do what I have to do, my day goes a whole lot better.

Prayer and Action

God, help me to do, on a regular basis, those things in my life that work. When they no longer do, help me to change. Just for today help me to....

Today I will....

_____

_____

_____

_____

_____

_____

_____

_____

_____

_____

_____

_____

_____

_____

_____

_____

_____

DAY 60
A bad day...

Once, early in my recovery, I had an extremely difficult day just prior to going on a trip. Nothing went right. I was ready to end it all and take a drink. Instead, I did what the program suggests and called a friend from the program.

Although I had a few more hours to work before I was to leave on the trip out of town, he suggested I leave immediately. Sometimes, he explained, it was helpful to get out of a tense situation for a while. A half hour removed from a potentially disastrous outcome was usually enough time to retreat and regroup. He quipped about going to the extreme measure of leaving town. The laughter broke some of the spell that the desire to drink had on me at that moment. During my eight-hour trip, I prayed and inventoried the situation, but the desire never really left me. When I arrived at my destination, I went to the first meeting I could find.

I really wanted to talk about my experience, but the leader kept calling on other people to speak. The last person to speak told us about a frustrating day she had had. After wallowing through an extremely bad day, she tried calling her sponsor, only to talk to an answering machine. She called close to ten other people, talking to nine machines and finally to the nonalcoholic roommate of the party she was trying to reach. The roommate said she really didn't know much about it all but remembered that she often overheard her roommate say, "Don't pick up; pray and go to a meeting." That night the woman wanted to tell us that the program works. She hadn't had a drink and the day, with its trouble, had passed.

Like the woman who told this story, I was grateful, too.

Prayer and Action

God, the program works. Help me to work it faithfully every day I am given to live. Just for today help me to....

Today I will....

_____

_____

_____

_____

_____

_____

_____

_____

_____

_____

DAY 61
Sharing my experience...

I've taken my share of science and psychology courses to better understand the functions of both the body and the psyche. I've read many of the popular self-help books churned out to help us put balance in our lives.

And yet, at an A.A. meeting the poignant and right-to-the-point messages come not from polished discourses of lettered people but from meek voices softly speaking from their hearts about the experiences they've had in their lives.

Prayer and Action

God, may I always speak from the heart and listen from the depth of my being to others as they talk honestly about their own life issues. Just for today help me to....

Today I will....

_____

_____

_____

_____

_____

DAY 62
Sharing my strength...

I often thought that there wasn't anything I couldn't do if I put my mind to it. Drink brought me to my knees. I discovered that by myself I was weak and vulnerable. I had no strength, no power over the demon alcohol and its cousin, drugs.

I had to surrender and hand my life over to a power far greater than myself to find the strength within to keep the disease of alcoholism in abeyance. It's amazing that when we totally hand over our lives in a leap of faith, we get it back with the strength and wisdom and power of a loving God so that we can do, with energy to spare, what, alone, we were never able to achieve. My strength comes from my Higher Power on a daily basis, when I hand my life over to his care.

Prayer and Action

God, I can't. You can. I think I'll let you. Just for today help me to....

Today I will....

_____

_____

_____

DAY 63
Sharing my hope...

There was a time late in my drinking career when I was convinced that I would never stop drinking and that I might as well just get used to it. It was the ultimate surrender to hopelessness. Despair became a constant companion. Death seemed like a logical and welcome termination to an unending, living hell.

Early in my recovery, I started looking forward to the coming of the next day. I not only saw daylight at the end of the tunnel, I could also hear the birds singing and was in wonderment at the power flowers had at brightly coloring even the rainiest of days.

Each new day brought change, growth and appreciation for even the smallest of things. Life was worth living and exploring. The worst of days sober were, in fact, a thousand times better than the best day drunk. There was and is quality life after drinking. It's the hope offered to all of us if we can take that leap of faith into the loving arms of a God who wants only the best for us.

Prayer and Action

God, take me. Mold me. Form me. Show me the way. Life is so much better when I do your will and not mine. Just for today help me to....

Today I will....

_____

_____

_____

_____

_____

_____

_____

_____

_____

_____

_____

_____

_____

_____

_____

_____

_____

DAY 64

Solving our common problem together...

I had lots of ways to solve my problems. When I look back at them, they seemed to all revolve around drinking, drinking and more drinking. When I didn't have a bottle in my hand, I'd point my finger at whomever or whatever was the reason for all my troubles. If only, if only, if only. Nothing I did worked. I was drowning my sorrows in drink, grasping for relief, but too far from shore to grab at anything on solid ground.

Together we can do what alone we were never able to achieve. Why it works is beyond my comprehension, but work it does.

Prayer and Action

God, thank you for the support and the strength I find in the fellowship. It is just another form of your loving grace in my life. Just for today help me to....

Today I will....

_____

_____

_____

DAY 65
Procrastination

Why do today what you can put off till tomorrow? A motto all of us alcoholics could have had hanging on our walls instead of the sampler "Home Sweet Home." Sometimes we didn't even have the energy to eat food because we had something more important to do: drink. The work, the obligations, the promises, even taking a bath were put off until tomorrow, so pressing and time-consuming was our relationship with the almighty bottle.

In most cases, tomorrow never came.

The program works if we don't pick up and use. We can get things done when they need to be done and have time left over, if we let our Higher Power be our motivating force and not let our disease consume us.

Prayer and Action

God, give me the strength to do the things I need to do today and not put off till tomorrow what I really can do today. Just for today help me to....

Today I will....

_____

_____

DAY 66

Relapse
S.L.I.P.
(Sobriety Lost Its Priority)

Not often, but sometimes, my brain tells me that I'm all right. It tells me that I've been at it long enough, and now I really could go out and have "a" drink. It doesn't tell me to get drunk—just to have one drink.

I need to go to meetings frequently so that I can hear firsthand from people who have been out there recently. I need to be reminded that it's not any different. I need to be reminded that one drink is never enough and a thousand is always too little.

Going to meetings isn't a guarantee that I won't relapse, but it is some insurance. It is a buffer zone between me and that first drink. Everyone who has ever come back from a relapse has indicated that before the relapse happened, they stopped going to meetings and working their program. That's more than enough proof for me. I don't want to slip (Sobriety Lost Its Priority).

I think I'll keep going to meetings.

Prayer and Action

God, that sleeping tiger in me stirs every once in a while. It wants to be back on that night circuit, prowling and stalking. It's lulled back to sleep by the conversations it doesn't want to hear when I go to meetings. One of your great blessings is the availability of a meeting whenever I want one or need one. Thank you for your goodness in my life. Just for today help me to....

Today I will....

_____

_____

_____

_____

_____

_____

_____

_____

_____

_____

_____

_____

_____

_____

_____

DAY 67
Denial

Denial isn't a river in Egypt. A dear friend gave me a poster with that saying on it. I had it framed and it hangs over my desk. It's a good reminder, because sometimes I forget.

It wasn't me. I didn't do it. I can hold my liquor. I don't have a problem. If only everybody would just leave me alone. I can handle this by myself. I don't need any help. You're just picking on me. You're out to get me. You're just jealous. You need to stay out of my business.

Sometimes I forget. That's why I need to frequent my meetings to get a reality check.

Prayer and Action

God, help me to remember, to *really* remember, because under no circumstances do I want to go back out there. Just for today help me to....

Today I will....

_____

_____

_____

_____

DAY 68
Anger

At some point in our disease we become angry. We're angry with the world, angry with almost everybody in it, and even angry with ourselves.

Why is this happening to me? I don't deserve this kind of treatment. Why me? We're angry about our upbringing, angry with our parents, angry about our schooling, angry with the government, angry with the authorities. Name it and we will find fault with it. We're even angry that we drink and can't stop, though we never admit that openly.

It's so wonderful to be in recovery and to realize that I don't have to strike out at everyone and everything. Life may not be fair, but that Higher Power of mine gives me everything I need to deal with whatever will come my way today. I may not like all the results that are dished out to me, but I will be able to live through the day without using.

Prayer and Action

God, thanks for allowing me to hand the day over to you. That takes the edge off many things and makes me realize that whatever I do today, I don't do it alone. You are there helping and supporting me all the way. Just for today help me to....

Today I will....

_____

_____

_____

_____

_____

_____

_____

_____

_____

_____

_____

_____

_____

_____

_____

_____

_____

DAY 69
Bargaining

At some point in our active drinking, we sense there is something going on, that maybe we are drinking just a little too much. We can handle it though. We switch drinks. We only drink in the afternoon and at night. We promise never to get drunk like that again if only God helps us through this one. We swear that we've learned our lesson. We'll never do that again. Trust us. We'll never do that again. Trust us. We'll never do that again. Trust us. All we need is one more chance, please. We can lick this. Let us try it on our own.

Prayer and Action

God, what a drunken baby I must have been. Help me to continue to grow up and change. Just for today help me to....

Today I will....

_____

_____

_____

_____

_____

DAY 70
Depression

When all that convoluted bargaining doesn't work, we become depressed. Nothing works. Nothings goes right in our life. There's no end to the misery. There's no way out. Is that all there is to life? We can't think straight. We can't work. We can't eat. We can't enjoy anything. We can't even get out of bed. Nothing has value. Even our drinking, once the elixir of life, offers no lasting solace.

Thank God that I'm in recovery, for today I realize that this too shall pass.

Prayer and Action

God, you give us emotions to help us experience, learn and grow. Help me not to get bogged down in the excessive preoccupation of any one of these; which can each become addictive in itself. Just for today help me to....

Today I will....

_____

_____

_____

_____

DAY 71
Fear

I was afraid of what they would say. I was afraid of what they were thinking. I was afraid of what they might do. I was afraid of the things I thought about. I was afraid of the things I did and might do. I was afraid to try something new. I was afraid of failing, of being ridiculed, of not being understood. I was afraid of the past catching up and what the future might bring. I was afraid of being alone. I was afraid of being in a group. I was afraid of standing out in a crowd. I was afraid of never being noticed or recognized. I was afraid I might be going crazy. I was afraid of going to bed and missing something. I was afraid of getting out of bed. I was afraid to finish a project. I was afraid I would never finish a project. I was in fear all the time.

They say that fear is false evidence appearing real.

Thank God that, in recovery, I can put one foot in front of the other and face whatever it is that I have to face today.

Prayer and Action

God, with you by my side, in front of me, behind me and within me, I can. Just for today help me to....

Today I will....

_____

_____

_____

_____

_____

_____

_____

_____

_____

_____

_____

_____

_____

_____

_____

_____

_____

DAY 72

We lose interest in church, community and service.

In the active days of our drinking, few things in life were left unaffected by the excessive use of alcohol. Many parts of our lives fell by the wayside.

As we closed in upon ourselves, service-oriented projects were not so important any longer. They took up too much precious time. The gains and perks from those endeavors were too imperceptible to calculate. We argued that our time could be better spent and more appreciated elsewhere.

Community matters received the same inattention. There was too much back-room politicking, graft and outright corruption to waste any time on community matters.

Church, for all practical purposes, was put conveniently on a back burner. Continuing to pray to a God who seemed impassive to our pleas became a charade whose sole purpose was to hide behind some purported normalcy.

Our disease chipped away at our supports and life-giving activities.

Thank God that in recovery all of these things are back in my life.

Prayer and Action

God, you were one of the first things to go when I
started to worship the spirits in alcohol. May you always
be the first thing on my mind when I get up in the
morning. Just for today help me to....

Today I will....

_____

_____

_____

_____

_____

_____

_____

_____

_____

_____

_____

_____

_____

DAY 73

We lose interest in friends and hobbies.

In the active days of our drinking few things in life were left unaffected by the excessive use of alcohol. Many parts of our lives fell by the wayside.

I always loved the arts, especially museums and the symphony. I enjoyed eating out and discovering new, interesting restaurants with unique items on their menus.

I stopped going to museums because they took too long to walk through without a drink in hand. I stopped going to the symphony because the intermissions were not long enough to consume a sufficient amount of alcohol to get through the second half of the program. I remember living in Toronto, Ontario, and going to a restaurant someone else chose. I was appalled and swore never to eat there again. They had no liquor license.

I stopped seeing some of my longtime friends. They didn't seem to have the same interests as I did. In fact, it was quite boring to be around them. Either they didn't drink or couldn't keep up with the way I drank. They just weren't fun anymore.

Thank God that in my life of recovery, these people and things are part of my life again. *Boring,* now, means listening to a bunch of drunks drone on about nothing in particular for what seems like hours on end.

Prayer and Action

God, thank you for allowing the creative beauty (the arts) that other human beings have shared with the world to be a part of my life again. Thank you for giving me true and lasting friends to share my life with. Just for today help me to....

Today I will....

DAY 74

We lose interest in peers and people in general.

In the active days of our drinking, few things in life were left unaffected by the excessive use of alcohol. Many parts of our lives fell by the wayside.

Peers—and people in general—got in the way. *If they would just leave me alone and stop prying and stop being so nosy. Didn't they realize how much work I already had to do? Didn't they know how pressed I was for time? Didn't they know that it was hard for me to say no? Why me? If I just had some time for myself, then, maybe when I was with people they might not be so bothersome.*

People wanted so much of us. They wanted more than we could give and still drink the way we wanted to, had to. One or the other had to go. The choice was simple and quick.

Thank God that in my recovery people are part of my life again. I wish I had more time in the day to do more things that involve other people.

Prayer and Action

God, thank you for all the wonderful people you have placed in my path today. It's so nice now not to be exiled all alone on that deserted island in my mind, with all the troubles of the world and with no one else to tend to them. It's nice to have people in my life. Just for today help me to....

Today I will....

_____

_____

_____

_____

_____

_____

_____

_____

_____

_____

_____

_____

_____

DAY 75

We lose interest in family and cut ties.

In the active days of our drinking few things in life were left unaffected by the excessive use of alcohol. Many parts of our lives fell by the wayside.

Don't answer the phone. Don't return their calls. Stall them. Put them off. Make excuses. Don't show up. Forget to come. Be too busy. Be overworked. There's not enough time in the day. There are so many pressing things to do; there isn't time for personal obligations.

Put the wedge between us and our family and cut ties. Make sure the smoke screen's in place, because if they ever find out who we really are, they'll hate us and shun us. We've got to get rid of them first, before they hurt and then get rid of us.

Thank God that in my recovery my family and those with close ties are there, nurturing and supporting me. And thank God I can give back some of that, in gratitude.

Prayer and Action

God, thank you for the way my family and close friends touch my life with warmth and love and friendship. They are wonderful extensions of your ever-abiding presence in my life. Just for today help me to....

Today I will....

_____

_____

_____

_____

_____

_____

_____

_____

_____

_____

_____

_____

_____

_____

_____

_____

_____

DAY 76

We lose interest in our professions and in work of any type.

In the active days of our drinking few things in life were left unaffected by that excessive use of alcohol. Many parts of our lives fell by the wayside.

I never missed a day of work. I don't know what they're talking about. I never even took all the vacation time I was supposed to. I came in on days off. So, sometimes I came in a little groggy. So, sometimes I forgot appointments and didn't get assignments in on time or just under the wire. So, sometimes my clothes didn't always match, or I wore the same ones all week. So what if I took off a little early or had a two-martini lunch? I was there, wasn't I?

They say that usually the last thing to go in this progressive disease that we have is our job. It keeps the pretense up. *(Alcoholics are lazy bums who don't have jobs.)* It helps us to feign self-worth. (We are *somebody* if we have a job. We pay taxes, don't we?) But, probably the best reason to keep a job as long as we can is that it buys the booze.

Thank God that in my recovery I am healthy enough to keep my job. All those years of drinking and using didn't completely incapacitate me once I dried out. My job does give me a sense of self-worth and accomplishment. It's nice to have that back in my life.

Prayer and Action

God, thank you for helping me not to drink today.
There's so much more time in my day, not only to do
things I need to do, but to do things I want to do. And
it's a funny thing. When I was out there drinking, I never
had enough money to make ends meet. Now that I've
stopped drinking, I always have money in my pocket.
Weird, huh? Just for today help me to....

Today I will....

_____

_____

_____

_____

_____

_____

_____

_____

_____

_____

_____

DAY 77
I acknowledge my disease.

The process of recovery sometimes comes in spurts and splashes. Sometimes it progresses in a well-defined and carefully crafted crescendo. It is a process, not a one-time event.

In order for me to do anything about the craziness that was going on in my life, I had to acknowledge the fact that something was happening that I needed help with. Even before we acknowledge and claim our disease, we have to become consciously aware that whatever it is, it can't go on any longer.

Figuratively, if not really, we kick and scream and fight until, with a sense of resignation, we are able to say, "Yes, I am an alcoholic. I have a disease."

Acknowledgment is a step fraught with setbacks and denials: *I may have a disease, but I can handle it. I'll try something new. I won't....It goes on and on, until I honestly acknowledge I have a disease and there is nothing I can do by myself to control it.*

Prayer and Action

God, I am an alcoholic. I am so grateful to know what all that craziness in my life stemmed from. Please help me on a daily basis to keep my disease in remission. Just for today help me to....

Today I will....

_____

_____

_____

_____

_____

_____

_____

_____

_____

_____

_____

_____

_____

_____

_____

_____

_____

DAY 78

I accept my disease.

The process of recovery sometimes comes in spurts and splashes. Sometimes it progresses in a well-defined and carefully crafted crescendo. It is a process, not a one-time event.

There was no sense ignoring it or hoping it would go away or denying that it really was a problem. There came a point where, in order to reclaim some semblance of sanity in my life, I had to accept the fact that I am an alcoholic and will be for the rest of my life. I accept the fact that at some point in the almost forgotten past, I had crossed over that thin line between being a heavy social drinker and being an alcoholic. I accept the fact that there is no magic pill to cure me of this disease. There is no way to jump back across that line of demarcation. I am what I am.

And the good news is that there is a simple procedure to follow that will assure me sobriety, one day at a time, for the rest of my life, if I so choose.

Prayer and Action

God, thank you for allowing me to do something positive about my disease. I'm one of the lucky ones, I know. Help me to take it and make it one day at a time. Just for today help me to....

Today I will....

_____

_____

_____

_____

_____

_____

_____

_____

_____

_____

_____

_____

_____

_____

_____

_____

_____

DAY 79

I surrender.

The process of recovery sometimes comes in spurts and splashes. Sometimes it progresses in a well-defined and carefully crafted crescendo. It is a process, not a one-time event.

I give up. I can't do it alone anymore. I have to hand it over. I need help. I can't get this monkey off my back. It has a death hold around my neck. The only way out is either to die or to surrender.

What a feeling of relief came over me the day that I handed it over and asked for the help I needed. It felt as though not just a monkey but a *ton* of monkeys had been lifted off my back.

And all I have to do is not pick up, just for today. Why hadn't I done that years ago?

Prayer and Action

God, I am thankful for my alcoholism. Its circuitous route has brought me back to you far more appreciative of all you have done for me. Thank you in advance for what you will place before me today. Just for today help me to....

Today I will....

_____

_____

_____

_____

_____

_____

_____

_____

_____

_____

_____

_____

_____

_____

_____

DAY 80
Socialization

The process of recovery sometimes comes in spurts and splashes. Sometimes it progresses in a well-defined and carefully crafted crescendo. It is a process, not a one-time event.

I always felt a little out-of-step with what was going on. Especially in my heavy drinking days (active alcoholic imbibing), I felt as though I didn't fit in. I found people in social situations boring. I wasn't interested in what was going on. Socializing and making small talk were loathsome drudgery.

By nature we humans are social animals. We live together. We work together. We play together. We even pray together. Thank goodness, in recovery I want to be a part of the human race instead of an antisocial misfit.

Prayer and Action

God, you created me as a social being so I wouldn't be alone. Thanks for doing that. Just for today help me to....

Today I will....

_____

_____

DAY 81

Time to restructure my values...

The process of recovery sometimes comes in spurts and splashes. Sometimes it progresses in a well-defined and carefully crafted crescendo. It is a process, not a one-time event.

Me. Me. Me. What am I going to get out of all this? What about me? What's in it for me? Me. Me. Me.

Recovery has helped me in all areas of my life. I used to think that I was the center of the universe, that everything needed to revolve around me and my wants and needs. The clearer thinking I have in recovery helps me to see and understand and accept that the universe does indeed revolve, but not around me. I have a place, but it's not in the center.

Being in recovery has given me time to rethink and restructure my values: selfish vs. selfless; giving vs. taking; vengeful vs. forgiving; outgoing vs. reclusive; loving vs. hateful.

I've some choices to make in recovery, but they don't seem so difficult to make anymore.

Prayer and Action

God, thanks for allowing me to be sober one more day. I have so much more energy now that it's not being siphoned into the bottle. Just for today help me to....

Today I will....

_____

_____

_____

_____

_____

_____

_____

_____

_____

_____

_____

_____

_____

_____

_____

_____

_____

DAY 82

A never ending journey...

The process of recovery sometimes comes in spurts and splashes. Sometimes it progresses in a well-defined and carefully crafted crescendo. It is a process, not a one-time event.

I'd love to have the magic elixir that would solve all the problems and right all the wrongs. When I was in grade school I prayed for the Midas touch, convinced that enough money could do just that. When I discovered alcohol for the first time, it seemed to me that it had the right formula to solve all my troubles.

I don't have an elixir and never will. However, I do have a way of life that is never ending, and brings me a continuous joy far beyond any unfulfilled ecstasy promised me by the spirits found in a bottle of alcohol.

Recovery is a continuous journey of growth, change and challenge. Recovery gives meaning, fulfillment and enjoyment to my life, which was once nothing but a bottomless pit where I wallowed in self-pity.

What I once thought was the fast lane turned out to be a dead-end road. Thank goodness recovery has turned me in the right direction.

Prayer and Action

God, every day I come across a fork in the road. Please help me to stay on the route charted out for me by "double A." Just for today help me to....

Today I will....

_____

_____

_____

_____

_____

_____

_____

_____

_____

_____

_____

_____

_____

DAY 83
In A.A. there is no seniority.

No matter who we are or how long we have been in recovery, we are all only one drink away from a relapse. Some may have had a longer time in recovery, but in this program, we only have the present. We live in the now. We take life one day at a time. Lest we become boastful or revert to our old egotistical ways, thinking we are better than the next, some in the program suggest that for today, the one who got up first has the most sobriety. There's no room in A.A. for seniority, pecking orders, perks or even rewards. Daily walking in sobriety is reward enough. Today, each of us who doesn't pick up is already a winner.

Prayer and Action

God, *sobriety,* not *seniority,* is the operative word. Etch it in my heart. Give me an unquenchable thirst for it. May I do today whatever it takes to keep it my most prized possession. Just for today help me to....

Today I will....

_____

_____

_____

_____

DAY 84
Never without a friend...

Most of them I didn't drink with. Most of them were not part of my group of acquaintances. Most of them, for me, don't even have last names. And yet, I know that if I'm ever in need of someone to talk to, to listen to my plight, to know just how I feel, to unconditionally love me till I can love myself, I know in A.A. that friend is just a phone call away. I know that friend is sitting next to me in any meeting room of A.A. that I find myself in. And sometimes that's what I really need to keep me from a relapse.

Prayer and Action

God, I need a friend. Thanks for having so many readily at hand in A.A. Just knowing that they are there helps a lot. Just for today help me to....

Today I will....

_____

_____

_____

_____

_____

DAY 85
It's spiritual, not religious...

It's something to think about. It's a way. It's a way of life. It's words to live by. It's a program. It's a step-by-step blueprint. It's a process. It's spiritual. It gets me in contact with that inner voice. It helps me to put balance in my life. It helps me to get in contact with powers of the universe. It helps me to be bigger than myself. It helps me to express my innermost thoughts and hear with eager ears the heartfelt thoughts of others. It allows me to get in contact with my Higher Power.

But it's not religious. I don't have to ascribe to any tenets or creeds. I don't have to pledge allegiance to one god over others. I don't have to follow prescribed rituals and recite a codified set of prayers.

It's spiritual. It's contact with a Higher Power. It's connectedness with the rest of humanity. It's wholeness within myself.

Prayer and Action

God, my religion means a great deal to me, especially now that I am in recovery, and A.A. has given me a chance to be spiritual in a way I have never known before. Thanks for both of these blessings in my life. Just for today help me to....

Today I will....

_____

_____

_____

_____

_____

_____

_____

_____

_____

_____

_____

_____

_____

_____

_____

_____

_____

_____

DAY 86
It's a daily action program.

Use it or lose it. If I'm not growing and changing, I come to a standstill or even regress.

Day after day, year after year without fail, I drank habitually. In a destructive and negative way, I was doing something.

In recovery I have to replace that sick thinking and sick doing with something positive, or the vacuum in my life will find something on its own to fill in the void.

Prayer and Action

God, sometimes I just don't feel like doing anything. They say idle hands are the devil's workshop. I've been there. I've done that. Help me to work my program. Just for today help me to....

Today I will....

_____

_____

_____

_____

_____

DAY 87
It's a group experience.

No one's an island. No one's adrift by themselves. They may call it self-help, but I can't do it myself. I need the group and I need my Higher Power. Any time I think I can do it myself, I ought listen a little more closely to those who have gone back out there and came back to report on it.

Together we can. Alone, I never could.

Prayer and Action

God, people who have come back from a relapse all say they just drifted away from the group. Help me not to become indifferent to my group. Just for today help me to....

Today I will....

_____

_____

_____

_____

_____

_____

DAY 88
It's voluntary.

The wonderful thing about A.A. is that it's completely voluntary. No one can make me go. No one can force me to go. No one's there begging me to go. I have the freedom to choose. I can go or not. I can either do it or not. No one can make me.

I can't fool myself though. There's a choice there. It's a life-and-death choice. I can voluntarily go to meetings and have a chance at life, or I can voluntarily choose not to go to meetings and have a rendezvous with, at the least, the living death of active using.

I've got a choice. No one can make it for me. For today, I freely choose life.

Prayer and Action

God, I don't want to lose the freedom I have gained by being a member of this voluntary organization of A.A. Help me not to give that up to the enslavement of the bottle that I once endured. Just for today help me to....

Today I will....

_____

_____

_____

DAY 89
It's simple.

Why didn't I ever think of this? It's such a simple formula: Don't use, go to a meeting and pray. I tried so many different ways to cut down or to stop drinking altogether. I had a thousand and one other plans of action. Each one was more contrived and convoluted than the previous one. Who would have ever thought three little things done on a regular (daily) basis would keep the tiger sleeping.

Nothing else has ever kept me sober even for a full day. It's so simple. You don't need to be a rocket scientist to follow these steps.

Prayer and Action

God, if I keep it simple I'll keep it forever. Help me to stay sober just through today. Just for today help me to....

Today I will....

_____

_____

_____

_____

DAY 90
It works.

Nothing I ever tried worked anything like this does. They tell us in the program that if you keep doing something over and over again and don't like the results, do something else.

I like what A.A. does for me. It works. I'm going to keep doing what they suggest on a daily basis.

Prayer and Action

God, grant me the serenity to accept the things I cannot change, the courage to change the things I can, and the wisdom to know the difference. Just for today help me to....

Today I will....

_____

_____

_____

_____

_____

_____

DAY 91
OOPS! It's longer than 90 days.

Ninety days is a great start, but that's all it is. I've had a long enough time in sobriety to know that I want this as a way of life.

And, I know I can have this one day at a time.

Prayer and Action

God, thanks for letting me feel your daily presence in my life. I can't, but you can. I hand it all over to you to do as you will. Take my entire being, body and soul. Mold me. Form me. Support me. Grace me. Keep me sober, and just for today help me to....

Today I will....

_____

_____

_____

_____

_____

_____

_____